We grew up in a big house that
designed and that my Daddy, a
working life caring for his patients, the sick and suffering. Judging
by the number of people paying their respects at his funeral Mass,
there were an awful lot. Daddy was so busy caring for others that
he was unaware of our sufferings and turmoil. We grew up
appallingly uncared for, unloved, rejected, beaten physically,
abused psychologically and emotionally. The black sheep,
destined to be dimwits and fail. A healthy environment existed
amongst the neighbours along the road, but we were never
allowed to witness it. We suffered a stolen childhood and
adolescence. We were then thrown into the mainstream of adult
life as social drop-outs. My sufferings continued, until I nearly hit
rock bottom. It was only through the help of my newfound
family,. professionals and wonderful neighbours that I was able to
discover all the terrible truths and intentions which hid behind
the lace curtains of Marian House.

This is my true story.

MARIAN HOUSE

Many Lost Years

Gerry Duignan

MINERVA PRESS

LONDON
MIAMI DELHI SYDNEY

ISBN 0 75411 123 7

First Published 2000 by
MINERVA PRESS
315–317 Regent Street
London W1R 7YB

Printed in Great Britain for Minerva Press

MARIAN HOUSE
Many Lost Years

To
Veronica and Paul,
For what you have given,
and continue to give me everyday,

to
all the wonderful neighbours
around Marian House, and
all the others who have helped me,
my gratitude is endless.

Thanks !

To all those who have suffered,
I say this:
You are not alone,
Courage,
the thoughts of many are with you

Saturday 14th September 1996

It's eight in the morning, I still haven't had breakfast, and my tummy is now a great sack of pains. The hotel night porter seemed to be rather busy with completing his duties, and preparing for his well-deserved rest, but I had to get to the airport early, and I do remember now that I hadn't even paid for breakfast. Upon arriving at the hotel I tried to negotiate my room price. I'm alone, and I can't stay for breakfast tomorrow, I'll have to be at the airport check-in desk to catch a wonderful flying machine by seven, 'Can't you give me some discount?' was my request. The pretty young girl looks at me, she's hesitating, she's probably following orders anyway, and I want to say to her, 'Well, my father always stayed here when he came to Dublin, Frank Colaghan isn't in by any chance?' I know that if Frank Colaghan, the hotel owner, would be in and if I got to meet him I'd have that room for free.

I didn't really want to mention that I'd been here before. It was however many years ago, what would it mean to her? I'd stayed here the night of the 30th May 1976, Dad was with me that time, as I was due out to Geneva the following morning. The young lady mightn't have been even born then, what do I know? I'd just like a small discount. Well, she's kind enough to allow me that, and I think what a nice country to be in, you can even negotiate a bit, and the £5 saved will probably buy me some fish and chips in the restaurant tonight. I don't know when I'll be in these parts again, so I might as well have a good plate of fish and chips before I leave.

Well I had some excellent fish and chips washed down by some good lager, and later on spent my time hovering between my television remote control in Room 126 and the bar downstairs, where I'd had some more lager and good conversation with the locals at the bar counter before I finally headed out.

Passing the reception desk I note that the young lady has now quit, and at this late hour is now replaced by a young chap whom

I judge to be the night porter. I move towards him, wait until he finishes a call, which he is treating, and then request an early wake-up call for Room 126, which he jots down on a pre-printed form.

Then I hit the sack.

All alone.

Trouble now is that the fish and chips have been digested and I'm hungry again, no breakfast tray for the moment, nothing but the bulkhead in front of me as I'm strapping into my seat, number 1-D upfront, nearly unaware of, and caring even less about the three other lady passengers in the same row. We are parked at right angles to the terminal building. Cockpit crew must be going through their pre-flight checks, I'm starting to dread this waiting, the minutes seem unending. I always dread these moments, I always have a Kleenex discreetly concealed in the fist nearest the central aisle to shield myself from the possible views of others, 'cause every time I leave the auld sod, I feel profoundly sad, even angered. But I don't want any of the others to see my emotions. That's what it was like too, growing up at Marian House. Never allowed myself to show my emotions. Saddened about what? What emotions, what reason to anger? Not necessarily about leaving my homeland, its people, their ways, but moreso that there's a job undone! Still another chance missed, another chance to find out why! Why?

Not what had gone wrong in my life, I know all about that, I don't need any repeating, but *why*? I can't understand, accept even less.

The lady to my right is still reading her book held steadfastly upright, one which she simply hasn't put down since taking her seat, maybe a good tale, she's into another world, she was probably luckier than me, being born into another world, at least another family. From behind, the hum of conversation which is picking up as people have now settled into their seats, and now they're on about the weather, the fishing, the golfing, the people and the whole lot of it indeed. From below and behind, I hear heavy thuds, which probably means suitcases and crates of all sorts being loaded into the aircraft's belly. The two ladies to my left are chatting, I can hear the French phrases, but I don't hear all the words. They seem to have enjoyed their trip to Eire, so much for them, they probably deserved it, and why not? Today's only Saturday, which might leave tomorrow as a day off for many.

Beautiful Eire.

That doesn't help me much though, because I'm still alone here. The two hostesses are now in their rear-facing jump seats, right beside the door, which has just been closed. Things are now in the hands of an air traffic controller, and the cockpit crew are waiting for instructions. I might just be sitting on board this Irish aircraft, which is still on Irish soil, but I really feel shut-off from Ireland. In a sort of no-man's-land. I want to unbuckle my seat belt and get off, but where to go to? Whom to run to? What could anybody do for me anyway? This is the point of no return.

Permission for pushback has been granted, chocks are now off, as I feel the aircraft being pushed tail-first out of its parking bay and then I hear the flaps and ailerons which are unfolding to pre-calculated take-off positions. The gentle whine of the engines, which have just started winding up many seat rows behind me, cuts in on my thoughts, and I realise that there's even less time left now. I will be in Geneva within two hours, and I start thinking of Veronica and Paul. Poor Paul, at least he doesn't know what I'm going through, though it's better so for him, Veronica would understand of course, but that doesn't help me much because they're in Geneva, and I'm still here.

All alone.

A temporary push on the throttles and we start moving, the Boeing 737 is now heading out towards the runway. The lady in 1-F is still reading, head bowed forward, it must be a good one, so I can't get a last good look at the airport surroundings. Do I want to anyway? I strain forward but give up, other things to worry about now.

Our big jet is still manoeuvring the numerous taxiways out towards the runway.

A right turn, which brings us swinging around to face the centreline and the full length of the runway. Over two thousand meters of hardened concrete up front of us out there. Then the brakes come on to hold the blue and gold painted jet, which is basking in the morning's Irish sun, and which is streaming through the window behind the lady in 1-F.

Time passes slowly again, as we wait here at the top of Runway 05 for control tower clearance to take off.

I listen to the engines turning over, and can imagine the impending instructions, which will soon be coming across the airwaves.

'Regenair 7008 cleared take-off.'

'Roger.'

The throttle sticks have just been pushed into forward position as I hear the engines surge and pick up power, the whine near instantly becoming a roar. Brakes are released, the aircraft nose pitches up slightly under the sheer mechanical force being provided by the underwing slung engines, some of its over forty ton weight coming slightly off the nose undercarriage. I am slammed backwards as the big jet starts accelerating down the centreline. With my feet pushed against the bulkhead, and my fists tightly clenched on the armrests, I can't hold on any tighter than in a roller-coaster ride as I'm pinned into the rear of my seat; I'm still feeling the buffeting and vibrations from the runway's surface as we continue through the acceleration of the take-off run. The twin jet engines are giving the maximum of their thrust and power as we reach rotation speed, the nose tilts up as the yoke is pulled back and up we go, the heavy jet is now being heaved upwards, ascending rapidly into the clear early morning air. We're on our way. Freed from the ground below us.

Slán Éire!

I can feel the tears refilling my eyes once again, just as had happened whilst waiting inside the terminal building, and waiting for the boarding call to come over the loudspeakers.

No winds to buffet us flyers, and glued to my seatback I can feel the continuing acceleration as we continue the climb-out. A wonderful flying machine, wonderful technology, a wonderful team, air traffic controllers, all working to take me back to Geneva, to Veronica and Paul.

Away, far away from this country, that cemetery and the grave.

The grave!

That was it!

Then for me, all hell let's loose.

We're still climbing fast, but the hostess nearest me is out of her seat fast and I wasn't expecting her.

She must have been observing me, the nervous state I'm in and all that, because she's already kneeling down in front of me.

'Is everything all right? Can I help?' she says, and her pretty eyes meet my reddened ones. 'My name is Susan.'

She's got my attention all right.

No clear air turbulence over the Irish Sea here, but I'm being rocked emotionally. The turbulence is in my mind right now. This is what I was dreading, this is what happens every time I leave the auld sod. But it's never been this bad. I think my Kleenex is already soaked wet, but I don't care. Susan is still with me, I look at her, she's a pretty young girl. She reacted quickly, to say the least, she's doing a good job. She's at work. I'm still on holidays. Well, sort of. Tomorrow will be Sunday, the last day of these holidays. Then there'll be life thereafter, however long that'll be, and whatever it'll be worth.

'Were you afraid of the take-off?' she asks me.

'God no,' I say. 'This has just been a hard trip for me. My father died whilst I was back on holidays.'

My body heaves from the increase in tension.

'I'm so sorry,' she says.

I nod in acceptance, the Kleenex still clenched hard in my fist.

I wonder if her dad is still alive. I wonder if things in her family were different than mine. I wonder if she knows what it's like to lose a father, even if he was someone you scarcely knew. I know that the legal term for a father is an ascendant. Everybody has two direct ascendants, a mother and a father. Well I never met my mother, I guess that I was lucky enough to meet my father, but I've never known any of them, as my father was more of an ascendant than a dad to me. I used to call him Dad, whenever I got to meet him, often out of fear, and other times in hope of some return of affection. But growing up at Marian House were years when the fear was quasi-permanent, and the affection was totally absent. The affection was what I'm still waiting for, could use some even as a grown-up now, but I sadly think I'll be waiting for an awful long time. Susan of course knows nothing of this, would she understand? Or anyone else on this plane? But the small amount of care she dispensed to me was already one drop less in the ocean of my sufferings and for that I am grateful. I suddenly ease up on my tensions, and hope for breakfast. Susan retreats towards her jump seat, and here I am again, all alone.

No father, never had a mother. Rhona certainly wasn't a kind or caring mother to me, never replaced the maternal one I lost the day she died at a hospital. Dad, from what I'd noticed and was submitted to, during all those early years at Marian House simply obeyed Rhona all along. That was probably one of the origins as to why I never got to know him. But why am I crying for someone whom I've never gotten to know?

Why?

Is it worth it?

I feel as if I'm in a shambles.

They'd buried my daddy out in Ballyheane cemetery on Thursday last. He'd grown-up in Ballinagarry, County Longford, went to school over there, and probably knew all the by-roads and boreens out to Kiltynagh. If they'd buried him in Ballinagarry, at least he'd be in his 'home country' and beside my mother, or so I would hope; she was a Coyne from An Cheath Rua, that way I'd always be sure where he buried my mother. Dad told me she's in the family plot there, but he never put her name on the tombstone. I see other Duignans mentioned there, but not my mum. I would like to know why, but will never manage it. Now that's another thing or two I can't understand, accept even less. Those are other parts of the undone job.

So they'd buried Daddy out in Ballyheane cemetery in the middle of farming country, nowhere near my mother Noreen. They said that that's what he wanted.

'Sure he has all his older friends buried out there,' Rhona had put it when we were sitting in the kitchen Thursday morning before heading down to Church for the funeral mass.

I know even less about his friends than I do about my dad, so I have to go along with that, have no other choice really. Closing my eyes I can see the grave now, near the top of the hill. Lots of graves around, so I guess that Dad must have some friends there after all. I see the hill too. You can see it long before you get to the village, especially because of the tall trees, which border the cemetery. Those tall trees are now increasingly many miles behind me with each second of passing time, but I can still hear the westerlies whistling through and around their branches and tall trunks. I don't know what kind of trees they are. I only know that they have that peculiar swayed look about them. They are growing with their tips and half their trunks pointed eastward towards Dublin. That's what they get for growing there, continuously windswept by the westerlies blowing in from the Atlantic. That's nature in those parts: everything suffers, the people from the weather and other people, the trees from nature, the sheep too from the weather, even with their woolly coats.

It's bad enough having your family spread out all over the country, the continent and the whole world too, and I've never gotten to meet or see them often, but now, not even my daddy is buried with my own mother in the same cemetery. That'll make for two cemeteries to visit whenever I come back to these parts. Whenever I might want to do so.

The nose wheels and undercarriage landing gear have been retracted into their wells, I hear the electrical motors winding in the flaps progressively, the throttles are being eased back, the engines responding accordingly as we start coming out of the climb towards level flight and are heading out faster than fast over the Irish Sea towards Wales.

Things start shuffling in the numerous cabin rows behind me. I hear belts being unbuckled, people changing position in their seats, the reduced engine noise now allows conversation to get back underway, Susan and her workmate are now in the galley. This means that breakfast must be coming, which will mean something else for me to do than think about my current state of mind, and what my future might bring me. I had even managed to forget for a few minutes that I was hungry, but now my brain is back on track, and I'm sure that there'll be a fine Irish breakfast on the tray. Sitting in row 1 also means no waiting to be served, off the plane in Geneva quickly, through passport control quicker than some others, and barring luggage delays I will get to see Veronica and Paul that little bit sooner. I am not deceived by breakfast this time, and I quickly settle in to my share of bacon, sausages and black pudding. I take it as another farewell from good old Eire, and I thoroughly enjoy it, as I don't know if or whenever I'll be back in these parts again. The lady in 1-F is still reading, and I wonder who could write such a good book as that, she's going to miss her breakfast and maybe Susan will remember my state of mind, and I'll be having two portions of bacon, sausages and the black pudding. I've got lots of fresh bacon, sausages and black pudding in my bags too, and if the Aer Rianta chaps didn't forget to load my bags into the airplane's belly, then Veronica and Paul will be having their share for dinner tonight. I can't imagine them waiting until tomorrow morning to have some of these Irish goodies. I've had my fair share of Irish breakfasts during the past week, and just about as much of many other things too. So I forget about any virtual second helping, we're speeding over England now, Eire is lying further and further behind us geographically and in my mind too, so when Susan comes around with more tea, I say, 'No thank you, but would it be possible to make a quick visit to the cockpit?'

She says that she'll have a word with the boys up front, and turns towards the closed cockpit door.

The thought of that eventuality being granted calms me greatly, and my Kleenex gets stuffed into my left pocket.

Shortly thereafter Susan tells me that Captain Nick and his co-pilot are expecting me upfront, and would I like to come forward? Holy Baloney, I think, I've managed it once again! I gladly move through the narrow door in to the cockpit, grateful for all the Irish hospitality once again. I have been in a number of cockpits through the years, but especially now I have to keep things off my mind.

And my Kleenex in my pocket.

I slide down onto one knee and we start talking. Captain Nick asks me if I've been on holidays.

'Well yes, I've been home for a week, but my father died so it hasn't been holidays really,' I explain, managing for once, to hold back any flow of emotions.

'Oh, I'm sorry,' he says, just like Susan said.

'Thank you indeed,' I say, and I think that if he announced the bad news over the cabin address system, everybody would probably say 'I'm sorry' too, and I think that that'd be kind of them, and aren't there lots of nice people with lots of sympathy on this earth?

But Nick senses that I prefer to change the subject. The co-pilot suggests I unfold the jump seat to my right and to buckle myself in with the five-point harness seat belt just whilst I'm up here. I settle in square behind the central console, and take all my time to admire the complex systems, the INS control and display units, panels with switches, dials and knobs in front, above and to all sides. The excellent Irish breakfast is way behind in my thoughts by now. It's rather quiet up front here, just a persistent soft hissing as the nose-cone of our big jet cuts swiftly forward through the thin air, the silence sometimes broken by the chatter from an air traffic controller somewhere on the ground way below us. Now my questions start coming out slowly, and amongst other details Nick explains our route. We've flown over the Sussex Downs, a change of heading to the right onto the Upper Amber One flight-track, our blue and gold painted wonderful flying machine is up at 31,000 feet now, and the European coast and mainland beyond is now approaching us at nearly five hundred miles per hour.

Spring 1958
Culligane,
Carraroe,
Co Galway.

My Dearest Sally,

It's about time for me to drop you a few lines, but I was expecting a letter from you any day since our poor darling Noreen died. May God rest her holy soul. I am sure, Sally love, that you got a shock and we all got it dear. If she was sick I'd go down to see her but it came so sudden that there was no time for anything. How I miss her God only knows. It's hard to believe it that our poor Noreen is gone forever. God look down on us all dear. Poor Jim Duignan, he got thin and worn out, he was here a few weeks ago and two others with him and my little Martin, oh he'll be all right and the baby, he is coming on fine, thank God. He was underweight but he's 8lbs and 10 ozs now. The sister-in-law is

15

taking away the baby soon, he is in hospital at present was since he was born.

I was down at the funeral and a few from Carraroe... I saw her she looked lovely the poor darling R.I.P. Well Sally love, I suppose you took it hard. I can't write this letter with the tears in my eyes, she was good to Coleen and to me too. Coleen took it bad, Sally, he wasn't as bad the first few days but worse he got then and worse he's getting too. He is in hospital but getting on well thank God. Jim Duignan went in to see him four times, the baby is in the hospital there too. I often thought about you Sally, very often indeed. Myself and Pat were talking the whole day yesterday about you, I do be lonely here, Sally love, my poor Coleen in hospital, and one of my children is not well. She is six years. I didn't send her to school yet she is not well, I had her in hospital at Xmas. I do have a hard time, dear, to look at my poor Coleen crippled up, it goes through my heart and soul you understand, dear Sally, you always did yourself and Noreen R.I.P.

...and dear heart answer my letter too, I'd give anything to hear from you. Noreen used to write to me often so write to me Sally. How is poor Frank and the kids? I am sure poor Frank took it hard about Noreen, I know he did... Well Sally love, drop me a line, tell me how you are and Frank and kids. I am sure you will get fed-up reading this letter but I am no good writing English but I am in Irish mait go leor.

I wish to God that my poor Coleen was at home, but he might be home soon. I do be very lonely now. This is spring now here and I am working hard, I have to go on the bog now seven miles in and out. I am worn out but I have my health, thank God.

Well dearest heart, I must stop. I am crying writing all this to you, I often cried, Sally dear, it's nothing new to me, but God is good.

From Megan

> Excerpts from a letter written by Aunty Megan in Carraroe, Co Galway to Aunty Sally in the States, Spring 1958.

1962

It's late winter and dark as night outside, and I guess long gone past six o'clock. I don't know exactly what time it is, as we don't have a watch between us. We always have to say the Angelus prayers at six o'clock after our supper for all those who supposedly need them. One thing of which I'm sure though is that we've been up here a while now. Same routine be it winter or spring or fall. Summer's different because we are often sent down to Mrs Ganaghan's for the holidays. Anyway it's winter now, it's way after six, and we aren't asleep at all yet, as we lie in bed listening to the gale howling and the rain pelting against the western gable of the house. I ask Martin something about Mammy, and he calls me over to his bed.

'Listen Gerry, that's not Mammy down there in the kitchen,' he says.

I don't understand.

'Where's Mammy then?' I say, puzzled.

'She's dead,' comes his reply.

'Dead?' I'm still young and hardly understand what to be dead means, and even less about why my mammy is dead.

'Why is she dead?'

He explains to me that she died in the hospital in Tury after I was born.

'Where's Tury, why did she have to die, what happened to her that she died?' I have lots of questions here.

'I don't quite know really, but that woman Rhona downstairs is not your mother or mine either. You see, as I'm older than you I knew what our mother looked like, her name was Noreen, but sorry for you, she died a few days after you were born. Daddy married that other woman whose name is Rhona, you see.'

I wonder for a while.

'Maybe Daddy likes the name Rhona?'

'Maybe.'

It's a winter's evening, it's dark out there and I can hear the gale still howling around the western gable of the house. Dead?

I can't really understand this at all. Martin tells me about that late morning a few years ago when Dad came out of the kitchen into the playroom to tell him about the bad news and then they drove down to the hospital in Tury, Martin sitting as usual in the front seat. If it wasn't bad enough at that, he goes on to tell me that neither Jane, Tadgh nor Fintan are my sister or brothers either. They're only half-sister and half-brothers to him, and that goes for me too.

I wonder too if the hospital at Castlebarry isn't better than the one in Tury, never have been in any of them, so can't guess really.

So there we are. A cold wintery evening, I've just learned that I have only one father, one real brother, one half-sister, two half-brothers, and a woman called Rhona living in the house. No real mother at all, never had.

'What was my mother like then?' I wonder.

Martin tells me that she was a good mother to him. So I hope that the Rhona downstairs will be a good mother to me, to Martin and to all of us.

12th February

Daddy comes to pick up Tadgh and I at the parking space behind the Hanley's shop because Rhona won't be at the house when we'd arrive. The big shop is situated down at the bottom of Main Street, right beside the river. I'm sitting in the rear seat as usual and Daddy asks Tadgh, who is seated up the front, if he has any homework to be doing this afternoon, and then asks me too. I tell him that I don't have any to do today. He can't understand that boys would be coming out of school without a bit of homework, which would need to be done, and that it wasn't like that at all when he went to school. We continue the drive up the Main Street and then out the Western Road towards Marian House.

We're just above St Patrick's Avenue, driving past the field where Martin and I sometimes play with Bertie and Maeve Glennon.

'Daddy, do you know that today is Gerard's birthday?' Tadgh blutters out.

There's a silence for a short while, then Daddy mutters

something which I can't make out, and he keeps on driving out the road past Sander's house.

It's clear enough to me that he's not interested in my birthday.

The homework, when we get it, is far more important.

Galway

One day Daddy and all of us head up by car for a trip to Salthill in Galway City, as he's going to visit an old friend there. The Mulligans live there and Mr Mulligan's a captain on a big boat spending a lot of time on the oceans, and they've a big house down there of which I don't get to see much inside as I have to spend the time out in the garden at the rear. I've got a fine view at the house though, and there are terraced levels full of flowers leading down from the back door to the lower garden level. This is much different to our house at Western Road because our back garden is much bigger but when you're down below the clothesline you can just about see the first floor windows at all. The clothesline divides our back garden roughly into two parts. Martin and I always have to stay down below the clothesline, where the grass is always well-cut, and never come above it unless we're coming or going back up to our big house, whenever we might get called.

'We have no business up there,' is what Rhona says.

After leaving the Mulligans house we head over to a big shopping place, because Rhona wants to look at something. She tells me to come inside with her whilst she's 'looking at things'. I follow her in, and we stroll around for a bit.

We're in a corner of the shop now.

'Take off your glasses,' Rhona tells me.

Take off my glasses? I wonder.

'Take them off,' she barks.

I obey and hold them in my hands waiting for further orders.

'Put them down there on the counter,' she says. The orders don't delay in coming.

'Here on this counter?' I ask, the counter being slightly higher than my head, and it has great dark brown wood panelling down its front. From my height I can just about see the peppermint creams, Rolo bars of chocolates, the potato crisps and marshmallows up there waiting for the lucky ones.

Not for me, for others.

'I told you, on the counter,' she repeats.

I follow her orders, and leave the new pair of glasses atop a pile of fruit and nut bars on the counter above.

Rhona then says that we have to go without dallying, and she pulls me by the hand before I can get hold of my glasses, I struggle but there's nothing to be done, and out we go to the car.

I climb into the rear seat but Daddy doesn't look rearwards so he doesn't notice that my glasses are missing and off we drive back to Castlebarry. When we are called into the kitchen for the Holy Angelus that evening, I keep avoiding looking in Daddy's direction, but when we've finished our Holy Prayers for all those in need, and whilst I'm getting up off my knees from the hard floor Rhona calls Daddy and tells him that I lost my glasses somewhere during the day.

'Ah, ah,' he groans, whilst my forward movement is blocked by him and he reaches for the heavy electrical cable hidden behind the big Virgin Mary calendar on the wall above the kitchen table.

And down I go, once again.

Seasons

The summer is still a while away, but as often on Sundays we all go down by car to Mrs Ganaghan's house in Rathagan, the other side of Baltrina. Mrs Ganaghan is Rhona's mother, so she's not a real grandmother for me either.

We'll stop at the tyre shop and petrol filling station shortly before we leave the end of town to catch the Pontarla road, and the twenty-five miles ahead to Baltrina, and five more out to Mrs Ganaghan's place. Tadgh, who sits up front beside Daddy will enjoy stopping here as he always asks for the Green Shield stamps that Daddy gets from the man when he buys the petrol. Daddy asks him how many more he needs for filling the book, and what might he be getting in exchange? Tadgh holds the stamps in his hand, counts them and starts calculating how many more he still needs to fill out his book. He promises Daddy that he'll be sticking in these new ones as soon as he gets back from Mrs Ganaghan's. Tadgh is into carpentry these days, so he'll be hoping for a wood saw, or maybe a pair of clamps to ease the job. But first he has to fill the book. I know of the book, but don't really know what it looks like, as he keeps it somewhere in the house, and I don't have any business in rooms other than the kitchen, the toilet and bedroom upstairs.

I never get any of the stamps, nor even an empty book that I could maybe do some drawings in. I know better than to ask for any, as I might get a flying thump from Rhona, who's sitting just over to my left.

Daddy never looks back either over his shoulder to ask me if I'd like to have some stamps from time to time.

When the summer comes we'll go down again on a Sunday, but as Martin and I will be out of school he and I will get to stay with Mrs Ganaghan.

'Ye'll stay with her then, and will ye be good boys and help her and the men on the farm?' Rhona asks.

I ask if Daddy, Rhona and the others will come and visit us from time to time, especially on a Sunday.

'Will you stop asking questions, and run out there to play a while?' is all I get as an answer.

So I get sent out with Martin to play, whilst the others stay put, and I don't understand. So I ask Martin if they'll be coming down to visit us, especially on Sundays? He tells me that if they're not going off to places like Longford, Dublin, or over to England to visit people, they might come down to see us.

The old house is nothing like what we have up at Western Road. One straight corridor runs from the sitting room along to the third bedroom. Then there's a part attached, with a flat roof where there's the main kitchen and the back storeroom. When you walk in the kitchen door there's a fine huge square table in front of you, with the sofa and the Aga over to the left. I always admire the table's beautiful wood and carved wooden legs. Mrs Ganaghan doesn't have a fridge in the house, which is a problem for keeping the milk fresh in the summertime, no phone either so there are lots of things to talk about when Sunday afternoon comes, and as for the toilet, well, you can go out the back and behind the trees in the orchard, as the turfbog's a bit down the boreen.

The farmgrounds are huge, acres and acres all over the place, out the front and the back, more room here than in our back garden at Marian House. You could yell for hours and nobody would be knowing if you were dead or dying from an attack of Jimmy's rams next door, or you were yelling for joy at all the freedom and space. So during the next few weeks we'll get to discover the place a little bit, setting traps for rabbits, weaving through the rushes in the field the other side of the road, some of which we can bring back to the house and make St Brigid's crosses out of, but minding my knees from the thistles as with my short pants on sure you'd be getting yourself scratched on the shins when going to the well for buckets of water, building dams with stones and bits of timber on the river over in the field, and plucking the grass around the house. When it's not raining Mrs Ganaghan and ourselves head off down to the bog to cut the turf. The bog is half a mile north of the house, and I'll often cover the distance barefooted, under Mrs Ganaghan's orders on the chip-covered boreen's surface, and once down there, and through the old rusty gate, sure I'd have to be minding myself and not step on a young thistle plant or sharp grass. That happened to me once, and by jove it hurts, especially as Mrs Ganaghan doesn't have the likes of ointments or anything for the pain, and anyway she never goes barefooted like I have to, even though I've brought my brown sandals along with me from Castlebarry, and so she couldn't possibly know what it's like to have your foot cut and keep walking and hobbling along on the pain. There's only one thing that I hate worse than going barefooted along the boreen. That's when Mrs Ganaghan decides to wash my pants, and she gives me a great piece of old tissue to wrap around my waist, and a nappy pin to attach down in the middle, that way it should look a little like pants, but I don't think so at all, and I feel ridiculous with such an outfit. She cuts the turf and we run to lay out the sods around the area, because they have to dry out for the winter. When Mrs Ganaghan's getting tired she'll stop cutting but we continue because all the sods we laid out the other days have to be turned over a quarter turn, to keep on drying. When they've been turned over a few times then we can start making small pyramids, starting with four sods so that with the air circulating between them they'll dry out completely. Then we can make great stacks out of a whole bunch of sods, until Jimmy next door or the Foleys who live a mile away will lend us a donkey and cart to bring it all up the boreen to the turf shed beside the house. We're the only ones working this bog because old Uncle Terence, Mrs Ganaghan's husband, who isn't a real uncle to us either, nor a real grandfather anyway, is too old, just look at him with his white hair and he has to carry a walking stick to get around. So he can't go to the bog, unless Mrs Ganaghan herself 'has to go someplace for the day, and speak to a man', and only then will he come along with us. He knows everybody living in these parts, so he spends hours standing by the ditch chatting with men who arrive up and down the boreen on their black Raleigh bikes; they'll stop when they see Terence, have a gawk to see if they haven't lost their trouser pins and then they'll talk about the weather, the government, the work in England, and the parish priest who's bought himself a new motor car, and isn't there a lovely colour to it? But we don't know these old men, and they don't ever get off their black Raleigh bikes to come over through the bog to say hello to us. Anyway it's better that way, says Martin, because Mrs Ganaghan won't be away for ages to talk to the man, and this evening she'll be wanting to know what we've been doing the whole day. Killing ourselves with our bare feet and all in the soft turf that is, is what we'd want to say, but she might laugh her head off at us, bog work being easy work and such, take the mickey, and tell on us to Daddy and Rhona and the others whenever they'd get back from travelling to Longford, Dublin, or off the B&I boat at Holyhead.

Some days we're all exhausted, and when evening comes we all settle down in the big bedroom, but the bed's not large enough for the old man and us both, so Mrs Ganaghan says that Terence has to sleep as usual with his head on the pillow facing the window, and we have to 'sleep that way', which means our heads facing away from the window, with the old man's feet stuck between our heads. Can't do it otherwise because Rhona's brother John Joseph, who can't be a real uncle for us either, has the middle room, and he's off to the Machine and Tool factory in Baltrina every morning with his toolbox, and five miles of road ahead of him, unless the parish priest might be going that way too, and John Joseph would surely hop in and take a lift to town, even if he doesn't agree with the paint colour of the motor car. So if John Joseph has to go into the factory, that counts him out from helping us out with the sods, the stacks, and the donkey's green teeth and frothing mouth too. I wonder what it's like to be walking all those miles to a factory, with a toolbox changing hands every two hundred yards, working all day and having to make the whole way back in the evening. Then at Holy Mass one Sunday morning Father Davey the burly parish priest gives a sermon about work and the divinity of it and all that. Everyone in these parts is into the farming business, and 'if only a few can make it to that new breed of worker who picks up his toolbox in the morning and goes to work in a factory all day, I say brave men take pride in your work.' I'm only a young fellow lost somewhere amongst all these grown-ups in the pews, but I have the impression that John Joseph and his toolbox are going places, and will soon be making it grand in this world.

After the Holy Mass that morning I've climbed the seven steps of the pedestal and am waiting below the church bell for Martin. He's gone off to the local sweetshop for the Sunday papers to bring home to Terence. When he arrives he shows me a front-page photograph of what he calls the Boeing 747, a new Jumbo jet that is now flying, and the paper is doing an article on it.

I have a closer look at the photo, and sure with all the windows to it, it looks like an awful big plane indeed.

'Where's Seattle?' I ask.

Martin tells me that Seattle is in America, which for me is an awful long way away from the back end of Mayo, and I wonder what it must be like over there in America and if I'll ever get to visit Seattle and see one of the big Jumbo jets.

From reading schoolbooks and looking at the pictures I know that all farms should have cows and pigs, goats, horses and sheep, and a dog to keep them in their places. Maybe chickens and even vegetables in a garden out the back. We have potatoes, scallions and rhubarb growing in the vegetable patch in our back garden at Marian House, and the place isn't even a farm. But there aren't any animals here at all, and Mrs Ganaghan even has to borrow the donkey and cart to bring home the turf. There's lots of grass out the fields in the back, out the front too the other side of the boreen, but no horse and machine to cut it. No horse and plough either to work all the acres, and sow wheat, potatoes, onions or any vegetables at all. Mrs Ganaghan's farm doesn't have any of these, so everything has to be carted out from Baltrina. Picking potatoes or onions must be easier than laying out sods of turf all day, and you wouldn't even have to turn them over or make stacks out of them. What's more you wouldn't need a donkey to bring them home to the house. So I really don't like this farm, it not really what I'd like to see around me. Old McDonagh beside our house on the Western Road has a farm too, but I believe that his farm is a real one. I think he even has cows up near the sheds at the top end of his field beside the house, but then again as I'm not allowed that far and have no business over there I'm not really sure. But he's got grass in the field, I can see that much from our side of the garden wall. He cuts the hay in the summer, 'cos when I was really young I'd seen him at it, and for me that's already more of a farm than Mrs Ganaghan's. Even the American Monsignors, whenever any one of them is here visiting us, be it Michael, Francis or Denis, roll up their sleeves and go over the wall to help him with the hay. They are all brothers to Daddy, which means that they are real uncles to Martin and me. They all live in America so we don't see them very often, and when they'd be here Martin and me share my single bed and they'd have the window bed. There'd always be a traveller's suitcase by the wardrobe, with steamship stickers all over it, and sometimes a bottle of whiskey on the bedside dresser. These are the first tourists I've ever met, and I wonder what it's like to travel to far-away places. I guess I'll have to wait until I'm their age.

The weeks go by and Mrs Ganaghan tells us that Daddy and

the others will be coming down soon to pick us up. They arrive on a Sunday, as usual, and Martin and I are told to run outside and play, whilst the visitors all stay inside the house and talk and eat cake and drink tea. I'm wondering where the others have been all summer, want to ask them, but they are still in the house, and afterwards when we're all in the car heading home to Western Road I daren't ask the question.

So I won't get to know.

After the summer holidays we still go down to Mrs Ganaghan's most Sunday afternoons. Sundays always seem the same to me. Martin and I have to get ready for Holy Mass. I go into the little storage room under the staircase to fetch the black shoe polish and the two brushes. The little room is one of the very few in the house that I'm allowed into, and it's only because the shoe polish and the two brushes are in a drawer there. Then out to the garage to polish my shoes. The black shoes are for Sundays, the brown sandals are for the other days of the week. The big black car is always parked to the left in the garage, and there is a bench made of cement blocks against the right-hand wall, so up go the shoes, and the brushes get to work. One morning Daddy is standing there in his Sunday suit, waistcoat tie and all watching me clean my shoes, and he sees that they are in a poor state indeed. He's giving out about the state they're in.

'Can't you buy another pair of shoes for me, Daddy?' I ask.

'Money doesn't grow on trees, son,' says Daddy. 'One day you'll see when you grow up and have to buy your own shoes, that the money doesn't fall down to be picked up like that.'

I don't know what it's like to be a grown-up, and earn lots of money, it's still a long way away, but I have to agree that money doesn't grow on trees, so I guess that Daddy is right about that, and I promise not to break my shoes any more. But I wonder if Daddy can't afford to buy me another pair of shoes, after all he's rich. Martin told me that Daddy's a doctor, and doctors always earn a lot of money. He said, 'Look at the big house Daddy has, he must have a lot of money.' I know that the house must be big, the garden goes around three sides of it, so when you've done 'the whole round of it' and picked all the autumn leaves or trimmed the garden rims with the shears then you know it's so, at least when you look at it from the outside. We have a huge fridge in the kitchen, I know there's a telephone in the dining room, and we have a toilet upstairs. So Daddy's rich and the house is certainly much bigger than Mrs Ganaghan's house down in the country at Rathagan, which doesn't have any of the modern conveniences or 'mod-cons' and maybe that's why Rhona married my daddy after my mother died in a place called Tury from God knows what sickness and she moved in to live in Dad's house with all his money and respect that he's earning from being a doctor.

Maybe.

We have trees around our garden, but no money ever falls off them. The only thing that falls off them are the leaves, blown down by the cold westerly winds coming in from the Atlantic ocean which is only a few miles away, and when it's late autumn, there will be leaves all over the garden which Martin and I will have to pick, but not today. Today is a Holy day, and we're going to Mrs Ganaghan's house again this afternoon, soon after the Holy Mass. I finish polishing the shoes, leave the big black car in the garage, and soon we're off down past the Trader's Rest Hotel, walking the mile down to Holy Mass in the big church in Chapel Street. The big black car comes out of the garage after we've left and Daddy will drive down with Rhona, and the others to Holy Mass in the church beside the Mental Hospital which is only three hundred yards from the house, and still a walk away from the Trader's Rest Hotel. Holy Mass isn't too bad for me, because the church in Chapel Street is just about the only other place in town apart from St Patrick's National School across the street that I'm allowed to go to, and it gets me out of the house. I'll listen to the parish priest and his Holy Mass, and the sermon too. Sometimes he'll talk about the Sins, which frightens me, and other times about the family, which frightens me too, how it's important that God's message is preached and practised in the Catholic household. We always seat ourselves near the front, but no parish priest ever notices that neither my daddy nor Rhona, or any of the others, ever come to hear the Holy Mass with us in the big church in Chapel Street, nor did they ask me why. So they couldn't ever hear the same sermon as we do, about the same Sins as we do, or anything likewise about the Catholic family as we do. Maybe I could go into the Presbytery on Chapel Street and ask what the other parish priest in the Mental Hospital's church talks about, but I'm not allowed in there either. And we don't ask the others about what they hear at their Holy Mass in their church.

This afternoon we'll be off to Mrs Ganaghan's house, which isn't bad either. Not bad because we'll be told to go out and play, which is fine because at Western Road Martin and I are only allowed out into the garden to pick the leaves.

'And don't leave one scattered anywhere now,' Rhona will say, and after that we have to stay in the playroom which, with the garage, is in the annexed building. Sometimes we get allowed into the back garden down behind the house. Some of the falling leaves arrive there too, but we don't have to pick those ones up because when visitors come to the house they are shown around the top garden only before they visit the house and settle in for tea and scones in the sitting room. So the top garden always has to be clean and tidy because visitors, the neighbours, or people walking up and down Western Road might see what state the whole place would be in, and wouldn't it be a shocking blow to a doctor's reputation if his garden wasn't in a fine state indeed? At least at Mrs Ganaghan's we can wander around the whole place, go over the wall and see if the well is still there and the water still flowing, if our dams on the river are still standing, and we can forget about Western Road. They forget about us too, and as the house has no phone in, then they must have many things to talk about. Many things must have happened during the week since the last visit to Rathagan.

Later on we're allowed in to have a bite to eat and I see Daddy all dressed up in his finest Sunday suit with the waistcoat, tie and all sitting in the big chair to the left of the Aga, and old Terence always sitting opposite him to the right, his hands clasped over his stick. Sometimes he stretches out his palms towards the Aga to warm them, and then back to the conversation about how the Government is ruining this country, and couldn't the Bishops do anything to stop all the young men going abroad to them foreign parts looking for work? I have my doubts about that, especially when I think about the Foleys down the road, they'd have an awful lot of pairs of hands in the house if they weren't all going off to England. With so many hands about they'd hardly need the donkey to do the turf hauling for them any more. Rhona sits on the sofa facing the Aga, which means that her back is to us, holding her saucer and cup of tea like a real what-might-you-call-it, and she keeps turning her head to see what we're eating, and I wonder if she'll ever get a strain in her neck from that, especially as it's no use, Mrs Ganaghan has portioned out any remaining slices of cake anyway. If we don't get much cake then we know that everybody else was hungry, helped themselves whilst we were out playing, and 'poor Mrs Ganaghan has to walk ten miles in and out to Baltrina to buy cake, and when she finally managed to get there yesterday there was nothing much left in the shops.'

I know Christmas is coming and we'll all get a present from Mrs Ganaghan. When December arrives and we go down to Mrs Ganaghan's small house in Rathagan, the weather in those parts is usually lousy cold and wet. She's not far from the Atlantic Ocean either, and she gets her fair share of the westerlies and the rain blowing in from America across the ocean. This means that we don't have to go out and play as much as other seasons, and chances are we'll all be in the kitchen at the same when the presents come out. Daddy always gets a tie and handkerchiefs. The tie will always go well with his Sunday suit, the waistcoat and all.

'Oh, oh, well thank you now dear,' he says.

'Oh that's all right, Jim, I know you like the ties and will you have another spoon of sugar in your tea there now, or another sup of the milk, it's fresh now you know?' Mrs Ganaghan says. I can well imagine that she'd have gone into town, and back out the five miles again, and for the Lord's sake sure you couldn't be going without fresh milk in the house when Doctor Duignan comes down on a Sunday afternoon for the visit and the chat, could you? Treating the son-in-law well is awfully important now.

Martin and I always get some socks and Rhona turns her head over rearwards to see if we have that happy look on our faces, and if we dare forget 'Thank you very much, they're nice now, Mrs Ganaghan,' she calls us rascals and where were we brought up at all? The others always have their birthdays in December so Mrs

Ganaghan explains to us all that she's giving them each one big present to cover for the two occasions. Rhona thinks that's a good idea, and she turns towards Daddy.

'Now that's very wise of you, Mrs Ganaghan, thank you too, Terence, for all the presents, and I think everybody's happy with all that now,' says Daddy.

Rhona butts in again with a glare so we all say that 'We're happy and thank you, Mrs Ganaghan.' Even if I'm really happy with my socks I might want to give a hug to Mrs Ganaghan, but I do notice that nobody within the Ganaghans or the Duignans ever give hugs, and I'm not the one to start. I realise that some presents are more important because of the birthday bit, and may I remind Mrs Ganaghan that my birthday is coming up in February next? Rhona turns her head, glares and stares again, and not even Martin now has the courage to tell Mrs Ganaghan that she's forgotten his birthday, which was last month only, and couldn't he have a big present too?

So we're all happy indeed and then Daddy says, 'Well Mrs Ganaghan thank you for the tea and the chat, but we'll be moving along now.' Then we head off in the darkness on the five-mile road to Baltrina. Driving up to the road to Farna I see the dark house coming near. The haunted house. I asked Martin about the house one evening, and he told me that it's a haunted place. From this distance I can see the shuttered windows and door, and the greying stone walls look spooky with the early evening darkness around the place. I close my eyes as we drive by, because I'd never know if there'd be a ghost who might be looking out at me through a hole in one of them window planks.

Keeping my eyes closed for a good minute I think too of all of the leaves on the lawn at home, and even if it's dark out there when I reopen them, through the darkness and the wilderness of the countryside and the hidden bogs out there I can see the leaves, and before we get back to the gates at Marian House I know they're still there, waiting.

Until after I come out of school tomorrow afternoon.

Fanta

Jimmy McLaughlin who lives on the opposite side and slightly down the boreen has a daughter whose name is Bernadette and she'll be having a birthday party soon. Her mammy tells me and Martin to come along down to their house in the afternoon on the following Monday at a set time, there will be other children along too, so we can both enjoy ourselves for a while. I'm happy too because we are never allowed into their place, the nearest I'd get to their front door is when I'd stand beside the big gooseberry tree which grows in an opening in the fence between Mrs Ganaghan's cowfield and the garden at the front of Bernadette's house.

This is the first birthday party in my life that I've been invited to, and when I ask Martin about it he's into telling me about all the cakes and the toffees which we should be getting. Sounds great for me, and I'm looking forward to it!

Lunchtime comes on the Monday, and when we sit at the bottom end of the table in Mrs Ganaghan's kitchen we find ourselves facing two plates stacked way high with buttered bread. Martin says that he's not hungry and he couldn't possibly eat everything on his plate.

Mrs Ganaghan says that we'll have to eat everything up to the last crumble, otherwise we're not getting let down to Bernadette's house, and that we shouldn't be eating everything else around us in other peoples places.

Martin shuts his gob and we stuff ourselves with all the bread and butter and we're nearly sick from all of it. An hour later Mrs Ganaghan tells us that it's about time now and we can head off down to Bernadette's house for the great birthday party.

There's a great day about it as we head off down the boreen, with the fine weather giving us great sunshine indeed.

As usual when approaching the place we keep a watchful eye out to our left side because we know that they have a huge boar, which waddles around that small patch of ground behind the tall fence, snorting and rolling himself in the muck. I've never seen him out on the boreen itself, but to look at him or hear him afar is enough to put the creeps into Martin and myself, and if he'd ever make it through a hole or such in the fence, or smash his way out the gate sure Jasus tonight wouldn't that put a devil of a fright into us indeed?

We creep cautiously along the gravel-covered surface and race in through the narrow garden gate, closing it firmly behind us. Still no sign of the boar. We're safe for a while now. We head in through the kitchen porch, and are bewildered by the decorations up and hanging all around the place. Plates and plates of cakes, and Smarties, sweets and toffees neatly set out on the kitchen table. Bottles of Club orange, Coca Cola and Fanta are to be seen waiting to be opened and enjoyed too.

Bernadette's mammy invites us to come forward and meet all the other boys and girls that we'd never met before.

'What'll ye be having there now?' she offers gently.

But we're so stuffed from scoffing all of Mrs Ganaghan's lunch of buttered bread that we can hardly even drink a full bottle of Fanta or anything, and we have to watch all the other children helping themselves to biscuits, sweets and toffees, drinks and the birthday cake too.

When we get back to Mrs Ganaghan's house we have to thank her for having let us go and enjoy the nice birthday party, and wasn't it lovely now at all?

But it's a good job that Bernadette's mammy gave us a few toffees and sweets before we left, which we stuffed in our pockets, that way Mrs Ganaghan doesn't get to see them, and they'll be for us only.

Milk

It's a roasting hot and grand day altogether, and Martin and myself are down in the back garden as usual, and today we are having the mighty fine weather indeed.

Daddy is doing some work in his vegetable plot at the far end of the garden, where he has rhubarb, scallions, potatoes, a blackberry tree and other bits and pieces to attend to, so he's coming and going up to the house and back again. Today he has told us to help him as with the summer period now he says that there'll be a lot of work to be doing.

Aunty Mairéad and Stanley are home on holidays from where they are living in England. Whilst Mairéad stays up in the house to chat with Rhona, Stanley comes down the back garden to see us all and how we are getting on with the job.

I'm standing at the outside corner of the bottom half of the vegetable plot, facing the neighbour's field. Stanley comes over towards me.

I hear him saying something, but can't understand what he's on about at all, he's using words that I can't catch, an awful foreign jabber to him at all.

'Oi said, wud you loik a glas of moilk?' he repeats.

'Eh?' I scratch my head as I look up at him. He's a great big strong man himself now, and I think that if he moves a little over to the right he'll be blocking out the sun from my eyes altogether. But I can't understand a word of what he's jabbering about.

Daddy comes back down from having delivered another bunch of scallions to the house again, and approaches from over to my left and is now standing with his brown trousers and wellington boots, and looking up at Stanley too.

Martin has heard Stanley's question and has moved closer between us.

'He has asked you if you want a glass of milk, he's English, lives in London,' he explains.

'Oh, a glass of milk?' I'm happy that Martin understood something at least of this English talk here because I didn't know what Stanley's jabbering on about.

Hot down at this end of the garden here I think, pulling scallions and others out of their rows and shaking all the earth off them.

I wonder.

I look up towards the back of the house, where Rhona is probably sitting in the kitchen and drinking her endless cups of coffee with Aunty Mairéad. I'm thirsty, but don't want Stanley to go up for me to the house because I know that Rhona won't be happy about that, and we're supposed to come up only when we get called.

I shake my head, and wait to get called later.

Back to the remaining scallions I go, and continue pulling and shaking the daylights out of them to get the earth off.

School

Martin has been going down to school at St Patrick's National School in town for a few years now, and one day Dad tells me I have to start too. The first day of school starts with Daddy driving me down to the school and we head to the first classroom, which for me is on the left when we arrive in through the main doors. I get a seat in the front row, my classmate Flannery is to my left at the double bench, and is in the row nearest the window. Martin goes to class with older boys in the other building nearest the street.

With time I get to like school a lot and am doing so well that one day I'm told to skip a class and move up to the next one in the corridor.

My Christmas exams have arrived, completed, and I've done so well in third class here that the teacher calls me up forward to his desk and as a prize I get a great bunch of huge oranges and a few bars of Cadbury's fruit and nut chocolate. It's been an awful long time since I've had some chocolate to eat, and have never seen such a fresh orange like this, and am so happy that I'm not going to eat anything of them right here, but will bring the whole bounty back home to Western Road to show to Daddy. But when I get home there's nobody there. They must all be away down the town somewhere. So I'll have to wait, and decide to settle down and sit on the hard concrete floor of the outside hallway which separates the garage from the annexe building on my own as Martin finishes school much later. I'm hungry, and wouldn't a bar of chocolate be a good thing for that now? But I prefer to wait, and that way I can show my prize for all to see. I guess that some time has gone by since I left the school as I notice that darkness is now setting in. But when I hear the noise of the motorcar's engine turning in toward the gate I know that the waiting is nearly finished.

A minute or two more and Rhona appears in the hallway with all the others trooping behind her. She sees me sitting there on the ground with my bounty.

'What do you have there?' she enquires.

'I won it at the school,' I say, holding up my prize for all to see.

'What do you mean, won?' she says, really wanting to know everything. 'What are you on about at all?'

'I got second place in the class exams you know, and this is what the teacher gave me,' I explain, turning towards Daddy.

'Come on now, you'll be giving that to me here, and I'll be minding it for you,' she says, and I have to hand over all the oranges and chocolate bars. She unlocks the annexe door, and I'm told to go in and play in the playroom.

Daddy hasn't even said a word, as all the others head into the house, and I'm left on my own out in the playroom. A short while later a few squares from one of the chocolate bars is brought out to me, and that's all I ever get to see of the great big prize that I'd worked for and even won in the Christmas exams.

After the first day Daddy doesn't drive me or Martin to school anymore, so we walk the mile down to school on our own each morning. We don't go home for the lunch break, as Rhona gives us each a paper bag with some sliced bread and butter, and a bottle of milk. We can eat and drink in the playground, play conkers in the autumn, marbles, or other games, and fight all we want but after lunch break we'll all line up for the call before going in to class again. We never leave the school playgrounds, except maybe on the occasions when we'd have heard one of the Army's helicopters which land from time to time in the grounds of the Barracks over to the opposite end of the town. So we race over there, and I get to have a close look at the huge machines parked on the open grass. Martin says they are called Alouettes, built in France, which is somewhere over there on the Continent. If Martin is lucky he'll even get to see them starting their engines again, and then the blades start rotating, but the deafening noise which echoes all around the courtyard and the buildings built in a quarter moon puts the frights into me, and when the blades start accelerating I creep rearwards and prefer to wait by the entrance gates. Back to class and I mustn't forget my milk bottle anywhere, or have it broken, 'cos there'd be a beating for that after the Angelus prayers in the evening.

Playing all we want is fine, but fighting all we want can be dangerous because when I get into a big fight I can't always win, and if I get knocked to the ground and get injured then one of the teachers will see my knee bleeding when I march in through the school door after roll-call. If a teacher sees that then he'll automatically call me aside into a small room between the main doors and the toilets to the right and put some of the terrible red ointment on my knee, and the red colour sticks so much that even by the time I get home after school the stain is still to be seen. Rhona knows where to look for the red ointment, and if it isn't already bad enough to have been beaten up by a big bastard and the ointment being put on my knee because it burns me more than the pains I already have, when I get home it means that Gerard hasn't been behaving at all again hasn't he, and all brats deserve a beating don't they? Never mind that it can't always be my fault if I get picked on most of the time, and then after I get the hell beaten out of me with an electrical cable after the Angelus prayers for being a brat, but there are times that I'd wish that instead of having buttered slices of bread three times a day, I'd have a proper meal to eat, and could be a stronger boy that way, I could beat the shite and the living daylights out of all of them big bastards, and they'd be the ones to fall on and finish up on the concrete floor or on the tar surface, and in the unlikely event of them being beaten by their fathers when they get back home then at least it wouldn't be my problem.

One day whilst playing in the field west of the school building I find the front page of a newspaper, and there are photos of a Bob Kennedy who has been shot and killed on the 05.06.68 in Los Angeles.

That's a long way from here I know.

After school we'll walk the mile back home to the house out Western Road. Sometimes we'll stop for a while and play with Bertie Glennon and John Hannon in the big field opposite Sander's house. The gate to the big field is at the top of the hill just after St Patrick's Terrace, which is further down from our house. Bertie is in Martin's class, and sometimes his sister Maeve comes to play with us. Bertie and Maeve live in St Patrick's Terrace, and John Hannon lives with a whole bunch of brothers and sisters right next door to us, but Martin prefers to play with John in the field down the road because we're not allowed into the Hannon's house to visit or play.

There is a small stream at the bottom of the field between the two rows of houses, a cemetery beyond the stream, but we never go further. Sometimes we'll stop too at the Glavneys house, which is just six doors from ours, and you can't see their front gate from behind the lace curtains at Marian House. The three girls Trina, Ciar, and Ailbhe become good friends to us, and if we're hungry their mammy, Ina, will make us a sandwich or two for us.

One day when the school should be finishing the teacher won't let us go because he'd like to explain a little about a play that the dramatic society would like to prepare for Christmas. He starts going into details, and as he winds on and on, I notice that the minute hand on the wallclock behind him is racing forwards, and it's now getting later and later. I start to panic, and become all too unsettled behind my school bench.

The teacher notices.

'Duignan,' he calls out, 'aren't you well at all, what's the matter with you, the fits or what? Are you in a jiffy?'

I'm so nervous that I can't even reply to his question, and I bow my head to avoid looking at him or the others.

'You'll have to let him go, Mr Mac,' I hear a voice say, 'because if he doesn't go now he'll be late home, and he'll get beaten for it.'

I can't even recognise who speaks up for me like that, or how he'd know about the way things carry on at Marian House, I just want to get going and fast.

A silence.

'Okay, Duignan, you can leave,' says the teacher.

I grab my school bag, say my blessings, and run.

I don't get to play any part in the school play.

Martin is getting near his end of year exams, and as he still has to spend some time on the gardening work, that leaves his homework in second place. As the dates approach he has to increase the rhythm and he has to do his studies down the back garden, so he gets me onto reading his classbooks and notes, and we walk miles and miles back and forth down the back garden, me reading stuff to him which is years ahead of my time. But I have to help him through those exams, though I don't expect him to get any praise if he passes, just like I got my oranges and chocolate bars swiped from me when I did well in third class, but judging from his state of mind I guess that failing them would be something near to a total disaster, and he might even get a particularly bad beating.

I want to help him, he's the only real brother I've got.

Daddy never comes down the back garden to us and asks Martin if he is doing well with his studies. Maybe he needs more time and less gardening, or more peace and quiet? The others always get lots of time to do their homework, and can even do it in the dining room, with the great big table in there you can spread out all the schoolbooks and exercise books you want. When they've finished with their homework they can then change rooms, and move to the piano in the lounge, so from time to time we'd get a few notes drifting out through the window onto the garden. Jane also goes down the town to learn traditional Irish dances, so with all their activities how could they possibly find time for leaves or weeds? We never get to meet Daddy during the day except sometimes whilst working and picking leaves out on the lawn, and he'd be racing back and forth with his lawnmower anyway. Maybe I could try and catch him when he is at the western gable end of the house, there isn't a window on that end at all, because with all the windows up front and out the back you'd never know which lace curtains Rhona might be hiding behind, and if she'd see me talking with Daddy, she'd be running out to see what business we're about, or to remind us to hurry up, we're a little late now, and she'd want to be serving tea a quarter of an hour earlier this evening because she's suddenly remembered that she has a Bingo session on this evening down the town, or out in Killabbey, and would you mind driving me over Dad, you'll have a pint or two in Walsh's pub whilst you're waiting upon me?

So there's no way we could get to talk to him about studies, exams, or anything else for that matter. We'd see him for the Angelus, but that's a time for praying for all the needful Catholic souls up and down the country and even the whole world, and mostly we see his back as he's kneeling and praying as he faces the calendar with the picture of the Virgin Mary above the kitchen table, and Rhona's there anyway and watching us both as we get off our knees until we leave the kitchen, so what would it change?

But whenever Rhona is due out for a Bingo session, then she's all excited, and we'll be rushed off to bed earlier, which means no beating for Martin or myself this evening. I don't know if she ever wins anything in them bingo halls, maybe if she would she'd be off down the town more often indeed!

When I start bringing homework back to the house, I have to stand in the kitchen to do all of it. There is a small work area to the right of the kitchen sink where I can spread out my books. Rhona will always be leaning on the workbench on the other side of the sink, drinking her eternal cups of instant coffee, and smoking a Carroll's cigarette or two. Whenever I look in her direction, I see that she's watching me, certainly wondering, and sometimes asking, if I'll soon be finished with my few bits, because the lawn has to be picked clean of all the leaves that have fallen since yesterday, because the whole place needs to have a nice look about it in case the strollers out the Western Road might be looking in, or I'd have to get out into the playroom.

One day our teacher starts talking about school projects. I'm wondering what all this caper is about indeed, but then he'll be telling us to get together in groups of two students and you'd have to pick a theme, and then you'd be doing a lot of research about what you've decided upon and then be putting together a huge board exposing all your work, drawings, samples and so forth. It's all part of the education thing he says, ye'll all be learning a lot from what ye've put together so now will ye all be off about yeer business, and get down to work. All the boards will be put up on display in the school corridors for the parents and everybody to see and admire.

I have to team up with Mark McGuire and we have chosen 'Trees' for our project.

Trouble is, that I'd have to be doing this outside school hours, and also have to go over to the library to look up books on our subject and research and then after over to my teammate's house to assemble and work on the whole thing at all. But the town library just as much as my schoolmates' homes are out of bounds for me, can't go there, so I can't help my mate with his project, and he ends up doing all the work himself.

When finished, my mate's board has a great look to it, it has a banner message across the top:

'One tree can produce a million fire matches, but one match can destroy a million trees.'

My mate Mark gets a lot of compliments for the great job he's been doing at all, but my teacher never asks me why I haven't helped him at all.

When Christmas approaches, the National School will be organising a Christmas Opera or theatre piece for the parents and all the other town residents, but I can't get any part of the action, because there's no end to them damned leaves and other work in the garden around Marian House.

Anyway, I'm always finished with my homework long before Daddy arrives home from the County Clinic where he must be awful busy caring for all the sick and people who are suffering with their pains and all the lot, so he never actually sees me doing anything the likes of such, and he never asks me if I like it or not, or what I'm learning at school, and do I ever have any problems with the sums, or the Gaelic and all that?

Man and dog.

It's a fine summer's evening and all, the strong yellow sunlight is streaming across the field opposite the house, towards the low hills on the horizon way beyond. There's not even the whisper of a wind to be heard outside. I watch as Mrs Ganaghan moves towards the round mirror, which is fixed, to the wall just inside the right side of the kitchen door. She has a powder box with her at hand and also the usual bottle of Oil of Ulay, which means that she's going to start putting her make-up on, do a beauty job, and soon we'll soon be off up or down the boreen for a casual visit somewhere.

Great!

The strong light radiating into the kitchen reflects upon her face and helps her get the creases out of her skin easier.

All of a sudden she starts a little cough or two, nodding towards the mirror, and old Terence, who has been sitting behind me in the corner chair near the Aga, butts in.

'Where would you be off to now at this time of the evening?' he asks.

'Oh, off for a short visit for a while with Martin and Gerard here,' she replies.

'But you couldn't be doing that, there's a man who'll be coming around to the house this evening,' he adds, leaning forward on his old stick.

'What man?' she enquires.

'Oh, a man who said he wanted to talk to you about things, about the dog,' he says.

I wonder who might be so interested about the poor old dog who spends his time locked up in the old farmhouse out behind.

'Well, in that case I might as well stop doing me nose here then,' she says, folding the powder box lid shut and swiping the bottle of Ulay off the kitchen table to remove them to the bedroom, and I and Martin know that we won't be going anywhere for a visit this evening. We'll just have to find something else to do and occupy ourselves.

The hours pass slowly, we keep waiting for the man to arrive but he never comes that evening at all, and the next day nobody talks any more about him and even less about the dog.

Glasses

I am used to wearing glasses, and that since when I was a small boy, because I have something wrong with my eyes. I don't know what exactly, and there's no point in asking or I'd be sent out to the garden to pick the leaves, or trim the edges on the front lawn.

At night I can't wear my glasses of course, so I always leave them on the dresser between the two beds. From time to time however, I find that the glasses are broken in the morning. Maybe it's just the rim or something, but I know that when the evening comes I'm in for a beating. The beatings always happen after the holy Angelus. For the holy Angelus we are all together in the kitchen, which is really the only moment of the day that such an event happens, Rhona kneeling against a chair, with a newspaper under her knees beside the Aga, the warmest place of all. Tadgh sits on a chair beside her, and Fintan and Jane get to sit at the white kitchen table. Daddy always kneels at the corner of the table facing the calendar hung above the table, with a daily newspaper under his knees too, his back towards the corner of the door, the big fridge and us both. He faces the yearly calendar hung above the table corner. Some years there's an image of The Virgin Mary, other years the words Bank of Innishland written near the bottom of the calendar. I always kneel beside the fridge, Martin to my left and us both with our short trousers, on our knees on the hard kitchen floor without any newspaper. After we've been down at six o'clock to say the Holy Angelus, praying for all the Catholic souls that need prayers, and whilst I get off my knees I try to make a beeline towards the kitchen door to head upstairs to bed, my head bowed forward.

'Gerard's broken his glasses again, haven't you seen it?' Rhona suddenly remembers to tell Dad, 'and what kind of a caper is this at all?'

Then Dad looks at me, and sure enough the evidence is there to be seen. A doctor might be rich, but glasses still cost a lot of money or so it seems, as I hear his roughed-up voice of anger growing.

'Ah, ah, ah here, down you go,' he says.

I'm terrorised, because I know there's no escape and this is what I've been dreading all the afternoon as I know that the moment is drawing nearer. I have no chance to tell what might have happened, not even an excuse, as my word has no weight in this house. Only Rhona's words count for anything here. Daddy reaches behind the calendar above the kitchen table, takes down the yard of heavy black electrical cable, which is always hidden behind. I am then pushed down on my knees facing him, then I feel my head being clamped between his knees, down with my trousers with my bare arse for all the others to see and for an eternity my little world consists of the downward view to the hard floor, and the heavy thrashing being meted out on my buttocks. I cannot hold back my tears, maybe some of the others are laughing their heads off, but I wouldn't hear them, my pain and resulting screams drown out the outside world and any noises. I know that Martin wouldn't laugh though, because he too gets beaten. Right now, he's totally silent, because raising his voice or complaining about me being beaten will mean the same treatment for him too. He doesn't wear glasses however, so he could never be accused of breaking such like, but there are plenty of other reasons to be found, and he'll get caught sooner or later for some of them. I beg Daddy to let me go – 'I won't do it again!' – but the lashing continues. It continues even though I'm not even responsible for the cause. I wonder if anybody else in town has been saying the Holy Angelus this evening for those in need, because right now I can't take any more of this.

Tomorrow evening it will probably be Martin's turn, not for broken glasses of course, but another trumped-up excuse.

Tadgh, Jane, and Fintan, who never break anything or do anything wrong are never summoned by Rhona to finish between Daddy's knees, just after saying the Holy Angelus and to be thrashed with the yard of heavy electrical cable which spends its days hidden behind the Virgin Mary calendar.

Visiting

Mrs Ganaghan and Terence don't even have a wireless to listen to in the long summer evenings. So when it's still bright Mrs Ganaghan will start putting on her Oil of Ulay, powder and make-up for the road, so Martin and I know that we'll be shortly heading off for a walk and a gawk about what's going on up and down the lanes. We head off out for a good walk and a visit in the area. She'll never tell us in advance where we're going, but off we'll head up or down the boreen. Nobody would know in advance that we would be coming around as everybody is without the telephone in these parts. The crows will be out chattering, and the red-breasted robins will be singing in the bright summer's evening sunshine. I enjoy the walking, because it gets us away from the house, and along the way there may well be some ripe blackberries just waiting to be picked off the briars or other shrubs in the hedgerows. There's also another variety with pods, which look just like fresh garden peas. One time we'd head up the boreen, and turn right at McDonald's house, out past the Clarks', Duffys' too, where sometimes we'd see the old man sitting with his boy in front of the house. They'd be sitting there with a pile of cooked spuds in front of them on the naked ground, and they'd be enjoying it galore. We might meet people cycling along on their black Raleigh bikes, and they'd stop, and there'd be a bit of chatter and questions about how we all are, and how's old Terence himself, and where might we be heading off to at all now on this fine summer's evening and isn't the weather keeping up grand now, thanks be to God Himself, but then after those awful rains and high winds of the spring isn't the grass growing mighty strong this year at all, and isn't the Government and all them Ministers up in Dublin ruining the country altogether, the whole place is in such an awful state of affairs, oh and by the way who are them two fine boys with you now, Mrs Ganaghan?

Past the little lane which turns off down to Gillespie's place, up over the hill wherefrom we have a magnificent view westwards over towards the Knoxes' castle. The castle was inhabited by English lords some centuries ago, and Martin says that they had lots of women slaves in their place, but now they're all dead and everybody's buried in the gardens around what's left of the castle. I can see the tops of the chimney stacks and other remains, the long straight boreen you'd have to walk through is now overgrown on both sides, and if they have dead people buried in the gardens, then there must be a ghost or two down there too. To look at the place from this distance gives me the creeps and I don't want to ask Mrs Ganaghan's permission to take a walk right up to the castle gates.

A left turn and across a small bridge under which the shallow flowing water is fresh and crystal clear, and we know that we're heading for Monaghan's house. I can see it now from the bridge's parapet. There's a great big field out to the front, the pretty thatched cottage being set well back from the road. I can see the white chimney smoke drifting lazily into the clear summer air, and I know the turf fire is doing well for itself. We arrive through the half-door, where a pleasant scent of burning peat awaits us. The half-door is a necessity on any real Irish cottage, it'll keep the geese, horses, or other farm animals out unless invited in to the kitchen. Right now there are geese all round in the huge garden, and I see the horse grazing leisurely further down near the stream that we've just crossed.

Once inside old Mrs Monaghan is there to greet us, her daughter-in-law is busy tidying around the place. At this time of the evening Justin would be out in the cowshed at the bottom end of the house. Sure the fire is going great guns in the huge open hearth, and there's a blackened kettle to be seen sitting on the hob to one side, and a huge round, deep baking pan is suspended from the centre above the roaring fire. They are baking fresh bread, and from another scent drifting its way through the old kitchen towards me I guess that they've put a drop or two of treacle into the dough.

I don't mind being told to go out and play over here, because there are geese to be running after, a cat has appeared, none of these animals to be found on Mrs Ganaghan's so-called farm at all. After that I wander into the cowshed and there's Justin to be sure, sitting on his milking stool hard at the evening's work, something that Mrs Ganaghan wouldn't know that much about as she doesn't have any cows at all. I like Justin a lot, he's so soft mannered, and even if he doesn't have any children I wonder what kind of a father would he make.

'Would you like to take a try at milking the cow here?' he asks me and I stare at him.

'Come on over, I'll show you how to be going about it,' he says and I pluck up the courage to be sitting beneath this huge cow with her huge udders full of milk, and I grab her teat. This is of course my first try, and I proudly give a good tug on the teat, but having forgotten to point downwards again towards the milk bucket below Justin gets his face squirted with a stream of the freshest Irish milk you can find anywhere for miles around.

He laughs heartily at all this, and I think that with all the animals and kind people around here wouldn't this be a great farm to be spending the summer holidays on?

Radio

Since coming down the last time, Mrs Ganaghan and Terence have made the acquisition of a wireless which spends its time under wraps perched on a small table to the right side of the back kitchen door. They'd rarely have a newspaper coming to the house at all, except maybe on a Saturday when we'd have made it the ten miles into and back from Baltrina to buy some fresh milk and other things, and then we'd have to buy a copy of the *Evening Press* and *The Western Weekly* for old Terence. We would also buy a Sunday paper the next morning over at Bredan's shop after coming out from the Holy Mass at Father Davey's church way down the boreen on the way to Kiltara.

Old Terence likes *The Western Weekly* because it's all local news, and will have some photos of the best cows and heifers around at all the local fairs. There might even a great photograph taken at the Baltrina cattle mart and showing Paddy Flannery with one of his prize heifers. He'll also enjoy reading Tom Hennally's *Farmers' Diary* where he'll have all the latest information on the current market prices for a cow, a pig, corn or potatoes. I wonder what use all of that could be to him, because he's too old to be farming now, and this isn't a proper farm place at all, nothing much grows here except weeds and the grass which gets to be plucked by Martin and I when we're down here on holidays.

I once had an idea about plucking the grass. At the house on Western Road didn't we use clippers to trim and finish-off the lawn edges after Daddy had been up and down the length with his lawnmower? So why not ask Daddy to lend us the clippers when we're coming down to Mrs Ganaghan's place? That way we'd do a better job indeed, and might even be able to do more in a day's work? Maybe we could even trim a few of them wild shrubs and the hedge that she has going around her small garden? Trouble is, I can never manage to get Daddy on his own. I'd have to be able to talk to him alone about that, but Rhona is always in the vicinity, so I can't manage a chance of me talking to him alone, between father and son that is, she'd interfere straightaway just to know what we're jabbering about, and if she heard anything about my suggestion of borrowing the clippers then she'd laugh her head off and I'd be praised just as much as the day I came second in the Christmas exams with my few oranges and chocolates as a prize, might even get a clout on the ear, and be sent off to be minding my own business. So it's down on our bare knees, and ahead with the grass plucking. One day Martin had it worse than myself. Mrs Ganaghan sent him out to pull all the nettles that were growing wild as hell, near the gable of the old farmhouse. She wouldn't let him have gloves to protect his bare hands, luckily he found a scrap of old newspaper outside to help him with the job, until it got torn to shreds. He's cursing like mad, and when she arrives out to see how he's progressing, she starts taking the mickey, and says that pulling nettles is easy work indeed, and that there's nothing to be all excited about

A good job we don't have nettles anywhere in our garden, up front nor down the back at Marian House.

No animals to be seen here either, they won't even allow poor old Rex to creep out for a while from his mucked-up lodgings, but I hear Terence going on about all these prices and things when visitors come round to have tea and biscuits at the house, or when he'd be having a bit of the gab with any man who might be going about his business up or down the boreen until he'd see Terence out with his walking stick. Weather permitting, any man on his Raleigh bike would stop and have a chat with old Terence, to hear all about the way the country is going now, the awful state it's in and all, and whatever might happen at all if we'd join the Common Market? Would it be the ruins of the likes all the small farmers up and down the place, you know, the likes of you and me, Terence?

Old Terence's given up any work he ever had many years ago,

but he's always into the chat, and has no limit to what might add to a great talk with anybody he'd meet on his way.

If he is happy with his *Western Weekly* I'm into the *Evening Press* a lot, lots of things to be reading about what's going on up and down the country, because the rest of the country and the world outside is what interests me, not just this lousy corner of the woods stuck up north of Baltrina, and there are lots of places that we never get to visit or see at all. For me there's no better way of passing the time, be it summer, or a long dark winter's evening. So the next best thing would be reading and asking questions all the time to Peter, who when he is on visits to his parents spends his time standing and warming his arse in front of the hot Aga.

'Where's Tralee, Peter?' I'd ask.

Cartoons too. Nice photos too of young ladies all dressed up and smiling for the cameraman at the Lahinch races.

'Where's Lahinch, Peter?' I need to know everything about Ireland.

Another few photos might show me a group of farmers and wives all geared-up for the hooleybooley at the North Connaught Farmers' Annual Dinner Dance in the Imperial Hotel back in Belnascully, and aren't they all looking so swell? Then there'd be a Reader's Column too, where people would be writing letters to the Editor, complaining about all the noise made by motor cars on the roads and boreens, and the state of all them roads and boreens too, about that bunch of TD's in Government who are doing next to nothing about the poor state of the whole country itself and if they'd do anything at all most likely they'd be adding another few pennies to the price of the great pint at the pubs up and down the country, and with the state of things here now, it's no wonder that our fine young men are all heading over to Liverpool and other foreign places with one-way tickets for the better side to life. Sometimes I find a short letter from a young girl or boy who lives in a town in Japan, or in Africa somewhere, and who is looking for pen-pal contact, preferably someone who collects coins, stamps or postcards. I'd certainly like to find a pen pal in a far away country, learn about their way of life and everything about their country, I could maybe steal an envelope and a few sheets of writing paper from Mrs Ganaghan's stock. I have very few stamps or coins to spare really, so don't know what I could possibly exchange. But how are they going to reply to me, at what address? I sadly realise that any attempt is doomed in advance, but I can always read their letter again and dream about these young people in far-away places, and hope that for them at least they're not stuck on a lousy so-called farm in a back-end of the woods behind nowhere every time they have school holidays.

It's midweek now, the weather hasn't been too hot recently and as the last of the bottles of milk bought on last Saturday's trip still hasn't gone sour as poor Mrs Ganaghan doesn't have a big fridge like we do at the house on Western Road, we're not going to go for an extra walk in and out to Baltrina for more bottles. That'll mean no papers today either, and Terence takes a bit of time to pull up the plastic covering over the wireless and listen to the news and the music during the late afternoon. Martin enjoys listening to the wireless too, any newsbits are always welcome, you'd learn what would be happening and going on in the great big world outside of Rathagan, and he adores the music to say the least.

Terence is seated in his favourite chair next to the Aga, which is puffing smoke up the chimney at a fair rate, and Martin is seated on the couch end, all ears towards the wireless.

Mrs Ganaghan goes to the mirror, which is near the kitchen door with a lipstick in hand. She starts giving herself a mini do-up, and suddenly I hear her coughing and then I see her nodding towards the mirror.

It's a pre-arranged signal, I've guessed it all, and old Terence knows that he has to switch off the wireless, and despite his old age, he's out of the chair and covers the yard or so swiftly, and suddenly the room goes quiet. Maybe he'd have liked to continue listening to the wireless, just like Martin and myself, but orders are orders.

We're not told so, but Martin and I know that we can go out and play instead of dallying around here in the kitchen, or find something else to be doing with our time.

Christmas Day

Christmas is coming again and Daddy has been in to McKee's butcher shop down near the town centre to buy a turkey for the Duignans' Christmas lunch. But our bird always comes with its feathers still on, so Martin gets the job of plucking the big fellow. He has to go into the garage on the other side of the hallway, the big black car will have been rolled back outside but I can't even go over to help him as I have to stay in the playroom whilst he's busy. He'll come back hours later cursing about the big bird with millions of lousy feathers on it and the worse ones are the tiny fine ones which float all over the place, and get into his eyes and up his nostrils.

Christmas Day is another Holy Day so Martin and I will walk down as usual to the big church in Chapel Street for the Holy Mass. Daddy, Rhona and the others will of course drive down the short stretch to the church in The Mental Hospital for their Holy Mass. Our priest will be giving a sermon a bit longer than usual talking about a boy called Jesus who was born into a poor family in Bethlehem. Jesus's father was a carpenter, and after he was born some wise men came to visit the family and brought presents. I wonder if a carpenter could be a rich man, as rich as a doctor? Martin and I hardly ever get visits, and whenever we do then they always come out to the playroom outside for the few minutes, as we aren't allowed into the house. We'll get asked how we are keeping and we always reply 'Very well, thank you,' because we don't know what else we could possibly say, especially with Rhona hovering around with her grand smile and great supervision indeed. The visitors might say what fine big boys we are becoming at all, and haven't we changed a lot since they saw us last time! They don't know of course that all of that's from eating buttered slices of white bread at least twice a day for most days of the year. Sometimes we do get a few shillings and pence in the palms of our hands from visitors, which Rhona always notices, but after they go back inside to the house she will always come back out to the playroom and collect the gifts, she'll be minding that for us she says, so we never really see anything more of our treasured coins. Not only that we don't get to buy any chocolates with the money, something with which we could nourish ourselves on, which would of course be a change from bread and butter, but we'll not be able to learn the true value and worth of money, which of course is part of any general ignorance.

After Holy Mass and whilst waiting for lunch we have to stay out in the annexe room, which is in fact called a playroom, as usual, and if I'm thirsty then I prefer to lift the cistern cover off the toilet which is in the adjoining room and use my small hand to ladle the water to my mouth and drink from there, rather than knock on the kitchen door, which is of course forbidden. The others have the run of the house by now, into the dining room or the lounge to admire the big Christmas tree. I know that every Christmas there's a huge tree in there. Daddy or anybody else has never showed me the tree, but I've seen it on one occasion. That was one evening after the Holy Angelus, and whilst taking the stairs for the bedroom I saw that the lounge door was slightly ajar. The few inches still allowed me a wonderful view of the huge tree, with its huge wide base, and its tip nearly touching the ceiling, and is well decorated with odds and sods, and little lights too. I guess that after Martin and I have been sent to bed Rhona will tell Daddy or one of the others to go in and switch on the small lights, don't forget to pull back the heavy curtains so that Dr Duignan's fine tree can be admired by all the walkers and travellers going up and down the Western Road. The tree reminds me that Christmas must be coming soon and I wonder what it's like when the lights are switched on, but I'm lucky enough to have seen the tree anyway, and maybe I could ask one of the neighbours what the Duignan's Christmas tree looks like from the front of the house when the lights are switched on in the evening.

We have to wait and wait for lunch out here, we could be starving or even dying from the hunger, that won't change much as we're not allowed inside the house until we get 'called', otherwise it'd be a 'beating' after the Holy Angelus in the evening a day or two later, because 'Them boys aren't behaving themselves and that's not a way to be carrying on at all!'

So whilst waiting I can have another read through the Christmas greetings cards which are hung up. Martin has attached decoration streamers going between the four corners of the 'playroom'. Thereupon we hang up all the cards, which Rhona has given us. There are many messages written therein, people writing sending their Best Wishes for a Holy and Happy Christmas to Dr James Duignan and all of his family. But we have noticed that the year mentioned doesn't correspond at all on many of these cards, and what Rhona has simply done is kept the cards that were placed somewhere in the lounge the preceding year, and have since spent twelve months in a shoebox somewhere and are then handed over to Martin and I for this year's decoration in our annexe room. So we read, with a year's delay, the well-mentioned messages coming into Marian House from all over the country and beyond. Anyway we don't know who all these people are, one card might even be from my godparents, but I never get to meet them nor anybody else much, don't know where they all live, what they do for a living; how would we feel concerned by those people, and what might they know of us both?

Finally we get called into the kitchen by Rhona. Of course Daddy, Rhona and the others have already helped themselves to the first portions of the bird and everything else, and as there isn't room for them five persons around the small kitchen table they'll have taken seats around the big table in the dining room which is covered with a nice cloth, fine pieces of silverware, and could seat eight people easily. From the dining room there's a great view indeed out to the front of the house and the big lawn which will be in a fine state of upkeep indeed, because when Martin is finished with the plucking of the big bird he and I will have to do a last tour of picking any leaves and general tidying-up in the big garden, because you couldn't have a garden full of dead leaves around it, and leaving it in a state like that for a Christmas Day at all. You know it wouldn't look well at all and that for a Holy Day, the walkers and travellers out on the Western Road might be looking in, and wondering what's with the Duignan's these times at all, with all the money that Dr James must be earning down at the County Clinic can't they afford a gardener at all and put a nice shape to the whole place? But the gardener's wages which have been saved through Martin's and my work will surely pay for the turkey, even if Martin still has to pluck it to finish.

The hatch between the kitchen table and the dining room is down and closed now and the opaque glass won't allow me to see Daddy or the others, neither are there any noises anywhere now, so I guess they're admiring the nice tree in the lounge. So Rhona lets us get seated on our own at the kitchen table with its plastic cover. I can't possibly take a seat at the top of the table, that's reserved for the others when they're at table, and for the Angelus prayers, so we have to sit side by side facing the hatch and the wall, and we can't see Rhona without turning our heads, but I know that she's there, banging plates and cutlery around a bit and coughing from time to time, and I think that comes from smoking all them Carrolls. But I know that she's hovering around behind us, and if I take a look away from the plate and the food in front of me the most I can do is look at the closed hatch, or stare at the Virgin Mary on the calendar hanging on the wall above my head. I know that it's Christmas today so we'll be allowed to sit at table, because there are times when we have to stand there to eat our food, because Rhona says 'That way, it goes down faster.'

Then Martin and I will have a portion of potatoes, Brussels sprouts and whatever's left of the big bird.

But every year it's the same, I don't know why Daddy couldn't buy a bigger bird than last year's, because we always get the leg joints with the dark meat and I'd like to taste the fine white breast meat for once. I remember that the parish priest at Holy Mass this morning said that Jesus the little boy was born into a poor family with a carpenter for a father, and I don't know what sort of a bird they'd eat down in Bethlehem on a Christmas Day, but I'm sure with all their poorer ways of living than what Dr Duignan could certainly afford, Jesus would sure get to sit together at table with his parents, and with any visitors too, and he'd certainly have some of the nice white breast meat and not just scrawny leg bits. But these must be hard times right now, as neither Jesus the son of God, nor God Himself seem to be doing anything for Martin or myself, because every year it's the same fare of potatoes, sprouts and scrawny turkey legs. But anyway this plate is much better than one full of buttered slices of white bread like we have many other days of the year, so I keep my gob shut on that one and don't complain to Jesus, God His father, or Rhona.

I'm busy scoffing this good food down, not even thinking of the bread and butter portions coming my way again next week and even looking forward to next Christmas's portion, but I can see that Martin is raging mad, because after all his work with plucking the millions of lousy feathers the day before and having them float into his eyes and up his nose all he gets is a piece of the bird's leg with its scrawny meat. Thank God he didn't have to peel the spuds! But I'm happy he did a good job with the plucking, because if he hadn't then Rhona would probably serve us some of them roasted feathers too.

Still no sign of Daddy, and he never gets to ask us if we've enjoyed the nice bird that he'd bought down the town in McKee's butcher shop.

After that we're despatched out to the playroom again because there'll be presents for opening later on. After all, it's Christmas so we'll be getting things, you know? The other children will often get a nice cardigan or something for a present because they'd need it and wasn't it grand of Santa Claus to think of that now just at this time of the year? Martin and I will get a big box with Animal Farm, Meccano, or Risk or something, and that's nice that everybody can play with Martin's and my present too. I'd never get a new cardigan or anything like that for myself only, and even if I'd be needing a new cardigan because my one has holes at the elbows from sitting at school desks, then it'd be my fault for having broken it anyway, that too deserves a 'beating' and sure it's none of Santa Claus's business to be bringing things for bold boys who are always into breaking everything they already have.

Daddy never comes out to the playroom to ask Martin or me if we're happy playing with our presents, and the other children too, as for once they've stayed out here with us for the whole of the afternoon. It's always like that on a Sunday as I know that sometimes there's a football match on the wireless in the kitchen, and the commentator Michael O'Harney will be talking about 'this great match with its two halves to it, the first-half and the second-half,' and even if it isn't Longford or Mayo who are playing today there's still no chance of seeing Daddy before the

Holy Angelus at six o'clock in the evening. But today is Christmas Day, and there won't be any matches on the wireless, so Daddy will probably keep himself busy with reading his medical journals or something else, but as I'm not allowed inside the house, I won't get to know what he'll be doing with his time.

But after all I like Christmas Day a lot because I can't remember having ever been beaten after saying the Holy Angelus on Christmas evening for a hole in my cardigan or other things which aren't my fault.

And if a beating is still due to me for something that happened recently, it won't come today, maybe another day, but I won't think about that until tomorrow at least.

Watch

We now have Easter holidays, and we've arrived down from Castlebarry in the afternoon as usual. But now Daddy, Rhona, and the others have left for the road back into Baltrina and onwards, and we'll spend the Easter with Mrs Ganaghan here.

We're sitting in the kitchen, I've taken a place in Dad's favourite chair by the window, Martin is sitting on the sofa to my right and Mrs Ganaghan has just sat down beside him on the storeroom side. There's not much talking going on, but all of a sudden Mrs Ganaghan looks at Martin's wrist.

'Where's the watch I sent you?' she asks.

Martin looks at her, a little surprised.

'What watch?' he asks.

'That valuable watch I sent you, you know the nice watch that I sent you at St Joseph's. I forgot your birthday, so I sent it later. Didn't you get it at all?' she explains.

Martin says that he never saw the likes of any watch arriving for him at St Joseph's. I think that that was very kind of Mrs Ganaghan indeed, sending a watch for Martin's birthday. I don't know what a new watch is worth, must be worth a few pounds though.

'Uh, uh,' says Mrs Ganaghan, shrugging her shoulders, 'them

people from the Post Office. A right bunch of rascals, they are now!'

Then I think that the watch wasn't a great one and that she's already forgetting about it, instead of wondering why it wasn't delivered to Martin at St Joseph's. Thereafter she changes the subject entirely, the watch is forgotten, and I wonder what sort of a watch was it at all?

Then I wonder if we aren't better off going over the wall into the field which is filled with thistles and rushes to see if our stone dams in the river over there are still holding up, if the well hasn't closed in entirely, or if we might be able to set a hare trap or two, that way maybe we'd have some fresh meat for an Easter meal.

The next morning the postman arrives, with some letters as usual, but Mrs Ganaghan doesn't ask him what should be done if the Post Office loses a valuable watch or anything else like that in the post.

Baltrina

Mrs Ganaghan tells us that we can go into Baltrina town for the whole day next Thursday, and if we like we can borrow Jimmy's bike next door to bring us in for the day. The horse fair at the Baltrina showgrounds will be on too, so if we'd like to spend some time over there it's no problem.

Thursday morning arrives. The great day. Martin is all excited and we already have the bike since yesterday evening and he has checked the brakes, the saddle, and even tested it up and down the boreen for a mile or two to see if all is well. He lets Mrs Ganaghan know that he's done all the work, so she's happy about that.

'Enjoy yerselves,' she says in the morning, handing out a few coins to Martin and me, 'and ye'll be minding yerselves, won't yee?'

I think that this is just as good as a Christmas. Martin is in a great humour indeed, and without delay we're up on our bike and pedalling down the dusty boreen which leads to the main road and then on our way to town. Begorrah sure Martin's so happy I think it must be the best day of his life.

Then onto the main road, and soon we're hurdling down the traffic free roads through the lush wild hedgerows.

The sun is belting down galore from the skies above, the whole place is basking in sunshine, only a few wisps of cloud to be seen for miles around, but Martin keeps up the speed which keeps us cool.

I'm sitting on the rear bicycle-rack, my legs dangling in the fresh air. Time to look around as we take turn after bend and keep advancing towards town, and time to admire the countryside.

I see sheep grazing lazily in green pastures behind stone walls, the fresh green grass of Eire is getting a bit of a chew, whilst others are lying around the field, some of them black fellows, their heads and noses turning towards the invisible but cool light breeze which is drifting slowly across the countryside. On the other side I see a great red-maned horse scratching the underside of his neck on the top of the stone wall, maybe he's waiting for his master or jockey to go for a saunter around the field? Red, a beautiful colour. Another one is stirring himself from his lying position further back in the field.

The turfbogs. Many bogs in these parts, lots of them derelict with nobody working them anymore. Better work is to be found in foreign parts. Further on there's a tinker's caravan parked on a lay-by, an old grey donkey is tied to a greying wooden pole out front, waiting for I don't know what.

Great bunches of nettles growing here and there, even right up to the road's tar surface, and with our short trousers we'd better keep away from them fellows and stay near to the middle of the road as we move along.

Signs up advertising potatoes and bales of hay for sale.

Turf and firewood too.

An old farmhouse lies as one of a few along our way, the old rusted gate at the front end of the garden has been mounted on two railway planks recovered somewhere from the Western Railways.

The fairgrounds aren't far from the town entrance, and I watch the traffic, which is amassing near the entrance gates. I see farmers waving their hands out opened driver car windows, and then I realise that they only want to turn right into the grounds, as they don't have any taillights or blinkers on their heavily laden trailers. We've arrived in town so early that Martin decides that we'll head over into the town centre for a while and have a look around first. We pop in to Kerrigan's bookshop. They always have a choice of Dinky toy cars there too, and Martin wants to offer himself one today. He picks out a beige-coloured Ford Cortina with a new swerving action explaining that when you press one side of the bonnet then the car will turn whilst moving forward. As we are rich today then we'll pick up a recent copy of *Ireland's Own* for Mrs Ganaghan who's been so kind to us for the day, as we know that she likes reading it galore, and when she and Terence have had their turns then Martin and I will read it from head to tail, all the poems, songs and comic bits won't be missed. Then we roam further, looking in through shop windows.

Many shops to have a look into.

Hats for hire in a drapery shop.

Another one with extra long wellington boots and other angling tackle and gadgets.

'A small deposit will secure any item' can be read on a small sign at the bottom of another window.

Then on to a shop selling lots of delph and crockery.

'Nice to handle, nice to hold, but if you break it, consider it sold' goes the verse in this shop window, sitting neatly between the Blue Willow teapots and cups and saucers. Arrah, sure there's no business for me in there I think.

Past the main junction and we arrive at Canola's restaurant down near the bottom of the street before the bridge. Walking through the front door I get the immediate and welcoming smell of the fish and chips. The vinegar too. With the shillings and coppers we have on us we treat ourselves to a delight of some chips and vinegar. When Mrs Ganaghan comes to town with us she brings us in here sometimes for a treat so we know the place quite well. Other times she might bring us into the Bonero café or Joe's restaurant for tea and biscuits.

When we've filled our bellies with the chips and licked the last drops of the vinegar off our fingers, we head back out to the fairgrounds. We walk in the driveway as the grounds are set well back from the street and on a slightly higher level behind the railway station. Farmers and country people strolling around lazily, many with a horse trailing behind them, wads of pound notes in hands and waging bets. One fellow has only a piece of a stringcord tied around his waist which is the only thing that'd stop his pants from falling down around his knees or ankles. Not a sign of a pair of braces to be seen over yer man's shoulders. Then you'd see other fellows, more money to them, with their ties on, and hats on their heads to keep the sun off.

Lots of stands with sweets around, and we can gulp some down for our remaining pennies.

We're having the best day of our lives.

But the hours have been passing away indeed, and now it's time to go, we have to start heading home, over to Gurteens on the Crosslanagh road, and then a right turn onto the older narrower road for the four miles out to Mrs Ganaghan's house.

Martin has now arrived at the top of a steep hill, and there's a great drop in the road before us. He gives a good push to the pedals, and soon we're speeding down the long slope, bordered by a long line of high trees to the right. We are moving so fast that before long we are already at the bottom, but then heading up the other side we start losing speed. Martin starts zigzagging with the bike and I wonder what's into him at all now?

'The laws of physics,' he says, 'that'll get us up to the other end, you'll see.'

I don't know what he's on about, but I have the impression that his hard pedalling and the laws are getting us somewhere.

'You have to take a slope like this by attacking it at a slant,' he says, 'it's much easier that way.'

It's fine by me I think, but have a look over my shoulder. You'd never know but there might be one of them Gardai fellows coming along with his motor car behind us, and if he'd see us swerving like that he might be stopping us and asking us where we might be coming from, and where we might be going to on such a fine day now, and have ye been into them public houses or what's with ye, have ye ever heard of the rules of the road but would you mind the swerving around the road like that because we'd might never make it home without having a traffic accident? Especially if he'd never have heard anything of the Laws of Physics.

We continue, Martin knows all the bends on this old road, and he travels along them with ease, just as if he were a country man himself. The only thing that worries us are the dogs. They'd run out through open gates or jump over a wall, and go for your shins, but it's the fright that gives us the creeps, and you wouldn't want to be swerving at the last moment, you might fall and have a hurt to the knee, and if Daddy and Rhona would be down on the Sunday they'd see our knees, and where have ye been at all and are ye being brats again?

Swerving is all right but you'd also want to be able to give a swipe at the fellow, teach the rascal a good lesson not to be going at us like that, we might miss giving him a good clout with our sandals. There are crows enough in these parts, and the fellow should try out his tactics on them. I don't think that I'll ever have a dog myself when I grow up, because if all the dogs in the world are like these mongrels that we can find here in the north of Mayo then I think that I'd prefer something else for a pet.

To be grown-up seems an awful long way ahead in the future, so I don't think too much about it.

Bull

Every morning Mrs Ganaghan comes into the middle bedroom where Martin and I sleep, since John Joseph moved away to Baltrina to be nearer the factory. I'm always on the window side and Martin near the room door. She arrives in with a great energy to her, ripping off all the blankets and sheets right off the big bed.

'Out ye come now, out of Blanket Street!' she'll be shouting at the top of her voice and I think what a way to be shaken and have to get out of bed in the morning, especially as there will probably be a lot of bog to be cut today. Breakfast is often limited to porridge and buttered bread.

It's early afternoon, and we've been at the turf for hours now.

She has been cutting with her turf spade at a terrible speed, no letting up at all. The weather is fine, not too hot, and I'm down with her on a level well below the top grass, about a yard below the upper level. Doing nothing much with my time really.

She's cutting wild with her turf spade and hurtling them heavy sods up above her head onto the bog floor with great speed. As I have to stay down below, I can't help Martin with the work of carrying off the great heavy sods to be laid out further away from the bog edge and where they'll start their drying-out process. So I'm dallying here, walking back and forward over the turf's surface. It has been raining a lot these last few days, so everything is soaked wild wet. I spend my time pushing my foot into the soft surface, and if I push hard enough the wet turf and rainwater oozes through my bare toes. Every time Martin comes back towards the bog edge to pick up another sod I hear him panting from the near exhaustion of the hard work. Each time he looks at me, I don't feel too comfortable down here at all, and I hear his rough breathing as he bends over and grabs hold of yet another sod. Old Terence is too old for any work, and is staying up at the house and is well out of sight.

Mrs Ganaghan starts giving out at Martin.

'Will you start getting on a little faster with it at all?' she shouts. She matches that with an increase in the cutting speed and within a short while there's a pile of sods building up above there, all unfinished work for Martin.

But I can tell that he is really getting furious and overheated with all the work, and I wonder if he can keep at this for long. He has now come back for another sod. He stoops right near the edge, and exhausted by the efforts already expended, has to take his breath for a moment or two before heaving another huge wet sod onto his outstretched arms.

'Come on, faster, come on, will you be moving?' shouts Mrs Ganaghan. Then with one swift movement she heaves the spade in his direction. His mind must still be boggled by the tiredness, and he doesn't see the sharp spade coming up towards him. The rusted cutting edge makes a direct hit into his right shin.

There's a second of silence, but from where I'm standing below I've already seen the blood flowing.

Then Martin heels backwards, his face all creased with pain. Then he screams and screams, clutching his wounded shin as the blood starts oozing through his clamped fingers.

I can't believe what I've seen, what Mrs Ganaghan has done to him and am waiting for Martin to say something, but I think he's having some difficulty there, he's completely blocked with the pain.

'The bull,' he shouts, 'the bull!'

Then he disappears running and hopping whilst he tries to clamp a hand around his shin, but I don't quite know in which direction because from down here he's quickly hidden by the bog edge and the nearest bushes, and the bull could be behind any of the other bushes near us. Jimmy the farmer next door to Mrs Ganaghan's house has this great bull, which has a ferocious look about him and he would usually be spending his time properly fenced in at the farm which is just beside Mrs Ganaghan's bog. He must have broken out! The thought of having him within attacking distance of me puts the jitters in my mind and legs.

'Let's run!' shouts Mrs Ganaghan, as she drops the bloodied turf spade on the soft ground underfoot and we set off and then start running, staying of course down on the lower level which will bring us back near the boreen which is some eighty yards distant. We then move cautiously up towards the higher level looking for the bull. But he is nowhere to be seen. No sight of Martin either.

We climb out through a small opening in the fence and up onto the boreen, which is on a slightly higher level than ourselves, and although keeping an eye out for the bull, we manage to make fast progress back towards the house. I think that we'll have to forget about the bog for today at least.

When we arrive old Terence is sitting by the Aga oven, his hands clasped over his walking stick.

'Have you seen Martin at all?' asks Mrs Ganaghan of him, as she tells him about the goings on down at the bog.

'No sign of Martin here at all,' he says.

My big brother's just run away, and I can well understand why, because I've seen the way that Mrs Ganaghan was making him work with the turf, he'd had enough of it all, but now I'm worried as I don't know where he could have headed off to, and whenever will he come back at all? What is he going to do for the blood on his leg? Have I seen the last of him forever? He's the only real brother I've got.

I'm told to go for a look out the back of the house and into the orchard too. But no Martin to be seen around them parts, and I report back to the kitchen.

Mrs Ganaghan doesn't delay in putting on a coat and heads off up to the post office up near the halfway house up on the Crosslanagh road. She's got to phone Castlebarry, she says. I get to stay at the house just in case Martin turns up. From the front yard I look up the boreen, and I see old Terence doing his walks the whole length up to McDonald's house. He's got his old brown walking cane with him, and he keeps poking it into the tall hedges full of briars along by the roadside.

'Martin, Martin, are you there?' I can hear him repeating in a loud voice, but I guess that that's not much use, because if Martin would be hiding behind that hedge he wouldn't come out for him quicker than he'd do for Mrs Ganaghan.

After an eternity Mrs Ganaghan is back at the house but still no sign of Martin. So we sit in the kitchen and wait, looking out from time to time up and down the boreen, just in case Martin might be coming. But from all the waiting it's getting dark now, and Mrs Ganaghan tells me what a bad brother Martin is to me, to be running away like that and leaving me all on my own. Many hours later I'm still sitting at the big table's end near the kitchen door, and Terence himself is settled in his chair to the right side of the Aga when Martin shows up in the doorway, his leg has stopped bleeding anyway now.

Mrs Ganaghan gets all excited.

'Where have you been, we've been spending our time looking for you all over the place?' she wants to know, her loud voice filling the room. Martin won't talk, he prefers to come over and sit beside me, and then old Terence gets up out of his comfortable chair, shouting and waving his brown walking stick at Martin. I think that if it wasn't for his big stick Martin would probably make it over to him and hit him a few good ones, and maybe even smash his old face in too. Maybe he'll run away again, I wonder, and the thought frightens me again, he's just shown he can do it once, so another time would be easy too.

Later, when we're tucked in to bed I ask him where's he been so long at all. He tells me that the story about the bull was invented so that he could run away from Mrs Ganaghan after he'd been wounded in the shin. He'd gone up to the Dolan's house where Father Dolan knows a little about Mrs Ganaghan's and Terence's antics and goings-on, and the way we are being treated. He says that he could have stayed the night over there, but that he didn't want to leave me on my own with these people.

The next morning we can have a sleep-out and the wake-up call is a much softer one as we don't get the blankets ripped off the bed like other days. Lots of time to dress, and for taking our breakfast too, and with our porridge there are even boiled eggs on the table for the both of us.

Mrs Ganaghan hardly ever boils us an egg, it's been so long since I've had a boiled egg served up like that, I hardly know whether to take a knife or a spoon to open it.

There'll be no need to go to the bog today, says Mrs Ganaghan, we'll finish it another time.

Rex

It's generally been a really lousy season down here at Mrs Ganaghan's place, sure it's been terrible weather at all now with the rain lashing all around for days on end and that damned wind would get to your inners and almost freeze you up. Then a few scarce days of sunshine, and it's back again to the rain. It had started again yesterday, but that was only practice rain, today it's for real. This afternoon Mrs Ganaghan has some visitors coming over from somewhere, and of course she doesn't have enough things to be serving them up at table at all, so I get elected to be off with myself down the mile and a half way down the boreen to the country shop to buy biscuits and bits and pieces for them people. Not even a dog would go for a walk in weather like this. So off I have to go through the rain and the worst of the lousy

Irish weather walking all the miles down and back to the little shop, the rain is soaking through my sandals and soon my feet are totally wet, but I have to keep moving. But I'll not be dallying at all, and before long I'm back up at the house again before the rain gets through my brown paper bag and the biscuits and cake would get all wet. Happy to be back into the warmth of the kitchen, the Aga's running hot as hell from all the turf in it. Turf sods that Martin and I would have cut the season before and carried, spread out and stacked, and loaded onto someone's cart to be hauled up by someone's donkey and unloaded into the old farmhouse which is now used as a turf shed round by the gable, and now that's being loaded in to the Aga. There's loads of conversation going on in the kitchen now, about the weather of course, the price of the pint, and the Government who's doing nothing at all for those poor young strong fellows who all have to head off to Dun Laoghaire and catch a B&I boat to foreign and better places.

Even whilst hovering about the end of the great brown kitchen table I'm enjoying the company jabbering on and it all well now, and sure Mrs Ganaghan must have just noticed it, and all of a sudden I'm told to go out and play. Go out and play! I've done three miles in the rain so that all these people can load their bellies with tea, cake and biscuits that I've been running for, and all I get to do with meself is to run out and play. Not even a cup of hot tea, tea drawn with the spring water that I've brought back in the big tin buckets from the well over in the field, to the house to be boiled, or a biscuit for me whilst I'm sitting on my own down by the end of the great big wooden table! I hadn't met a single dog outside in such weather at all on the way to the shop!

So now I'm outside in the hay shed annexe, the whitewashed walls are gone grey from the years and the dampness in the air, the rain is pounding down on the sloped corrugated tin roof above me, and then streaming over the edge in a continuous flow. Outside you can see the holes drilled into the concrete from all the gallons of rain that have been let down since the concrete was poured God knows when. The rain lashes and lashes at the grass out front, and the sandy road surface beyond. Looking over towards the field the other side of the grey stone wall, and all I can see is rain, rain all the way as far as the low dark clouds touching the horizon in such a greyness that not even the dogs would dare go for a walk. A few cows have grouped themselves under a great tree in a field way beyond to try to protect themselves from the pelting rain. But looking at this dog's weather that the heavens are letting us have now, there's no sign of it stopping in the near future. Dog's weather! I wouldn't mind having a cuppa of that hot tea myself and maybe a Jacob's wholemeal biscuit to go with it! None of the likes for me today! I'm fed up with it all and as I don't know how long the visitors will be talking to finish their tea and biscuits and their conversations about the pint and the Government and all that, I've no idea how long it'll be before I'll get 'called' back inside.

The dog.

I think of the young dog, which has his quarters locked up in the top room in the old farmhouse. His name is Rex, he belongs to Peter really, but spends his days and weeks locked away and nobody except Peter is allowed to take him for walks or anything else. Peter will always come back home on Saturdays, but with driving Mrs Ganaghan and all out to Baltrina to do her shopping, he'll have a pint or two in a Market Street pub and by the time that all are back to Mrs Ganaghan's place and have had some sandwiches and tea, and as like sometimes Mrs Ganaghan will have the fire roaring in the black range and manages to boil a chicken that she'd have brought out from Baltrina, Peter will have little time to visit his dog or ask about him. Dogs don't talk anyway, and Mrs Ganaghan would never tell him that his favourite Rex spends days locked away in the top room full of dogshit and piss in the old farmhouse behind and that the door is opened only to bring him a basin of swill now and then. The room of course never gets cleaned out at all, so the poor fellow just lives in his own stink in there. Peter'd probably have a fit or two if he knew anything about that. I dash back out into the pouring rain and head around the back for the shortest way to get the dog back over to the hay shed.

I have him on a piece of cord, which acts as a leash, and we run back towards the covered annexe adjoining the big hay shed. The dog thinks he's being let out for a walk, and he seems to be happy about it all, his tail wagging all over the place from the excitement. The roof is still being pelted from the heavy rain so there's a continuous drumming as I can hear it coming down above me. To the rear there's an old horse cart parked, not going anywhere these days at all, and I'd use it sometimes for climbing up on or as a toy of some sort. Just forward of that there's an old donkey cart which is also well into its retirement age. There's a good space left free out to the front of the shed, the ground being covered with a mixture of damp earth and turf powder, from where the raindrops can be seen overflowing the corrugated rim. I tie the dog to one of the rafters above and sit back on the donkey cart and start hoping that the visitors will soon be on their way.

I'm getting fed up with waiting, and the dog's probably fed up with being tied up to a roof-rafter too. He might have thought that he was being taken for a walk, something which he hardly ever gets.

He barks.

That rain just won't give up, and it's boring me really stiff. Of all the places in the world to be on a lousy afternoon full of the worst of Irish weather. I forget about the dog for the moment as I keep looking outside hoping for better things to come.

That dog certainly wants his walk, because he barks again.

Tea and biscuits! What's in it for me? Rex barks again and then gets into a rage of barking. I'm having enough of being shut out in this weather, enough of the rain and enough of Mrs Ganaghan's rough treatment. That dog! Right now I have enough of his barking too!

I head into the rear end of the hay shed where I find a nice big stick. Back to sit on the donkey cart and wait. Rex starts barking once again, and too right he's now getting on my nerves.

'Shut your gob will you!' I shout at him, wielding the big stick. He quietens for a bit, but it doesn't last for long. Then I jump off the cart and lunge for him, lashing out with the stick which was handy. It comes down hard on his rear end, he yelps from the pain of it, and starts running in a great circle still being tied by the cord to the roof.

Tea and biscuits!

The dog has now gone a few complete circles, and I lash out again, shouting at him at each go. Lousy weather! Another lash.

Mrs Ganaghan! Again a lashing.

Broken glasses!

Another whack.

I've had enough. Enough of all the injustice, and each time that I see the dog coming towards me I already have another excuse ready to lash at him to him with all my force. I stand in the doorway between the big hay shed and the annexe so that I can judge my swing well.

Buttered bread!

Heavy buckets of spring water to be carried back to the house which will later go into the blackened kettle on the iron range and ends up as boiled water for filling the hot water bottles for Blanket Street, whilst the others are up in Longford or on the boat to England. Plucking the grass at Mrs Ganaghan's house instead of using Daddy's garden shears, picking all them damned leaves in the huge garden around Marian House by hand instead of being able to use a rack to do the job, you name it, I've got more than enough excuses to be tired of this life and anything it's got to it. The dog is now terrified from fright and howling with pain as he completes more and more circles on the turfdust covered floor.

Holes in my cardigan!

The cord is also getting shorter as each turn shrinks its length which means that he doesn't make such a wide arc anymore, and his area for manoeuvring is getting limited. This makes it easier for me to judge the distances necessary and it's easier to place a direct hit.

Holes in my shoes!

Whack. I keep up the rhythm of beating and shouting because I've just had enough and nobody to turn to, nobody who I think could possibly help me in my situation.

The little dog is now in pain, he howls louder and louder, and I shout louder and louder at him, but I don't care because I know that Mrs Ganaghan's still inside with them folks with their cups of hot tea, cake and biscuits, the Sweet Afton cigarettes too, and with this bad weather the kitchen door is still certainly shut tight so they certainly won't hear me shouting or the dog howling. Right now he can hardly move any further from me in any possible direction, and all of a sudden I've vented out all my anger and force on him, and can't shout any more from the sore throat I've just given myself.

I let go, and settle back to lie on the donkey cart.

Rex is all caught up, and nowhere to go now. He's nearly stopped howling but his black and white body keeps shivering from the fright I've given him as he cowls low down to the ground. His tail isn't wagging any more now, he's got it stuck tightly between his hind legs. I'm starting to get shaken too, because I now remember what it's like to get beaten by Daddy after the Holy Angelus and that mostly for things which I'm not guilty of. I can remember what it's like to get a heavy electrical cable on my bare backside, and judging from the state of the dog I wonder if he's had it any easier with my stick.

So if I've been beaten a lot by Daddy for things that weren't my fault, and now I've beaten the living daylights out of poor Rex, and he's never done anything wrong to me where does this put us both? It's bad enough for him squatting whole days and weeks in a rotten room full of his own muck and piss, and he didn't do anything wrong to get that either. Why did I hit him so badly? I'm not sure why.

I throw the stick back into the hay shed, and Rex watches it as it flies in the opposite direction.

I feel sad now.

Even sorry for what I've done to the poor little fellow. He'd seen me throwing the stick out and I guess that he's understood that much. I get off my backside and start calling him in a quiet manner. He won't come to me at all, so I get down on my knees and crawl over to him with my outstretched hands. If I'd had a slice of white bread, I'd give it to him, but I don't even have that much for myself, and as for a biscuit not the slightest chance at all! I manage to take him by his front paws, edge him towards me and into my arms, and I try to comfort him a little. The time passes, and I feel him getting somewhat relaxed, and at least for him I'm happy too.

The time passes slowly indeed and then I notice that the rain is still pelting down, the two us are now against the cold wall and then suddenly I hear the car engine starting, but I wonder if I'll have to stay out a while longer until being 'called.'

'Gerard,' I can hear Mrs Ganaghan shouting, this time she hasn't delayed.

I don't answer, but I take the little dog tightly in my arms round a long back way to his room, that way we can be together for a little more time before I give him a last gentle pat on the head, but I still have to force him in to his stinking room and bolt the door shut.

Spanish

We don't have any books to read whilst we're out in the playroom, or down the back garden, and aren't allowed either into the County Library which is on the way home from school and beside the Post Office up on Western Road. But from time to time, Martin manages to borrow a comic book, such as the *Beano* or a *Dandy* from one of his classmates, because we don't have any pennies to buy the likes of a *Beano*. Sometimes we'd find a scrap of a page or two by the roadside whilst walking to or from the National School. But we have to be very careful, and not let Rhona see anything of the likes of them comics, nor any sort of a book upstairs. So we'll fold them a bit and stuff them underneath our jerseys whilst we're going into the kitchen to say the Holy Angelus prayers, and that way we'll be able to smuggle them up to the bedroom.

So, it may be comics only, a poor choice of reading material really, not much to educate myself on, but I have to do with that much. At least it's amusing, which is by far better than playing with little else than dull wooden blocks out in the unheated annexe building whilst waiting to be called into the house for slices of buttered bread for supper. The others do have real children's books, like Enid Blyton's *Famous Five*, or *Secret Seven*, and we do manage to catch glimpses of them if any of the others bring one out to the shed which is the so-called playroom, but it's for a short while only, as those books don't belong either to Martin or myself. As there are no bookshelves to be seen in the kitchen, which of course is largely out-of-bounds for both of us then they must be stored somewhere on a bookshelf in the dining room or the lounge, but we don't know better.

So evenings after we've been on our knees to say the Holy Angelus, and pray for all those in need, and maybe after a thrashing or two, but before it gets dark in the bedroom upstairs we whip out our bits and strips of comic books from their hiding places, and we're into the antics of Dennis the Menace or Blondie.

It's great to be having a smile and a laugh with the characters from time to time, but we're also onto something, which is even better. Another session of Spanish, that is.

Comprendes usted?

We keep the volumes hidden between the carpet and the old newspapers covering the wooden floorboards below because Rhona might find them, and we know what would happen then. We've noticed that the way we make the beds up in the morning, and appear in the evening, that she has been ruffling under the mattresses, checking anything and everything out. So daytimes they stay undercover, and evening times we are at our studies, just like the priests during the nineteenth century who said Holy Mass for the believers in secret hideaways up and down the country for fear that they might be discovered by the English troops or occupiers. They too knew what awaited them in the event of discovery.

Martin gets the little magazines from a classmate, so every evening we go through the lessons in an edition of 'Hoy'. We'll start with a recap of the preceding lesson, and then move on to a new one. I learn phrases like *'Donde vas hombre?'*, or *'Que ora es?'*, and Martin is even surprised by the progress I'm making, every time that he congratulates me, I feel like I'm on the top of the world I help him too, as I put other questions to him, and we work on everything together, and that way we both know that we're making progress, and when we grow up we might make it to Spain one day and try it all out on a real Spaniard, because in Castlebarry we don't have one single Spaniard within sight. All we have around here is Castlebarry-speak, and the Irish of course, but we have enough of that in school anyway, and it'd be no use in trying that out on any Spanish *'Muchacha'* or *'Torero'*.

So we are having a whale of a time and moving along smoothly with our studies, *comprendes*?

Until the evening that we want to start another session, and when Martin goes to the hiding place under the carpet, the magazines are gone, we know who's taken them, but we can't ask the question out of fear of Rhona, and Daddy for the beating which we might get for doing something which isn't allowed nor known about.

Martin and I were so happy with our part-time education that we are now profoundly saddened and totally blocked in our progress.

Is education a crime in this household? I can't learn Spanish at St Patrick's National School, so what's the problem with learning it in the evenings before the sun goes down? Am I condemned to let my quest for knowledge, education and self improvement be quenched and suffocated by Rhona?

I wonder what explanation Martin is going to give to his classmate because the magazines are on loan. Some months later Martin creeps out of the bedroom late one evening and into the storage room beyond the landing. He rummages around a bit and by sheer chance what does he find but all the 'Hoy' magazines stuffed behind odds-and-sods? We could of course steal them back, but whenever Rhona finds that out that'd be a crime too, and then we'll be into another beating for going in to rooms where 'we have no business'. She wouldn't of course tell Dad what was 'stolen', but maybe a 'fine flowerpot' might be 'found broken' in that room, and even if Dad asks to see the proof then the 'tale' will be that the 'smithereens' have already been thrown away, and she 'forgot' to tell Dad about it earlier but anyway Rhona's word is good enough for Dad and we'll be in for a 'thrashing.'

So now without our Spanish magazines to help us while away the time in the evenings we'll just have to find something else. Martin has an idea. Whilst he'll lift up the end of one of the beds or rock the great dresser slightly to one side I'll whip out the pages of the national newspapers which are lying on the floorboards. That'll make for something to read, and we'll repeat the process to put them back into place.

One evening he's looking at the death notices in a paper, and he sees the name of a Duignan mentioned.

'Hey Gerry!' he calls, 'have a look at this.'

I creep over to his bed, and he passes the page to me.

I read.

Fr Michael O'Duignan, late of Kiltynagh, who has died in the USA.

I'd remembered Father Michael, whenever he was home in the summer he'd be over the wall into the McDonagh's field to help with cutting their hay.

Now he's dead. But Daddy never talked to me nor Martin about that. Why? After all he was family to us, but as we are slowly being denied contact to any family, even those in Longford, then what interest is a dead uncle out in the USA?

Hasta luega!

Coppers

The day for Martin's first departure for St Joseph's in Tury has now arrived. It's autumn 1966, and on this late afternoon the sun is streaming down and exceptionally Martin and I are above the clothesline which separates the bottom end from the top end of the garden. Enjoying the swing for once.

Jane is here with us too.

Mrs Ganaghan appears out from the house.

'So you're off to St Joseph's then?' she asks of Martin.

Martin, who seems to be happy with his forthcoming change of situation smiles.

'Here, here are a few coppers and shillings,' offers Mrs Ganaghan, as she hands them over into Martin's outstretched hand, 'something for you, you know, just in case.'

Martin's smile grows even wider.

How kind I think she's become, what with Martin going off to college and that, and won't she be missing him when the rest of us will be driving down to visit her at Rathagan on the Sunday afternoons during the winter which is somewhere ahead?

'Well, I'll be going back in to the kitchen then,' she says, disappearing.

Martin shows me the coins, which he then puts into his trouser pocket.

Shortly thereafter, we are all called into the kitchen.

Rhona is standing by the Aga, and us others around the floor area.

'Here Martin,' says Rhona, 'I have a few coppers and shillings for you now somewhere.'

She's about to head for her bag.

'But Mrs Ganaghan has already given him some just now, down in the garden,' blurts in Jane.

Rhona stops in her tracks.

'Show me!' she says.

Martin reaches into his trousers pocket, and brings out the coppers, which he'd just gotten as a present from Mrs Ganaghan.

'Here, take the ones that I'd prepared for you,' she explains 'and Mrs Ganaghan's coppers, I'll be taking them, and I'll be minding them for you.'

Martin has to hand over the coins.

Daddy stands watching the proceedings, without saying anything.

He's probably thinking what a kind mother-in-law he has to be giving away coppers and shillings on such a special day for Martin like that.

But I've read between the lines, I've seen the message, which has gone through, and I've seen to what extent Rhona and her mother are capable of scheming and engineering. I'll have to watch out for further set-ups like that in the future.

Martin comes back for the Halloween break, and I'm curious to know how he likes his college. He seems to enjoy it for many things.

Except one.

He's the only boy in first year who wears short pants, and all the college takes the mickey out of him for that.

If he'd managed to take Mrs Ganaghan's coppers and shillings with him I guess he'd have bought a pair of long trousers, and so be much happier off.

He can't tell the other boys that he's a farmer's son, can he?

Dinky

It's a Saturday morning, the 12th February, which is my birthday, and I'm still in bed. Wide awake of course, the room is still dark as the heavy curtains block out any daylight which is available, but I'm not allowed to go downstairs until I'm 'called'. It's always like that, any day of the week, Saturdays, and even today on my birthday too. I know that I can get beaten for things less than 'leaving' the bedroom before being 'called', so I don't dare it.

I can hear lots of noise coming from the kitchen below which means that the other children are already down there with Rhona and Daddy too maybe, which is only something else normal too. This morning I don't get 'called', but Jane comes upstairs with a message and a small packet for me. She calls before entering the bedroom.

'Mammy told me to tell you that Mrs Ganaghan sent you a lovely present for your birthday, here you are now, and Mammy also told me to tell you that you can come down now,' she says.

What luck!

I wonder what's gotten to Mrs Ganaghan, she never remembers my birthday, even if it's soon after Christmas, but anyway it's very nice of her, and what do I have here? I open the small packet, and find a nice new Dinky car, and as I like Dinky cars this one will be a special one, the first birthday present of my life! Tomorrow it'll be Sunday, so I guess that after the Holy Mass in the Chapel, and lunch we'll all be going down to Mrs Ganaghan's small house in Rathagan, and I mustn't forget to say a big 'Thank you Mrs Ganaghan,' because that was very kind of her indeed.

As I'm allowed downstairs now I can sit at the table in the kitchen, and there'll be some porridge for me as it's Saturday, which I like just as much as my new Dinky car, which is sitting proudly in front of me waiting to join the few other toys that I have out in the playroom.

So the next day we all go down to Rathagan for the afternoon, I jump out of the black car, but before I get to say a big 'Thank you Mrs Ganaghan for the lovely Dinky toy,' Rhona calls her down to the sitting room at the bottom of the house where they spend a few minutes, but when they come back up I still get the chance to say a grand 'Thank you Mrs Ganaghan for the nice Dinky toy you sent me.' She seems all happy about my pleasure with the new toy, but Daddy looks puzzled. So Rhona tells him all about the story that Mrs Ganaghan sent me a Dinky toy for my birthday.

'Oh, oh, that was very kind of you, Mrs Ganaghan,' but he doesn't ask when my birthday was.

Yesterday was my birthday, so I don't get sent out to play like other times, but whilst eating my slices of bread and butter, I can admire my Dinky toy which I was allowed to bring along with me all the way down to Rathagan, and is now parked on the big kitchen table in front of me.

A few weeks later Martin comes home from St Joseph's in Tury for the Easter holidays. The following morning we're together out in the playroom. Jane's there too, and I'm near the door at the top end of the big table. All of a sudden Martin notices my Dinky car in the midst of other toys scattered out on the table.

'So you got the present I sent you?' he asks. I look at him.

'What present?' I ask.

'The Dinky toy there, that one,' he says, picking up the one that Jane told me that Mrs Ganaghan had sent me for a birthday present.

'You didn't send it Martin, Mrs Ganaghan sent it to Gerard, and Mammy said that,' she starts to say.

'No, no, I sent it to you, I posted it from Tury,' Martin repeats, looking at me, and I can't understand who's to be believed here at all.

That evening, whilst upstairs in the bedroom, Martin insists on the fact that he, and not Mrs Ganaghan as previously mentioned, sent me my Dinky toy, the first birthday present I'd ever received.

So now I believe that Rhona is a liar!

Hospital

It's Christmas time again, Martin has gone back to work at the Beltree House Hotel in Westbary, so I'm alone at home. One day Rhona gives me an awful big portion of potatoes and food to shove down my throat, and sure the next day I have these awful pains in my tummy. It hurts and hurts, but I daren't catch Daddy's attention to my plight. But when Daddy comes up to the bedroom one evening to talk about my tummy pain, I know that Rhona has been onto him about it, because she had noticed.

The next day I am suddenly packed into the car. I don't know why nor where we're going, and anyways I'd never ask the question.

'Down to Galway we're going now,' Rhona says with a voice to her as if I'd ruined her day as she looks my way, 'down to the hospital, and see what's wrong with you.'

I sit there not asking why they'd not just bring me to the local hospital which is just down the road opposite the Trader's Rest Hotel, and anyway my tummy isn't hurting me as much as it was last night and I think I'll be grand really. But I judge it wiser not to ask that question or make any sly remarks either, because you'd never know when a thump might come flying this way, so I keep my gob shut tight, and Daddy keeps driving.

We arrive at what is called the Regional Hospital in Galway City. There's a huge parking place out the front, a building further over to the right which I'll find out later is the nurses' home.

In we go, and then through these great wide corridors, the place has these winding staircases and lifts too. I've never been in a lift in my life, nor in a hospital either. People all dressed up in white clothes chatting, holding piles of paper, or moving back and forth in the corridors. So many people, never seen so much going-on in my life. I decide that I'll have to try one of those lifts when I'm on my own.

We arrive at what Daddy says will be my ward, and that a friend of his works as a doctor in this great hospital.

'It's the finest hospital for a long way around, and my good friend will take care of you whilst you are here,' he says before leaving.

I wonder what's the matter at all with the hospital in Castlebarry, it's so near the house and they must have good doctors over there too, and Daddy must have a friend amongst them, and anyways I'm much better now.

But before I can pick up the courage to talk about it to him, he is already turning to go back out to Rhona in the car, so I get left with the nurses.

Two nurses show me to my bed, which is the first one in the third row in from the ward door. Fourth bed from the window. A plain wall across the passage to my right. I have to get undressed out in the changing rooms, and will have to wear hospital bedclothes for my stay. I have a look around my ward, lots of sick men in here. I wonder if any of them are from Castlebarry, if any of them ate too many spuds at one go, or what did they do to get themselves sick and that and have to go to hospital.

'The doctor will be in to see you tomorrow, are you all right there now?' asks the young lady, 'so you can take it easy there now for today?'

'Ah yes, and thank you now,' I say. I appreciate that I'll have time today to roam around. No need to be in a jiffy here. I have a look at the other beds about me, there's not much to see in here except a few empty beds and sick men, so I decide to head out into the corridor.

Through the ward doors, and I arrive at the nursing station again. There are great windows to it, so the nurses and doctors can see all the patients and others coming and going, and what they're up to. The walls inside the station are covered with boards and sheaves of paper and charts all pinned up around the place.

After the station there is another ward to the right. A huge place this one. I think it must be three times the size of my little one.

I have a gawk inside, and apart from the size of it, it looks just the same as my place. The same dark walls, the same windows, the same model of bed, the same uniforms carried by the nurses. Nothing changes except the faces. I retreat back into the corridor. The wall colours are all the same in all these corridors. The floor covering too. People coming and going, doctors and people dressed in whites talking in small groups. The toilets and changing rooms are to my left. I continue, and there is a small waiting room to my left. I glance out through the windows only to see a drab backyard, with some concrete blocks and stones strewn here and there. I turn in my seated position, and look at the door facing me. It has a great big sticker with 'Intensive Care' written in red. I don't know what that could possibly mean, and don't want to ask the question to any of the staff who seem eternally busy moving in both directions in front of me.

Then a nurse approaches, and heads for the door. I lean forward. She opens and goes inside, leaving the door slightly ajar for a few minutes. I have the chance to have a gawk inside. I see a man lying in a bed on the opposite side, there are curtains pulled on both sides of his bed, but the bottom end is free, and I see a board with charts at the bottom of the bed. Then I raise my attention towards the patient's head. He has tubes, wires, and yokes of things attached to his mouth and chest, and dangling to both sides of the bed and connected to kinds of electrical machines. The poor fellow must be awful sick indeed, because nobody in my ward has so many tubes and wires about him, nor have I seen the likes in the other ward either.

Then the door is pushed closed. I get up from my seat and continue towards the point where the exit should be. Suddenly corridors branching out in all directions. I take a left turn. I arrive near the main entrance hall, and see the lifts again. Beautiful wood panelling to be seen here and there. I head into one of the lifts on the left side. A nurse follows me just before the door closes, she presses a button, and we start moving upwards. I don't think she has even noticed me, and she gets off before me so I'm left on my own to discover this new item. I press the button for the top floor, and when arrived up there, I don't like the height when looking out through the windows, so holding the central handrail, I gently let myself back downstairs to the great hall, where I can still wander around for a while before dinner comes.

'Hello there, I'm Doctor Kelly and I'd like to ask you a few questions,' says the owner of the outstretched hand which comes towards me as I'm lying in bed the next morning when this young fellow appears.

He pulls himself a chair and sits down to the right side of my bed. I have a gawk at his doctor's coat, the pockets filled with papers, and he has lots of coloured biros in his top pocket. He starts asking questions about what I eat, and how much, and all the likes.

I don't tell him about the scrawny legs of roast turkey that I'd get for my Christmas Day dinner, but I tell him about the spuds.

'Arrah, do you like the spuds there now?' he wants to know more.

'Oh, yes I do now meself,' I repeat, because I can't tell him either that most evenings for tea, and before going on my knees for the Holy Angelus prayers I'd get just some slices of buttered bread to fill my tummy for the evening and the whole night too. The spuds that I told him about would be for another occasion. Maybe a Saturday or Sunday's dinner, because going to school on a weekday I'd have my paper bag with slices of buttered bread and a bottle of milk with me, no spuds for sure. Maybe the others would get spuds for their dinner, after Daddy would have driven down from the County Clinic at the midday break and picked them up to drive them back out to Marian House for their dinner. But Martin and I have to stay down at the National School for our dinner, and we never see the others arriving back down from Marian House after theirs, and anyway they'd never tell us if they'd have had spuds or not. When Rhona cooks up spuds for dinners then it's something near to a treat for me, because as I rarely see her cooking anything better than the rashers and lads, don't know if she can do anything other than a roast of some sort. Even down at Mrs Ganaghan's place it's sometimes better than at Marian House, because in summer when the weather's just fine she'd bake a great treacle cake from time to time. She has a huge deep circular blackened baking pan for that job, and I don't mind going for a run out to the turf shed for extra loads of them turf sods, because when Mrs Ganaghan is going to bake one of her great treacle cakes then she's in a great humour today indeed, and her cake will be excellent and we'll tell her such, and what else would you get but another chunk of the great cake indeed. Sometimes and if the weather itself isn't too hot now, sure she might have some of the fresh country butter from Monaghan's in the house, and then I'm in heaven. Sometimes when Peter would bring her with his DKW motorcar into Baltrina on a Saturday, and whilst he'd be off for a sup of the cool stuff, then she'd be going wild in them shops indeed, and she'd even buy a chicken, which means more sods from the shed, because you'd need an awful roaring fire to itself in the Aga range to boil such a bird. But boiled chicken is another one of her treats, we like her for that and I don't even mind running for them sods at all. Martin is always on the watchout for the wishbone, and he holds it in such a way that I can hardly ever make out which is the heavier and stronger side, so he nearly always wins the game with the wishbone. Martin tells me that our mother Noreen was a great cook indeed, but that's of little help to me now she's dead and gone. All I can do is wait and try to win at playing the wishbone, and then I could hope for a new friend or two, because at Marian House I'm not allowed into the neighbours houses and have friends, but I don't see many children of my age in the parts around Rathagan either.

The young doctor is looking at me, I've been gawking up at the roof, happy as I was with the first dinner I had here last night. Here I don't get called for my dinner, and face some miserable slices of buttered bread or the odd rasher or two like back at Marian House. Here all I have to do is sit up in bed, and the nurses will even bring me my tea, which they call dinner here, which I can't understand because Rhona always gives us dinner at twelve o'clock in the day. Anyway, I get to understand what the lunch and what the dinner is, and the ones here are delicious.

More questions. I try to find answers.

The dinners here. I get spuds here too. Meat and vegetables, and a little gravy.

'Well, thank you very much now,' says the doctor, who has finished writing things down on the board that he had on his knees, 'and I'll see you again later in the day.'

I'm left to dreaming about my next lunch and dinner.

During the afternoon, two other doctors come to see me and they want to ask me questions. Now they are both seated to my right side, papers in their pockets, and biros in their top pockets.

The questions start. Funny, I think, that they are very much the same questions as I had to answer this morning. One of the doctors is making notes on his board, and the other seems to be reading things off his. So I have to tell them both all about the spuds again, and all the works.

The next morning another new patient is wheeled on his bed into our ward. They bring him past my bed and then towards the opposite side. A great stocky man he is himself, and I'd say about fifty years old. When my lunch tray is placed down on my bed table, I straighten myself upwards and am ready to enjoy another of these good meals. The nurses have brought all the lunch trays for our ward, and I have a glance towards the new patient's tray. He's only two beds to one side of my position, but facing him I can easily see that he doesn't have the same meal on his plate as I have. I turn to my neighbour on my left.

'Why aren't all the meals the same?' I ask, nodding in the direction of our new patient.

'Oh, I know yer man there, and he's had a heart attack now,' he explains, 'so they won't give him any potatoes.'

'No spuds?' I can't understand.

'No, none of them spuds there for him, they're not good for you if you've had a heart attack, you know?' he wonders if I understand.

No spuds with the meals for yer man because of a heart attack?

I don't know if a heart attack is a bad thing to be having or not, but not getting any spuds for your lunch or dinner certainly seems to me a bad situation to be in.

I shake my head, I have a look down at my portion of spuds, meat and turnips all well arranged on the plate in front of me, and by God aren't I an awful hungry lad now there again. Definitely no signs any more of them terrible tummy pains that had upset me the other day at Marian House.

That evening after dinner a nurse tells me that I can't have anything more to eat or drink for the evening and no breakfast either in the morning because I'll be having some tests, so I'll have to be fasting. Now having no breakfast in the morning is nearly as bad as having no spuds with your meals like yer man opposite me, but I guess that it's still better to miss out on breakfast than having a heart attack whatever that means, like yer man.

'And about lunch?' I'm getting worried here. But the nurse has understood my state of anxiety.

'Oh, you'll be back in time for lunch,' she says smiling, before she disappears.

Not too bad, I think, they can do their tests, and I'll dream about my lunch.

A nurse brings me out to another part of the building, and I get to drink this terrible tasting white stuff which keeps coming my way in glasses. I try to let it down my gob, but it's just too hard to swallow.

'Come on now, you're a grand lad yourself, you have only three more glasses waiting for you there now, it's for your Barium test,' I hear the voice say. How can they do this to anybody? What's this all for? All because of a pain in my tummy, which I got after Rhona had forced me to gulp down all what was on my plate a few days ago? This is downright uncomfortable, and it's even starting to ruin some of the quietness and even pleasure that I'd found since arriving here within these walls. Nurses who bring me my meals, and what good ones they are too. Nurses to chat to when it's all quiet in the evenings.

I bring another glass of the stuff to my lips, close my eyes, dream of the spuds and the meat with the gravy that will be coming my way at lunchtime, and swallow. I continue so with the two last ones. Then we wait for a short while and then I have to come into the Radiology room. It's cold in here, and I have to stand with my bare chest and belly pinned up against a cold metal frame type of thing.

'Hold yourself now,' says the lady all dressed up in a heavy metal type clothing, and from time to time I hear the whirr of the black machines as they move around my back and sides.

A few minutes more and the lady says that I can go back downstairs to my ward and the doctor will be coming to see me.

When I arrive between my bedsheets the nurses have just started bringing around the meal trays, and isn't it great to be settling in and being served like this? I wonder if it's as good as this in the hospital in Castlebarry, but right now I don't care to think about that possibility as I reach for my fork.

The doctor won't be coming this afternoon, but he'll see me in the morning, I'm told.

The afternoon off! Great! Time to stroll and observe the comings and goings within all these walls. One of the patients on the other half of my ward has a chessboard, so we get together for a session until it's checkmate. Time to stroll through the other wards. In one waiting room I meet an elderly gentleman, and time enough we do have to talk. His name is Von Stampen, and he now lives in County Galway. He starts talking to me about the war years. I wonder about the war years. Not the Irish wars with the British, he says. He was with the German troops in Northern France in the 1940s. I listen to him, to his story, listen to all he had to tell about the conditions of fighting a war, firstly against the local French, and then against the other invaders. But now it's far behind him, and he lives peacefully in western Ireland. I'm only a young boy, have read about wars, but had never come so close to someone who had actually fought one. But I find a certain quietness in his voice, and I wonder what it'll be like to be a grown-up, and is that when peace and quietness comes to you?

'What's that you said?' I ask of the nurse, because I couldn't quite catch the word.

'A colonoscopy, I said,' she repeats.

'A what?' I'm having some difficulty here.

'Oh, never mind, it's a test,' she says.

A colonoscopy? The nurse returns later in the evening and asks me to go with her out to the examination room. I wonder if I have to drink any glasses of their lousy milky looking drink like I had to the other day. But none of the likes comes my way, I simply have to lie down on an examination bed, on my left side, and pull up my knees hard against my chest whilst the two nurses manage to push a great piece of tube up my rear end, and they have a gawk in there to see if all the bits and pieces are still in there and if everything is all right with my rear.

A doctor comes to me the following morning, saying that they can't find anything wrong with me at all, even with all their tests and things. Then I think that I'd felt like telling them that much a long time ago, that I'm not a doctor myself like Daddy is, that I was grand all this time really, no need to keep me in here longer, but when I think of all the good meals, the cheerful nurses, the liberty that I have to roam and wander around the whole place, and even if Daddy or Rhona don't have the time to drive down the fifty miles from Castlebarry to visit me during the ten days that I've been here, sure isn't this a better place to spend some time at than at Marian House?

Ten days without seeing or hearing anything of Rhona herself, sure isn't it a holiday in itself?

Knife

As of late Daddy and Rhona would be late coming home in the afternoon from time to time, so when it happens I'll arrive back from school and not hearing from Rhona then I know that I can walk into the kitchen to which I've got access, where they'll leave out a piece of fruit or bread for me. I can't go further though as the door to the hallway and the rest of Marian House will always be locked, and closed off for me. It's now December 1967.

Today there's a fine ripe banana sitting there on a small bread plate placed on the right hand side of the sink, in front of the window overlooking the garden, and I'm looking forward to it. Then I wonder instead of peeling the banana lengthways as usual, why not cut it acrossways and make segments of it?

I look towards the cutlery drawer situated to the left of the sink, and hesitate a few moments. But I want to choose a knife to do the job. So I make my mind up and head over to the left. I pull on the heavy wooden drawer, which opens to reveal a whole range of knives, forks and spoons. I choose a knife and move back to the place where the bread plate is. One clean incision and the peel is sliced through. I take my time to savour the fruit, and wash and dry the knife before putting it back in its storage place.

I'm back out in the playroom when I hear the car approaching the gates, so Daddy and Rhona are arriving home, and judging from their footsteps I know that they've headed past the playroom door and straight into the kitchen, as usual.

Barely a few minutes pass until I hear the kitchen door opening.

'Gerard!' I hear her calling in her high-pitched voice.

I open and peer out through the playroom door, to see Rhona standing in the kitchen doorway, a furious look upon her face.

When I arrive into the kitchen Daddy is there too, standing by the kitchen table. Rhona pulls me by the ear towards the window.

'Have you been into the drawers?' she shouts.

'No, no, I haven't,' I reply, but I have a feeling that she knows I'm lying.

'So you haven't been into the drawers then, have you?' she shouts again, putting more pressure on as she pulls me nearer the sink by the window. The bread plate with the banana peel is still sitting there. The knife is of course gone back to its place in the drawer.

'Come over here and see for yourself.' Daddy is invited over to the sink to see the piece of evidence. I have no line of defence.

'So you go sneaking around in the drawers, and then you have the cheek to lie about it all?' she says defiantly, holding up the peel for all present to see.

'Have you seen the way this brat behaves?' she calls to Daddy.

By now she's shaking the wits out of me, and then Daddy heads to fetch the heavy electrical cable hiding behind the calendar above the kitchen table. This time he doesn't even wait until after the Angelus prayers, and I sense a real boiling anger in his voice and in the swiftness of the beating right there in the kitchen. Martin is a long way away in St Joseph's in Tury, he won't know about what I'm going through now, he's far away from this, good enough for him.

That evening whilst lying in bed and crying my eyes out from the pains I scribble a small note for the neighbours. The next day I wrap it around a pebble picked up in our driveway, and throw it through a hole in the backyard fence and it lands in the Hannons garden. Because I couldn't be caught dead going into their house or front garden this is a pre-arranged signal which I can use if ever I need help. Now they'll get to know what happened and why.

I don't know how, but within forty-eight hours, Rhona has gotten word of my message, which means that the Hannons have well received it and therefore reacted in some way.

Now it's late afternoon, and I get hauled out from the playroom. Going up the staircase, and whilst on the third step, I get a violent kick from the rear, and Rhona's pointed shoe reaches me just at the bottom of my spine. The pain jolts me, and up to my bedroom I have to go. Rhona has wrenched me up here, and before my pants are hauled down I get a look out through the window in the direction of the garden fence where my message went through. I fear that now I'm going to have to 'pay' for my bad behaviour.

She is growling and jabbering as she forces me down on my knees against the bed.

This time it's Rhona who has the heavy electrical cable in her hands, and she's yelling about my getting in contact with the neighbours and telling fibs.

'You have nothing to be doing with them people, and let this be a lesson to you,' she says and starts a savage beating. She lashes out again and again, and I come to realise that she's just as good as Daddy with the heavy rod.

Daddy has now arrived and takes turns with her for meting out the punishment that I seemingly deserve. Then suddenly he leaves the room saying that he'll be back. Rhona continues meting out the blows on my bare back and buttocks.

Daddy does indeed come back to the room, and straining to my right I can see the broom handle he's got in his hands. I really get the frights now, because if he's going to start beating me with that wooden stick, then the 'rod treatment' will have been nothing to compare with it.

I fear the worst, heavier pain and suffering is coming my way.

I feel like a cornered rat. I start screaming intensely, trying my utmost to wrestle myself free, only that the first part of the beating and all my struggling has sapped my energy considerably, and anyway Rhona has a terrible hold on the back of my neck.

She's not letting the pressure go one bit, and with my head and chest still pinned to the bed covering, my knees barely touching the carpet, and my legs flailing everywhere from the pain, she moves aside and Daddy moves forward.

With the broom handle.

He hits, swings again, hits, and hits repeatedly, on the back of my frail legs, my buttocks and all along my back up to my shoulders. I start losing all track of time, it seems to be an eternity since this hell let loose.

Another heavy stroke on my back and I hear the snap as the broom handle breaks in two. I pray to God that he doesn't have another one downstairs. It's either the broom handle or my back. Daddy curses, and as Rhona lets go of my neck I get another view to my right. Daddy is still standing there in front of the big wardrobe, the two smashed bits of the handle in his hands.

They must have 'judged' that I've had enough of the lesson which has to be given when I've been telling stories to the neighbours, because all of a sudden I hear them leaving the room and closing the door behind them.

I remain lying face down on the bed for a long while, unable to move because of my pains. I'm all alone and in sheer agony. Martin can't help me, can't comfort me nor help dry my tears as they stream down my cheeks. Nothing but the bed covering to do that.

Because I borrowed a bread knife to cut my banana in two?

A cornered rat would at least have a chance to jump at his aggressor's throats, to counter-attack and at least defend himself. I remember the day I tried cornering one in the school playground shelter down at the National School in town. We were a few boys who dared get down near to the black slimy animal stuck with his tail in a tight corner, but when he showed us his teeth we rapidly decided that it was wiser to let him fight another fight or die another death. But here I am alone, and in face of all this violence I have no defence, no exit either. I just have to submit and suffer the consequences.

The rat, he was luckier. After a small fright he went free.

Then I remember the Hannons, again. When the pain eases a little and I can start moving a bit I search around the room for another scrap of paper. I'm lucky, and get down to writing another note. The next day it will go through the same hole in the garden fence as the first one. Rhona doesn't know how I get the messages through, and I sure won't tell her.

I have all the time to think and write my thoughts down

because Rhona doesn't call me down for supper or to say the Angelus prayers for all those in need. I wish somebody would say a whole string of prayers for me, because right now I sure need some as nothing ever improves here in this house.

I remain lying on the bed, trying to get to sleep, but with a battered back and an empty stomach it's not easy.

I manage to write another note and the following morning before heading down the mile to the school my scrap of paper goes through the hole in the fence like the first one.

Once again the reaction doesn't delay, coming just a few days later.

But this time I don't get called into the kitchen or upstairs to my bedroom.

Instead I get called by Rhona into the sitting room at the front of the house. I can't understand why as I never get allowed or invited in there, not even to admire the bright lights and the great green branches of the Christmas tree which I know goes up in there every year. I arrive in the room, and have a look all around at the fine pieces of furniture, the record player, and the set of three flying geese hanging on the wall behind the door.

Then I see a man in a dark suit sitting just beyond the fireplace, his back to the rear garden.

'Hello, I'm from the ISPCC, do you know what that means?' is his question.

I shake my head as I don't have an idea.

But I do know that somebody out there is worrying about my well-being, trying to support, but can't just walk up and ring the front doorbell, so they can't get through to me. But the thought is comforting to say the least!

'Have you been beaten recently?' he wonders aloud, but I don't know what to say.

He repeats the question, and whilst Daddy watches from his seated position near the door I manage to tell the man that because I borrowed a butter knife to cut a banana in two instead of peeling it with my bare hands I've been beaten twice. I can see Rhona hovering just inside the door, so I keep to the minimum of details. Then the man asks me to come over near him. I approach the stranger, but I am not afraid of him, he even has a gentle manner to him. I wonder what sort of a man he his, does he have children? Maybe, but I don't think they get beaten like I do.

He says that I must get undressed as he wants to have a look at my back. My clothes start coming off, but the room here is well heated in comparison to the playroom outside so I'm not uncomfortable at all in here.

The man puts a few questions to me, studies all the marks and bruises which I can still feel up and down my back. He scribbles some words on his notepad. A few more minutes and it's already all over, he tells me that I can get dressed again.

He says his goodbye, and I leave for the cold playroom, hoping that he will come soon again.

But I never see or hear from the man again.

Donilaun Hotel

Across the bridge over the River Moyna and a left turn brings us onto the Sligo road. Dad tells me that he has found a summer job for me at the Donilaun Hotel. He's talking so much about the fact that he's been many a mile indeed looking for such a job, up and down and even across the whole county to find one, and it hasn't been easy at all.

Another bridge over the Brosneen River, a right turn at the junction with the Enniscaragh road, and we are now heading down a narrow road towards the hotel. Daddy is still talking about all the efforts and miles he's been doing to get me a job in such a fine hotel, so I'll have to be doing my best to keep it. I nod my agreement, hoping that he'll have noticed in the rear mirror and am most grateful but I wonder why he's been travelling the high roads and the low roads indeed, and what's the point in having a telephone in the house at all, when all you'd have to do is phone around the town and county to see if there are any jobs going at all? Maybe there's a job going at the Beltree House Hotel where Martin is already working?

Anyway, I don't know what's awaiting me, but I have a feeling that this summer is going to be different than the ones I'd usually spend at Mrs Ganaghan's house cutting turf, plucking the grass, and running to the well across in the field for buckets of the freshest spring water that you'd find in the North of Mayo, and all those sort of jobs.

Daddy parks out the front, and we head in through the double glass doors, where there are a pair of great brown leather-clad armchairs to be admired. A man sitting comfortably in another armchair to the right greets us as we head towards the reception desk. Daddy whispers to me that he's the hotel manager, and I think what a soft job he has at all. The green carpeting underfoot is plush, the carpet in my bedroom at Marian House is nothing like this, it quietens the noise of our footsteps as we approach the reception to the right side of the spacious hall. There's a total calmness reigning in here, and the interior coolness contrasts sharply with the hot summer's day outside. The hotel owner shows up and we talk about various bits and pieces, I'm told that I can start in the morning and that will be for three pounds a week now, and then Daddy comes with me through the kitchen out the back to my new room in the staff quarters. The building is at the back of the hotel, and I have a fine bedroom facing the hotel ballroom.

It seems that a beautiful day is in the making as I turn up to have some breakfast in the morning. I keep an eye on the refectory clock as I have to start at nine. The head chef gives me a quick tour of the kitchen and then he leaves me to get on with the job. I'm standing in front of a sink that's deep enough for me to drown myself in, and it's already overfull with pots and pans. A bottle of Teepol, sponges and metal pot scrubbers on the ledge in front of me and I have all I need to get to work. Pots and pans all over the place. Before I can even start I need to find and pull the stopper as I have to empty the amounts of cold greasy water which must have been there since yesterday evening, and then clear all the pots and pans out of the sink. So the pots are all over the floor now, to my left and right, and even behind me.

I start working through yesterday's pots before I can manage the new arrivals from this morning. Behind me I see the ladies busy with the washing machine for plates and cutlery and glasses. To my right I can watch the team of cooks in action, and even before they've finished the breakfast trade they are already getting into the preparations for lunch in the main restaurant and bar, and the noise level increases accordingly.

Chef tells me that there's a wedding on today and I'll have to be doing a great speed to keep up with all the work.

Three pounds a week.

A fortune, or so it seems to me. I've never had so much money earned by myself in such a short time, beats poker games at Mrs Ganaghans by far. And she rarely gave me pennies for all the work I'd done over there during a season.

I wonder what I'll be able to do with such a lot of money. But then I remember that Rhona said I'll have to be spending none of it for bits and things excepting of course what I'll be buying for Mrs Ganaghan when I'd be going to visit her on my days off.

Mrs Ganaghan.

Rhona says that I could be bringing her whatever things she might be needing, do you know?

Milk.

If the weather keeps up like this then I'm sure that Mrs Ganaghan will be running out of fresh milk at no speed at all what with her having no fridge in the old house, so I'll have to bring her out a few bottles when I'll be off from work. If she's not going to be happy with a few bottles of the freshest Irish dairy cream from the North Mayo dairies then I don't know what I'll have to be doing.

Work.

Lots of it coming my way today, and my day off seems to be somewhere in a distant future. I've got my arms more than elbow-deep in hot soapy water now, and whilst fishing around I'm keeping an eye open to see what's happening around in my new world. A bedlam of steaming cauldrons, clanging pots and shouting cooks, one who's doing the meat joints, another the vegetables, a pastry cook too, she takes care of the Tutti Fruttis and the Peach Melbas, a nervous head chef supervising the whole set up, add to that the noisy washing machine behind me and me banging a pot or two around, and they'd hardly notice for a short while if I'm watching their goings-on, and I'm enjoying it all.

This to me is a real kitchen though, the first time I've seen the likes. Real work going on here, real cooking too. This isn't a bread and butter kitchen like we've got up at Marian House. The most Rhona can manage seems to be rashers and sausages, a roast from time to time, and of course a turkey for Christmas. Otherwise it's bread and butter. In Castlebarry I don't have the right to be dilly-dallying in the kitchen at all, and my time there is limited to a few minutes to gobble down my slices of bread and butter, another few for homework, and of course an eternity whilst I'm on my knees for the Holy Angelus at six o'clock. Here I can spend hours in the kitchen, working, but also admiring the orchestrated manners of a whole team of cooks and staff, and here's meself with a bottle of Teepol, a sponge, a potscrub and looking busy too.

Arrah, sure doesn't it beat turfing any day.

Turfing.

I wonder if Mrs Ganaghan will have enough turf out in the barns to heat the house and boil the water from the well for her hot water bottles late nights this coming winter? Aw, what am I worrying about that for anyway, it's not my problem, not any more.

Sometimes I see the hotel manager approaching the kitchen, but he'll never put a shoe further than the small ledge, which separates the stillroom area from the kitchen. He'll stand there and have a few words with the head chef, who he never comes forward to greet like yer man. Even the hotel owner never puts a foot forward off the red floor tiling of the stillroom. One day I ask a cook about those manners, and he tells me that in here the head chef is the boss, and no one comes into his kitchen unless he gives his approval.

When the lunch business finally dies down, and all the cooks have finished sending their greasy pots and pans flying in my direction, I can finally get around to hosing down my sink, and then move on to other jobs. I have to get on with cleaning the other kitchen areas. I heard that Rome wasn't built in a day, and this place is so big that there's no way that I'll manage to clean the whole place thoroughly in one afternoon. So I set up a rota system. Mondays I'll clean out the kitchen store, starting by wiping down and washing the top shelves and moving downwards, getting rid of all the sugar grains from burst packs and raisins which are lying around instead of finishing up in some cake. Finally a good wash to the floor. If I do a good job this summer here then there's a chance for next year, no? It'll certainly be better than turfing!

The next day it'll be the turn for the meat fridge, and thereafter there's enough to do with the walls, and the sweethouse too.

The sweethouse.

It's a small oblong area adjacent to the kitchen. A sliding door separates it from the hot steamy kitchen, and there's a small latch to the front facing the stillroom and the restaurant. Through the hatch I can see the swinging doors which lead into the hotel dining room beyond, which seems to be a world away for me. Standing on the tip of my toes I can see waiters and waitresses coming and going with a lot of bustle, sometimes nervously and with shouts and foul words too. The sweethouse is Hilda's world. She's always dressed in crisp whites, she's a lively person, when she hears an order for a 'Peach Melba' or 'Banana split', or 'Tutti Frutti' she'll have it ready in no time at all, and even if she lets a drop of syrup or chocolate sauce hit the wall or floor she knows that she won't have to worry about it, because Gerry's on duty today, and she can count on me to give the place a proper clean-up.

With all the hot summer weather we're having, there's nothing better during the afternoon, having cleaned for hours on end, than sliding the door open and heading into the sweethouse, opening the freezer lid, and carving a nice chunk of vanilla or strawberry ice cream which I'll then slide between two wafers and that'll cool me off for a short while at least.

But the ice cream isn't all that's to be found in this kitchen. Lunch-time and even dinner, I can stand at the hot kitchen counter where I'll have a plate of meat, potatoes and vegetables, sometimes topped off with gravy all served up piping hot to me, and then all I'll have to do is settle down at table in the staff refectory at the bottom end of the kitchen with a bottle of fresh Irish milk for which I don't have to have permission to take like anything at Marian House, and I enjoy it all. Nothing like that to be found elsewhere.

Shortly after my ice cream I'll be heading off duty for the evening, and the cooks won't be delaying in getting back for the evening shift.

That also means that a lot of pots and pans will be piling up again until I return in the morning.

A few weeks after I've started, Daddy comes around for a visit in the afternoon. He was in the town anyway he says, and wanted to know how I'm getting on. I don't know what the hotel owner or manager might have been telling him about me and my work, but as we're standing in the courtyard behind the kitchen door he has a good look at me and my growing potbelly.

He smiles as he adjusts his glasses.

'I see that you're putting on some weight, you're looking well, son,' he says, putting his arm over my shoulder.

'Oh yes, I'm happy here, and everything is working all right,' I tell him, surprised by his fatherly jest.

I don't tell him about all the portions of meat potatoes or vegetables however, neither about the vanilla or strawberry ice creams.

The hotel owner says that in the evenings I can always come forward to the television lounge adjacent to the hotel bar. I can even offer myself a Club orange soft drink whilst watching Bonanza and other programmes.

My cosy bedroom faces the rear of the hotel and on Saturday evenings I can hear the country and western bands who are on-stage just inside the ballroom rear window opposite me playing their live music. I can hear the chords being strummed, the drummer's beats, and various instruments.

The lead singer's at his piece again.

'Hey, did you happen to see the most beautiful girl in the world?

'…if you did, was she crying?'

The music drifting in through the top of the open window is putting me in another world altogether, a world where there are people actually singing, dancing, and I guess that they must be really enjoying themselves.

'…Won't you tell her that I love her?

…tell her that I'm sorry.'

What a cosy way to slip into a deep comfortable sleep, instead of listening to the westerly gales blowing in continuously from the Atlantic, and howling their way around the gable end of Marian House.

Tomorrow it'll be Sunday, which often means a day off, time to go up the town and maybe go to Mass, and take life at a leisurely pace.

But sometimes I'd have my two days off during the weekdays, and for such an occasion I'd head up to Central Hill to hire a bike for my time-off. I could pick it up late in the afternoon, on a Tuesday, and return it late on Thursday. Having the bike already on the first evening would of course give me a sense of mobility and freedom so I'd find myself going way out the Enniscaragh road, or up towards Kiltara for the few hours. With all the force stored in me from eating huge portions of meat, spuds and veggies twice a day, and the odd ice creams too, add to that the three-speed gears on my rental bike, and sure there'd be no stopping the likes of me. I don't have an Ordnance Survey map in my possession nor a road map, but no fear of me getting lost anywhere north of Lough Connagh.

So the next morning, and after a good breakfast, I'll be slipping on my seat, into first gear, a good push to start, and I'm roaring off down the road to town leaving the hotel behind me. I'll let somebody else worry about the pots and pans, ye've seen me for the day. Sorry Hilda! I stop at the far end of the town, at a shop opposite the cattle marketplace, just before hitting the open road out to Mrs Ganaghan's.

Have to pick up a few bottles of the freshest milk for her. She doesn't have a fridge like the hotel nor Marian House, so I'll be careful in choosing which ones I'll take with me.

She'll be all happy to be seeing me around.

'Have you been cycling out all this way here, isn't it grand of you, Gerard, to be bringing me out the milk now?' she'll be marvelling about what a good young fellow at all I'm being, and playing surprised that I'd have thought about the milk.

Rhona tells me that I should always be bringing out milk and things that Mrs Ganaghan might be needing do you know?

Spending money for those items would be all right and acceptable, but not for other amusements now. But Mrs Ganaghan never gives me any shillings or pennies back into my hand to pay me for the milk or other odds and sods, which I've paid with from my weekly wages of three pounds. But then she's certainly never seen the insides and workings of such a great hotel kitchen as the one at the Donilaun, and never knows how much I've sweated for my three pounds a week.

'Ah, that's all right now,' I say, proudly handing over the bottles which are still cool from the shop's fridge, 'it took me less than twenty minutes to be out.'

I decide that paying to rent a bike to bring out the pints of milk to Mrs Ganaghan's place is also an acceptable charge to be deducted from my wages, and that'll be so much less savings in my hands at the end of the summer too.

When I've cycled out the five miles with the milk and odds and sods, I'd never ask Mrs Ganaghan if she has enough turf out in the barn behind the house at all, or if it's drying out properly at all in the bog down the Kiltara road. I'll let her worry about that, today it's my day off.

Whenever it's my day off and if I turn up for lunch or dinner to be served at the kitchen counter, I can't help seeing the pots and pans piling up around the place, and can imagine the others hidden below the water's surface like the bottom of an iceberg. A jeering stare from a cook or two won't budge me a bit into going towards the sink. Not today.

'Do you know what now, Gerry, sure, if you'd be doing half an hour there now at the sink, sure tomorrow you'd be having it easy on you at all, and did you ever think of that one?' is what I'd be asked.

Then again, I might just do it for Hilda, because I like her more than the cooks, but all the buggers would see me at it anyway, and they'd take the mickey.

But I've wised up a wee bit since coming this way and I now know that if they'll be running out of a pot or a whisk during the day, well, a curse or two from a cook, a dash of Teepol, a flying scrub and a rinse, Jack's me boy, and that'll be one fellow less for me in the morning.

After all, today's my day off, and Mrs Ganaghan needs the milk. And sure if I'd been gone to the Beltree House Hotel like Martin, sure who else would bring her the fresh dairy milk at all?

Donilaun II

It's still a fine hot summer period indeed, we've been having such a spell of warm evenings that I'm always strolling and passing my time outside. Sometimes I'd head up through the town, maybe stop to play a bit of handball up on the court behind the empty secondary school, or go down beside the river and try to count the salmon in the clear water. Otherwise I'd hang around a while at the back of the hotel before bedtime.

There's an old metal barrel lying out on a rough patch in the back grounds, so here I am doing a balancing act, and moving back and forth through the rough ground and grass, and I have to be minding myself galore now.

The rolling job is going well until suddenly, I lose my balance. I fall, and to add to my danger there's this big stone lying on the ground below me. Lying right there at the wrong place, because it's right in line with my flight path, and I hit it heavily with my left shoulder as I keel over.

Sure isn't the rock itself harder than my shoulder, and the pain starts killing me. I edge up from my awkward position, and when I come to my senses I head dazedly towards the kitchen. I think that I'll need to see a doctor. Not Daddy, any other doctor will do.

There's a lot of activity going on there at this time of the evening, but I get the attention of one of the cooks who's seen me clutching my arm. He races towards me, panicking as he can't imagine what's been putting me in all this pain.

I explain.

'Quick, quick, let's take my car,' he offers and in no time we're racing through the parking area in front of the hotel restaurant and heading towards the small hospital at the other side of town. From my lying position on the rear seat I'm looking upwards and outwards and can make out the rooftops of the various familiar buildings and street corners that are along our route to the hospital, and despite the searing pains, I know that he's making fast progress and that soon we'll be there.

We're heading out the Crosslanagh road now, past the pink shopfront where there's a sweetshop, a place where I'd often buy a few whilst cycling out the road to Rathagan, but this time I'm not going that far. My evening off is being ruined.

The cook can't stay with me at the hospital as he has to get back to all the work that's awaiting him.

I'm left in the care of the nurses, but seemingly they can't do much for me here, I'll have to get to the bigger hospital in Castlebarry.

Rhona.

The Castlebarry hospital is only a short drive from Marian House.

I don't know what's really wrong with my shoulder, they won't tell me much either, and without delay I'm lying in an ambulance which heads off out the Castlebarry road. I don't want to go to Castlebarry. I've been so happy down here in Baltrina enjoying all the work at the hotel, and all of a sudden I have to go back to Castlebarry!

The pains from my shoulder jolt me sharply, and now I'm more worried about any more pains on the way than the possibility of seeing Rhona so soon again.

It's late at night when we arrive, and whilst waiting for a bed to be organised I have to sit and wait in this cold emergency room. The first time in my life in this place which is only half a mile down the road from Marian House. The screams coming from behind a curtain beside me tell me that there's a woman in there who really is in agony. Sure I still have pains from my shoulder but it's nothing to scream about. I hear voices trying to comfort her, help her. Is she going to die? It certainly sounds like it to me. What a place to have to die in! When I'll have to die I'd prefer to be outside in a field where there are geese, or cats and maybe a horse. Maybe even a lone donkey, even with its green teeth would do.

But I believe that I'm not going to die from a pain or two in my shoulder, so I'm not that bad off.

After a while the lady stops howling for a bit, and the staff seem to have quietly left the place to attend to other affairs. I quietly get off my chair and have a gawk around the curtain end. Poor lady sitting there has started at it again, and I don't know whether she's going to stop breathing or cough all her insides out or what. Rushing footsteps to be heard, and I retreat to my chair.

A nurse arrives on my side of the curtain to tell me that they've finally got a bed ready for me upstairs, and would I be following her at all now, so I'm guided into a ward and through the darkness by another nurse holding a torch. The other poor lady gets to stay downstairs behind the curtain, with all her misery.

Judging by the snores, which I can hear from around the room, I think that everybody must be asleep up here. But my bed is in the second row only and right near the door, so at least I'm not right in the middle of the snorers. The nurse props me up with lots of pillows behind my back, because I shouldn't fall over on to my left shoulder. It's really late now, I'd never be going to bed so late in my life, I'm tired, and even with the pains in my shoulder, and the snorers around I have no problem falling asleep.

I hardly have time to finish my breakfast before Daddy arrives. I have an impression that he's not very happy indeed to be finding me here in a hospital bed just down the road from Marian House, and that when I'm supposed to be down in Baltrina earning my three pounds a week, and doing the good job which is to be expected of me, especially after all the miles he's been doing up and down the county to find such a good job for me indeed! I try to explain to him what's happened to me to have put me in a state as this. Maybe the nurses in Baltrina told the ambulance driver who told the nurses here in Castlebarry what's the matter with me, and they'd have told Daddy all the story, because he's coming and going to the nursing station just outside in the corridor and isn't very much interested in listening to my version, or of my pains either.

When the nurses have finished with my treatment, the ointments and the bandages I can leave the hospital and Daddy brings me up to the house. I don't know what's gotten into Rhona, and I don't like the look of her at all.

'What have you been up to, what's gotten into you?' she yells at me.

'I was playing with a barrel, but fell off it and hurt myself on the shoulder,' I explain as she's having a look all over my armband. I have a feeling that that's not what she wants to hear from me.

I wonder if playing and getting myself hurt at it is a crime or what? This is the first time in my life that I've had an accident that sent me to a hospital. Is that what she's so mad about? Has she forgotten the day when she deliberately pushed one of my fingers between the cog and chain of Tadgh's bicycle out in the playroom, and spun the pedal until my fingertip got crushed and the blood spurted through the chain grease? Wasn't that an accident? She left me with just a roll of toilet paper to rub off the grease and blood pouring from my finger and flush down the toilet. No Dettol to clean and disinfect the open wound. She didn't call a nurse or even give me a bandage that day! She didn't turn to Daddy after the Holy Angelus, and ask him to have a look at my bruised finger and see if it would be all right, did she? He's a doctor, so he should know about caring for the sick and the suffering, shouldn't he? But if my finger had kept bleeding through the night, and if any of it would have stained the sheets then I'm sure it would have been worth a beating! Another one!

She turns to Daddy.

Since arriving in the ward this morning Daddy hasn't asked me how I am, if I'm still suffering from pains or anything, or if so what could he do for me?

But he's listening to Rhona now.

'Do you know who's been calling on the phone to me whilst you were down at the hospital?' she announces.

'What have you been telling the Glavneys?' she now directs her anger towards me.

I think that she's gone slightly crazy.

'Eh, eh, nothing, what could I possibly have been saying to the Glavneys?' I offer.

'Do you know what I've been hearing, he's been phoning the Glavneys and telling them that he's not happy at all about being sent down to work in the Donilaun,' she says aloud to Daddy.

'No, I haven't,' I butt in, because I'm damn sure about what I've done and what not. I've never had the chance to use a public telephone in my life and why would I even attempt to call them, being so happy about my new summer job situation? How could they even know where I am or what I'm doing? If you'd ask them any questions I'm sure they'd think I'm down cutting turf in the bogs north of Baltrina like last year and the years before. I'm living in a world of so-called grown-ups here, and I wonder why Daddy wouldn't have the idea to call the Glavneys themselves on the phone? They live only six houses down the road, so why doesn't he walk down and ask them what is true and what isn't? But just like myself who isn't allowed into those neighbours' houses, he wouldn't be caught dead having any contact with them either.

Rhona calls them the bogside people of North Mayo.

So Rhona's version of the story will be just good enough for now.

Because she probably told him and made him believe that the class of neighbour we have on the Western Road are tinkers and aren't worth having around us.

Neighbours.

What's the point in having neighbours when you can't even visit them or talk about the weather to them or about anything else? Our house is just about the only house out the Western Road where the driveway gate is permanently closed, and we don't even have a dog or a cat in our place. Even cats and dogs can live in perfect harmony, but neither Rhona nor Daddy can live in perfect harmony with the neighbours.

I defy all her attempts to crush me on this one, I'd like to ask Daddy to go and check for himself with the Glavneys, but I know that Rhona would still be one wiser than myself and my suggestion would be cut short.

So I get packed off down to Baltrina. We arrive down at the end of the narrow road, which passes by the hotel. We turn off and are edging up the last slope towards the first of the two parking places out the front.

Rhona tells Daddy to stop the car right there. He follows orders and the engine is cut. Looking out towards the front I can see the facade of the building, I can nearly see the pile of pots and pans waiting for me in the kitchen way out the back. I'm happy to be back in these parts.

'If you don't tell me now about you phoning the Glavneys then we're turning the other way around and back up you're going to Castlebarry,' Rhona announces.

Now I feel like a cornered rat.

Once again.

Why did she have to come this far to make such a statement and leave me with such a choice? Why couldn't she have stayed in Castlebarry? It would have been extra time for her to drink a few more instant coffees, and smoke a few more Carroll's whilst gawking out the kitchen window at her fine garden.

A choice?

I don't have one!

I have to say what she wants to hear and that Daddy can hear it too.

I look forward again towards the hotel building. It's just out there in front of me, but it's really a world away. I think of the pots and pans, of Hilda, the plates of meat spuds and veg, the ice creams. I think of all the kind people that I've gotten to know within those walls. Three pounds a week. The fortune of it. The television lounge. Club orange and ice. I can nearly hear one of the big bands with their country and western music drifting out from the rear of the ballroom on the Saturday nights…

'…Hey, did you happen to see the most beautiful girl in the world?

'…if you did, was she crying?'

I'm near to tears because I'm about to lose some of the most wonderful things that have happened to me since a long time in my lifetime, and I just want to live my newfound lifestyle without interruptions. I know, however, that I wouldn't be going back to Castlebarry because Rhona wouldn't be having me there, but instead I'll be brought out straightaway to Mrs Ganaghan's place, and when my shoulder heals, then it'll be back to cutting turf, trimming grass and running with a heavy bucket to the well for the fresh spring drinking water.

I'm not sure, but I have an uneasy feeling that my whole small world is starting to crumble in, and all that's the fault of one and only person.

If I have a choice to make it's between going back to the hotel where I'm so happy, or returning to slavery.

'…Won't you tell her that I love her?

'…tell her that I'm sorry.'

I lie.

I've broken one of the Ten Commandments and I know that it's against the rules of my Catholic religion to lie about things, but under the pressure of the present circumstances I have to do so. I wonder if I should go to church on Saturday and confess what I've done bad today, but I don't know if I'll be able to find the courage or the words, and I don't know if the priest in his confessional box would have time or patience to listen to all I'd have to tell him about Rhona or even understand a little of what I've been going through.

But Rhona's got what she wanted.

That's all that counts here.

As far as I'm concerned Daddy doesn't know what he wants, he lets her tell him what he should want, and that's the only way to be having things.

But then again hasn't she lied to Daddy about me having phoned the Glavneys, so me lying about it, just to save my chance of getting back to the paradise of the Donilaun Hotel isn't that much worse, is it? The parish priest would understand that much.

My shoulder and arm is still all bandaged up and can't start back to work straightaway, so I'll have a few days to rest. Everybody is excited to see me again, and hear about how they treated me up the town and in the great big hospital in Castlebarry, because they couldn't find me at the hospital up the town. A good job nobody asks me how I was treated when I got brought back to the house at Western Road because I wouldn't know what to say, I've already had enough on my back for things that I didn't say, and what would really happen if I started telling the truth?

'Are you all right there now, are you grand with that on you?' asks one. A good job too that they have nurses in the Baltrina and Castlebarry hospitals, ladies who took care of me, changed my bandages and ointments when necessary. I'm going to need it if I have to heal, and get back to my job of three pounds a week.

Daddy hardly even noticed that I've got my left shoulder and arm all tied and strapped up, and didn't ask me how I was, if I wasn't suffering too much.

He's a doctor, you know?

But this is just one brick on top of my wall of suffering, so I'll have to live it through.

The truth will just have to wait for another day, another year maybe, and maybe even more than that.

When I ramble back into the hotel kitchen and over to the hot counter for my meals, I'll find my meat already well prepared in small pieces, lots of them good mashed spuds, and an extra knob of butter on my garden peas.

'Will that be all right for you now, Gerard, at all?' I'm asked. Those cooks sure know how to take care of me indeed, just you guys wait until I'm fit again, and I'll be taking good care of cleaning yer kitchen again.

Even the barman gives me lots of ice in a pint-sized glass, that way I can have all my Club orange at one go, whilst watching the television set in the hotel lounge.

A few evenings later, the place is packed, and the crowd are all excited with the chat and the jabber indeed.

It's now 21st July 1969, and during this coming night the Americans are landing on the moon for the first time in history.

I ask if I can stay up to watch the action, because I don't want to miss this one.

'Sure Bejasus Gerry, who on earth and who above it could be refusing that to you now?' says the barman, and permission is granted.

I'm not sure about the distances, but I have a certainty that the way from earth up to the moon is a way longer than the main road from Castlebarry down to Baltrina.

Even with all the bends on the way.

June 1970

Martin, who is home on holiday says that he's had enough and indeed I cannot but have to share his feelings. One evening whilst in bed we talk about things over and over again and he promises that tomorrow he'll ask to talk to Daddy about the situation. Next evening comes, and in defiance of the ban to leave the bedroom at night, he goes halfway down the staircase and calls for Daddy. Daddy emerges from the kitchen, but when Martin asks to have a talk with him, he objects.

'No, not today,' Daddy replies.

So that's it! He just doesn't want to dialogue!

This is the first time that we approach him in a direct way, the first time that we try to get his attention on a particular problem, and what does he do? Not today! He doesn't want to enter into any such discussion! Does he have to ask Rhona's permission first?

'We're going!' Martin says as he comes back up to the bedroom. Whilst we're waiting for Daddy and Rhona to go to bed and fall asleep we make our plan. Martin suggests that he could push the car backwards out of the garage, whilst I open the gates without making any noise. Driving during the night we could try and make it to Belfast, and then sneak on a ferry boat which would bring us over to Scotland.

We delay and then in the quiet of the night we get heavily dressed and sneak downstairs, keeping to the edge of the staircase steps because one solitary creak from a wooden plank and Rhona might awaken and wonder what kind of a brat might be crawling downstairs at this hour at all? When in the kitchen we find Rhona's handbag in the corner behind the fridge. We'll have to find some money to buy food along our way, so a quick gawk inside her bag reveals some twenty pounds, which we take. There are also some wholemeal biscuits handy beside the sink and we'll have them with us too. Rhona will certainly find something else to go with her cups of instant coffee later.

All of a sudden from where I'm standing in the outside corridor, I hear some sort of noise from upstairs. I head to the garage door and whisper to Martin, who's in there.

'Psst, I think I heard something from upstairs,' I whisper, straining to keep my concentration on anything further that might be coming our way.

'Are you sure?' he asks.

I say that I'm fairly sure, so we have to change our plans. Damn it!

'Let's run,' says Martin.

'Where to?' I ask.

'Not out to the front,' he says, 'down the back garden, and move it!'

I whip up the packet of biscuits, which were placed, on the corridor floor, and we hightail it to the back garden. A last look at the house from behind the hedge out the back. No lights have been switched on, but as Daddy and Rhona's room is at the front we can't be sure about the situation. So down we run down through the back garden and over the wall into McDonagh's field. We thread our way through the darkness, through another field and push on towards the lake. We keep moving fast, some moonlight has now come to help us on our way, and soon we're crossing the wooden bridge behind St Patrick's terrace. I never like crossing this bridge because it's got wooden slats and you can see the water through the separations between the wood. No time to think about that now though. We arrive at the bottom of Chapel Street, where we take time to stop and rest. Also to think about what we'll do from here. Judging by things, the whole town is fast asleep. We start searching around until we find a Raleigh bicycle propped up against a wall in an alley, and Martin decides that we'll cycle down to Baltrina and take the train from there.

'Why not from the train station here in Castlebarry?' I ask.

'The station is out of the question,' says Martin. 'If somebody's awake and notices anything now, then they'll check there first thing in the morning.'

Sounds fine by me and I hop onto the bikerack behind Martin, and we pass the Parochial House and then the Holy church and off we set out the Pontarla Road. We're doing a fine speed all along, and finally there's a nice long slope down towards Hanly's Hotel by the lake so Martin can ease up on the pedalling. He asks me if I know how to give hand signals in case we need to turn.

'No problem,' I say, as I wave my left arm out in the cool air, even if there's no motor car for miles behind us.

Further along the lake we make a stop and go bathe our feet in the cool water. We bike across Pontarla Bridge and still not a car in sight. We make another stop before leaving the Lake District, leaving the bike in the deep grass by the roadside, and we climb up a small ridge just to keep out of sight. As we finish off the biscuits and we are still hungry, Martin says that we'll stop at a corner foodstore, which is further down the Baltrina Road. We stop a hundred yards after the shop, and as I stay put Martin walks back to buy some bread. Sure enough the lady in the shop asks what his name is and where is he coming from, and what's his business in these parts at all? He tells her that his name is John Flannery and he's from Westbary. She's happy with that, Martin has the pennies to pay, and he gets the bread.

Back to the pedalling, and the miles to cover before reaching Baltrina. It's a good job that Martin is older and stronger than I am, because if I had to do any of this we wouldn't be at Lough Connagh yet. Having covered the twenty-five miles, we arrive in Baltrina late morning and we stop at the station, which is on the left roadside about half a mile from the town entrance. We must check the timetable at the station. There's no train for Dublin until the afternoon, so we ride further into town and as my shoes are broken Martin says we'll get me a new pair, which we find for a few pounds. Arriving back at the station we leave the bicycle hidden in a corner, before boarding the train.

My first time travelling on an Irish train, but especially the first time going anywhere without Rhona's supervision and control.

Since arriving at the great big Euston Station in Dublin we spend a lot of time walking back and forth wondering what to do about our situation. What to do in this great big city? My first time being in such a big place, and it frightens me. People, lots of people scurrying back and forth, busy into shops and jumping on and off double-decker buses the likes of which I've never seen in the West. People who I don't know, and who could hardly know anything about me or my plight. So they're people who can't help us. From a phone box in Dame Street Martin decides to phone the Glavneys. Martin even calls them a few times, which costs a lot of pennies and shillings, which are going into the great black box, and I think that he's nervous about something. It's now dark but we walk back over to O'Connell Street again, but with all the walking back and forth in these new shoes I'm getting blisters and sores on my feet, so we have to take a rest. We sit down on a bench at the foot of the statue facing the bridge. I'm tired, just stone tired.

But now it's time to relax, nothing but relax.

Martin says something.

'Eh?' I am still dazed from the travelling.

'I tell you don't look now, they're watching us,' repeats Martin, as I hadn't heard him the first time.

'Who's looking?' I ask.

'The Gardai,' he says, 'they're in the car just in front of us.'

I straighten myself up and there I see them. The car is just some ten yards away in front of us. The driver's window is down.

'Who are ye waiting for?' asks the guard who's driving. Martin gets up and moves towards the car where he spends some time talking to the Gardai. When he comes back to me Martin says that one of the guards has recognised us as the Duignan boys from Castlebarry, and my young age has already attracted their attention at this late time of the evening.

'We're going over to the police station with them,' says Martin when he comes back from the patrol car. I'm so tired from not sleeping at all last night so all I need is a place to lie down and rest. I follow him to the car, into the back seats and they set off in the direction of Store Street police station. On the way one of the guards is asking questions, but I leave the talking and answers to Martin. The questions continue after getting to the station, and a guard brings me down to the floor where they have cells for prisoners. He slides back the latch on a heavy metal door and lets me have a look for myself.

'Is that where you want to sleep?' he asks, and I don't know if he is trying to frighten me or what. I shake my head so he brings us back up to the kitchen, where they're going to lock us for the night. That doesn't worry me, and soon I'm fast asleep on a bench.

Morning comes, and I've had a great sleep indeed. A great burly policeman comes into the kitchen. Judging by the looks of him I wonder how he'd ever fit into a police patrol car at all and go and chase robbers or the likes of runaways, maybe he was a real cop in his earlier years, but now with his great tummy he's sticking to doing the tea and biscuit rounds in the Gardai barracks here, and attending to the kitchen which is indeed in a sparkling clean condition.

'Do ye have any mooney?' he asks with a great accent. I find that funny and Martin tells me it's a Dublin accent, but he seems to be a nice chap, nothing severe about him at all. He says that we can go out for a walk, and to come back later as there are more questions. Martin says that we have some money with us, so we head off for a stroll. Over to the Busaras station, and hop onto a bus that takes us out to the airport at Collinstown, and we spend a sunny afternoon up on the terrace looking at all the coming and goings of those great flying machines. I wonder how long I'm going to have to wait before I too can get on to such a great Aer Lingus flying machine and go visit far-away places.

When we come back to the police station late afternoon we are guided up to a big room upstairs. But this huge place is nearly empty, and we have to sit at a small square table facing the window. To our left there's another table of the same size. There's a rough looking fellow at that table and he's going through a set of questions.

He tells the guard that he wants to speak to a lawyer.

Then our guard arrives, and we get the same questions as last night. Martin is answering as best he can, and then yer man at the other table starts butting in.

'Ye're awful fellows to be running away like that from home, what do ye think yeer parents would be thinking of yee at all?' he asks as he bends over in our direction. I feel like telling him to mind his own fecking business and you have the looks of a right old crook yourself now. Maybe his wife ran out on him, and he's on the lookout for her, or is it the other way around I wonder? Maybe I should put the question to him, but I keep my gob shut, because I have an uneasy feeling that we're in enough trouble already.

In the evening we are allowed over to the Hannons flat out in Ballsbridge where we'll be staying the night before having to go down to Castlebarry. Late evening Daddy and Rhona arrive and are parked outside. There's a guard with them. From behind the curtains in the darkened lounge I can see Father Hannon talking with them on the pavement at the bottom of the Georgian steps leading up to the main door. The mere sight of Daddy and Rhona puts the frights in me, they're so near me now, and I start worrying about meeting them again tomorrow. I hadn't seen her in nearly forty-eight hours, and it suited me fine to say the least. When Father Hannon returns into the lounge he tells us that the guard had insisted that we come out from the flat and return with them to Castlebarry. Father Hannon says that it would certainly mean a beating for us both, and that the guard would be held morally responsible if that would happen, and the guard backs down on his demand. It is agreed that we will head back down to Castlebarry the next day. But after a fine dinner and all I need to drink, I can have another calm night's sleep before all of that.

The next morning off we are to Euston Station, accompanied by one of the Station Guards, and off down to Castlebarry with the CIE train, where we are met by Father O'Malley who drives us over to the police station. The room is rather a long one. I sit in the corner near the bottom, Martin's near me to my left so I feel somewhat secure. There's a guard at a big table to my right. Father O'Malley is on Martin's left. We can talk to the guard for a while before the others arrive.

Daddy and Rhona finally arrive, with Daddy sitting near us, and her a long way off up near the door. The discussions continue for a long time, my mind is getting blurred by all the words and questions and I'm slowly having enough, and don't even have any faith in any possible solution.

We have to hand over the remains of the money, which we'd stolen from Rhona's bag.

The guard then turns to Martin and myself, explaining that they can only say that food, clothing, and shelter is being provided to us so there's no justification available which would allow us to be placed in a home. I remember the buttered slices of bread, yes it's food, so I can't object. The roof above our heads isn't leaking on us either. I have a pair of open-topped brown sandals for my feet, which I get to wear be it sunny weather or the worst of a rainy Irish day. I'd never wear socks, but am I going barefooted to school? But their laws don't say anything about the right to use the other rooms in the house, go shopping with the others, and the many other privileges such as piano and dancing lessons, or trips to Longford or England, the front seat in the car and others which the other children enjoy; I'd like to admire the big Christmas tree in the lounge every Christmas too, and that without getting a beating because I've been into rooms where I have no business. But their laws don't say anything about affection either. Maybe I'd like to learn to play the piano too, but nobody asks me the question. The guard asks Martin if he wants to press charges. But Martin is really nervous, and he says no.

Nobody asks me either if I want to have a lawyer just like the crook did in the Gardai station in Store Street. But then I am only a child. When the talks are over and done Father O'Malley takes us with his car down Main Street. Into the fish and chip shop we go, and I get offered my first porterhouse steak and real French fries in my life. Yum! This beats bread and butter, and rashers and lads anyday, and we even get to stay seated at table for as long as we like to enjoy it.

But I know that the feast will have to come to its end at some time of the day, and Father O'Malley then drives us out the long road to Marian House.

We get parked in the annexe room again. Back we are indeed to the cold sterile environment of Marian House.

Jane comes on a visit to us out from the house.

'Mammy says that ye stole forty quid, which is more money than ye say ye did,' is the message she's been told to bring.

Martin defends us and repeats what was said down at the police station, and she disappears.

A few minutes pass and she's back out again.

'Mammy told me to tell ye that ye'll never run away like that again,' is her message this time.

Martin is standing with his back to the heater, and I'm facing the window. He tells her that she can go back into the house again to tell her mammy that we've maybe done this just once, but that we'll do it again if we want.

The next day we are allowed out onto the main road for a walk, and in the company of the other three children, we can even take a stroll to the top end of McDonagh's field. This is my first time being up this far out the road, and from here I get a view of the town which has always eluded me.

Later we learn from neighbours that the first thing Daddy did in the morning upon discovering our escape was to head down to the railway station, and he checks every carriage on the Westbary to Dublin morning train.

Later on we discover too that life is continuing as it had ever been, that our running away and the Gardai haven't managed to change anything at all, and the promises that we'd be allowed to visit the neighbours houses were worthless.

Donilaun III

'Gerard, you have to come around out the front, you have visitors for ya,' the girl says.

'Visitors,' I wonder who this might be at all?

Rhona?

'Visitors, I don't know them but they're at the reception desk and waiting for you, so come on now,' she insists.

I follow her as I make my way back in through the kitchen and stillroom, and out through the heavy door leading into the hotel hallway.

I arrive at the reception desk, nobody to seen in this area, in fact everybody seems to be out enjoying the hot weather, and then the receptionist appears from the back office.

'In the bar, Gerard,' she beckons to the right back up towards the hotel bar.

'Who is it at all?' I enquire, but she doesn't know who these people might be and shakes her head.

So I retreat from the desk, and cautiously make my way up the two steps and continue moving further back to the bar doors which are now wide open. A glance to the right, still no signs and then to the left where there's a surprise for me.

I see Father Francis, Father Denis, and Mother Alouise who are seated comfortably in the great armchairs around a coffee table. I haven't seen any of them since ages now, but will always manage to recognise them.

What a surprise! They live so far away from Castlebarry, and haven't gotten to see me in so many years and here they are all of a sudden, as if having strolled in right off the street! They are on holidays in Ireland, and wanted to know how I'm keeping, and if I'm happy about working in this great big hotel.

I can only reply that I'm most happy here, happy about all the people too, but don't mention anything about how different it would have been if I had to spend my summer season working on Mrs Ganaghan's farm at Rathagan. I don't believe that they've ever seen the place, nor know what it's like to be cutting turf, and hauling it up to the house, and plucking grass and other jobs too. Jobs where I don't get to meet many people other than those of her family. Here, I even get wages paid to me every week, and that's far better than anything that Mrs Ganaghan ever gave me, and trying to win pocket money on poker isn't a safe bet at all.

Father Denis orders tea and coffee and chicken sandwiches. Whilst the lounge waiter is preparing our order we have a little time to talk about things.

The light is streaming in through the overhead sunlight and I sit back and relax, enjoy the sandwiches, the fresh bread is so soft, and the meat is delicious.

Father Francis says he has a present for me, and he produces a brand new watch from his jacket pocket.

'It's the latest model from Timex,' he says, as I stare and wonder at the wonderful timepiece, which he is holding out for me to take.

'It's for you only,' he says.

I don't know what to say really, except a meek 'Thank you' because at my age I'm not used to receiving things at all, and therefore don't know how to value them or express my gratitude. Whenever visitors would come to Marian House, and in the event that they might be brought out to the annexe building to get to meet Martin and myself, they might give us coins in the palms of our hands, but we would always have to hand over the shillings and pence to Rhona shortly after they'd have left, because she'd be minding them for us. So the value of money and gifts is something new for me. It's something I'll have to learn for life later on.

Something I do know, however, is that Rhona won't be taking this watch from me as she used to with the chocolate bars nor oranges, and as this is a man's watch, what could she be doing with it? But then again, maybe she'd want to give it to one of the other boys?

Before they leave Father Francis also has a silver-plated comb and clothes brush which he leaves me too as gifts.

His initials 'F. O'D' are engraved thereon.

I've never received so much in one day of my life.

Donilaun IV

All the months of the school year have gone by and Daddy announces that I will be able to go back down to the Donilaun Hotel for the coming summer. He says that the manager was so happy with my work last time that he'll be having me back again. I wonder how the manager could arrive at such a decision, because as I see it he spends most of his time out the front of the hotel, he mightn't know all of what I've been doing at all. Well I'm happy anyway, but Daddy tells me that this summer I'll be doing hall porter out the front hall.

That'll be something new for me.

That way I might get to see more of the hotel manager and the work he really does, and whatever he might be up to at all in a day.

Four pounds a week. Wow! That's a pound note more in my hand than last year!

It's an early start here too.

I have my own porter's desk taking up a position in the corner of the hall on the left hand side when I arrive in through the main glass doors. To my left and above the huge open fireplace I can see the stuffed pike, which was caught in Lough Connagh many years ago. I have a view towards the stairs leading up towards the guests rooms situated on the two floor levels above. Great armchairs adorn the spacious hall, two steps and the plush carpeting leads one towards a guests reading room, the hotel bar, and the main dining room to the rear of the spacious hall. The reception desk, where often more than one lady will be busily occupied, is opposite me, I need a few good strides to get over there, the manager's office lies behind, and a guests lounge slightly over to my right. There's a small gift-shop just behind me.

My daily rota starts with me giving a thorough clean to the public toilets down at the end of the corridor. I then move over and clean all the glass door-panes at the entrance side, then into the residents lounge for a thorough dusting and wiping down. The residents lounge overlooks part of the second car parking area, and from here I get a fine view of all the potted shrubs and flowering plants in the garden just below the great windows. There is a great expanse of other shrubs and flowers out the front too, where there's a huge lawn well laid out. There's a gardener who works full time here and that's his whole world. Beyond the car park I can see the salmon locks on the river, and the water is cascading down over a series of rocks and natural waterfalls. No time to dally here though, as I have to give a good hoovering to all the carpet areas. I push and pull the heavy armchairs back and forth and out of my way as I head into corners, and under the coffee tables for the slightest bit of visible dust, or breadcrumbs from yesterday's afternoon tea. The heavy armchairs remind me of the ones I've seen occasionally in the lounge at Marian House, but now I've hardly time to betake of their comfort.

A short stop for breakfast, and off to the kitchen to get a wee bite of some buttered toast and marmalade with a pot of tea from the stillroom and down to the canteen.

My Timex watch tells me that my break is up, and I head back out again towards the front. Lots of other cleaning jobs to be done, lighter ones now, like polishing all the brass doorknobs and various other brass furnishings around the hall.

Some days, when wedding receptions are due in, then I'll have to head over to the ballroom entrance and clean the whole access hall, toilets and carpets. A good sweep out in the forecourt too to get rid of any leaves or stray papers before laying down the red carpet.

The receptionists would have their eyes out for me whenever a guest checking out would be phoning down for bags to brought back downstairs. Not a problem in the world I say, and sometimes I hurdle up the stairs so fast that the guest wouldn't have time to put the phone down on the hook, and here I am already at Room 21.

'Are you here already, you're a mighty fast fellow yourself?' a startled fellow would have to say when he sees my boyish face gawking at him through the open bedroom door.

'Oh, if you're not ready then I'll come back in five minutes,' I can always offer, and with my new Timex always wound up to the limit and working just fine I'll never miss getting back to a room on time.

On the second floor there are a load of single rooms for what are called the 'travellers'. These are travelling salesmen, who generally stay one night in the hotel before moving on to visit clients and factories in the neighbouring parts. They always carry their smallish bags themselves, and anyway they don't have great pieces of luggage like the Americans and the others who look as though they're here to stay until Christmas.

The Americans can arrive at any time of the day, stepping out of rented cars, which they pick up at one of the airports. If I'm cleaning the forecourt or just standing out the front of the hotel I'd hear them coming up the driveway with the car's engine still revving from having driven most of the way up from Shannon or Dublin in second gear instead of fourth.

They dress in great tweeds too, lots of checkered green colours and shades in their shirts and trousers which puts them standing out a mile from us Paddys.

I'm standing at the reception desk, wondering about these people, where they're from, and what they're after here in Ireland.

'Here's the auto keys, boy, we got all the luggage out there in the trunk, in the green one you see,' one says, and the keys are dropped into the palm of my hand, and reaching the great double glass doors I see that if they have a green car to spare at the airport the Americans will surely rent it. These Yanks, they must like everything and anything that's green. Even their dollar notes have a green look about them. I've gotten the keys in the palm of my hand as if I'd been on this job for years. The guests have long disappeared before I can finish getting all the bags out, and remembering which key is for the trunk and which one for the passenger doors.

Firstly, all the bags into the hall and neatly arranged in front of my desk. Then the hauling starts. The Americans like the suites which have a lounge area adjoining the bedroom, which must remind them of when they're back home. Problem for me is that these are the rooms furthest away from the reception area, and when I've managed to get up the flight of stairs there's still an awful length of corridor to go. I quietly deposit the first bags just outside the bedroom door and return for the remainders. I load on the bags for the last trip so when I finally get to knocking on the door, I'm puffing and panting like a donkey who's just hauled a ton of turf up Croagh Patrick and down the other side and then out to Clew Bay, and won't that show them that I'm hard at me work indeed?

I deposit all the bags on or beside the luggage rack, hand over the automobile keys to the gentleman, and am about to close the bedroom door behind me.

'Boy,' I hear a loud drawl calling my attention, and I turn in my tracks to see yer man coming after me towards the door.

'Yes?' I enquire.

'What do they give you, boy?' I hear the great burly fellow drawl out, his great width and girth nearly blocking out the sunlight filtering through the sunblinds way behind him.

I don't know what he's on about, and stare at him.

'I asked what do they give you for the bags, boy?'

'Oh, oh, you mean the bags?' I'm catching up now.

'Yeah yeah, the bags, boy,' as he dips his hand into his shirt pocket and whips out various coins and notes.

I've been told that when I've been hauling bags and bags upstairs I shouldn't forget to stretch the palm of my hand out and I might get a tip for the good work indeed. But I don't like this idea, it's more like begging to me, and anyway with the few pounds a week, the meat spuds and potatoes, and all the new goings-on in my new job and meeting all these people from places near and far, I couldn't hardly wish for more could I, so why stretch out my hand? The guest will be able to decide for himself if he wants to make a donation.

'Arrah, sure whatever you'd like, sir,' I say gratefully, and if I don't get a green dollar note, I'll have lots of Irish coins from the great burly American, who stares at me gawking at him.

It keeps going like that for a good part of the day, and again tomorrow, the day after too, and with all the coins rolling in I have to find a small box to hide them all in my bedroom, and from time to time I'll bring some of them back out to the reception and ask one of the girls for pound notes. They always smile when they see me arriving with the coins, and even after smiling whilst counting the coins, I have to smile again. At this rate sure I'll be able to pay for the bottles of fresh milk for Mrs Ganaghan and even a few odds and sods too each week, and why not an evening from time to time at the Central cinema up the town, and that without touching any of my four pounds wages at all.

One evening I go to see *Tora Tora Tora*, which costs me only 10p, and I enjoy it so much that I go again the next evening, and the evening thereafter. I watch the same film three evenings in a row.

Another evening, they are showing a film called *The Go-Between*. It's a story about a young boy who does all the message carrying between an older chap and the lady he calls his girlfriend, as they can't really meet each other. So the young fellow is scouting back and forth, dropping messages and letters, like I used to have to drop messages through the fence and into the Hannon's garden when I got badly beaten by Rhona and Daddy for having borrowed a butter knife to cut a banana.

Well the boy and the girl do finally grow up, and they run away from their households, like I did with Martin in June 1970, but they are luckier than we were, as they manage to find a house to live in, and one day the girl is expecting a baby to be born, and when the great day comes and the baby comes out of the girl's tummy, she asks him if it's a boy or a girl, and he looks closer, but says he doesn't know. I wonder what it's like to have a girlfriend, and be into making babies, but I hope that they'll all live happily ever after.

I've become friendly with a photographer who lives up the town, and he's at the hotel often, what with all the wedding doos that they're having at the place, and yer man comes down for the photo sessions out the front on the beautiful lawns. He even invites me to his home on the edge of town, where I can admire his work on weddings, but on many other subjects as well.

He is impressed by my curiosity in photography, and he suggests that if I'm interested, he has a second-hand camera to sell. So for a few pounds of my money earned on tips at the hotel, I become the proud and happy owner of my first camera. All I need is to buy my Ilford films at a chemist's shop up the town, and away I am with a curious eye trained on various landmarks around the town, and out the country when visiting Mrs Ganaghan.

I won't tell Rhona about all them pennies and shillings coming my way for running up and down the stairs and panting like a donkey after I've been carrying loads of heavy bags for people, and even if she'd be wise enough to cop onto it then I'll say something like 'Arrah, a few pennies here and there now, hardly enough for all the bottles of milk I've been bringing out to Mrs Ganaghan at all.' I'll tell her even less about the cinema tickets, because that's not money to be worked or saved for, and sure for God's sakes tonight you'd never know what kind of rubbishy pictures they might be showing on them cinema screens and it's not even a place for a fellow like me to be hanging about at all.

But as far as I know Rhona never goes staying in hotels or the likes, and she's hardly the one to be giving out shillings or even pennies to a boy, so I'm not worried about that one.

With the weeks flying by I'm running back and forth, upstairs and nearly everywhere else and getting to know the ins and outs of the whole front of the house, and sure know how to change light bulbs or fuses when needed. I can whip you up fresh chicken or ham sandwiches and pots of tea if you'd like to have a seat in the residents lounge, and I won't be a minute about it at all, sir.

With the Timex watch that the American uncles, Fathers Denis and Francis, and Mother Alouise offered me I know how fast I'm moving.

St Joseph's

Martin is now in his fourth year at St Joseph's. Daddy drives me to Tury late spring as I'll have to sit an entrance examination. This is the town where I was born and where my mother Noreen died in hospital, but it was mentioned so seldom that I'd nearly forgotten about this.

I'm standing beside Daddy in the great studyhall. The vast expanse of dark brown floorboards and the school desks are something that I'd never seen before.

'Son,' Daddy calls me, 'you come first in these exams, and I'll buy you the best bike that money can buy.'

'Yes,' I nod in acknowledgement of the message just passed to me. But I'm not very optimistic about getting that far. I look around at the great number of other boys who are already seated to all ends of the room, and that's far more than my class at Castlebarry. I'm not optimistic, because I don't feel well prepared to affront and win, how could I when I'm more used to picking leaves and trimming the lawn at Marian House? The other children at the house would have a far better chance because they can use all the time they need and wish to spread their books out on the dining room table to the front. Anyways, I'd never have madly wished for a brand new bike in my life. If Daddy had ever cared to ask, and he wouldn't have had to have waited until I was twelve years old, then I'd have been ever so happy with an old second-hand thing, even half rusted, because that'd already be better than having no bike at all, which is my current situation, unlike Tadgh, who has his own in the garage at Marian House.

A whole day of examinations before heading back to Castlebarry.

A few weeks later the answer comes back. I've come sixty-first, out of a maximum of seventy places available. In the meantime, at the school year-end exams at Castlebarry I'd come ninth. I can't understand, but it seems that the world beyond Castlebarry is different, tougher.

Anyway I'm in. That's what counts for me. Away from Marian House, from Castlebarry. Life at St Joseph's can only be better than what I'm used to.

After my summer stint at the Donilaun Hotel, it's time to get going. It's autumn 1970, and Martin will be starting his fifth year. So we'll be together for a full year, which he says is a good thing, and so I'll be able to adapt as best as possible. We have two beds in one of the small dormitories provided for brothers.

The day's schedule is of course far different from that at Castlebarry. The great bell downstairs inside the main doors wakens us all out of our sleep. The cold water with which I wash my face is a thermal shock, and certainly gets any sleepiness out of the system. The single sheet toilet paper is rather rough on my backside, this sure isn't the Donilaun Hotel here.

After a breakfast of cornflakes and cold milk, then it's time for study, or Mass, and then classes. I enjoy all the classes and the subjects, except one. The Physical Education on Wednesday mornings. Mind you, not every Wednesday morning, but if I get wind on a Tuesday that tomorrow we're off to the swimming pool for lessons, then I get all frightened. Castlebarry is only eleven miles from the coast, but I was seldom over there to be able to waddle around in, and get used to water. When the public swimming pool was built in Castlebarry on grounds near the National School, I wasn't allowed over there anyway, so I never had the chance to get used to deep water. Until I came to St Joseph's. That's when I felt that I'd finally have a chance to do so. But one day, whilst at the shallow end of the pool, and whilst Martin was somewhere about the college grounds, I was grabbed and hauled out by two of the fourth year students to the edge of the deep end. Whilst one has a solid grip on my short arms, the other is firmly holding my legs as they start swinging me back and forth over the pool edge. I see the deep water below me, and I get the frights. I scream. They keep swinging.

122

'I'll call Martin on ye,' I hurl at them, but that doesn't stop them, and even so I'll probably have a deep bath coming.

They keep laughing, and swinging.

Until one of the arms of the fellow who's holding me by the head end comes dangerously close to me. For a few split seconds I stop screaming as I grip him, and start sinking all my teeth in.

Nothing so far had convinced them bastards to let me go. Being big bastards, and being in fourth year, had given them unwritten powers upon first year fellows. I knew that the fellow I'd managed to bite was a chap from Inishboffin Island. He could probably swim like a shark. Probably a fisherman's son. Unlike myself. But for me he was far less than any peasant.

From that day onwards I dread any water, deep or shallow.

That's why I dread the Physical Education classes, and the possibility that swimming lessons were on the schedule. I'd even tried a few, with the floating blocks that we use, but I am completely blocked.

Blocked to the point that instead of coming down for breakfast, I'll stay up in bed and shortly before nine a.m., I'll rub some toothpaste into my upper and lower gums, and wait for Sister Bee. She's the college medical chief, and she bumbles around the place all day, taking care of sick students, and the burst lips and black eyes that come from falling onto non-existent blocks of cement, or walking into goalposts on the tennis courts.

The violence here, it's all free for those who have the physical strength to mete it out.

She arrives into my ward, and sees me crouching in the bed.

'Bee, bee,' she announces. She's not very articulate in the language. I try not to smile as I see her waddling up towards me. The game would be up.

'Sick?' she nudges forward. 'You're telling no fibs?'

I shake my head.

The thermometer comes out from her black medical bag, into my gob. She takes my arm into her hand, she holds her fine watch in the other, and starts counting. If I want to say anything, well with my gob shut, it sounds more like a moan, which only adds to what seems to be my physical suffering. A minute later she starts shaking her head, and with another 'Bee, bee,' she shows that my heart is doing well for himself Thank God, and then she whips out the thermometer.

'Hmmm,' she nods, 'better stay in bed today.'

It's worked again! The toothpaste trick has worked again! It also means that she still hasn't copped onto the trick invented by God only knows whom, but it's damned useful! It's a good job too, that she never tests my temperature under my armpit nor up my arse, because I never put any toothpaste there. Can't afford to waste any of it anyway.

But under other circumstances the days are different, and class continues until the lunch break. Even on Wednesdays I'll be down for lunch.

The college refectory is a huge room on the ground floor level and is split into two parts. The tables are rectangular, seating five or six along each side, and one seat at each end. The boy seated at the tabletop is the one who is responsible for ladling out the portions of food, the boy at the bottom is responsible for clearing off the dishes and cutlery and bringing everything out to the wash-up area. This for all the meals of the day. There is a rotation system which must be respected, meaning that each boy occupies a position for the whole day and thereafter shifts one place, clockwise per day.

As to what is available for ladling out, well there are things that most of us like, some that none of us like and so forth. The spuds can be soapy, the baked beans aren't bad, but when you've had enough of them, you've had enough. Someone's even written a little poem:

Beans, beans, they're good for your heart,
the more you eat, the more you fart,
the more you fart, the better you feel,
so eat your beans at every meal!

I don't know who he is, but maybe his father owns a factory for canning baked beans. For vegetables we'll have lots of carrots. One day I haven't finished my portion. The Dean, who supervises the meals, and especially the behaviour of all these, sometimes unruly, boys, pipes up.

'Not eating your carrots there now, Duignan?' he asks of me, looking at my unfinished plate.

'Ah no, don't like them much,' I say to try to satisfy his curiosity.

'You should be eating your carrots,' he continues, 'and they're good for your eyesight, did you know that?'

I stare at the half portion still on my plate, and then lift my eyes again to meet his. Carrots good for my eyesight?

'Have you ever seen a rabbit wearing glasses, Duignan?' he asks, a sly grin to him now.

'No Father, never,' I reply.

'Well, there you are now,' he adds, smiling as he moves on to the next table.

A rabbit wearing glasses would indeed be something to be worth gawking at, but in the meantime I gobble down what's left on my plate. The rabbit will probably be for another day.

Some sort of a dessert will be coming along too. It too varies a lot, and we all have our favourites. The creamed rice goes down well with everybody, it tastes excellent, and it's nourishing too. Trouble today is that O'Donnell, that roughneck from some mad suburb of New York has been selling the desserts that he doesn't like for the last fortnight to his famished tablemates, and God only knows how he's done it again, but he has calculated whack-on, and out comes for our table one of the great deep trays of the piping hot creamed rice from the kitchen.

The tray is now in front of him as he takes the ladle into his hand. He lets his eagle's eyes roam around both sides of the table. I'm seated at his right side, bottom seat.

He picks up one of the deep dessert plates, and starts the work. The plates are then passed out in order down the table, clockwise too.

There are fourteen boys, so fourteen plates, therefore fourteen portions.

Nobody takes to their portion until O'Donnell serves himself too. He's the last to be served at the table. By himself. Even from this end of the table I can judge that there is still a hell of a lot of the delicious creamed rice at the bottom of the deep tray. He keeps helping himself.

Help yourself and the Lord will help you is what the priests remind us from time to time.

He dumps the ladle into the tray, and looks in my direction.

'Duignan!' He's after me.

'Uh?' I try to stall.

'Your dessert,' his hand is up in the air, waving in his bodily direction. 'Don't you remember, the jelly that I sold you last week?'

'The jelly?' I am still hungry, and fearful about my nourishing dessert heading elsewhere than my belly. 'Ah, yes.'

Reluctantly I hand over my plate to the boy on my left, and I watch as it floats from a pair of hands to the next, and settles down in front of O'Donnell at the top of the table.

'But my jelly was good, wasn't it?' he insists, despite the fact that the portion was unlawfully small last week.

'Yes, yes,' I offer.

So small that I'd already forgotten that it had saved me that day too from hunger pains, but a debt is still a debt. O'Donnell's memory seems to be working fine.

Especially when it's in his favour.

'O'Reilly, your dessert!' he has already continued with another tablemate, and I notice that I'm not the only one at table who owes him their dessert. But it's little comfort for me.

Especially when I have a closer look at the portions which are awaiting to be scoffed down by O'Donnell. I notice they are generous indeed when compared to those dished out to those who didn't owe him anything.

A good job that we aren't allowed out the town to be betting on the horse races. Because with a fellow of the likes of O'Donnell in town, the bookies would all go broke and close down shop.

He had told me that his father is a cop in New York. Whilst his father is trying to keep the law over there, his son is over here making his own ones.

But he's good at buying and selling portions of dessert at table in secondary school, so he might do well working at the New York Stock Exchange later.

Only six more days, and it'll be my turn to be at the tabletop.

After lunch we have some time free for recreation, and then back to afternoon classes.

On today's schedule we have Latin, which bores us slightly. We learn about Julius Caesar who left Rome and has been up and down a few boreens during his trips, but apparently he never came this far to learn anything of the likes of Gaelic.

Latin is a language,
as dead as dead can be,
it killed the ancient Romans,
and now it's killing me…

I prefer learning the modern European languages, because if I continue to enjoy working in the hotel business like I do every summer down at the Donilaun Hotel, then I know that the world is a big place, and there are hotels far and wide. But I have to learn the languages.

French lessons are already on our programme. This I enjoy. We have a special auditorium, with audio-visual aids for our lessons. With the help of our book, the headphones and the images projected onto the big screen I can learn fast. Our book is based on a Frenchman, Monsieur Thiebaud.

Monsieur Thiebaud va en vacances
Monsieur Thiebaud va visiter la grande ville.

We follow Monsieur Thiebaud everywhere, and learn about the French ways and customs of life. He likes his café et croissant for breakfast, will have some escargots or cuisses de grenouilles for lunch, to be followed by some Camembert, which is apparently a smelly cheese, et une baguette du pain, all washed down with some of their Côtes du Rhone red wine, and when he is en vacances he'll maybe have a café with a glass of Cognac. I wonder if they've ever heard of the great pint of Guinness over there at all?

Having Father Walson as a teacher is indeed a great pleasure, he being fluent in French, he's such a kind soft spoken man, the eternal smile to his somewhat round face, and by God, I'm near to Heaven.

But as we have many German fishermen coming to the

Donilaun Hotel every summer, I need to be able to get on with them too, *verstanden*?

One day, with some of my spare shillings, I head out the town, and into a bookshop, where I buy a copy of *Deutsch leicht gemacht*. I'm the only student studying German, and as the college doesn't have any teacher in this language, then I'm on my own for my studies. Martin is doing the same with Spanish, he too has a small guide book to help him along, to carry on from where we got left off when Rhona stole our little magazines from under the carpet at Marian House.

We also have lessons of Gaeilge. But there again, I can't find the utility of it long-term, am having difficulty gripping it, and can't enjoy it.

We have more study time again in the evenings. I'm sitting near one of my classmates and for the first few weeks he spends his time crying and crying onto his studydesk. I turn to a studymate on my other side and ask what's wrong with yer man.

'Homesick,' is the answer I get. 'He wants to go home and stay with his mammy.'

I can hardly believe what I hear. I certainly don't want to go home to Castlebarry and Marian House. I've found a newer sort of home here, I'm happy to be away from Rhona, and the food even if not perfect is better than what I generally get to eat at home. I wonder who invented the word homesick.

Studytime is also the time to be doing my homework. Here I can concentrate on my work, don't have to worry about picking leaves, nor trimming the lawn. Problem though is that we have very little pocket money on us. So little in fact, that I don't have enough pennies to buy enough copybooks for each subject. So very quickly, I've started using one book for four subjects. I start my sums at the front, turn over and start my history from the other end, and then quarterways through, on both sides, I'll fill in with the Gaeilge, and the geography too. It worked for a few days until my mathematics teacher and my Irish teacher needed the copybook to do their checking.

I couldn't give the book to the both of them the same day.

'Why?' bawls the maths teacher at me.

'Because I needed it to put my Irish lessons in there too,' I answer.

'What, show what this is all about!' he continues, clearly angered at such an answer and behaviour.

I hand over the copybook. He scrolls through all the pages, only to find texts and sums spread out in four separate sections.

'But you've got four subjects in here!' he exclaims, waving the book high in the air.

'No money,' I meekly manage the two words. My thoughts go to the pounds and sums of money that I'd earned down at the Donilaun Hotel during the summer. Rhona is of course 'minding it all' for me, and I see very little of it coming my way. I could live comfortably with some of it indeed, and have enough for my copybooks, biros, and odds and sods too.

I bow my head to avoid looking at him further.

'What, what's with you Duignan?' he shouts. 'You, a doctor's son, with no money?'

His shout jolts me, and for the first time within these walls I have the living daylights scared out of me. By another grown-up person.

I shrug my shoulders, because I have nothing else to say, to add as an explanation.

I just hope that the story doesn't go too far, because if it gets back to Daddy, then he'll tell Rhona about it and she'll invent a story such we've been spending too much money on sweets or suchlike. For her, the £1.50 spent on my *Deutsch leicht gemacht* book would have been a waste of money.

But copybooks, pencils and biros aren't the only items that we need to buy for ourselves here. We need toothpaste and soap for our body hygiene, for example. Clotheswise, we've gotten the strict limit with us here. Martin enjoys going to the hops every Saturday night when the girls from the convents across the road come over for the evening.

But he has only one fine yellow shirt, so come Saturday afternoon, a bit of soapy suds, a rinse, and I'll supervise and watch it drip-dry in front of the huge boiler below the kitchen level. He manages however, from time to time, to borrow a cardigan, a pullover *col roulé*, or another item from a classmate, just for a change. He tries his best to get on with the girls.

Or wouldn't a pack of sweets be a pleasure too, when the college shop opens on the Saturday afternoon, or for a football match out the town on a weekend, or the film on Sunday evening? So I start borrowing from another student who is leaning against the wall waiting for his turn to get to the top of the line. Not all are willing to lend however, but sometimes it's managed. But like the desserts at the rcfectory table, a debt is a debt. Sixpence and sixpence is already a shilling.

Even for a doctor's son.

Sweets or not, all the boys are kindly requested to assist at all football matches, be it out the town or on board the chartered coaches which might bring us to Charlestown, Athlone, or elsewhere.

Before leaving, we'll have a training session on the ground floor hall in the middle wing.

All together now lads:

Oh, when the saints, oh when the saints,
oh when the saints go marching in,
I want to be in that number,
oh when the saints go marching in…

Then off to the match after lunch. With or without sweets and toffees.

Donilaun V

The summers are coming and going just like a schoolyear at St Joseph's in between them, and for another change I'll be doing the service in the great big dining room and ballroom this time. This makes of course for a real early start to the day, having to be in for the breakfast service to start.

'Hey, can I have a pitcher of iced water there, sonny?' a Yank seated at a window table asks me, 'and I'll have my eggs sunny side up.'

'What's a pitcher?' I wonder quietly to myself, and manage to get the attention of a waitress who's not too far away from my station.

'What they really want is a jug of tap water and ice-cubes now, they always do with their meals,' she explains, and then I realise that there are other jugs of iced water on many other tables, and I guess that we have a great bunch of them Yanks around this week. I tell the breakfast cook about the eggs, he'll understand what's needed.

For a good Irish breakfast they really put on a fantastic show here. You can have stewed prunes or grapefruit segments from the buffet up at the restaurant-top for starters, thereafter a choice of cereals that go crackle, snap and pop, or smoked kippers. Then comes a hearty portion of freshly-cooked Irish bacon and sausages, black pudding, eggs and grilled tomato, with lots of toast or brown bread, the best of Irish creamery butter and marmalade, and all the tea or coffee you'd like.

Not to be forgotten, the pitchers of iced fresh Irish water as an extra for the Yanks.

The real works.

The cooked breakfasts keep me on my toes for a good while up and down the four steps between the main restaurant level and that of the double kitchen service doors, taking orders, scurrying to the stillroom where the smell of fresh toasted bread fills the air and seems to last for hours, trying to get the stillroom girl to do her best for me too, or to the kitchen beyond, then clearing off after guests have left their table, and resetting. The round tables by the windows are the favourites with most people, as the view towards the river is not to be missed, and these have to be cleared and reset without delay. The 'travellers' will settle easily for the small square tables in the middle row as they continue to work on their sheets of paper and drawings with which they couldn't finish last evening.

After breakfast I'll have to help get the tables ready for the lunch service, and then do the carpet hoovering all over the whole restaurant area.

It's summertime now and it seems that nearly everybody who isn't already married at this end of the country will be doing it this year. The busiest days are Saturdays, there will always be a banquet, so if I manage to finish early in the main dining room then I'll be 'called over' to the big ballroom to help out there.

After a first few weeks then the manager leaves me on my own to set up nearly the whole table layout.

Piles of tables are stocked at the end of the banqueting hall. Heavy tables are to be carried way up towards the front, unfolded, and secured before being set up according to the number of guests expected and the table plans which the banqueting manager will have set down.

One day I've swept the whole ballroom floor and am now unfolding one great heavy table, and I note that some fellow has written a little inscription underneath: 'John D. was employed here, but he never worked here.'

I can't quite read the year, which is written, but I have a smile and continue. I wonder who he was, and where is he employed these days, maybe he's actually working somewhere too and not just being employed.

Tables to be carried around from their storage corner and set up, crisply ironed tablecloths and napkins on next, chairs pulled up and neatly placed. Then comes the round of cutlery, starting with the meat knife and fork in their position. Then comes the knife and fork for the entrée, and according to the menu planned, a soupspoon to the outside right. Dessert spoon and fork placed to the front. Then after a bread-plate for bread rolls and butter, glasses, napkins, salt and pepper cruets on plates with doilies, and table flower decorations will follow. The seating cards for the bride and groom and their close families will be set out on the top table, which generally runs along the back wall of the ballroom.

Today we are expecting some one hundred and fifty guests for a wedding breakfast, and we're far from the limits.

Loads of small jobs to be finished before the first guests have arrived. The wedding cake with its number of layers will have been delivered by an outside caterer from up the town and sits majestically in the centre of the top table. There will always be a miniature couple in plastic holding hands atop the cake. Holding hands but never kissing is the way I see it. If you kiss someone doesn't it mean that you love that person? I wonder what it's like to love someone so much that you can get married for, but my thoughts get back to my work before the manager might give me a bollocking for dilly-dallying.

But everything is well and ready as the manager arrives in, casting a glance over the great wide room, to tell me that the motorcade has arrived at the hotel entrance, and that I can start helping the barman who is now emptying the float money into the till's drawer. The happy couple will of course be having photographs taken out now on the hotel lawn for their huge wedding album, and this is all part of the whole ceremony indeed. But some of the men haven't really great interest in the picture-taking out the front, the photographer doesn't stop changing people around, and then looking for other spots for another shot and would ye all keep closer together now, side by side for one more, and that's it now? But they've escaped from the photographer's and any wives' attention and are already on their way to the corner of the ballroom bar.

'Ah hallo there, will you be serving ourselves with a few pints of the cool stuff at all?' says this chap who has just waddled up to the bar counter and is pulling out a barstool.

'Oh Mikey you're looking grand and lovely there, aren't you doing very well at all?' says a second newcomer.

'Ah well I'm mighty now,' Mikey shifts position on the barstool, 'you're not too bad yerself, you're looking terrific at all.'

'A grand day altogether, isn't it?' adds yer man, 'a mighty day for a wedding now.'

'What'll you be having now, Jimmy, a Harp or a Smithwicks?'

I expect that the first orders won't delay in rolling in.

'Ah, I'll be having a Harp meself, still faithful to it you know, thanks now Mikey,' says Jimmy, who hasn't delayed in taking up an offer and an invitation.

'Well make it a pint of Harp and a Smithwicks too will you now, lad?' says Mikey, who by the looks of him is waiting for the serious things to go, 'and you won't be dallying about it will you now?'

I choose two pint glasses, and the Harp is flowing. The Smithwicks on the next tap too.

A glance towards the customers to see how they're keeping and sure all seems to be going well. Still no sign of the bride and groom. Camera shutters must still be clicking outside.

Yer man is eyeing me.

'I didn't see you here last month, young man,' enquires the man called Mikey, 'are ye new around here in these parts, lad?'

'No, no,' I say, 'last month I had to stay mainly at the other side, over in the restaurant.'

'Hey Jimmy, did I tell you at all about Joe McKearney's wedding here last month?'

Jimmy has now turned to his drinking mate.

'I heard about it now myself, you mean Joe from out Crosslanagh don't you?' says Jimmy.

'Jasus, they did an awful doo here at all,' he goes on, 'there was great craic going on too, it's a pity you missed it now, great craic indeed.'

'Oh, how's your mother then now, Jimmy?'

'Didn't she have an awful bad sprain to her ankle there last week,' says Jimmy, wincing as if he was the one who had tripped up.

'I didn't hear of that one now.'

'Oh, shocking pains to it at all.'

'Oh. We have all day to ourselves lads, no rushing to it now, we're not in the slightest of a jiffy there now, are we?' Mikey has the plan laid out.

They're having another slow sip of the cool stuff to sustain themselves for the first few minutes of the near future, the day and evening ahead won't be a short one, but the later minutes will be worried about later. The later kegs of the cool stuff too.

Other chaps are now coming in in small numbers and are joining together around Mikey and Jimmys' barstools.

'What's your name there now lad, and where are you coming from, oh, we'll be needing a few more for them boyos here,' says Mikey, who is sure splashing around his punts today.

'Gerry's me name, from Castlebarry,' I say, and the first two pints are already on the bar counter.

'Sure meself and the lads, we're all down for the day from Kiltara,' says Mikey.

Both men have a wee sup of the cool stuff, and wipe the froth off their upper lips.

'How are ye doing now fellows, didn't drop dead from that heat out in the garden there did ye, I couldn't stick it meself, it's so raging hot out there, roasting isn't it?' Mikey is wondering, curious if he's missed out on anything whilst he has been cooling himself off inside here, 'I had to come in to get into the shade.'

'Well now with all the heat and drought going on out there, a man like meself wouldn't be sticking it out for longer than for yourself now Mikey, oh, and begorah you're looking well now there yourself, got the Sunday suit out again, will you be keeping it on until tomorrow?' asks one of the newcomers.

'Ah, two pints of Harp, a Highland cream and a drop of todays, there now will you please?'

The first sales are already rung up on the cash-till, and pound notes and coppers are landing in the drawer.

Mikey's into a fit of laughing.

'Well, it depends a bit maybe on how long the bride keeps ye all dancing at all, and how many kegs Gerry the lad himself here has in the cellar,' he's nodding my way and the others are into the habit by now, 'and if Father Reilly will be staying round for a while tonight sure he mightn't be up himself in the morning to say the Sunday Mass?'

Pulling the two pints is easy, but I don't know what the drop of todays means.

I turn to one of the barmen, and he says that means fresh water.

'Wasn't it a lovely Mass now?' The gabbing and blathering is going full guns.

'Well, I did get to hear bits and pieces of it, but wasn't Breegie in a great state herself, she's grown into a fine lovely woman, the likes of Dermot himself deserves a wife like that, sure he's a mighty fellow himself, he has the ways and the means to talk the hind legs off a trotting horse, the dead spitting image of his father, don't you agree there now, Jimmy?'

'Sure Dermot's been making loads of it over there Manchester, you can see that by the size of the house and the whole place he's finishing off, no flies on him there now.'

'Arrah, will you be getting married yerself, Donal, before the year's out?' says Mikey, who must be interested and on the know about any forthcoming weddings in the area.

'Oh, sure I don't know meself at all now,' muses Donal, having a sip of the cool stuff.

'But you're still doing the line, aren't you?' says Mikey, who has to get to the bottom of this one. The bottom of his pint glass will wait for once.

'Oh, sure I'll have to ask Katie about that one now,' adds Donal with a laugh and a blush. Mikey's probably after another wedding invitation indeed.

The crowd has now started moving in slowly from the sweltering heat outside, women taking seats at the various coffee tables laid out around the lounge bar area, the men hurrying over to the bar for orders, the young boys and girls all immaculately dressed are running around the whole place, in through one corridor, out through the other, whilst waiting for something to drink to be served up to them.

The pints of Harp, Smithwicks, and the Highland Creams with the drop of today's come first, the Club oranges, Cokes and ice can follow later.

The barman has just whipped up the phone and dials the restaurant.

'We need extra hands over here in a jiffy, the crowd is in,' he barks, 'are ye nearly done with over there or what are ye up to at all?'

The bride all dressed up in white, and groom have appeared and are now moving towards the top table. Most of the women seated at the low coffee tables are turning their gazes, once again, towards Breegie, and isn't Dermot a fine handsome man at all? Most of the men keep their attention turned to their neighbour, or gawking towards the bar counter and the beertaps. Breegie and Dermot arrive at the top table from where they go through the checking of seating arrangements in the great ballroom.

The bar trade is going swiftly for a while, and when I hear the gong being rung I know that the manager has been through the kitchen, and according to the head chef it must be time for the meal to be served. The bar trade might be roaring along, but the head chef doesn't give a damn about that, he wants those platters of roast turkey and ham out and served, and the baked Alaska too.

Because when everybody in the kitchen is finished, they still have to clear off, have an hour or two off if they can manage it, and be back again for the evening shift.

'Listen, right now ye're portions of roast stuffed turkey and ham are ready in here in the hot ovens,' is the way he explains it, 'leave them around for another hour, and it's not roast turkey ye'll have, it'll be grilled turkey, okay?'

Bar sales aren't his problem, and his kitchen has a reputation to be preserved, and especially that of his roast turkey and ham.

The gong is ringing loud and clear a second time, as apparently it had gone unheeded. The crowd finally starts to move towards the tables, pints and glasses in hand. What a crowd I think. What's his name Dermot sure must have been making loads of it over in England to be able pay for such a lot of people coming to his wedding lunch. They must all be making loads of it wherever or whatever they're doing in life. From one wedding to the next, you'll never see a small crowd, just as much as you'd never hardly see anything other than roast stuffed turkey and ham as the main dish. But the roast turkey and ham is a favourite seller, and before the *Western Weekly* is printed on Monday sure the whole village of Kiltara will have heard once again of the great portions of roast turkey and ham served up at the Donilaun Hotel. I hear the saying goes that every wedding gives ideas to those who are still unmarried, and the chances of one or two of today's guests sitting at the middle of the top table sometime next summer is more than likely. If they make it to the altar then they'll surely be making it over afterwards to the lawn at the Donilaun Hotel for the wedding photos, and the famous roast stuffed turkey and ham in the ballroom.

The baked Alaska too.

The bar rush is now over, but this doesn't mean that my day is over. The manager has already told me that I'll be needed for meal service, so the cleaning of the bar counter and tables, the glasses, drip-trays and ashtrays will just have to wait. So there's no time for dallying at all. But today it'll be easier for me, as this time I have the first table near the kitchen exit. The other tables are allocated to the other waiters and waitresses, some of whom are called in as 'extras', and they'll be doing the farthest walks today.

Mikey has a glance around the great big ballroom before seating himself amongst his company.

'Jasus, would you think there's anybody left at all back in the village?' he wonders aloud when he's seen the crowd.

Today there'll be a choice of soups to start. The manager has set up a table for distribution just inside the kitchen door. I'll manage two soup-plates between my left-hand fingers, a service cloth and two more plates on my forearm. But then I have to move before the heat gets through to the skin of my arm.

'Thick or thin soup, sir?' I say as I'm moving swiftly along the side of the long table.

'Ah, what sort of thick soup do yee have today?' is the reply, and things are starting to get delayed already.

'Ah, cream of mushroom it is, sir,' my offer is swift.

'Well the thick one will be grand and lovely with me, and thank you now,' he says, and the great smile is still there.

There's hardly nothing better to be doing with one's time than enjoying a free lunch, with thick soup and all at the Donilaun Hotel.

No time to acknowledge the word of thanks and down goes a plate of the mushroom soup and I'm moving at speed up the length of the table. I see a waitress approaching with other soup plates on her hands, and I know she'll be coming along with the 'thin' soup, which in culinary terms is also known as beef consommé.

The conversation is going great guns at table now, and if it's not about how well Breegie herself is looking and hasn't Dermot been doing well for himself and making loads of it in Manchester at all, and they're a lovely couple now, the likes that haven't been seen in these parts in many a year, then it's about the Government and the way they're running and even ruining the whole country itself.

All my soups are now down and served on the table. Everybody keeps up the conversation and nobody wants to pick up a spoon and start their soup, because with one oval formed spoon at the top and another round formed spoon to the right in the place setting you might just go for the wrong one, and that wouldn't be the right thing to be doing at all, especially in such a fine hotel.

But Mikey himself knows just about everybody who's living north of Baltrina so every time that someone from up by Kiltara or Belcarrig would be getting married sure he would be having his invitation and out comes the Sunday suit for the weekend. Mikey knows the ins and outs of all the hotel bars and ballrooms in the region, and must be familiar too with the rules of the game with the thick and thin soups, which knife, fork and spoon on the table in front of him goes for what, and the roast stuffed turkey and ham served up at the Donilaun Hotel.

He doesn't hesitate and reaches with his right hand for the soup spoon, and within three seconds time the conversation all around the table goes dead as everybody else has gone for their soup spoons and the thick and thin soups are being savoured, and isn't this what we all came for now?

Back to the kitchen to check on the final details for the platters of meat and vegetables. Soup plates are then to be cleared off, and into the kitchen towards the washing up counter. Over to the hot counters and out with a pile of twenty hot main course plates from the inside shelves. Keep moving. Out to the ballroom. Plates out in front of the guests.

'Mind yerselves there, the plates there, they're hot!' shouts a cook.

Thanks a lot I think, but I've already noticed!

Speed!

Back to the hot counters. I've the first table inside the ballroom so I'm at the head of the queue now, service spoon and fork poised for action. The cooks are now going wild all over the place. Head chef barking orders. Steam rising upwards from the bain-maries all over the place. To the rear the veg cook is ladling out the roast potatoes and buttered peas into veg dishes.

I readjust my service cloth draped up the length of my outstretched left forearm. I'm still standing here, and getting heated up somewhat.

'Will ye flippin' move it now, otherwise we'll be here all day!' the head chef yells to the joint cook behind. Up come the platters, onto the counter. Chef has a final check of each platter, and I heave mine onto my arm. Securing it with my service fork and spoon, I rush for the ballroom through the service door, which is now blocked in an open position. Ten portions of meat on my platter. Enough for half a table, so just for the meat I will need a return trip to the kitchen.

I have to remember, food service from the left side, drinks from the right. Mikey and the neighbour to his left are busy with the conversation about the whole country and the awful state it's in. Food service from the left. I have to interrupt the boyos with their conversation, and manage to wedge in between them. Down onto Mikey's plate goes a portion of the roast turkey and ham, stuffing and gravy too.

'Ah, thank you now,' he says, still grateful it seems.

What a great free lunch, a mighty meal itself altogether now that they're all having here at Breegie's and Dermot's wedding, a grand style of living at all to it now.

I straighten my back again and keep moving. Still many portions to go. Each portion less makes the platter lighter, and therefore it's easier on my back and arms.

More speed. I finish my ten portions, so it's back to the kitchen firstly to the wash-up, and then over to the hot counter for the second platter.

More speed!

Halfway along one lady doesn't like the turkey and ham that much.

'Do you have any roast beef in the kitchen today, lad?' she wonders.

'Ah, I don't know now,' I explain, trying to dissuade her, 'I'll have to have a word with the chef himself, and I don't know what he'll be saying about it.'

I don't mention to her that the chef himself can be in a very bad mood from time to time indeed.

'Would you doing that for me now, and you're a grand big boy yourself,' she says. The compliments are not lacking at all here, but I'm more worried about what chef is going to say to me. No compliments to be shared there! Waiters and cooks might all be working in the same hotel, but they aren't on the same team! Anyway she'll have to wait. I'm going to finish serving all the other portions of turkey and ham first, before I dare approach the chef. The sight of a fine portion of roast beef appearing at table now might just entice a few others into going for second choice, and I'd be in for a real bollocking by yer man himself.

Back to the kitchen with the remaining portion of meat, and over to the hot counter. I try to get the attention of the cook who has been preparing the meat platters, but head chef is posted defiantly in front.

'What are you about, Duignan?' he booms at me. 'What is it you flippin' want now there, what are you after?'

I put on my best smile.

'Ah, would you have a bit of beef at all for a lady who doesn't like the turkey, chef?' I wonder aloud, as I'm standing there and ready to hightail it in case a roast spud might come flying my way. I'm trying hard to keep the smile on my face, which isn't easy with all the heat and steam they have in here.

'Ah no, I won't be having that one now, and anyway, do you have a docket there, Duignan?' he asks, adjusting his tall head chef's hat, which means he's the boss here, and he might want to remind me, his left hand going for the biro in his top pocket.

I shake my head, keeping the smile under control.

I know I'm upsetting the schedule, but I think that he's going slightly mad if he has time to take care of paperwork right now. He must be taking the mickey, asking for a docket like that when all hell is letting loose around him, which means at least that he won't get too angry with me.

'Bleedin' woman, she's givin' me a pain in me corn,' he wheels around and looks towards the meat cook.

'A portion of beef for Duignan there,' he barks. 'But only one portion now, Duignan, nothing for anybody else,' he says. He's got a carving knife up in the air. 'Did you clean your ears this morning?'

'Yes chef!' I keep the grin on.

'Well, if you've washed them, you've heard what I've just said!' The tall hat is readjusted once again.

But I'm happy that my request hasn't thrown the whole place upside down and especially as I haven't met any flying potatoes or big words yet. Chefs in good humour today I think. Maybe because everybody heard the gong on the second call, or maybe had no time for breakfasts in the morning before going to the church for the Holy mass which makes them all starving to death, but anyways the bar trade didn't dally for too long.

Maybe because I gave him the widest grin that I could, and anyways with my young age I might get away with a few odds and sods more than the older waiters or waitresses.

A small platter with a nice portion of beef is coming my way, and I wonder if I'll get the remaining turkey and ham for dinner.

I stand staring at him.

'You'll be moving now Duignan, before I take a flippin' swipe at ya,' he barks.

'Thank you chef!' I say, and I'm off like a wild fellow out to my table.

A waitress is following close behind on my table with a huge veg dish holding buttered peas and the roast potatoes that I didn't get thrown at me. Out go the portions. As I've started with the table nearest the kitchen door, so it's the first one to be served and finished. Apart from the top table, that is.

This means that I'll then be taking the veg dishes to the next table and following on where another waiter has just served his portions of turkey and ham at the same time and with the same speed as myself. We keep rotating in this swift and orchestrated manner and within no time everybody has a piping-hot portion of everything in front of them. Empty meat platters to the washing up area, any veg dishes with remains go back to the hot counter.

It'll be taking them a while to get through those great portions so I head back to the bar and the unfinished work there. Glasses off the coffee tables and back to the bar counter and then into the glass washer. Ashtrays to be emptied and washed. Drip-trays to be emptied and rinsed out. A drop of the Teepol, a wet cloth and a wipe down to the bar counter, and all the areas behind. A check in the cash register to see if we have enough pennies and shilling coins to keep going afterwards, if not, down to the reception desk in the front hall with a wad of notes to exchange for bags of coins.

I hardly have time to put everything back into shape, the manager is calling me as the guests have nearly finished the main course. So there'll be little time to rest. Back to the ballroom and clear off the joint and bread plates and cutlery. The baked Alaska is taken out of the freezer to be quickly passed under the salamander for glazing. Twenty cold dessert plates out on my table.

After dessert comes tea and coffee service. I move along my table, and sure Mikey has finished his plate of dessert too. With all the pints of the cool stuff, the thick soup, and plates of roast turkey and ham, and dessert too, I wonder where he's putting it all away.

'Tea or coffee, sir?' I offer.

'Yes please,' comes his reply, calmly.

I don't know if it's the cool stuff that's gone to his head or he's tired from all the gabbing about the state of the country and the price of the cows and pigs at the cattle market out the Crosslanagh road, but I have an impression that he's not listening to me at all.

'Tea or coffee, sir?' I repeat the offer.

'Ah no, sure I'm grand meself now, and thank you,' he manages.

I keep moving up the length of the table. Time is certainly moving along, and the manager tells me that I should take some time off as I'll have to be back for six o'clock and prepare for dinner.

With my short break I won't be going too far down the road today, I'm feeling tired from all the running for the wedding breakfast and from Mikey and his crowd too. As I lie back on my bed I can hear the band drummer checking out his sticks, and the guitar chords are being strummed and tuned, everybody getting geared up for the dancing. Sunday's Holy Mass is still a long way away and I guess that Mikey will be having another glass or two of the cool stuff before the evening is out.

I head back in again for six o'clock to have a bite to eat for myself first. I don't get the portion of roast turkey and ham, but a huge slice of baked ham and potatoes. I'm so hungry that I cut a great chunk out of the meat, and into my gob it goes. What I haven't noticed however was that the cook had literally coated the underside with hot Tabasco sauce. It nearly burns me to death, and I run to the fridge for a pint of cold milk to quench the fire in my throat.

Maybe it's the fault of the portion of beef.

Things are going mighty guns over in the function room, so for me it's into the dining room for the travellers and the Americans we're expecting for dinner. Don't forget the pitchers of iced water I tell myself. Heading into the kitchen from time to time I can hear the strains of music coming through from the ballroom where the festivities are going great indeed.

This evening Monsieur Hervé, a French client, is in again. He has reserved himself again a small table to the right when you arrive down the four steps. A lot of the other staff are still busy over in the ballroom with Dermot's and Breegie's crowd. There's no wine-waiter here, so the manager asks me to do any orders that might be coming in.

'You ave ze list of wines, Monsieur?' Hervé wants to have something with his meal, somebody told me that they all drink wine when at table over there in their country.

I oblige by bringing over our list and leave it to him for a gawk.

'Monsieur, I will ave zis half-bottle of Chateau Lagrange, please,' says Hervé, who has clearly gone for a French wine, and as I can't find one in the wine stocks in the restaurant I have to go down to the store opposite the reception desk. Hervé's been lucky this time, out come two bottles, one goes into the restaurant stock and without delay I'm back to his table, the corkscrew is working down just well into the cork, and I pour him a drop into his glass for tasting. The seconds are passing, even the minutes too. With Mikey's crowd, I'd probably have served six pints of the cool stuff in this lapse of time. Then Hervé slowly takes his glass and with a cool steady and calculated move brings it towards his face. Then he lifts the glass to the light, has a gawk, then brings it to below his nose moving it back and forth, and he starts sniffing at the few drops of wine. I'm standing there, waiting with the little bottle still in hand, giving a fast gawk around the dining room from time to time. Then with one swift move he has the glass to his lips, and some of the wine disappears. Then he starts swishing it around in his closed mouth, holding the glass a little lower to the tablecloth now, and by the looks of things he's thinking like only a Frenchman could when he has a sup of the wine in his gob. He must feel like being back at home.

'Ees good,' he pronounces, settling the glass on the tablecloth. Finally, I thought! I top up with some more wine, and am about to put the bottle down in front of him. Then I have an idea.

'Would you like me to put the wine in an ice bucket?' I ask obligingly.

'Monsieur!' Hervé has bolted himself into a rearward position, and is staring the living daylights out of me.

God, what have I done wrong?

'Just... put the wine... in an ice bucket?' I repeat.

'Monsieur, in my country, in France, we never put ze red wine on ze ice, ze white wine, yes, but not ze red one.' I have a fast look around me, the manager isn't around and nobody else seems to have heard. I've been lucky this time!

'Yes sir, I understand,' I offer as I hastily place his bottle in front of him, and retreat. I try to keep myself busy in other parts of the restaurant but the main dining room is quiet tonight, not many extras this evening, so when we've cleared off most of the dirty tables, I'm called back by the manager to the ballroom bar again. I'm happy to keep out of Hervé's way, leaving him to his bottle and meal, and if he doesn't want to finish it this evening then someone will shove the cork back in again, scribble his room number on the label, and he'll have the rest tomorrow. At least I now know that red wine doesn't go onto ice. That's something new that I've learned.

Back in the ballroom, and sure Mikey himself is keeping well, he has the best seat in the bar corner, where he has a grand view of the dancefloor indeed and that'll be fine for him as he doesn't like the dancing anyway and Gerry here must still have a few kegs of the cool stuff in the cellar, and he sure knows how to keep it flowing.

The hours pass, the band keeps up with the music, and the whole bunch are having a great hooley-booley indeed. Many hours later the bride and groom decide to call it a night, which is the signal for the band to stop their tunes and for everybody to pack it in. Mikey and his crowd in the corner don't have much of an intention to leave. They want another one for the road.

'For the life of Reilly tonight, are yee all in a jiffy?' he asks of his drinking mates. 'What's with yee, are yee already tipsy now or what?'

'Gerry, open the back doors will you?' asks the manager.

So I head down to open wide the big rear doors at the end of the ballroom, then the front doors too, and with the cool evening air now rushing through the whole place the remaining ladies start feeling the wind moving around their legs, and we know they won't dally in dragging off their husbands with them up to Kiltara, Belcarrig and the north. I'm too busy with cleaning up the place which looks half-wrecked, so don't have much time to listen to Mikey and all the ways that'd he'd reorganise the whole world next week when he's finished with the work down on the farm, and the Sunday's Holy Mass too, and soon he runs out of pound notes and company to keep up the conversation with, and he finally gets a seat in one of the last cars leaving for the north.

Glasses back to the bar counter to be all washed up. Ashtrays to be emptied and cleaned. Empties to be collected off the tables and the bar counter and into the bottle skip with them all. I'll sort them out tomorrow into their plastic cases in the hotel backyard, but not tonight. Drip-trays to be emptied and rinsed out. A dash of Teepol, a wet cloth and a clean up to the tables, the bar counter and the whole area behind. The cash till to be checked, emptied, and the sales deposited in the safe at the reception desk.

In the early hours I manage to finish and head out for Blanket Street.

Hard work but a great life, the nearest thing to paradise that I've ever found! I'm glad that Daddy drove all those miles up and down the county to find such a god job in such a fine hotel indeed.

Even if I know, that when returning to Castlebarry at the season's end, Rhona will be 'minding' what wages I've saved.

Joseph's II

Autumn 1971. Martin has now finished his secondary education, and has hit the road in the direction of Dublin. He had told me that he had no wish to go back to Castlebarry for any reason whatsoever, and I can understand him.

So that leaves me all on my own. Alone to defend myself, and try to face up to everybody and all situations which may present themselves.

On my own too to vent my anger, at others. I slowly become rowdy, and will seek out any chance to go 'overboard'.

One day, I'm standing on the fourth floor level in the Monroy wing. I lean over the banister, and am at one of my favourite pastimes again. I have collected a whole bunch of empty soda tin cans, and am ready to let fly.

A few have already gone earthbound, and I still have a stock to go. I am not alone up here, there are a number of boys surrounding me, moving, and coming and going. I choose another can from the pile, which is at my feet. I reach out over the banister again, I dally a little, and then let another one go. I watch as the can sails down, turning over and over, but keeping its course remarkably well.

Then suddenly, I see the black gowned sleeve, which has just joined other sleeves moving up from the basement below.

One of the priests! And he has his hand still gliding along, as he continues his travel up the staircase.

Bang! I can see the can coming to hit squarely beside the hand. I had hoped that it might continue and head somewhere on the ground below, and roll out of sight.

Out of luck! Out of luck too, because there are witnesses to what I've been up to. They've seen everything. I'm in trouble. I retreat back into the great big gymnastic hall, and the whole way back to the stage. To wait. I look towards the doorway and escape route, which is behind me. Should I run? Where to? Why? I'll be caught anyway, sooner or later. It could be at supper this evening, and the priest will know where to come and find me.

I continue waiting.

Then the black gowned figure appears in the doorway, way ahead of me.

The College President! Not just any of the college priests!

I couldn't have possibly chosen a worse target than him. I glance around the room. There are lots of boys in here. They are all frozen still. Not a word to be heard. Total silence. The

President makes a beeline for me. He doesn't stop to ask any of the boys who the smart fellow might be throwing cans down like that.

I press my body against the wooden structure, which I'm leaning against for support. He's still coming at me with a slow but definitive pace, so I know that someone has squealed on me.

The single, but powerful slap hits me with such a force, that it literally flattens me, on my back onto the stage surface behind me.

Scrapping with others has now become commonplace.

One afternoon, I'm on the third floor in the Monroy wing. But I have to get down to the new building for a physics class. One bastard from Achill, Dermot McManus, won't let me go, and is intimidating me.

'Come on over here, nigger,' he says. He wants my blood. 'I'm going bash the frigging daylights out of you.'

It's the nickname, which I detest the most. I'm now having difficulty controlling my anger. The great fecking shower of shites they have here is really getting on my nerves. Makes me wonder if they shouldn't mention it on the entrance examination papers.

Can you do your sums?
What's the capital city of England?
Are you any good at scrapping?

Two correct answers, and welcome to college is the way they should be doing it!

But the Dean had witnessed one day that I was being upset by a nickname. Sticks and stones can break my bones, but names will never hurt me, was the way he had put it to me. The phrase comes into my mind now.

'Ah, go and frig yourself off,' I answer.

'Do you want a scrap, Duignan?' He's getting heated up now. 'I'll smash your bollocks to smithereens, you'll see!'

'Let me go, go feck off!' I order.

'Whilst I'm at it, I'll put a squint to your eye too!' he says. He is now tugging at my cardigan, and if he wrecks it then I'm in for a beating from Rhona or Daddy next time I'm home. But time is running out for me now. He probably can stay in this building, but I have to get down to the next one. Joe Space will be starting his class in very little time, and if I'm late then it's a bashing from him.

McManus is somewhat taller, and seems stronger than me. I've never had to hit him in a serious scrap yet, so I don't know what he's worth. He could hit, and hurt me. But so could Joe Space. He's an adult, and the way I see it is that all adults are taller, bigger, stronger, and are certainly good at beating the living daylights out of me. Be it Daddy or Rhona at Marian House, or the priests here in the college.

'Mind your bollocks, Duignan!' he comments as he restrains me from running.

I've had enough. A scrap with him, or a beating from Joe Space? What the hell of a difference does it make for me? I am getting beaten up a lot here, sometimes by the priests for my unruly behaviour, which has already made me lose all respect for religion by now, and if not then it's by the others for I never know what.

I let fly with my clenched right fist.

I go for his throat and hit him square in his Adam's apple. I know that it was a strong one, and I watch as he keels rearwards, onto the flight of stairs just behind him. His hands go towards his throat, and I watch for a second or two as he starts choking.

Then I start running. I let him suffer. The violence here is for free, and now he's had a portion of his own medicine. Self-service.

But I've learned to fight, and defend myself. That's important for me. Martin had told me the one about the Adam's apple, just in case!

St Joseph's III

An awful lot of the other boys have butter or sauces such as HP stored upstairs in their dormitories, with which they can of course better enjoy their meals. I don't have money though for such items, and I can't continue borrowing from the others. I have to find some kind of a plan.

Then one comes to mind. Why not raid the kitchens and the

priests' refectory during the night, that way I should certainly find something worth putting on my plate? I talk to O'Donnell about it, and he agrees to join me. So we have to take turns at sleeping and staying awake, and when all is really quietened down, and listening to the hours pass by on the clock tower outside, we decide to move during the dark of the night.

Wearing stockings underfoot, we creep down the big flight of stairs and start by going through the priests' refectory. There are full bottles of sauces in a cupboard here, and we help ourselves. Then onwards towards the kitchens, where we'll search for whatever scraps of food we can find in fridge's or on shelves.

We manage to fill our bellies too a bit, and we retreat to our dormitory. The whole place is still fast asleep, and as my bed is the first one inside the door, and O'Donnell is opposite me, we don't arouse any suspicion at all. It's worked.

I've now learned how to steal.

I've broken another one of the Ten Commandments. That's against my religion.

We repeat the operation from time to time, whenever we start running low on our stocks.

It works a marvel, until the evening that I'm called out from the dormitory, and Big Johnny is waiting with the cane for me. I get badly beaten by him. Big Johnny is the tallest and the most feared of all the priests. His height, his powerful swing through three hundred and sixty degrees, using a fine cane, which stings badly.

I'm not sure, but I have a feeling that the American has squealed on me. But he has a reputation of being a fierce fighter, I'm not going to put the question to him.

I still know more about the colour of the westerly winds that blow in from the Atlantic than I know about my relations or family in Carraroe or in Longford. This also goes for the origins of the Duignan family, never having had the chance to talk to Daddy about these people or this situation, just like as in many other ways.

I feel like a tree with no roots, no attachment anywhere.

One day, I decide that on the following weekend, I'll make an excursion over there, as I want to get to met anybody, and get to know them. Martin had of course talked to me last year about those people, but now I'll be on my own for any visits. I ask for permission to leave the college, and this is granted. I haven't of course written to Daddy to tell him about this. He might only object, talk to the College Dean about it, and that'll get me nowhere. So I'll just have to turn up with no information, no addresses. With the small sum of money I have I get to Galway first, and then another coach out to Carraroe. The coach is full of people speaking the Gaeilge, so I must be in the right direction. Otherwise I don't quite know where I'm going. I haven't been so far since the early sixties. I'm afraid to ask anything of the other travellers on the bus, and I get off at a point where I think the house that I see might be it.

But I'm out of luck, the place is even empty, and I am miles away from anywhere. Through the darkness I can see the bus tail-lights disappearing in the distance, so I start walking in that direction. The weather is somewhat cold, but at least it's not raining. I eventually find the village, and head for the church. Beside the church I can see the Parochial House, and I ring the doorbell.

When the door opens who do I see but a certain Father Mannion, who was in Joseph's until the previous year. He recognises me all right, and invites me inside. I tell him the little that I know of my dead mother and her family. I don't know how he manages, but within a few minutes, he gives me indications and sends me to a house, which is some three hundred yards from where we are standing. I am grateful for his help, and finally believe that I am now on the last stretch Uncle Jimmy and Aunty Megan can hardly believe who is standing on their doorstep on a blustery winter's night.

But from the welcome, which they extend me, I know that I've finally located my family.

St Joseph's IV

Most of the students are into some hobby or another here at

college. They have a chess club going, a debating society which I participate in, and quizzes are regularly organised between our team and the Christian Brothers' boys and others from the town.

Since I've bought my Halimex camera at Baltrina during a summer stint, I'm interested in joining the photography club, which already has a number of members. The problem is, however, that I'll need money for buying films, and paper for developing, this apart from my normal budget.

Then I have an idea. When we're off to inter-college football matches nearly every second Sunday, I'll have my camera with me, and before match begins then I'll have the players all lined up for a group shot on the pitch.

That evening, whilst all the other students are at the cinema over in the great gym hall, I'm crouching over the worktable in the darkroom on the first floor. First to develop the film, have it dry, and then over to the exposure projector, and start my six by five black and white prints.

Into the tray with the developing solution. Tweezers at hand. Check the temperature from time to time. Judgement as to when the print is ready. Out into the middle tray with plain water. A back and forth movement to rinse the picture. Out into the third tray, which is holding the fixer solution. The seconds are again counted and then into a tub of warm water for a wash before putting on the drying machine.

By the time that the others are out from watching *Cat Ballou*, or *The Thirty-nine Steps*, I'll have my prints up on the college notice board inside the main doors, and I'll be standing with my copies ready.

For all the football minded, my prints sell like hot buns.

The profits earned will more than cover my general expenses for photography, and will even allow me other treats too, like buying a handball from time to time. I don't intend to spend all my time in the darkroom, and enjoy when the handball courts aren't crowded, that way I can get on to play and whack the ball for a while. They're always crowded on the weekends, but that's not always a problem, because I sometimes receive a visit from Mrs Conlon and Mrs Glavney, who come down for the Sunday afternoon, and they take me out for a drive through the countryside, we'll have a good chat, and they always have 'goodies' of fruit and chocolate bars with them. Rhona and Daddy hardly ever come to visit me whilst at college, and whenever they do then we'll sit in the car parked up by the great cathedral near the college grounds instead of driving out into the countryside like Mrs Glavney would do, but they always come to pick me up when the holidays are started.

The handball is not just for the exercise, but it gets my mind off things when I need such. It's also useful when exam days arrive. Be it year-end, or the InterCert or Leaving Cert exams, the other boys are so busy cramming themselves to the last minute, in the dormitories or classrooms, there is all the place I need down on the courts, and from studying all year long, which is no great problem for me, I am well prepared, and spend my final hours and time having solo sessions, before heading into the examination hall.

For many others, the 'hops' which are organised every Saturday evening are a hobby, but not for me. They would enjoy the girls company, they coming over from the convents across the road, but because of my shyness my world has become so small, is so restrained and limited, that finally I know very little of the great wide world out there, and don't know what to talk about, and from the state of my teeth, which are lacking dental care for many years now, I have difficulty in trying to smile. I have become so painfully shy, and feel that I have little character nor charisma, no personality. So instead of trying to enjoy the dances, I prefer to remain alone, in my classroom, and to indulge in my studies.

At least that should help me through all my exams.

Daddy would be happy about that.

Suit

We're all on our way home to Castlebarry. It's a winter's evening, and it's dark as night out there. All's quiet in the car as we advance, bend by bend, mile by mile.

'He's talking to you,' says Rhona.

I look in her direction, as I hadn't caught anything that Daddy might have said.

'What would you like to do when you leave St Joseph's?' Daddy asks.

I'm startled, as Daddy rarely ever puts a question direct to me like that. What's gotten into him at all?

Do what when I leave St Joseph's? Do I have a choice? But he's just asked me. He hardly ever asked me anything, like if I was enjoying school or am I happy with life or anything at all down through the months and years. I can remember the evening many years ago, that he'd come up the staircase and into our room to ask us if we wanted some water because he had found that the rashers which Rhona had cooked and served us for dinner were rather salty indeed. Since then, nothing. But now he's asked me another question! What's going on here?

'Well?' Rhona has her gob open again.

I was caught out by the total surprise, and hardly have time to start thinking about what to say. I could never decide on things like where I'd like to go on holidays, or whom to visit on Sunday next. And now I have to decide something! Got to say something before Rhona starts taking the mickey. Thoughts go filtering through my mind, but what to say? Will Daddy or Rhona be happy or unhappy? I falter, but know that I have to get something together, especially as Rhona might just take the mickey if I don't have something serious and good to offer.

Then I remember the Donilaun Hotel. All the enjoyable days and evenings I had spent working there, all the kind people and customers I'd met. The hotel manager O'Coonealy had noticed that I was a good worker, and had one day asked me if I wanted to continue in this business when I'd left secondary school. I'd replies yes to him, and he had had some advice for me.

'If you want into this hotel business, you'll have to know a lot about the world, and know how to keep people taking,' is what he'd said. 'You'll have to be able to talk about a breed of dog to a dog-owner, or a species of tree to a gardener, whenever you'll be meeting the likes.'

How to learn a lot about the world? Whilst growing up at

Marian House I was never allowed into the town library which was on the way home from school, never had a book to read up in the bedroom, just as much as a teddy bear, nor a bike downstairs.

Then I asked him about the town library in Baltrina. So off I head, into the modern building beyond the town centre, and ask to become a member. The lady says that I can even have two tickets, that way I'll be able to borrow two books at a time. With my time-off I'm now into borrowing and reading books on the dogs, the trees, and everything else like famous buildings, cities, transport, photography and the like that is to be found.

But as I won't be going back there any more, and as Tadgh will be spending some time there this summer, he had asked me to give him my two membership tickets.

I know that he enjoys reading, as he has done a lot of it in the rooms at Marian House, and he says that he'll be taking out two tickets too in his name.

That way he'll have four books at any one visit.

My mind's attention drifts back to Daddy's question.

'Well,' I start, 'you know all the months that I have been working at the Donilaun Hotel?'

'Yes?' Daddy has heard me and is still waiting, just like Rhona too I guess.

'Ah, well I'd like to go to hotel management college,' the words come out.

No reaction from Rhona, which I can't determine is a good sign or not.

'Do you know where there's one?' Daddy enquires.

'Yes, down at the Shandon Airport in County Clare, I even have their address, which I got from the chef at the Donilaun,' I add on, glad that things seem to be moving along smoothly, and isn't that a great thing for once?

'Well, you'll have to be writing to them, and see what they have to say, yes?' asks Daddy.

Daddy tells me that if I want to go to Hotel College and become a hotel manager I'll have to be going to an interview, and I'll need to impress these men with my knowledge and wiseness indeed.

A fine suit too is needed for such an important occasion, that

I'll be having the best three-piece one that money can buy, because I'll be deserving that much on such a great day. I'm looking forward to this.

So he's talking about the suit again when they arrive down from Castlebarry to visit Mrs Ganaghan the following Sunday. Daddy explains to her about the interview in the Burlaston Hotel in Dublin, and isn't there a fine draper's shop in Hill Street in Baltrina? She agrees to go into Baltrina with me during the week, as I'll be staying with her and we'll have a look out for a great suit indeed.

It's a beautiful day, and Mrs Ganaghan and I set out walking the five miles into town. Lots of things to be doing today whilst we're in there, have to find some fresh milk, and other bits and pieces. But beforehand we head down to the drapery shop.

It seems to be a quiet day for business as we're the only clients to be seen. The weather's too fine for a drapery shop to be overfilled with customers, maybe they come on rainy days or on market days.

'Hello yerselves, now,' says yer man as we head towards the rear of the shop, where he is idling, his elbows down on the great long wooden counter, his measuring tape dangling from around his collar.

Mrs Ganaghan tells the man what I'd be looking for.

'Sure we have lots of fine suits here, have a look at all the tissues I have here,' he announces, hands waving around the whole shop to show off everything he has for sale, whilst he still keeps one eye on me, 'and sure you're a fine looking young man yourself here now, and what age might you be there now?'

'Seventeen,' I reply, but I'm more interested in a suit than the gab. All I need is one tissue, for one suit.

I spend ages going back and forth looking at all the samples. Sure, he has lots: black, which I guess would go well for a funeral suit, and then all kinds of tweeds for a Sunday suit, followed by everything I've never seen before in tweeds.

But I want to have a second if not a third look at what I'm ordering. After all, this is going to be the first suit of my life, and Daddy said he'd pay for the finest one, which pleases me. My eyes keep roaming around the shop, maybe there's something on a rack up there, somewhere that I have missed.

Then I see what I was looking for, this one here is what I'll be having. Yer man smiles, and he says he'll have to take my measurements. The man now has his measuring tape held between both hands, and as Mrs Ganaghan keeps moving back and forth in the shop, he starts making notes. He's already measured my leg length, and as Mrs Ganaghan comes back toward us he moves up to my shoulders. I can't understand why, but at every chance he says that he has to check my hip width again, and then fiddles along the inner leg length again. I'm getting fed up with him with his queer manners, hovering and touching around my hip and legs. Can't he keep his bloody thumbs off my body and on his measuring tape instead? How many times does he have to take my measurements down there, every time that Mrs Ganaghan has her back turned?

So now I've chosen my suit, and a shirt and tie to go with it too, and yer man finally has all the measurements he says he'll be needing.

'He'll be needing the suit for Easter,' Mrs Ganaghan says. 'The bill you can send to Dr Duignan in Castlebarry, who's my son-in-law, do you know?'

'Oh, and how's your daughter Rhona then?' he enquires, happy to be having such a nice class of client in today. Must beat selling trousers to farmers who never seem to make any money at all on selling cows or heifers at the market in town, and with the bad prices, and bejasus tonight, aren't the times going to the dogs indeed? And will the days be any better when we get to join all them others in the Common Market at all, and what kind of a suit would a farming man wear over there on the Continent at all? He seems to be so happy having served us, he had a great pleasure at all now, and even made a fine sale indeed and he'll probably be charging full price for Dr Duignan. No point in even mentioning a discount here.

I'm wondering if I couldn't have a sample of this tweed to show it to Daddy when I get back up home, but the man says that that's not possible. Mrs Ganaghan tells me not to worry, and that we'll be back in again to pick up the suit.

The weeks pass by and on my next visit to Baltrina we're

heading back to the draper's shop, and I'm looking forward to having a look at the finished article.

We arrive back at the shop, and yer man's there all right. A few customers in here now, and he finally reappears with my suit.

What a horror!

I can't believe this! The fellow disappears as he has other customers to attend to. Mrs Ganaghan is hovering all over the place, looking grand, and I keep staring at my suit.

It's not the same colour nor tissue! This beige-coloured one with its big squares in the tissue has nothing to do with the choice I made a few weeks ago. It doesn't even go so well with the shirt and tie, which are still in the plastic bag since the day that I chose them.

What to say, what to do? I can't get yer man's attention at all. Mrs Ganaghan seems to be totally indifferent indeed, she's looking all over the whole place as if she'd never set her foot in here, and she keeps getting stopped by people who know her already or want to know her and what business brings her into this fine drapery shop at all? Where are the other samples, maybe I'd find the one I was after since the first day! Daddy hasn't even been with me to the shop, so he can't possibly know what a good choice I'd probably have made!

So now I know what's gone wrong!

The old fecking bitch!

Whilst I've been back up in St Joseph's, the old one hasn't lost time in getting back to the shop, and with some excuse has changed the colour and tweed that the chap's supposed to be using for my suit. Who ordered that?

'Aren't you happy now at all?' she asks.

I nod some sort of an acceptance.

'A nice suit you have there now for a nice young man of your age,' says the draper, smiling, 'and it goes grand with you, fits you like a glove.'

You're an old bastard too, I think to myself quietly.

Mrs Ganaghan is full of kind words to thank the draper, and without giving him too much of a stare, I walk out into the street as he holds the door open to bid us goodbye.

We've still got the five miles to walk home still ahead of us, me holding the great big drapery bag along the whole way, and whilst doing so I have all the time on earth to remember and dream about the three-piece suit I'd chosen in the drapery shop for my interview, because I have to impress those men Daddy had said, but that I will never get to wear.

Shandon

In the late spring of 1975 I attend an interview at the Burlaston Hotel in Dublin. I pass the test and get to start at the hotel Management College at Shandon Airport in Clare. Instead of going to the Donilaun Hotel I'm to be spending the summer period there working in the big airport kitchens.

I've never worn cook's clothing before and the huge square apron goes way down to my feet. Day one starts and I'm nervous. I get assigned to the vegetable cook. My first job will be washing a huge deep sink of cabbage. Yer man leaves me to it, and goes about his business. But washing the leaves one by one leaves me way behind with the pile, and when yer man is back I get my first bollocking.

I've been at work only fifteen minutes.

This sure isn't the Donilaun Hotel.

The days are heavily charged. When needed, I'm called over to the production part where the meal trays for the aircraft are prepared. Rows of small plates running to all four corners of the immense table. I'm still so young and small, that even standing on my tiptoes I can barely manage to reach the plate nearest the table centre. I ladle and ladle the food out.

I have a room up at the barracks buildings beyond the control tower. Rapidly the whole place and my clothes and set of knives become stenched in the smell of onions, soaking into everything. Tons of onions every week. Tons of everything really. Tons of tricks too. Not all of us young students have worked summers at a hotel like the Donilaun. We get the mickey taken out of us because being new to this place and job sure you can't be wise-on to everything. One chap gets sent to look for a bananastraightener. Another is sent away to search for a spaghetti peeler. I'm told that they'll be needing the key of the ramp. There's a whole bunch of smart-alecs in this place.

One day my vegetable chef boss calls me over to where he is busy in the hot kitchen. There's a big jet coming in for an unannounced stop, and the kitchens have to prepare a load of omelettes for the meal trays. Yer man is there, busy all right. He has nine omelette pans lined up on the cooking range in front of him.

He has just ladled out a portion of whipped eggs onto the last pan.

'The one to the right is for you, Duignan, and hurry up with it,' his tone of voice gives him repeatedly the title of most hated guy in the whole brigade.

I watch my mixture, which has just started cooking and bubbling. I glance to my left to see how he manages with the eight remaining pans. I see that like a circus juggler, he ladles out a portion so that his first pan is a raw mixture, the others are cooking progressively, and the last one to his left is cooked and well turned, and thus ready for distribution to the flight preparation area.

I'm giving loving tender care to my pan and omelette.

I glance at him. His huge overweight body fills out all the creases in his oversize kitchen whites, which I believe comes from picking, munching and chewing something every time he stops in another area of the huge kitchen, be it bakery or the cold kitchen. Probably spares having any food at all in his fridge at home, I think. But he has this knack to his arm, so that whilst I'd say 'Bob's your uncle', he has flipped over two or three omelettes.

'In five minutes, you'll be taking the second pan too,' he barks.

The bastard!

I know that he wants to test me to the limit, and when I've reached that far, he'll take a laughing mickey, and have another tour of the kitchen to tell the sauce chef, the sweet chef and the cold kitchen fellow too, whilst he'll stop to taste something new and different, that these young fellows aren't worth anything, and however for the sakes of Reilly did the college interview board ever manage to find such a bunch of gobshites for this new season?

I hope however that he doesn't go as far as to tell the head chef. The small Frenchman, André, his crisply starched tall hat adding a quarter to his whole height already, spends a great part of his time running round the whole place cursing everything. 'Zee fucking students' is all he calls us, never has a word of praise nor encouragement. So I'm at the mercy of my bosses' whim whether or not he cares to complain.

'That'll be it for today,' the heavy chap suddenly announces, and boy with all the heat coming off those roaring cookers, I'll be happy to be able to step rearwards, and wipe the sweat off my brow.

Happy too, because I haven't reached my capacity limit. André is nowhere to be seen.

Lots of airplanes coming and going out there on the tarmac. Lots of movements of big jets coming and going again to the States and over to Europe. Charter flights with American soldiers moving back and forth to their NATO bases in Germany. I am, here at Shandon, at a gateway to the great wide world out there, but as yet have never been out of Ireland, nor ever been on a plane. I wonder what it is like to be travelling.

I'm busy working, and when off then I start spending my time over at the airport buildings. I manage to buy myself a pair of binoculars, and an airband radio. The frequencies allow me to listen to the tower, ground, and other VHF frequencies. I get to know a great number of the airport security guards, and the airport buildings and operations inside out.

The first year of college then gets underway, with lots of practical work. Cooking, housekeeping, service, food costing and so forth.

The evenings are devoted to study, and when finished I'm always off down to the terminal to watch the activity, whilst my classmates are off down to Shandon town or further. I don't have money for the pubs.

I hear from Daddy from time to time, especially when I've asked for more money. The winter evenings set in, as does the cold weather coming in from the Atlantic.

The hunger too.

Weekends are off, and as first year students aren't allowed to take a weekend job, I'm surviving on little money. One evening, I've left but a few coppers in my pocket. I wander and gaze at the small packets of biscuits, which are on sale at the staff freeflow restaurant. But I don't have enough money to buy any, so have to just return in the darkness to my room, and wait for breakfast in the morning.

Saturday mornings I can remain in bed, listening to the air traffic jargon on my little portable radio. One morning, early spring, I've picked up from the control tower that there are a number of overhead flights arriving eastbound from the States and which normally are destined to Heathrow and eastern England, and that they're coming into Shandon Airport. I wonder what this chaos is about. I change my radio frequency and when I hear the weather report for eastern England I understand. They're completely fogged in over there. That'll make for a hell of a lot of Boeing 747's and other 'heavies' here. It's still early but I alert all the classmates. Before we get 'drafted' into the airport restaurants to help out with their problems, we're all scattering like zebras when the hyenas come feeding. On the next bus into town. A discreet visit early afternoon, and I count thirteen big jets still parked all over the place. But our day off has been saved. Especially as they wouldn't pay for our work.

It's the 30th May 1976. I'm about to leave for Dublin. Daddy is coming up with me, as I'm due out to Geneva the following day. I'm starting my second year of college. It'll be practical work, on the ground level so to speak, which means that I'll also be getting a salary. The college had of course explained that to Daddy and Rhona. When translated into Irish pounds it seems to be an impressive sum. Daddy tells me that I'll have to be saving my salary during the coming twelve months, because what with all the bills and repairs they have on Marian House, they won't be helping me to pay my way through third year. I'll have to pay for all my tuition fees, meals and schoolbooks, lodgings and general expenses too.

To me third year sounds a long way away, the money in Switzerland is going to be great anyway, and so I accept this condition.

I've got my camera slung over my left shoulder as I'm still standing in the kitchen near the fridge.

'You can leave your camera here,' Rhona says, 'you'll only be wasting money on them films.'

I stand defiantly.

'It's my camera, I paid for it with my money that I've saved at the Donilaun, and it's coming with me,' I have to say.

I turn and head out through the door to the waiting car. Daddy doesn't delay in arriving and we start the drive to Dublin. He's taking a turn down by the Market Square in town, and he makes a remark.

'You'll have to be careful with your aircraft spotting when you're over there,' he says. An Irish spotter had recently been stopped and jailed in Belgium, which made for great coverage in our local press.

I wonder how he has found about that one. How does he know what I do with my free time? I reply that yes, I'll be careful.

We stay the night at the Western County Hotel, and the next day we're out to the airport.

The airport was the one that I'd visited, with Martin, when we'd left home a month of June many years ago, and where I'd gotten to admire the wonderful flying machines during an afternoon.

Now there's one of them waiting for me and my classmates.

The view of the hordes of sailing boats on Lake Geneva and towards the Alps is impressive on our approach to Geneva Airport, and once on the ground the summer temperatures are soaring. I've never had anything like this in Ireland, and we all have to buy ourselves tee-shirts, as we don't have such in our possessions.

But the price tags on the tee-shirts and many other items which we need to buy, even if they are only at Sfr9.95, or Sfr14.95, or Sfr19.95, are expensive and are of a much higher price level than what we are used to in Ireland, and soon my monthly salary is not worth much. A succession of months, and I'm knocking at the personnel office each time to ask for an advance of a quarter of my next month's salary. My lodgings and meals are deducted from gross wages, then come the taxes and the insurance premiums too. Little money left then for travelling, nor for going for a day's skiing. Even the price of a pint of the cool stuff is steep, and so I start feeling a sort of social exclusion, which had already started at Shandon and is simply continuing.

When working in the kitchen or in restaurant service we have of course a great number of split shifts to accomplish, and the work schedule is hard indeed. Nothing like this in Ireland, and the small satellite kitchen on the ground floor is worse than a sauna. But we have to keep going, remembering amongst other details, that a rare steak can always be put back on the grill, but when it's well-cooked, then it's too late to make a rare one of it. Little or no food to be wasted here. It's a professional operation, a hard school, but I learn fast. But the café and croissant for breakfast isn't much of a comparison with the hearty Irish breakfast which we were used to for a start to the day's work.

One afternoon, whilst the others are out boozing in the pubs in the city, I'm spending time on the airport terrace. But my activity attracts the attention of somebody, because suddenly I am requested by one of the airport security guards to follow him for questioning. They want to check what I'm doing, what I've scribbled down in my little notepad, and of course my identity. I don't have my residence permit papers with me, so the police phone the restaurant to check everything out. Damn it, I think! My employer will certainly make a report to the college, and the Director there will write to Daddy. That'll mean a real bollocking the next time I meet Daddy! The thought of that worries me, especially as he'd warned me. If the Swiss kick me out for security reasons, then I won't be able to finish my year, and that might mean getting kicked out of the college completely. Then a bollocking wouldn't be enough, it would probably mean a severe bashing from him.

In the late autumn Daddy writes me a letter with news from Ireland. He encloses a cutting from one of the Irish national dailies. The photo shows a group of students from the Shandon College. The shot is taken from their Graduation Day ceremony, and thereon I see a group of four students, all dressed in their graduation gowns and mortars, having been successful in their exams, and Daddy tells me that this is what I have to work towards.

In the spring of 1977, a young girl starts working at the restaurant's buffet.

Her name is Veronica.

I invite her to the jig for St Patrick's night. In our staff quarters on the third floor we have three bedrooms, two students per room. I'm sharing with Harry. The beds go up against the walls, the wardrobes against the windows to block off the sound for the neighbours opposite. We'd heard that the Irish are renowned here for organising parties, and the restaurant director doesn't want any problems like he always seems to get each year. We promise that it'll work out just fine.

Excellent cooks and organisers that we are, we have no difficulty in drumming up the best of an Irish stew. I do a load of trips over to the restaurant, and carry back tons of crushed ice, which gets loaded onto the beer bottles which are waiting to be cooled off in the two bathtubs. Everybody from the restaurant, except the Director is coming at some stage or other. They are all invited. Bets are running as to who might manage to knock off Dominique, the heterosexual girl who loves walking around the kitchen in her tight chef's trousers trying to look like a man and getting us all thinking of the excitement whilst trying to concentrate on our work.

Early evening the ceili gets going. Then the crowd comes, the Italians, the Turks, they're all there, to be sure. Looks like more of a European feast day than just an Irish one. They've certainly heard from the previous years about the craic that the Irish are capable of organising for their St Patrick's Day. The restaurant director too.

The police too. Word was that they've marked it down every year on their calendars at the local station: the 17th March.

The food is excellent, the beers flow, the craic has attracted the crowd. Attracted them so much that I start noticing people and total strangers have appeared off the streets, guided by the music blaring down from the third floor level, and have started partaking of the Irish hospitality. The place is overloaded.

Then we hear the pistol shot. Apparently somebody who lives just across the street has a starting pistol, and that it gets used every 17th March, at least.

They must make a note of the Irish national feast day too every year. Every 17th March.

Then the police with their machine guns turn up. They've got to empty the place. We turn down the decibels and the chat, and manage to have a great number of people out, and the cops think that it's over.

Veronica's apartment is upstairs on the fourth floor, so she can stay anyway.

The cops finally disappear, and we can keep up the craic, but with lower voices. The last party stragglers are leaving, and I find a total stranger selling some of our remaining beer down in the street in the very early hours of the morning.

The summer season is now approaching real fast, and both myself and Veronica know that I have to make it back to Ireland, work and study obliges me.

We bid our farewells at the airport on the 27th May 1977, both of us unsure what the future holds. The craic, or what I've managed to have of it, is now over.

I have to work towards achieving my Diploma. That's what Daddy had said.

Donegal

After finishing my year of training my return flight from Geneva takes me back to Dublin on the 27th May 1977, and I spend the night in the capital before heading down with the Aer Lingus flight to Shandon the following day. I haven't put my foot near Castlebarry, so haven't seen Daddy, nor Rhona, for a year now.

I get off my flight at Shandon, and instead of heading north, I'm off to the CIE station in Limerick where I can catch a coach down to Cork City, where I can visit and stay with the Glavneys for the night. From there, a longer coach trip brings me back up through central Ireland, bypassing Castlebarry, and I find a room for the night in Sligo.

The next day I continue my journey northwards, and I meet

my classmates Barney and Harry at the bus station in Letterkenny. We have an appointment to meet Declan, who is the owner/manager of the hotel where we will be spending our summer period. Without delay he arrives, we pack all our bags into his car and we head north to the Shannaun Hotel at Port-na-Glagh for the season. This is because we have to fill in our remaining months within the Irish hotel industry before we return to Shandon College. Declan's an ex-student from the college, and he's also been 'away' for a year's work and romp in far-away places.

'Any broken hearts there lads?' he asks.

He's gawking and leering at the rear-view mirror. Harry and Barney take the mickey, but I don't care, have other things to think about, to worry about. The only thing I'm now sure of is that Geneva's a long way behind me, Veronica too, and right now the only place I'm going is an unknown hotel stuck in an isolated corner of Donegal.

I don't want to see him leering any more, so I keep my gaze fixed out the right passenger's window.

We settle in to our new abode. Staff quarters behind the hotel, two separate dormitory buildings, one for the girls, and the second one further behind on the hill up from us. Barney and Harry take a room together, I get a room for myself, next door to what's supposed to be a bastard of a kitchen chef, O'Rooney. There are only four guys and Declan to run the kitchen, bar and management, a few girls for the stillroom, the restaurant, and reception, the two boyo brothers for the potwash. We work like the hammers of hell, but as we've just come out of a year in Mövenpick's schedule, it's absolutely no hassle for us. The weeks fly by, and we're so busy with guests arriving every Saturday for a week's stay, often more. The scenery is simply fantastic up in these parts, and with all the work we nearly forget that the whole of Ireland still exists south of Letterkenny. Yes the work, but also the play.

Afternoons we are off to the fine uncrowded beach down below the hotel, late evenings off to a local dance hall along the Dunfanaghy road. Barney's doing well with a young lady, she's got one big pair of you-know-what-up-front, I've seen her in a bikini on the beach one afternoon and if it isn't enough, evenings she's got a grey tee-shirt with a blue message 'HARP – WAY OUT IN FRONT'. Wow! You can qualify or quantify it whatever way you want, flying the flag, or displaying the wares, but Barney's having a whale of a time. He's even onto an auxiliary barmaid, who declares 'Anytime you want Barney, and as long as you like.' He's in heaven, who needs the French Riviera near St Tropez when you've got all the craic up here?

Affectionately speaking I'm becoming a bit starved myself, and then one day Kathreen, who works in the stillroom squeezes in beside me at the lunch table, even starts helping herself to bits on my plate. Is she going to sit on my lap next or what? The others are now finishing their meals and slowly moving back to work, and Kathreen tells me that she wants to talk to me and would I mind coming over to see her when we shut down the kitchen this evening? Later on when the company have all headed out the Dunfanaghy road, and instead of heading out for a pint and a hooley-booley, here I am treading into the womens quarters, with Kathreen's room being the second on the left. Poor girl, she must be so tired as she's already in bed, but we get talking which is more than we can ever do in the stillroom, especially with her mates watching and listening. Mind you, she's got one mate, Angela's her name, who's got a right look of a tomboy about her, with tight leathers and heavy boots. I wouldn't mind her treading upon me, but I keep that for my dreams.

'Come on, Kathreen,' the old laundry lady next door has heard some foreign voice in Kathreen's room, and now she's pounding on the wall, 'I know there's a man in your room, and would you get him out of there, or I'll be reporting you in the morning.'

Damn it!

Kathreen's is a little embarrassed, somewhat frustrated, and maybe even sheer angry I think.

'Listen, I'll give it to ya tomorrow,' she proposes. 'A promise.'

'Give it to me? Oh, all right, what's a day in a lifetime?' I wonder to myself, and she gets a hug before I creep out the door, hoping that the old one isn't going to ramble out all of a sudden and have a great gawk at Kathreen's visitor.

The next evening, whilst Barney and Harry are out the

Dunfanaghy road again, and O'Rooney is getting himself pissed drunk in some pub, she pops up to my quarters 'cos she hasn't finished telling me her story that she had to cut short last night. We're on our own in the barracks up here, no banging on the wall to be heard this evening, and we can listen to the Rolling Stones with their *Goat's Head Soup* album and other cassettes that I brought back from Geneva, and would she mind me lending her that one and some Status Quo and Slade too, and she even autographs them, she's so happy. She also tells me a little about her life up here in these wild parts of Ireland, yes, yes she has a boyfriend who's a banqueting manager in a hotel in Letterkenny, but he's not much interested in keeping her happy.

'But you're different, but don't worry,' she says, 'I get all my supplies from across the border so you're safe.'

Then she keeps her promise.

I get, and I give in return.

Too bad for yer man the banqueting manager I think, he can take bloody well care of himself, but I'm sure that I can take good care of Kathreen. The summer's not worn out yet. Neither am I.

She won't stay for the night now do you know, because she'd be missed by her roommate, and they'd need her for the stillroom in the morning, so she'll be off down now whilst the laundry woman is probably sleeping and what she's been doing with any of them new college students won't harm the older lady's way of thinking, and it's better off to be down before the whole company gets back from the hooley-booleying out the Dunfanaghy road.

I wake up in the morning, a beautiful day, the ocean is a deep blue, life's a beach, and I'm urging to get to work. A final brush of the hair, I adjust my chef's scarf which is great for absorbing the hot kitchen sweat coming down the back of your skull, but right now it's got to hide the love bites on my shoulders and neck, but I think I'll not be able to get to the beach for this afternoon at least. Oh well, no regrets, I've had my share, so don't care about not maybe seeing the Harp lady in her bikini outfit today. I pass Barney's room, wondering where he's been the night, but even if he tries to impress us today with a score better than the ten positions he'd done the other night and all that without waking Harry, I won't let him bother me. I just hope that Harry's managed to get some sleep, and if not maybe learn a trick or two, but today's another full house, and there'll be work on the chopping block and at the hotplates.

Into the kitchen, have to start getting ready for lunch.

'What's on the menu today?' I enquire.

'There, it's all marked up over there,' answers Barney, who is already down, and active.

Then down to work, saucepans, mayonnaise, whisks, plates, eggs, tomatoes, warm the ovens, late breakfast orders for some, after that on to sauces, the dessert, don't forget the dessert for goodness's sake.

'Where's O'Rooney, for God's sake, what's he up, to the ould bastard?' I ask.

'What's that word supposed to mean, Cauliflower Mornay?' the receptionist has appeared and is worried about a spelling for the menu cards.

'Come here, love. I'll show you how things should be done, you know, the right way,' Barney says.

Up with them roast joints here and into the oven boys, otherwise we'll be the laughing stock of the Hotel College.

'Can someone go upstairs to shake old O'Rooney?' Barney asks. We have a lot of unfinished work here.

Not even one of the two poor brothers who do the pan and pot washing would dare go up to wake old O'Rooney. He's bad enough at lunchtime, and it's only ten o'clock here now. We're even grateful for his absence, even the potwashers are at the height of their motivation, absorbing without effort all the dirty utensils coming their way.

'Keep this momentum up boys, we might even make a fine profit for Declan this week!'

Then all of a sudden yer man turns in, smiling because he knows that he can always count on us to keep the show going and thataway he can hide behind his foulness and headaches too. He looks at me, my kitchen attire all white and crisp and with my chef's scarf neatly tied around my neck, something I actually never wear. He is sloppily dressed to say the best, his jacket half-open, no chef's scarf to be seen on himself, but no lovebites either. I might tell him that I'm after his lousy job, but let's forget it! He seems to be in a lousy mood this morning, probably got bounced out of another pub last night and couldn't find an off-license this side of Sligo. I feel that he's out to get at someone, but he knows that I'll not take any of his nonsense. He heads for the younger of the kitchen porter boys, angry that neither of them went up to 'disturb' him from his drunken sleep, especially with so much work to be done.

'Here, would ye take a pound of this flour to the chopping board over there, and chop it all up for me, and would you hurry along a little with it now, I'll be needing it for lunch?' he barks an order.

The young boy scurries to fulfil the order.

'What's the count for lunch? How many packed lunches went out this morning?' I ask, as we need to make a rough calculation of the number of guests expected for lunch. I have to deduct the number of packed lunches from the number of people on full board to give me an estimate of clients expected for lunch.

The waitresses are still scurrying back and forth, busy with the late breakfast trade, through the dining room doors to the right and the stillroom area to the left.

The stillroom.

Kathreen.

'Chef, not enough greens here, can we get another veg out of the freezer in time?' calls Barney. O'Rooney curses, 'cos he's got to make a decision, he's in a poor shape for that and then he sees Declan coming through the kitchen door. By the looks of things Declan's seen it all before I think, but what could he do without O'Rooney, who's been here for years for each summer season, earning lots of punts which will keep him afloat during the long Irish winter, and keep his line of credit running in all the pubs and off-licences south of Sligo? North of Sligo nearly nobody wants to serve him anymore. What's the point in selling a few pints of the good stuff to a man who's going to drink it all, and then after, on some pretext, will pretend that 'your pint' is the worst to be found in the whole county, if not with the other five as well, and 'If you don't serve me up another, but a good one this time, I'll smash all yer fecking faces to bits, and that'll be a lesson for ye to be serving pints like that to me, O'Rooney, head chef at the Shannaun Hotel and the whole of my kitchen brigade all the way up from the Shandon Hotel College!' We'd never of course be anywhere near his whereabouts at any given time or any given pub in an evening, so if he wanted to count upon our moral support, he could always take a long run and jump for himself.

Problem was he'd tried it on so often, and was never happy with the replies of the barmen, who generally sober, knew what a good pint looked like and was worth moneywise. So poor O'Rooney, even after a hard day's work was getting refused in a growing number of pubs in the region, and when he found one with a new barmaid, he would abuse her until someone spotted him, and then the 'troubles' always started. Then the fights. He might be a small chap to look at, but he's well fed, and has lots of calories waiting to be burned up.

One of the local fishermen arrives by the back door, with a fine catch of fresh salmon and lobsters right out of the bay. It's a great excuse for him to get away from Declan, and he always likes having some fresh lobster in the house. The goods are checked, weighed, the price is debated, and a signature on the docket means that O'Rooney has made a good choice and a great purchase. It also means he has a few fresh lobsters in store.

Then he remembers the kitchen porter and the pack of flour. The college students will sure keep the real kitchen running.

He runs toward the boy with the chopping block. Chopping flour seems to him to be a far more pleasant occupation than heaving heavy pots and pans around the place, and maybe he is hoping that this could lead to a cook's apprenticeship one day.

'Are you still chopping away at my flour?' he glares at the young fellow. 'Look at this, you fecking eejit, it's far too fine, why didn't you stop and call me before?' He seizes a fistful and lets the fine-milled flour drift down from above his head as if it were a mini snowfall, and from the wild early morning look to O'Rooney's face, sure the poor young chap can't understand what he's done wrong at all. He knows a lot about dirty and clean whisks, pots and pans, but this must have been the first time he had to chop finest milled flour.

'Now you go for another pound of the flour, chop it, and don't you waste any of it!' he says and wheels towards me, grinning aloud, and obviously proud of his managerial skills. 'You stop sooner, do you understand, you fecking eejit?'

The young boy has the next packet of flour already on the chopping block, ready for the big knife.

'Awf,' O'Rooney sighs. Those bloody college boys won't play his games, and the potwash brothers, well he can't do much mickeying with them either. Then he remembers the fresh lobsters idling around in their water-tank, and wonders if the new waitress has ever had a close-up look at a fresh lobster who'd rather be crawling around the Atlantic seafloor than being in captivity and gripped behind his back by meself, a right bastard of an Irish chef, having nothing else on me dirty mind than scaring the shites of a poor young lady who's only here for the craic, get laid maybe, and also to earn a few punts during the summer? I mightn't get around to laying her or any of them, but I'll give them some of my craic!

One day Declan calls me out to the reception desk, there's a man on the phone for me and would I come upfront? Daddy's on the phone and he's real angry. He can't understand why I haven't been down in the western parts since getting back from Switzerland, and all this puts me off and the argument starts getting heated.

'Oh, I think there's a bad line here, Dad, but I'll call you back soon, agreed?' I have to find an excuse to finish with him.

He agrees.

I never phoned.

A few weeks later Declan calls me to the phone again. I'm nervous.

'Is it a man?' I ask.

'No, it's a woman?' he says. I get even more nervous, what the hell does Rhona want from me? I make it to the phone.

'Hello?'

'Gerry, hello it's Veronica calling.'

'Veronica, oh hello, nice to hear from you, how are you, where are you, you seem so near?'

'I'm calling you from Switzerland, and I'll be coming over with Annaliese for holidays soon for a fortnight, okay?'

'Great, great, I'll sort out a room for ye here at the hotel. Give me more details when ye have them.'

All excited, I tell Barney about Veronica's and Annaliese's forthcoming visit, and Barney starts telling O'Rooney, and he's never seen a Swiss lady in his life, isn't this lovely now, we'll sort it all out and you have to have some time off with them. He tells Kathreen about the visits coming, and she gets all worried about my 'Swiss Miss' coming over, and how long is she staying at all?

Declan hears too, and he starts talking about Switzerland again.

'Did you get any skiing in?' he asks.

'No, I didn't have a chance,' I say.

'Did you go up with one of the cablecars then?' he enquires.

'No, I didn't,' comes my reply.

'Well, what did you do then whilst you were over there, no craic?' he asks, all curious.

'I worked and worked,' is all I can find as an answer, as I bow my head to avoid giving him any further explanations.

What I had to say was of course true, I did have my two days off each week like everybody else, but what I couldn't explain to him was that instead of going skiing or travelling as a tourist in the world renowned Swiss trains and cablecars, I had, on Daddy's orders, to be saving my wages and money for paying all of my way through the third year in Hotel Management College. No money could be wasted on such niceties. On the one occasion that I'd left Geneva, with Rod Costelloe who was visiting us from Shandon, for a day trip, I'd made it as far as the village of Mürren, from where the cablecar leaves for the Schilthorn. But when in the village and reaching into my pocket I could only note that I didn't have any money left for the trip higher up, so that was the nearest that I ever got to a Swiss cablecar. A good job that I had at least a return train ticket to Geneva! And when in Geneva, the price of the pint wasn't an easy thing on the budget either!

One Saturday morning I'm off duty and idling my time in the hotel forecourt. There's a family there packing their bags into the car, just like many others on a Saturday morning. Then the man calls me over, says he has a question for me. When I approach the stranger has a gawk at me.

'Would you be one of the Duignans from Castlebarry now?'

he enquires.

'Yes I am, my name is Gerry Duignan,' I sure wasn't expecting this one, but I do reply.

A closer gawk and he has all my attention and curiosity. Who's yer man I wonder? What does he want? Did Rhona send him?

'Well, we're all from Castlebarry too, and we know all about your family,' he says. He sees that I want to know about him.

'I'm Padraig O'Flaherty, and I've got the Badgers lounge bar on Market Street.'

I know where that is. I nod my head, don't know what else to do.

With the work here, Kathreen and all, I had nearly started to forget that Castlebarry down south ever existed, and here it's all coming to me flat in my face, something which I didn't really need right now, with the holiday job finishing within a month and all.

'Well see you then,' he says, reversing the car towards the driveway. I don't tell him to give my best wishes to anybody in Castlebarry.

I take the CIE bus in the morning from Letterkenny, and the trip takes me through Northern Ireland, and across into County Monaghan and further down to Dublin Airport.

Veronica and Annaliese are looking just grand and swell off the Aer Lingus flight from Zurich and I'm happy to see them both again. I've been speaking no German since leaving Geneva at all, so it's not so easy giving the introductions to Ireland in a smattering of French and German. We won't make it back to Port-Na-Glagh this evening so we look for a B&B near the Store Street Busaras station.

We find what might be a fine little place, and when the door is opened, there's a big chap of an owner having a great gawk at us.

'We're looking for some accommodation for the night,' I say, me doing the tourist guide.

'Will it be three singles then?' he wonders aloud.

'No, a single and a double would do us just fine, would you have them to spare?' I insist.

He's having an awful look at my youngness at all, probably figured out that these young ladies are from the Continent or another far-away place, but this young chap here has a bit of an Irish gob about him. I think that yer man is probably wondering where the good old Irish Catholic standards are going to all these days, and isn't the whole country and its youngsters in an awful moral state at all, and what might the mighty powerful Catholic Church and the Government be doing about these kids in ruins. He's giving me such a stare, and the two girls too, that I think it's just as well for me and all of us that he's never heard of an Irish colleen named Kathreen who works up in north Donegal, and the way she does things, he'd be kicking us out of his noble Georgian house and probably be up to calling the Gardai Siochana on us too.

Anyway we manage to get the two rooms, and head out for some grub down by O'Connell Street. We are all tired from the travelling, so after me giving my guests some information about the geography of the country, it's time we hit the sack.

Declan's reserved a nice room at the Shannaun for the two girls, for a fortnight at attic level, where they have a fine view of the Sheep's Head Bay to the front, and the Atlantic ocean to the left.

Head chef O'Rooney, as he likes us to call him whenever we have important visitors present in the hotel kitchen, is into his element with the new visitors coming around to taste his excellent cooking of fine Irish specialities. Would they have the likes of any of this or that over there at all? He knows that it's their first time spending holidays by the oceanside, that the saltwater is new for them, but he doesn't dare give them a close-up view of what a fresh Irish lobster looks like. No chef, they've never seen a fresh lobster firsthand. But I let him know for sure that if he'd even try it on them, then the Shandon boys would give him a rough time.

But the fortnight flies indeed, and now the holiday job is over so we say or goodbyes to all at the hotel and head off to Letterkenny to catch the CIE expressway bus down to Dublin. Myself, Veronica, Annaliese, Barney and Harry occupy the rear row of seats in the coach. O'Rooney himself is sitting a few further rows to the front and we can hear him effing non-stop to the passenger on his right. He must be happy to be below the Sligo-Dundalk parallel once again, lots of pubs to choose from again for the coming six months.

We come to the border crossing with Northern Ireland, and thereafter keep moving as the bus is not allowed to stop within the six counties. A lot of armoured patrol vehicles to be seen along the route, when all of a sudden our coach comes to a screeching halt. A lone soldier in British combat fatigues has climbed aboard and is now approaching the rear. He's holding a machine-gun at hip level, and he keeps staring at me. I wonder why, and then I realise.

The telephoto lens! I have my Canon camera with a 300mm telephoto lens astride across my laps. He keeps moving forward, not looking at any of the other passengers seated to his right or left. He is now standing straight in front of me, the machine-gun is now at my chest level. I don't budge an inch, keep looking him in the eye.

'So you like photography then?' he asks in a heavy accent.

'Yes, I do,' is my calm reply.

The soldier seems to be happy with that, I now see him turning in the other direction, and he leaves quickly towards the front door.

Goodbyes and goodbyes again at the Busaras station before we start splitting up. O'Rooney doesn't delay at all in heading off, Veronica, Annaliese and I head off to the Granges Hotel on O'Connell Street. Whilst we're having a sup at the bar there I slip out to the Aer Lingus office next door, to confirm their seats on the flight next day, and also manage to get myself a return flight into the bargain. The savings from the Shannaun Hotel can well pay for that I say. So instead of heading down to Castlebarry for the fortnight before college opens again, I'm going back to Switzerland where I'll get to meet Veronica's family. Maybe I should send a postcard to Castlebarry!

It's a total surprise for Veronica of course, as I hand down my ticket on the bar counter once back at the hotel.

The next day, and we're off to Collinstown Airport where one of Aer Lingus's wonderful flying machines is waiting to take us to Zurich. Annaliese's brother is waiting for us there, and we hit the motorway. The first stop is at her house facing the Zurichsee, and then we continue the eighty miles left to Sumvitg.

Within a few hours we arrive, in darkness, at Veronica's house, where she is so excited and she can't wait to tell them all about her Irish trip.

With my smattering of German, and a few words of Romantsch, I get along really well with her parents Joseph and Barla, her sister and her brothers too.

I awake in the morning to the sounds of cowbells ringing in the field just below the house, and the occasional shell being fired by a military training camp who have set themselves up down by the Rhine river in the valley below.

I don't waste time setting out to discover this Alpine resort, with its architecture, the towering mountain peaks, the family farm.

The family farm.

This one's a real farm, a family enterprise to say the least. When I think of Mrs Ganaghan's place in a hole north of Baltrina, I'm in a different world here. It's even prettier than old Joe Monaghan's farm, but then again even with that in those earlier days wouldn't I have been happy?

I discover a home here.

A house where I can roam from one room to the next without hesitation. At mealtimes I get to sit with all the family around the one big table in the kitchen, and evenings we might hit a deck of cards, and play some Remy or a new version of poker, something, which never happened for me in Castlebarry.

I've found a new family, and a new mother too.

In Romantsch, Barla can't be translated, so I call her 'Mumma.'

This place becomes my adopted home.

It's now well over a year since I've seen Rhona or Daddy.

Year 3

My return to Shandon, for the third year happens without me going to Castlebarry. I arrive in Limerick, and as I don't have any place to stay even for the first night, I have to find accommodation and fast.

Checking through the daily paper, the first phonecalls don't bring anything of success. Out to Shandon, and enquiries there. Nothing available for the moment. Then a stroke of luck finds me sharing a room with classmates over at Shandon town. Pricewise it's okay too, and I don't believe that I'll be able to improve on it. I have all my savings with me. I have to survive from now on. On the 28th October 1977 I pay £441 for my tuition, education travel, and examination fees for the Academic year '77–'78, and that takes one hell of a whopping chunk out of my saved monies. I still have to worry about all the other expenses, which I'll have to face during the academic year, such as the books account which is to follow. Luckily however, I managed to save an awful lot whilst working at the Shannaun Hotel. Lucky too that I haven't decided to go into medicine or such, how would I have managed to pay fees for up to seven years straight without earning anything from time to time?

But again, I underestimate the sums of money, which I'll be needing, and my reserves start drying up.

I have to find a solution. Fast.

Then a good friend of the students, Rod Costelloe, finds a weekend job for me in a small hotel in Adare. They need somebody to help on weekends in the restaurant and bar. So a rhythm for me starts every Friday afternoon after class. Rod drives me down to the hotel, where I start work immediately. I can however sleep there, and then up early the Saturday morning, busy with breakfast service, then on to preparation for lunch. A break during the afternoon, and back for dinner. The cycle repeats itself on Sunday, except that I'll leave for Shandon during the afternoon.

Then there's a little time to rest, as studies get under way the following morning for the whole of the week to come.

But the few pounds preciously and strenuously earned manage to keep my head afloat. The people at the hotel are happy with my work, and I'll be able to go back for the holiday periods, I promise the manager. So I even return for the Christmas break instead of going up north to Castlebarry or anywhere else.

That'll make for more money however. Less fun, lots less than the other students. My money problems and constant worry about it keep me isolated very much from my classmates. I can after all spend time on the airport terrace watching the wonderful flying machines coming and going, and needing little but the batteries for my airband radio. It's a cheap sport. But going over to the Shandon Arms in town or into Limerick is very much out of the question.

One day, whilst at the lunch-table, I'm sitting two tables away from the Director's table, which is by the window. He has some visitors who have been touring the college installations, and now they're invited for lunch.

'Your students here must be rich,' says one of the gentlemen, obviously impressed by the college, and the fine lunch which is being served.

'It is not the students who are rich,' replies Mr Boulens, 'it is their parents who are rich.'

I hear the remark, but daren't make an answer to that one.

I am a poor student, even with all the money that I'm earning at the hotel every weekend, but luckily Veronica starts sending some money too in the springtime, so with all and all I manage to pull through.

The year's committee are planning the annual dance in a hotel in Limerick, but I am dreading this date: firstly, I don't know who to invite, and that means me paying for two tickets as well. So I don't invite anybody, and end up turning up there, on my own, and sitting around with the classmates during the evening, listening to how they are amusing themselves.

Partaking of the festivities as if I am a bystander.

Brighton

The 31st May 1978, and my third year is at its end. It's a cold blustery day as my Speedbird jet heaves off from the runway at Dublin airport. So instead of going by Castlebarry, where I haven't been for some two years now, my travels take me to Heathrow airport and south to Brighton. I feel like it's a one-way trip. A one-way ticket to the wide-open world. A religious medal which had belonged to my mother Noreen, this on a chain around my neck, and a framed certificate signed by some representative of Pope Pius which blessed my father's and mother's wedding on the 10th September 1952. A few masscards too. I have no toys, no books, nor souvenirs of my empty youth whilst growing up at that place, only the memories of those harsh empty years. At least it's easier instead of having to haul loads of baggage.

I will be working the fourth year in a hotel there, a year of practical work.

Veronica has since found a job as an au-pair girl with a family who live in north London, so my visits up there start becoming frequent.

Nearing the end of my year down south I am on the lookout for a job, and want to move to London.

The big city. The bright lights.

Maybe the big money too.

I get a job working as Assistant Banqueting and Conference Manager at the Regency Towers Hotel in the city centre. It's a giant place, with over eight hundred rooms. I soon have duty management responsibility for the restaurants and bar areas, plus a disco.

In Brighton the job was a live-in one, and now I've had to find lodgings in the city. The salary which I'm earning here is twice what I was on at Brighton, but I quickly realise that life in the big bright city with all its lights is expensive indeed, and I hardly manage to save much.

There are a great number of us in pinstripe suits working as managers in this huge place, I'm just one of them, but I feel unlike them in that I'm having difficulty in getting on with the others on a social scale. Difficulty in joining in their conversations at the lunch table, having a laugh and a joke, and even less getting invited to any social events outside of the workplace.

On the 28th August 1979, Veronica and I are married at the Registrar's Office in Hounslow, West London. A few days earlier I'd been to my bank manager to ask for a loan, because the big money earned so far hardly sufficed to cover the cost of living in this big city, I was way down on funds, and I wished that Veronica and I might have a damned good meal on the evening of our marriage.

She becomes an Irish citizen. I write a letter to Marian House telling Daddy about the good news.

He does reply, but he's angry as hell, saying that he can't understand that I couldn't find myself an Irish colleen, and that them Continental girls have no morals to them at all!

Exams

The final exams of the fourth college year are approaching, so I'm working on finalising all the various details travelwise and so forth. Our budget is low, and we do manage to split the travel expenses with Murray, who will be driving back and forth to Limerick for the same occasion.

Paddy O'Kearney has kindly arranged to offer us the accommodation at the Glenilaun Hotel in the city, we will of course be settling for our meals. I am still going through various formalities when back in the Shandon region, and remember that I must phone Daddy about the invitations to the Graduate Diploma conferring festivities, especially as I haven't heard from him for some time now. From our hotel room, I choose to call, during office hours, the clinic on Western Road opposite the Trader's Rest Hotel where Dad is based. The secretary finds him without delay, and we exchange a few niceties, and I tell him I'm staying in the Limerick region.

'Oh?' he says.

'Did you get the college invitations?' I enquire.

'What invitations?' he murmurs.

'You know, the invitations to the conferring ceremonies, all the parents get them,' I say.

'No, I didn't see any invitations here,' he says.

'It's not possible,' I say, 'the conferring is on the October 26th next.'

'Well no, I haven't seen any letters here about that,' says Dad.

'You mean that no letter with the official invitations has arrived at the house?' I ask.

'No letters here about that,' he repeats.

'Can't you understand that the Diploma date is for next week?' I ask him.

'I haven't heard anything about it,' he continues.

'Well listen, can't you phone the college, Mr Boulens will certainly confirm that the ceremonies are taking place, and confirm that you're invited?' I try.

My memory goes back to the newspaper clipping which he'd cut from the Irish Times two years earlier and even sent it to me whilst I was working in Geneva that year. There were four students to be seen in the photo, all dressed in their black gowns and mortars for their graduation day, a lecturer is with them, and in the background you can see the faded forms of an older generation, students' parents without doubt. So he knows that graduation day is part of the college programme! It's the grande finale, it's a feast and celebration, there's the ceremonies at Bunratty Castle and there's a sumptuous meal prepared and served up to all of us by the college students at the Airport Hotel. Two years later they'll be the honoured ones.

'Oh no, I couldn't do that,' he asserts.

I have the feeling that there are lots of people coming and going around him in the office or in the corridor outside, and that I'm intruding on his time.

'So you're not coming down to Shandon for my graduation day then?' I make a final attempt, vainly.

I'm sitting here in this hotel room, Veronica is near me, I'm grateful for a few things in life, but here I am with my father on the phone line who won't believe a simple message that I'm trying to get through to him. I can't believe this.

Then I remember that on a June evening of 1970, Martin had crept down, in defiance of the ban, the landing stairs, and asked to talk to Daddy, and he didn't want to hear us out on that occasion either. All we wanted to do was talk, we didn't even ask him for a goodnight kiss, did we? So we mean nothing to him, and despite the number of promises made in the Garda station in Castlebarry on a sunny afternoon shortly thereafter, nothing, but just nothing has changed since. Britannia may rule on the high waves, but Rhona rules at Marian House! Right now my word has no value to his eyes, he is blind to my questions, to my suggestions even, and there's no point in continuing.

I hang up the phone, after all, why pay useless phone charges?

My heart is empty. My stomach is a sack of pains. Four years of hard work and study behind me, and my own father won't even be interested in seeing my diploma, the diploma that I could show him as proof of my success! What to expect now? What to do? Call the College Director? That would serve little purpose! It's not even his business to consider the particular family situation at Marian House! It's not his fault, and therefore not his responsibility to untangle things! I have to finish the exams! I need to get my diploma! When I have my diploma, there'll be no reason to come back to this damned place!

The conferring day arrives, weatherwise a fine day, but there's no sign of Daddy or Rhona anywhere, and even as we arrive at Bunratty Castle I am still on the look-out and still hoping for some appearance. There is a photographer moving through the groups of people formed here and there, getting snapshots for the local and national newspapers, and memorial photos of the students, with other students and with or without parents, you name it, they can choose. I carefully avoid the photographer's attention, preferring to wander around aimlessly around the spacious grounds. No Daddy or Rhona to be seen.

'Gerry, I haven't seen your parents,' I hear someone calling.

'Couldn't come,' I murmur, and I move on.

'Duignan, where are your parents?' I hear an authoritative voice calling. I guess it must be the College Director, but my footsteps change direction, preferring not get talking about the general situation.

I get my seated place, amongst my classmates in the left row within the great hall, its great walls towering high above my head, and await my turn to be called. Just can't understand.

'Duignan, Gerard!'

I catch the name being pronounced, and slowly glide my way towards the aisle, and move forward towards the conferring table, where I am presented with my scroll, the beeswax stamp has dried, and I read the mention 'Passed with B Honours'.

Whilst returning to my seated place, I keep watching the floor or the high walls above, have no interest in looking at the joyous crowd to be seen everywhere in this great hall, but I know that Veronica is there somewhere. That's comfort!

In the dining room at the Airport Hotel, Veronica and I have two fine places seated at the end of a table near the restaurant door. After the sumptuous meal there are various acclamations and speeches to be made in honour of, and by various of, the students and lecturers alike. Towards the end of the ceremonies, the College Director calls for silence, and from his standing position he announces a round of applause for the only college student to be married before the conferring ceremony.

Veronica and I stand momentarily to register the cheers and applause.

Something at least!

The College Director does not, however, mention that I am the only student out of the thirty-three finishing college this year whose father or parents are not present at the conferring ceremony, because 'a letter never arrived'! I know however that the Director, with his typically Swiss precision, would have despatched the letter with its invitation to Dr James Duignan at Marian House, Western Road, Castlebarry, for today's ceremony.

But I've already guessed that the letter did arrive safely whilst Daddy was busy down at the County Clinic opposite the Trader's Rest Hotel, and as the college wouldn't consider it necessary anyway to send such documents by registered courier, Rhona disposed of it as she deemed fit.

A good job, however, that the initial letters from the college in the spring of 1975 did 'arrive' at home to Marian House, otherwise I'd never be here right now, never gotten so far. Would probably have never met Veronica.

At least I've got that much.

Shortly thereafter we leave for London again, and as Daddy never visits me abroad, he'll never get to see the College Diploma scroll that I worked for and paid so hard at to achieve.

London

Life at work since returning from my graduation ceremony is becoming more and more difficult. Not necessarily because of the pressure of work there, but that I'm starting to feel uneasy about the effectiveness of my role in this career.

Then slowly through 1980, a gangrene starts setting in. It starts with an inner inadequacy to be able to face up to others, feeling painfully shy, to stand my ground, to 'face the group', a feeling of 'unknown factors' which are surrounding me, a feeling of very low self-esteem of myself, a complex of inferiority, and what I am capable of doing and achieving. Failure and its possibility seems very high to me indeed, so I start avoiding initiatives, preferring to be happy with the status quo, fearing that I might become the laughing-stock of the group.

I now realise that I simply haven't been allowed to learn the strong communication and interpersonal skills that are needed of me here, what should have been a sturdy education turned out, deliberately to be a stunted one, which could well condemn me to a lesser life, one of ignorance in social skills which could bring further shame upon myself. Without those skills I can't be a good team player, so I'm having difficulty defining my contribution to the group.

All this despite me having a professional training and background, having learned much in the Hotel College and on the ground level so to speak, but finding that I'm increasingly unable to 'sell myself' and whatever capacities which I might still be harbouring within myself to others, and especially to my upper hierarchy. They are the ones who employ me, represent the company that pays my salary. But every salary deserves results and achievements. That's normal. But now I get to feel that I've lost my ambitions, my intuition has been killed, and my spirits are sapped. That's not normal.

How to progress, how to move on, how to succeed in such an environment, and then start moving upwards on the management scale to higher achievements, when I'm already unprepared and having great difficulty 'associating' within the situation and with the people at this lower level? But I need to succeed and prove myself to those who would laugh at my failure. But who can help me here? Castlebarry? It's a long way away, and for me my daddy is even further afield. I don't believe that he can, nor will he be able to help me. Anyway, I'm now twenty-two years old, and am supposed to be a man at this stage! Be on my own feet!

Sadly, however, and whilst not daring to mention it to Veronica, I am becoming increasingly blocked in this social and professional context and life. I try to keep my head high, my face up, I put on a show, a front to pretend that everything is okay, even great! I've put myself behind a mask, as if I was at the Venetian Carnival permanently. Whilst doing nothing socially, I have become too busy for others, no time for anybody who might want a help for this or for that. I continue living as a social hermit, increasingly avoiding contact with others around me, and the flat-sharing situation out in Chiswick is hard too. Even going to the hairdressers for a trim becomes a nightmare.

What frustration, what helplessness!

One day the catering manager calls me into his office. He tells me that I've been doing an excellent job recently, but that he feels that the atmosphere of such a big place isn't the best thing for me, and that he is searching for a small country hotel, where I'll be in a small team, and better on my feet. A small team! How can I associate better with a small team, rather than a larger one, I wonder? I'm having difficulty with individual contact, and those contact situations are to found anywhere and everywhere.

The evaluation, and the result: I now have it flat in the face!

Oh, oh, the vultures are coming, I think!

I feel my body sagging in the seat, my mind worn out, what with trying to surmount unfavourable and unfair obstacles.

So here I am, I had hoped that things could continue onwards, but this chap must certainly have had a better start and follow-on to his life than I had, and now for me, it's telling. He has seen my difficulty, but I guess that he can't analyse it totally, understand its sources. But he has seen that something is going wrong here.

I wasn't prepared for this meeting, just as for much of life in general.

I sit there nodding to his talking and accepting his arguments, a monologue really, I can't offer him much for an exchange of ideas, my brain is washed-out, he's the wise one here, he's got what the job needs and what it takes to get on in the rough professional life out there. He certainly has had a happy and correct childhood and adolescence, schooling too, and support from his parents when needed. Learning how to fill hot water bottles for the dark and cold winter nights ahead and other household chores down at Mrs Ganaghan's place is hardly much of a preparation for schooling and development.

I didn't get any of that support. And I won't get any now at this late stage.

What to do now?

For a choice, I think that the pickings are slim indeed! The dice have been thrown, and I'm getting the low numbers.

Go driving buses for the public transportation company?

For a loner, it's a job that might suit me!

In my stomach the pains of total angst are welling up.

I start envying him, even despising him, not that it could be his fault, just that he can't or won't be able to do anything against my father and Rhona, the two persons who fundamentally are responsible for what has become of me, and where I now stand and sit.

Two persons for whom I now have real hate in my heart.

A small country hotel, instead of the big city and the bright lights! If I was strong enough, I'd be the one who's deciding where my next career move would take me, and not the other way round.

Just as results are needed instead of a diploma printed on parchment, I know that social skills are ever as much important as college training.

I have been allowed to fail.

I leave yer man's office, agreeing to meet him as soon as he has some precise suggestions for me.

Life, with its unhappy and unpleasant situations simply has to continue. Just like the earlier years at Marian House.

But I have an idea.

I have to move away from this city.

The 7th February 1981 takes Veronica and I to Zurich, and then to her parents house in the Alps for holidays. Whilst there, I manage to find two jobs for us, both working in a local hotel. Upon returning to London, my notice is accepted by my boss for the end of March.

I now have a new chance! At least I believe so! Maybe a stepping stone to a new future? A new life on the professional level, maybe on a social level too?

The 11th April I start working as a waiter in this small hotel.

From day one, despite my weak knowledge of German, I get assigned to the busiest station in the restaurant. It's a hell of a rough life to start. Veronica, when working in the next station, will try her best to help with traductions for me. The important thing is to keep pushing, to win over.

Little by little, my language knowledge picks up, improving my German, and the local dialect, Romantsch, allows me to be accepted by the locals. Veronica's parents live five miles down the road.

I get to the stage, however, that I'd like to start having responsibility, moving back onto the ladder again; the hotel here is rather small to offer anything.

Then one day I see an ad for a job in Geneva. Geneva, the city where Veronica and I had met in the spring of 1977. The Hotel des Béarns. A five-star hotel built in 1834, the oldest in Switzerland.

It's part of the same company that I'd worked for in England, but a different division.

They are doing considerable renovating and reorganising within their set-up.

One phone call late week to the General Manager, and I'm asked to make it to Geneva as soon as possible.

We drive the two hundred and fifty miles to Geneva on the following Monday, as my meeting is due for the next day, and before the weekend I have their reply.

I have the job. They want me in Geneva.

I will have to start on the 1st February 1982.

Chair

Mid-December 1981. We've covered a great number of kilometres in the last ten days. I'd bought our first car last month and as we had time off before moving to and starting my new job in Geneva, Veronica and myself leave Switzerland, travelling through to Normandy and the coast at Calais. From there we take a ferryboat which brings us to Folkestone, and we disembark late one afternoon.

Driving off the boat I notice that I'm low on petrol, and stop at the first filling station that we see. I step out and the lady attendant approaches me.

'How much?' she enquires.

'Forty gallons, please,' I reply.

She's standing there, the petrol pump still in her hand, and gawking at me.

'Won't get forty gallons in there, luv,' she says in astonishment, her heavy cockney accent shows that she's not too far from home. Unlike myself.

I'm standing there looking at her and my small car too, wondering if I haven't miscalculated. Then I realise that I'm no longer on the European mainland, rather on one of the British Isles, and that here they buy their petrol in gallons and not litres. I'm trying to do the conversion table but give up.

'Oh well, just fill her up please,' I resign.

Our journey then takes us up through London. We miss the circular road, and as I was used to riding my motorbike in this city the last time I was here, I find the traffic situation really stressing. Add to that driving a continental car with the steering wheel on what's the wrong side for the British traffic. We manage to make it northbound and spend a few days with Stanley and Mairéad up in East Anglia.

Then we take a gamble and decide to head for Ireland. To Castlebarry. Going home to the green fields with the rushes and the thistles, of Mayo. From here we then cut across central England, driving into Wales and catch a huge ferryboat for the crossing of the Irish Sea.

I haven't been at home in Castlebarry since May 1977, before leaving for Geneva, and that's now some four and a half years behind me. Haven't seen Daddy or Rhona in that long time. They have never seen Veronica either. But they know, through Mairéad that we're coming. Coming in off the Turlins road and approaching the town, however, I start getting an uneasy feeling in my stomach, and I'm not quite sure what sort of a welcoming committee to expect. Maybe they'll have headed off down to Kerry on some trumped-up excuse for a few days just to avoid us. Maybe they just won't answer the doorbell at all, and stay retreated in the lounge.

I decide to try a trick. Rhona might be wise, but I'll have to be wiser.

It's now late afternoon as we drive out the Western Road and by Marian House. Arriving there, I slow down on the speed, and without stopping I notice the car which is parked to the side of the garage. So far so good. I know that if the car is there Daddy and Rhona are sure to be home. They wouldn't be going anywhere for a walk without taking the car first. You wouldn't ever see them going for a walk up or down the road, they might meet neighbours, which they treat as a class of bog people; if they'd wanted to hide they'd have certainly put the car in the garage out of sight for all prying eyes.

I continue driving out for half a mile, and do a U-turn before heading back into the town. We stop at the Trader's Rest Hotel for a break, a pint of Harp and a moment to think over what we're doing.

I don't admit it to Veronica but I'm afraid. I'm real nervous. Has Rhona changed since I saw her last? Daddy wasn't at all happy about my marriage to Veronica. He had written me, asking why I couldn't find an Irish colleen, as them Continental girls have no morals to them at all! Why judge her before he's even met her for the first time? Is this him speaking, or is it Rhona who is speaking through him? Will his attitude have softened up any?

This is of course Veronica's first visit to my home.

Marian House, which is supposed to be a home to me.

After a while I go to a phone box and call Marian House. Rhona picks up the phone. I tell her that we're approaching Castlebarry town and just wanted to check if they're in. Yes we're here and ye can come over, she says.

I hang up, somewhat relieved.

We finish our pints and drive out the road for the second time this afternoon. The driveway gates are open and we drive straight in to park. Daddy answers the doorbell, this being the first time in my life that I've dared use this front entrance, and he greets us. I cross the threshold of the house which I haven't been into for over four and a half years and we follow him into the kitchen where Rhona is seated to the left side of the Aga, her cup of tea awaiting her on top of the cooker. She rises to greet us both and then reseats herself immediately. Daddy pulls over two chairs from the small kitchen table, and places them in front of the Aga. He already has a chair to my right.

The Aga fire is going great guns heating up the kitchen on this cold December afternoon as I stand facing it.

'What are you taking your jacket off for?' asks Rhona as the left sleeve starts sliding off my arm.

What am I taking my jacket off for? Is that what I've just been asked?

I can hardly believe what I've just heard! Here I am back in what is supposed to be my own home after more than four years of absence. Back in the home where I grew up, even if it was in the annexe building beside the house. Is it a home or is it just a house where I am a stranger, and am to be treated as such? If the wise men who came to visit the infant Jesus in the cradle at Bethlehem wore jackets when they arrived by camel, did they have to ask permission from Mary or Joseph to take them off? When I arrived in Veronica's parents' place in Sumvitg in September 1977, did her mummy ask me what I was taking my jacket off for?

No, she didn't.

Judging by the remark she's just made Rhona certainly hasn't changed a bit in all those years. Maybe she was comfortable too in having me out of the way for so long, and that this new visit was an intrusion on her regular and comfortable life. This is the house that my mother designed and lived in for a number of years with my daddy and Martin before she had to die from complications after I was born in a hospital in a place called Tury.

I didn't know what kind of a welcome I was to expect, but I certainly wasn't expecting this much!

My impression of relief found earlier has just worn itself out.

Do I have to ask permission from Rhona to take my jacket off and have a seat in the kitchen in what is supposed to be part of my home? Do I have to tell her that me and Martin lived in this house before she ever was lucky enough to able to marry my daddy and arrive to live within these walls, and benefit from it socially and wealthwise? The death of my mother has suited her well indeed to say the least!

I remember some of the last words that we exchanged face-to-face standing in this same kitchen the day I was leaving for Dublin to catch my flight to Geneva. It was the 30th May 1976. Shortly before leaving the house she had noticed my camera on its strap hung over my left shoulder and told me to leave it behind.

'You can leave your camera here, you'll only be wasting money on them films,' is what she had to tell me.

'It's my camera, I paid for it with my money that I've saved at the Donilaun, and it's coming with me,' I had replied defiantly on that occasion, as I hadn't liked her sharp words.

So she hasn't changed in all those years, and well I'm just going to adopt my attitude according to the continuing circumstances.

What am I taking my jacket off for?

'Because I intend to stay a while,' I reply.

The defiant answer is out so fast again that I hardly realise that I've had time to compose my phrase, and I drape my jacket over the back of the white chair.

'Now, now, dear,' utters Daddy, as he has obviously heard our exchange. I settle into a seated position on the white painted hard wooden chair, but even without any cushion I feel comfortable now, as I've managed to put my message through, and Rhona shuts her gob for a good while.

The conversation gets going, Daddy is curious to know whether Veronica likes Ireland and all the rest. Rhona then starts becoming all smiley and curious too about Veronica. We even get cups of tea and Rhona enjoys playing host to the visitors.

'Will ye be having a bite to eat, well, I mightn't be having much in the house now at all, but should have some rashers and lads in,' is her suggestion. 'Wouldn't they be grand for ye?'

I guess that Rhona's habits and expertise in cooking is something else that hasn't changed much either since we last met.

Veronica, who is sitting between Daddy and me, is puzzled as she doesn't know what the lads are meant to be. I explain that those will be Irish pork sausages. She smiles, nodding her head.

So we accept gladly.

So out come the frying pans from the cupboards, the rashers and lads from the big fridge, and soon Rhona is whipping up an Irish breakfast. It's nearly eight o'clock in the evening here. I believe that it's the first time I've had an Irish breakfast served up to me at eight o'clock in the evening. I'd be used to having a full Irish breakfast at eight o'clock in the morning, but I guess that you'd have to be not only in Ireland, but also in the kitchen at Marian House, to have an Irish breakfast served to you at this late hour.

But it's also a change from slices of buttered bread. The thought amuses me.

We're soon seated at table in the big dining room to the front of the house, from where I can have a view out at the garden. I'm now over twenty-three years of age and this is the first time in my life that I can get to sit at table in this room. This is just one of the rooms which were strictly out-of-bounds for me down through the many years I spent growing up here. This is the room where Daddy, Rhona and the other children would sit around the big table with its linen tablecloth, napkins and silver cutlery and have their Christmas lunch of fine roast turkey with all the stuffings, the potatoes, and vegetables too, whilst Martin and I would have to wait out in the playroom, our stomachs aching with the hunger, and waiting to be called in and sit at the small kitchen table with its plastic tablecloth and metal knives and forks, and be served up the remainders of the turkey, and especially the scrawny legs and dark meat. The turkey that Martin would have cursed on many an occasion because of the millions of fine feathers which would have floated into his eyes and up his nostrils when breathing, whilst he sweated, plucked, and prepared the big bird for the whole of the Duignan family.

Whilst Rhona is finishing the preparation of the breakfasts out in the kitchen, and whilst we're sipping tea and chatting with Daddy I'm admiring the amount of silver plates and other fine ornaments that are on display around the various buffets and shelves so as to decorate the room. I'm seeing them for the first time, just like Veronica. I have no idea what all the whole lot would be worth at purchase price, and when I consider that I had to pay all my way and bills and pocket-money through hotel college during my third year, instead of having the right to enjoy myself as much as my classmates, and maybe go skiing, or take a trip on one of the famous Swiss cablecars, or enjoying as many pints as they do after a hard day's work in a busy Swiss restaurant, I now feel like revolting, and slamming my fist down hard on the table and opening my gob about the injustice of it all like I've never done before. But I'm behaving here as if it were the usual habit around here to be sitting in such a comfortable armchair at a table with clean white linen and having a full Irish breakfast at eight o'clock in the evening.

How would it have happened if I had chosen to go into medicine, and become a doctor like my father? How many of those long years would I have had to pay for from my pocket?

So we have breakfast served and the inevitable and endless cups of tea. We'd already had an Irish breakfast at four o'clock in the morning before getting off the B&I boat at Holyhead, so this is my second Irish breakfast of the day. I wonder if this one might be valid for the Guinness Book of Records.

Daddy enquires if we have a B&B for the night. As we haven't had time to sort anything out, and Rhona seems to be getting on great with Veronica and thank you now, she says that we can stay for the night up in the front room. I have a feeling that the hospitality is growing on them, as this is the second time that the rules are being broken, not bad for one day I think.

No arguments so far. We accept.

We've been travelling the whole day, so falling asleep isn't a problem and we have a sound night's rest.

We awaken when it's broad daylight, and you can imagine what we have for breakfast.

Whilst travelling through England and now to the auld sod we had noticed that the weather conditions were worsening. The garden is somewhat snow-covered and this morning's weather forecast says more snow for Ireland and even into England. So instead of staying for a day or two more and getting to taste more of Rhona's Irish breakfasts at all hours of the day, we decide to pack our bags and try to head back to Switzerland, in the hope of arriving there before Christmas Day.

Still no arguments in sight, so before closing our bags I leave out the box of Swiss chocolates for Rhona and the bottle of cognac which I'd bought on the boat for Daddy, as I know that that'll be a pleasure for each of them.

As we head eastbound through the Midlands we notice that they have far more snow in these parts than in the western seaboard, and soon the green Irish countryside is now carpeted in white snow. But our little car is well prepared for winter in the Swiss Alps, with snow tyres, so we can keep up the speed and the driving isn't too dangerous for us.

The driver of one armoured cash delivery van wasn't that lucky. I'd seen where his truck skidded off the road and finished flat on its side in a ditch up in County Westmeath.

Out to Dun Laoghaire and catch a ferryboat to Wales. We arrive shortly after midnight, and decide to start driving eastwards. The road is really barren and we cover miles and miles without seeing a village or even a house. The night temperatures are bitterly cold, and we stop to cover ourselves with a blanket, leaving the car doors locked shut and the engine running to supply us from time to time with hot air. Barely an hour's sleep, and we're on the road again. The motorway conditions further south are atrocious, the lorries keep throwing snow and dirt onto our windscreen. The cleaning solution for washing the windows has frozen solid in its container from the cold temperatures of the night before, and I have to stop regularly and with handfuls of snow I manage to clean the windshield.

We arrive in Kent and stop to spend the night with Mother Alouise, who is of course over the moon to see us. The cuckoo clock, which I'd brought along on my trip in February 1977, is still hanging and ticking away the hours and days in the hallway at the convent.

Another ferryboat takes us for the short trip back to Calais. I sit at the steering wheel and wait for the bow doors to open. I tell myself that I'm going to have to concentrate on the changeover, as it's back to Continental driving. The car ahead of us gets going and I follow along the quays towards customs. We're stopped at the bottom of a humpbacked bridge and there's a queue of cars in the right lane and front of me. I forget where I am, and after many days driving in England and Ireland I can't understand what all these bods are waiting for. They're on the wrong side of the road. I shift into first gear, cut a solid line and pull out to the left and start overtaking. I'm nearing the top of the bridge just before the blind left turn when I suddenly realise that I'm on the wrong side of the road, and that all the others are waiting for passage through customs. An emergency braking, me and Veronica get the frights, and it's a good job that customs people are more interested in people's passports than their driving.

The car radio had broken down whilst in Ireland and we have hundreds of miles to cover without any music at all. We pick up a French motorway, which brings us east of Paris and start driving and driving. We're tired of all the driving, boredom and fatigue set in. Hardly a car to be seen, which is a stark change from the English motorways. I'm awakened by the rumble of the car tyres running on the gravel, which covers the emergency lane. A shock.

At the speed we were doing I would certainly have finished up like the armoured truck driver in County Westmeath, and at worst I mightn't even have gotten to have another one of Rhona's Irish breakfasts ever again.

I manage to push on until a motorway restaurant and order two of the strongest coffees they can possibly brew for me.

We've had enough for one day, so we stop at Strasbourg for the night. The next day is Saturday and we cross into Germany, and after many hours of more motorway driving we finally arrive at Veronica's parent's house in Sumvitg.

We've spent exactly two weeks on the road, and when I look at the dashboard counter I see that we've covered a distance of 5,600 kilometres from Sumvitg to Marian House and back again. But at least I've managed to take my jacket off whilst over there at Marian House, even have a good night's sleep before hitting the road again.

Christmas is coming and I don't know if Veronica's mummy will be cooking a turkey or what for the Christmas lunch, but I don't give it too much thought.

It's just great to be back home again.

Béarns

February 1982. I start at my new job. It's one of back-of-house management, with a team of sixteen persons. I'm in charge of all back-of-house cleaning, and public areas of the hotel too. All the stock control, the washing and polishing of all the cutlery, silverware, porcelain and kitchen utensils within the hotel.

Shortly thereafter, they need someone for purchasing and food control, and I get picked. This involves food costing and restaurant menu preparations in conjunction with Head Chef.

Time passes, and then the position of Assistant Food and Beverage Manager opens. Once again, I get promoted, and am now responsible for the cost controlling and profitability of the entire food and beverage operation of the hotel.

This brings me into contact, and increasingly constant use of a personal computer, with very detailed stock control programmes.

Responsible too for the planning, discussion and organisation of all the banquets and conferences in the various function rooms on the banqueting floor.

Mother Alouise

My aunt, dear old Mother Alouise, died on the 17th November 1984, after a lifetime given to the church and to the faithful.

Help us to witness Christ is still living,
service to others cheerfully giving,

Teach us to pray, and work for God's glory.
Ave Maria, ave.

Jane phones me in Geneva to give me the bad news, and tells me that I should come over for the funeral. I tell her that I don't want to do that, can't understand the purpose of it, that it's better for me to keep away from family. She insists, saying that I really should make an appearance. I don't know what to do, tell her as much, and hang up.

I really don't know what to say, what to do. For family reasons I have met Mother Alouise on such few occasions that I hardly know her, but I have also heard so much about the good she has been doing for many parish people in the south-east of England, and if only for that I feel I need to get over there fast. I'm confronted by the choice I have to make, to go or not to. If I don't, I run the risk of regretting it later, and not being able to correct my wrongdoing, and then suffer even more because of that.

But I remember Mother Alouise's good humour and chuckle from the last time I'd seen her alive, when Veronica and I had stayed with her and the other nuns during a wintery night in mid-December 1981.

I decide to go.

I can manage an early morning flight on a British Challenger BAC 1-11, and it's a short hop to Gatwick. Jane doesn't even know that I'm due in. When I arrive in Gravesend nearly everybody seems to be there. Daddy is happy to see me in any case, and I'm slightly nervous about meeting uncles and other family members I haven't seen, and who haven't seen me in ages, but for them it's easier. I hardly recognise anybody, and this my own family you know! I'm feeling uncomfortable here, I'm keeping behind Jane, asking her politely to go through the 'Who's who' in this place for me.

The Swiss cuckoo clock that I'd brought the nuns whilst on a short visit in spring 1977 is still to be seen in its place in the hallway.

Daddy tells me that funerals are great occasions. I wonder why, and look at him strangely. He says that they are great moments because they bring people together. I wonder what the hell of a family is this we have here? Do we all have to wait until somebody dies and moves on until we can all have an excuse and reason to unite? What's the point in me uniting with my dead Aunty, when during all the years gone by I wasn't ever allowed to visit her in England like the other children did, or even see her when she did come home to Longford during the summer months, Longford which is only a few miles down the road from Castlebarry?

But then again when she'd be home for her summer holidays, where would I be for my so-called holidays? Turfing, that's what. Down cutting turf and working on a lousy so-called farm north of Baltrina, turf with which Mrs Ganaghan would be able to heat her old farmhouse and boil the spring well water atop the black iron range to fill her hot water bottles at nights during the long winter ahead. Cutting turf for her and her family is more important to some people than me getting to know my relatives? Her two boys, who aren't real uncles to me, are of course too busy earning money in the tool factory in Baltrina, or on the building sites all over England. And before we'd start the day's turfing, then it was emptying their bedpans in the morning. We weren't family to them. We were their servants, no identity, and they were our masters.

You wouldn't catch them cutting turf or even being near a bog. Maybe they'd hardly know what a donkey's frothing mouth with its green teeth really looks like.

Plucking the grass barehanded too, all around the house, so that the place would have that tidy look to it.

But for me, my real family and relatives, be they in Carraroe or Longford, aren't supposed to count, and for them I don't exist. That's all there is to it, simple isn't it?

Not even the turf is an excuse, it's just a cover up. One more cover up in a never-ending line, one more to keep myself in ignorance, and others about my whereabouts and my well being.

If it's not turf in North Mayo in the summer months, it's the leaves and weeding on the great big lawn which surrounds Marian House in the autumn and winter months.

For Mother Alouise's Requiem Mass on the 21st November

there's a great church ceremony indeed, as befitting such a fine woman. It seems that the whole parish and lots more people have turned out to pay their last respects. All I hear is praise and compliments for all the fine work she had done down through her life's service to those within her church and parish, and all those in need. But I remember that I too am a Catholic, only that I couldn't ever get near to her during all those years. There were many times in my life when I too was in need, saying my Angelus prayers for all the others, but nobody ever did anything for me. Maybe Mother Alouise could have helped me, I don't know. But then she couldn't know all about the real situation within my home. When she did arrive with one of the Monsignors from America at Marian House shortly after Martin and I hit the road towards Dublin and were caught there by the Gardai, the door was shut in their faces. So they knew that something was wrong! Had they heard that some years ago one of the parish priests had been out to Marian House to read 'the riot act', but sadly to little avail? Who told them? What information did they have in their possession? Given their life-long 'marriage', as was their duty to the Catholic Church and all its belongers, they must have been concerned about my well being and that of Martin too. But if they didn't get far in their research, I can't fault them about that. Their access to Martin and myself was being blocked systematically!

They'd travelled a long way that day looking for us, only to find the door opened but immediately being slammed shut in their faces!

Sorry, no funeral today, so there's no reason that we should unite and meet and talk.

And if ye don't mind at all we'll have to be on and about our business now, do ye know?

Is that part of the traditional Irish hospitality and welcoming we are famous for? To strangers, and above all to your own family?

When the three wise men travelled by camels to Bethlehem to visit the newborn infant Jesus who was lying comfortably in his cradle, did Joseph the carpenter slam the door in their faces? Did Jesus's mother Mary, a prostitute, slam the door in the men's faces as they stood there with their gifts of gold, frankincense and myrrh?

So where does that put my father, a doctor, who is supposedly richer, financially and intellectually, than a carpenter, and his beloved wife Rhona, on the social and humanitarian scale?

So here I am sitting on this church bench with Daddy, Rhona and the others up in the front row. Then I think that it is unusual for many reasons, because my thoughts go back to my earlier years when they would all drive down to the chapel in the Mental Hospital for their Holy Mass, whilst I would have to walk the whole way down the town to my church to hear my Mass and that this might just be about the second time in my whole life that Daddy is beside me in a church for a Holy Mass. Not bad for an Irish Catholic family, eh?

Funerals are great occasions for reuniting people.

I remember the Castlebarry National School Christmas plays, which were always organised before Christmas for the parents and the other local people from the town. Wasn't my voice good enough in those days to be allowed to stay behind at school after school hours were out, to prepare and participate and sing with all my classmates upon the school stage? Or even help out in the million and one other ways of preparing?

No.

Leaves and trimming lawns.

Turf.

There's always something serious and needy to be worth doing now at all, and it might even keep a boy out of mischief, do you know?

So here I am, supposedly a good Catholic, expected to be giving the best of my voice for all those behind me to hear, praising the Lord and his good works on earth.

I sing.

> Christ be in all hearts,
> thinking about me,
> Christ be in all tongues,
> telling of me.
> Christ be the vision
> in eyes that see me,
> in ears that hear me,

Christ ever be.

Mother Alouise's coffin is being lowered into the grave. Her final resting-place is what they call it in the Catholic religion. I'm still too young to be not too far away from my 'final resting place', but with all the goings-on on the face of this shitty earth for nearly twenty-seven years now, I sometimes wonder if it mightn't come sooner than later for me. Then and only then might I have the chance to have a long-overdue chat with Mother Alouise. If the Gods in heaven can't arrange that one, then there's no more hope at all.

Let's wait and see.

I start crying. Just can't hold back. I don't know whether I'm crying for my Aunty that I've never really gotten nor was allowed to know, never will, or because of the pure hypocrisy of some people standing around the grave which now contains the coffin.

I feel like fainting.

Funerals are great occasions, they bring people together don't they?

Then I swear that one day, when I have Daddy in front of me, and I'm in a really foul humour, and that either he or Rhona will irritate me just one step too far, I'll repeat his words to him, maybe even let him swallow them.

'Day is done, the light of God shines…'

Béarns II

Back to the work schedule, heavier and heavier than ever. Then I start getting duty management assignments. This means spending twenty-four or forty-eight hour periods within the hotel walls, sleeping there too, having total responsibility for all events and problems. I cover the whole building in an evening's shift, from the staff quarters on the fifth floor, down to room service on third, the restaurants and bars, the ballroom and conference rooms on first, down further to the huge kitchens in the basement, all of this non-stop – stopping, checking, questioning, enquiring about operations, the well-being and potential problems of a sector or a member of staff.

But with the passage of time, I start experiencing, once again, the same uneasy feelings that I'd gone through during my London years. The same inadequacies and unhappiness reappears within me.

I start abusing of alcohol.

In the spring of 1986, my personnel boss at the hotel leaves her job.

She gets a job working at the County Hospital in town.

We had formed a good team together, working closely when solving the various staffing problems at the hotel, and sharing very much in general our opinions on life, the world, and so forth. She was also aware, not of my personal difficulties, but in my work the insurmountable problems that abounded. To see her leaving was like a loss to me.

But a few months later she is back, as she has a job proposition to make me.

I need to change, but what to do? In which direction?

But her proposition is just what I needed, because the social strain, once again, is getting the upper hand of me. I've learned many things in this business, such as cooking or bedmaking and tidiness, met many people, but I feel that the time has come to turn my back on this business. I can cook up a vitello tonato, or a saumon au tomate, but I can't sit down and enjoy it totally. And in spite of what I haven't achieved, or learned, I am still suffering, the treatment continues and I am still submitting. I want, and need, to change jobs. I have to tidy up my mind too. I have but one life to live on this earth.

It takes me less than forty-eight hours to decide.

October 1986

On the 2nd October I start working at the hospital. Having turned my back on the hotel business, I feel as if a huge weight has been unloaded off my burdened back, a sort of reincarnation.

My job function is one at various reception desks, taking care of the continuous flows of people who arrive there, the accidents, the appointments, sales representatives, phone communications, bleepers, the ambulance bay, the whole lot.

I'm happy, and the salary is well above what I was on beforehand.

Our son, Paul, is born on the 1st November 1987.

On the 24th May 1988, we return to Ireland for a short trip. This time we are joined by Veronica's brother and family. We rent a small cottage up in the Midlands where we can be in touch with Jane.

We decide to visit Castlebarry, as Daddy hasn't seen his grandson yet. We arrive early afternoon and we all get seated in the lounge. I try to remember if I have been seated in this room since the day that the man from the ISPCC came to visit me and look at all the bruises and marks on my beaten back and body one certain afternoon in December 1967. I can't remember.

Rhona is asking us questions all about where we've been, who we have been visiting and have we seen Jane at all? But I refuse to answer her questions honestly, and bypass with other snippets. After all, it's my own business whom I go to see and meet, and if she's having a fight with her daughter, I won't intervene. I dislike her snooping around, it's part of her ways and means of trying to control me and my movements.

The general chatter continues for another while, and then it's time to start thinking of the miles to cover before arriving back at our holiday home.

Arising from my seated position, I move towards the sitting room door. Rhona is waiting for me in the hallway.

'What are ye doing on Sunday, where's your cottage, can we phone you and meet there?' she asks. At this point she's making me truly irate.

'Listen, I can't give you the exact location, I could draw you a map, but we don't have a phone in the place,' I answer, turning towards Daddy to see his reaction. 'I tell you what, if we don't have anything planned for Sunday, then I'll call ye, all right?'

'Now, now, dear,' says Daddy.

She nods her agreement, and then hands me over a small

present, which she thought, would please me. She then shuts her gob for a bit. I express my thanks, and say that we really will have to be going.

When I arrive back in the Midlands, I open my 'present'.

Rhona has given me a mug from the Ailwee Cave in County Clare. How thoughtful, I think, she doesn't give gifts often.

But concerning my Sunday plans, I don't call Castlebarry at all, and we all return to Geneva on schedule.

Jane and Danny had gotten married, and they have given birth to a daughter, Aisling. The proud parents would like me to be the young girl's godfather, which I accept. So on the 25th February 1991 we are in the air again, back to the auld sod. Ten days holidays in front of us. Danny comes to pick us up at the airport and we stay in Longford for the duration of our trip. Jane and Danny are still having a great fight with her parents in Castlebarry, so for solidarity reasons we don't even approach County Mayo. The Castlebarry crowd don't know that we're in Ireland.

As usual, the company in Longford is greatly enjoyed, and the Baptismal is held in Longford town.

James and Rhona Duignan don't attend their granddaughter's ceremony.

Help!

It's well past midnight on the night shift at the hospital. I'm working the shift with Pietro, an Italian, and all's quiet for the moment. Then one of the hospital security guards comes near our sector, and without greeting me he calls Pietro over towards him. My workmate joins him, they take seated places, and from this discreet distance I can hear them jabbering on in their southern Italian dialect further along in the hall.

This is of particular significance to me. There is a summit here. Is the other chap avoiding me purposely? Isn't he interested in conversation with me? Why is he avoiding me? Don't I have anything to offer him, conversationwise? Since some time now, I have been persecuted by a number of unwell feelings, which have crept back into my daily existence, once again. Feelings that I've had once before, in London, and again at the Hotel des Béarns. The same ones of rejection by the 'group', an uneasiness in facing up to strangers, and others in general. Questions abound about what could I possibly bring to the 'group', will they listen to me, how will the 'group' judge what I have to say? A social phobia.

Fearing failure, I am finding myself once again retreating from all social contact, no sport, no hobbies no activities, no friends.

Whilst settled in with my new job, and feeling reasonably happy with this new team, I am well aware that any further progress upwards will be severely limited, as in this place, you need excellent social skills to move forward. Skills that I have never learned, skills, which have been, denied me since my infancy.

Now it's too late to recuperate, I'm too old. I'll have to be happy with the current salary, which I'm now earning, and that's it!

What I need now is help!

One day I read an article about psychotherapy.

The article is composed of a series of short stories about people who have had problems in their lives and ended up talking and going through psychotherapy. Behind these stories are real people, and through reading and rereading the article I suddenly find that I can associate myself with those people. I can even sympathise with them, as many of the details therein are exactly about how I'm living things now, how I'm perceiving things and especially the people who surround me.

Part of my job here entails being based at the ambulance bay at the hospital. Over the years I have been here I have been confronted with a number of dead bodies. Accidents of all sorts, but also suicides. Gunshot wounds, defenestrations, overdoses, people who walk off twelfth floor roof levels, and so forth.

One night the hospital ambulance comes back with a middle-aged man on the stretcher. He's got a clean 9mm hole to the side of his head. The blood has stopped pumping.

He's dead. Whilst checking the man's identity, one of the ambulance chaps finds a hand-written letter in the man's pocket.

He opens it and starts to read. The dead man has clearly outlined his sickness, the failure of his family to support him through this, and now he can't take it any more.

He's made a choice.

Even the specific location of his parked car is given. So he has premeditated all of this.

All he needs is a gun. The courage he must have already.

What could have prompted him to go so far? Pain and suffering, injustice, lack of care?

In the obituary notice in the local papers the message reads:

Our dear father, brother, uncle…
is sadly mourned by…

A few days later I'm talking about this case, and suicide in general, to one of the hospital priests. He tells me that once you've made up your mind it's easy to do. He doesn't say that it's a sin or anything like that. He says that when you're so far, it's nothing more than a solution to a particular situation. But he doesn't say that it's terrible, and this frightens me.

Easy to do, once you have the courage.

That frightens me.

I find that prospect somewhat shocking. That man was sick. He had his problems. He was let down by a number of people. Maybe he suffered physical and psychological pain, injustice, and lack of care. He took a decision. I feel concerned by all of this.

Because I too am sick, only in a different form. I have my problems. I have suffered injustice, and lack of care.

There had been an increasing number of occasions recently where I've been in a state of mind and low spirits that I'd seriously considered the different possibilities that I have to 'finish off' the situation. Like walking off the kerbside when one of the urban transport buses is speeding to its next bus stop, or in front of the high-speed TGV French train as it leaves the outskirts of Geneva for Paris. I've suffered physical and psychological pain, injustice, and lack of care during my early years at Marian House, and those elements have continued for a long time thereafter.

But I've never taken a final decision. Yet the elements are

there. The unhappy bits. The many lost years. The empty years, empty ones, except for the cruelty and the violence.

But Veronica and our boy Paul are there too. I have to care for them. My father never cared much for me nor Martin during all those earlier years, we were left, abandoned to ourselves in the annexe building at Marian House, left to grow up on our own, left to try to find about life and what it's worth or what it entails. All on our own. We were the black sheep in the family, destined to remain ignorant, destined to be dimwits, and fail in our education. We were then thrown out into the mainstream of life in this great big world, totally unprepared for the social and professional challenges that awaited us, nor the defeats either. I'm still very much on my own, except for Veronica and Paul. But the mechanisms which have accompanied me so far and have driven me to become what has been made of me are far too difficult for them both to understand, and there is a natural limit in what way they can be of help and benefit to me, but they are there. They are part of my life, and if I take it, then I won't be there to care for them, and that won't be of much use to them. Taking my life may well be a solution for me, but not for them.

And I have only one life.

So every time that I get near the brink, I think of Veronica and Paul who I'll be seeing at some time of the day or evening again. It won't be for the recital of the Holy Angelus at six o'clock, but maybe for a game, a joke and laugh, a meal, the cinema, a game of ball, the shopping, or some of the other daily activities. That'll be a hell of a lot more than I ever participated in any one day with my daddy whilst growing up at Marian House.

So for the parts where neither Veronica nor Paul can be of much help, I'll just have to get help from a professional.

The professionals are mentioned in the stories of people who set out to overcome their problems, and I say to myself that if they have managed to pull through and win, then I can do likewise.

I need a solution.

I need to find a good psychotherapist.

I make a decision.

A stroke of luck, one of the psychiatrists who has just left the

County Hospital has established his own cabinet in town. He can take me for a first consultation without too much delay.

The address is easy to locate, and I hover in the lobby waiting until nobody's around to find his letterbox. His cabinet is on the first floor. A small waiting room. Whilst seated, I avoid looking at the door, and bury my attention in the daily newspaper which is available.

A few minutes preceding my session, I hear the next room door opening and footsteps approaching the exit. I keep my attention turned to my newspaper, as I don't want to see the face of the person who is leaving, just in case I might be identified. Geneva's a small place.

My turn comes, and the doctor invites me to come inside. I sit down and observe him as he starts adding a few titles on his folder. With his huge beard, and the look to him in general, I think he sure looks like what Hollywood would call a psychiatrist. A few moments more, and I start wondering why I'm in here at all. Me, sitting in front of a psychiatrist? Am I mad? Me? What would Rhona say if she saw me here? Would she split her sides having a great laugh at all? She'd probably look at me queer and ask me if I'm well at all?

'Sure if you have to talk to the likes of such a man, then you couldn't be well at all with yourself, aren't you about it now?' is what she might ask of me.

I push those thoughts out of my mind.

'What's your problem?' he finally asks.

After explaining my origins I tell him the story about the oranges and chocolate bars that I'd won at the Christmas exams whilst at National School, and how they were removed from me by Rhona and shared amongst the others, whilst I got only the smallest part of my bounty. This without any congratulations on the part of my father, or any intervention on his part as to why I was then sent into the annexe building, to be left alone.

Then I told the doctor a lot about my life.

About growing up in the cold and sterile environment at Marian House and beyond.

For the following hourly sessions I started turning up at the last minute, fearful that I might meet someone leaving the cabinet who might recognise me.

From July 1991 to November 1992, I sit a total of forty sessions. All of these were based on my interpersonal activity, and the problems that I faced therewith. Specific case studies were discussed, based on an event, which would have happened more or less recently. My perceptions of the situation, the actors therein were discussed, and the debate evolved about what to make out of all of this.

After a few sessions, I started feeling really settled in with this psychiatrist chap and we managed an excellent work relationship. I didn't feel uncomfortable any more about sitting in his waiting room, and even started turning up early. I had by then realised and accepted that I had a problem, many problems indeed. So why might I be ashamed to meet another patient who is leaving before me or just as I arrive, that the person recognises me or not? It can only be someone else who too has a problem, who too has started treatment.

With hope.

The sessions always happen when I've just finished my workshift, or on a day off, and my employer is thus never aware of my problems, nor what I am undertaking to settle this mess. My sickness insurance covers most of the cost, but I still I have a part to pay from my salary and savings.

Then slowly with time, and after much reflection, observation and study, even whilst outside the cabinet, I start realising that in fact my perception of people and situations has been rather harsh, even unjustified, and that they are in fact not judging me, as I thought.

I start cooling off.

I've learned to understand that the hospital security chap is entitled, just like myself, to be free to choose whom he wants to discuss and associate with.

I start smiling. With time I've finally learned to smile, an honest smile which comes from my heart, not just because the other person may have smiled first, something which I would have so often avoided in the past, not wishing to get entangled in any contact, not wanting anything of the other person. Now I can offer the smile first, and if the other person replies with a smile or simply a few words, it's become easier for me, even totally natural for me to continue. After all, the other person maybe has their problems, and they need a smile or a chat to forget, even if it's only for a short while, what might well be a misery of life for them. That much I can do. It's even my duty as a human being.

I start associating with people. I take out a membership in a local computer club, and increasingly enjoy the company of newfound friends and contacts. I start contributing to the club and the group, helping where I can, sharing too.

I start laughing. Laughing about life, about what others have to talk and laugh about. I start feeling well in other people's company.

I stop feeling being uneasy in groups. I don't have to blush anymore when I'm with female company. The days of the 'hops' which I never wanted to attend when I was at St Joseph's College are over.

I don't feel the sweatdrops run anymore from under my armpits and down my thoracic cage when confronted with strangers or somebody who in earlier times would have been seen as, and judged as, an aggressor who wants my skin.

I have unwound with regard to many things, many potentially difficult situations for me.

It's late 1992 now, and mentally I feel like a teenager who is now approaching his adult life.

The world and the people living therein, in my eyes is and are now considerably different than in the past, but still there has been much lost time. Many lost opportunities, lost chances, lost occasions, the twist, the cha cha cha and other dance movements never learned. Much time which cannot be recuperated, but some things are now looking favourable. I feel that some of the wounds have started to heal.

But there are still all those lost years.

Many lost years.

Kerry

As happens regularly, Martin is inbound on a Swissair flight from New York for a short stay. He takes advantage of his travel benefits, and for a handful of dollars he's back with us again.

We start talking about Ireland. He says that he'd be interested in going back, and even meeting Daddy again. He tells me that a few years ago, he'd sent some photos of his girls to Daddy, but he never got a reply, so this time maybe he'll bring the photos personally.

I remember the letter from the Hotel College about the graduation day ceremony, which must have been sent, but curiously never arrived at Marian House either.

I say that I'll set the groundwork. I fly to Ireland, and even spend a night at Marian House. The next morning Rhona has to go to work, so I spend a while with Daddy in the kitchen. Just general chat. Then I suggest that we go for a drive. I'm not totally comfortable sitting in this kitchen, and anyways I have an important question for him. This he accepts and we head off out in the direction of Nephin Beg. We've covered a few miles.

'Daddy, Martin would like to come over to Ireland soon, and pop in to visit you, what do you think?' I ask of him, my hands gripping the steering wheel harder than ever.

'Oh yes, we haven't seen him in these parts for a long time now,' is his answer.

I feel an almighty sense of relief, a battle's won, as I was fearing what his reply might be.

I wonder if he realises why Martin hasn't been in these parts for such a long time now. Did he ever receive the photos of Martin's cute daughters? What with working in the aviation business, Martin could have on unlimited occasions, travelled on standby, and that for a ninety per cent discount off normal airfares, and visited this country and even his own father often. He could even extend such travel benefits to Daddy and Rhona too. But they hadn't made life an enjoyable thing for him nor for me, so why should he be the kind one now? The thought of Rhona 'jetting' to London every fortnight and boasting about it to all the people who might care to listen to her and her high lifestyle probably upset him sufficiently to have the idea dropped.

So it wasn't to be so for Daddy nor Rhona. No gifts to be made.

We turn back on our journey, and head back into Castlebarry, as I have to start heading eastbound already. I tell him that I'll be writing to Martin in Miami about our talk. Daddy seems happy.

We hug and say our goodbyes at the east end of town. I had suggested bringing him back out to the house but as Daddy says he likes the walk back through the town centre, we part here.

I leave Castlebarry, my heart considerably lightened.

When back in Geneva, I write to Martin. We start planning. I suggest to Martin that we spend a few days in the south first to discover a little of the country before heading to Castlebarry. He agrees. Martin will rent the car from the Miami end, as the prices proposed in the American publicity are far more interesting than what I can find in Switzerland. Veronica, Paul and I arrive in Shannon on the 10th August 1994. Martin is due in from Amsterdam. Aer Lingus is on strike so there's a whole mess. Jane and Aisling are already with us, and waiting too.

Martin finally arrives, and I sort the car out. We decide to split into two groups, as Jane has her car with her. We head down to Kerry, as we had never visited that part of Ireland, and also wanted to stop in the Burren area too, and visit the famous singing pubs there.

Castlebarry will wait until further in the week.

Jane hadn't met Martin for some years now, but we all enjoy her company. I notice however that Martin is slightly nervous, but I can't figure it out. There are a great number of tourists travelling these roads, and changing address every night means that mid-afternoon, we have to start thinking about finding a place to stay for the night. But it's not easy, even stressing. I guess that's why Martin is nervous. Our journey brings us progressively northwards, and we decide to stay in Longford for one night before going to Westbary for the second night and then Castlebarry.

Whilst we're in the house, Jane's phone rings, and she answers.

She spends some time standing there in the lounge, the

receiver pressed against her ear.

Then she hangs up.

'Mammy told me to tell ye that ye're not welcome in Castlebarry,' she has to say!

'What?' I ask. I'm astounded.

'That's what she said, that's the way it is now,' is all she can offer for an explanation, shrugging her shoulders.

But the message is clear as can be. Jane is simply caught in the middle.

I don't believe what we've just heard. Just like the afternoon when we were brought back up from the guards' station in Castlebarry and out to be parked again in the annexe building at Marian House a certain month of June many years ago, Jane once again gets elected to pass on a message to us. On that occasion Rhona had told her to tell us that we would never run away again. Jane had come out from the house to announce that one. Now she has another message. I don't like what I hear this time either.

Is this to be a repeat of the welcome and the question that I was asked when I started taking off my winter jacket in the warm kitchen at Marian House a certain December afternoon in 1981? Rhona had asked me what I was taking my jacket off for on that occasion.

I've been to Ireland already, to get the ground work set, Martin has travelled many thousands of miles the whole way up from Miami, and I too have spent time and money flying and travelling from Switzerland, paying for Veronica and Paul too.

Martin has certainly been waiting for this occasion for many months now. More so than I, I can well imagine. He hasn't put his foot inside Marian House nor seen his father since leaving St Joseph's in June 1971.

Over twenty-three years, without any contact between father and son whatsoever having passed, and we now have worked on, and firmly believed in this chance of reconciliation of some sort.

With only less than forty-eight hours to go, we're not welcome!

Why did Daddy accept to have Martin visit the house when I'd put the question to him many months ago? If he had changed his mind in the meantime, couldn't he have written to us, and advise us of same? Why announce this at the last minute? But then Jane did say that Rhona had been on the phone, so she was the one giving the orders here. That was not our daddy thinking there, it was Rhona who was plainly thinking for him! White simply isn't white any more, it's a darker shade of grey, if not totally black, and that's what our father is being told!

Unwelcome! In what is supposed to be our 'home'?

I'd started the preparations for this trip, and the goal has to be fulfilled! That's what I think about it right now!

Martin is becoming really nervous. Maybe deep down, he was expecting this from Rhona or some other form of confrontation? Maybe that was why he was so nervous all along.

Paul and Aisling are playing together at the kitchen table.

The rest of us are standing there in the lounge, then moving nervously back and forth to and from the kitchen. Totally numbed by the news! I start thinking real fast. We are going, I decide.

But I need to invent some sort of a scheme.

We'll just have to tell a lie. Even if it means breaking one of the Ten Commandments.

'You didn't tell Rhona that we are all present here in the lounge when she called, did you?' I ask of her.

'No,' Jane replies.

'Then officially for the moment, she doesn't know that we with you when she called?' I ask.

'No,' Jane answers, 'but she'll be calling later again.'

'Fine,' I say to her, 'whenever she calls back again, and if she still insists that we aren't welcome, you should tell her that we have already left for one night's stay in Westbary anyway, and that therefore you can't transmit to us her message.'

She hesitates.

'When you requested, a few years ago, you could count upon our solidarity, then we didn't go to Castlebarry when you were having the problems with your mother because of Danny,' I remind her. 'She's your mother, but apparently she hasn't changed much now, has she?'

Jane agrees to pass on the message, even if she hasn't much of a choice.

Well, doesn't the phone ring a little later on. We all slip into the kitchen, closing the door, and stay real quiet.

Jane answers the call.

We stay hushed up. When Jane finishes on the phone she explains that she has given the message through to Rhona, who has seemingly believed her story. Rhona insists, however, that Jane arrives at Marian House well before we should be expected to do. Jane had said that we were thinking of arriving early afternoon, so that for her to arrive mid-morning is no problem. Rhona seemed to be happy with that solution.

Daddy hasn't been on the phone. Only Rhona.

But we had to invent and tell a lie. It's even against my religion to do so.

I am somewhat happy too. But we still have to face Rhona. After what she has tried to achieve, she has in any case shown us clearly what she thinks of Martin and I, but she has betrayed herself there. She has just shown that on the triangle between the three of us, nothing, simply nothing, has changed in the twenty-three years that Martin has now left the house.

To safeguard the situation, I have had to invent a lie, and convince Jane that she'll tell that lie to her own mother. But Jane, who has also been on the receiving end of her mother's wrath, knows what she is made of, what she's like, and doesn't need much convincing here. I figure that we will just have to be stonehard with any further attempt on Rhona's behalf.

But we're going. That's what we've come so far for. Rhona or not.

Martin is mighty uptight. Me too, somewhere deep down.

The following day Martin, Veronica, Paul and I all head towards Westbary to spend the night there. Jane stays in Longford, and we'll see her again tomorrow. Driving westwards through Castlebarry is somewhat emotional for Martin, and as I drive out the Westbary road I slow down as we pass Marian House. Martin stares at the place as if it were a haunted house. He doesn't seem to be very happy about the prospects of being within those walls within the next twenty-four hours.

'Aw, shucks to it,' he says, 'let's go somewhere else tomorrow. I don't want to go into that place!'

I swallow hard.

'Martin,' I say firmly, 'Veronica, Paul and I are going there tomorrow. And you're coming with us, okay?'

'Well, I guess so,' he nods hesitantly. He doesn't really seem convinced. I keep driving westbound.

The tourist season is running full steam here too, just like further south. We can't find accommodation in town, so we head back out the Castlebarry road to find a B&B place. We manage to find a small place. We are still only ten miles distant from Marian House. Collectively, many miles from Miami and from Geneva.

For Martin, it's twenty-three years timewise, thousands of miles flown around the planet for his job within all those years, and now we're within ten miles of Castlebarry. But we're a world apart from Marian House.

'What name will it be in?' asks the owner of theB&B.

'Ah, Duignan,' I say.

She has a gawk at me.

'The Duignans from Castlebarry?' she enquires.

I suddenly remember that the Irish still have this innate curiosity for searching from strangers all the titbits of information, which they could then talk and chatter about. Like where are ye coming from, and where are ye going to, and how long will ye be staying, and isn't the weather keeping up mighty well at all now recently?

'Yes, from Castlebarry,' I offer, before anybody speaks up.

The woman is eyeing me up and down as they say here. Probably curious to know why we aren't staying at Castlebarry at all.

'We have a lot of friends to meet in Westbary this evening, have just arrived from the south side, but will be over in Castlebarry tomorrow,' I try to justify things.

'Oh, sure don't I know Dr Duignan well at all now, a great man himself now!' she says, 'and Rhona too!'

I sense that Martin, who has been standing to my left, has started having enough of the gab. I throw a glance towards him. He doesn't seem to be impressed at all by the lady's politeness. But this is Ireland, I know of that. Martin has been away for so many years now that he has probably lost a little of the feelings and niceties of the auld sod. He must have, in the back of his mind, his memories of the real Rhona, and what she had said, concerning us, over the phone to Jane yesterday, not what the lady's perception of her might well be. Playing bridge is one thing, playing family members off, pitting one against the other, is another matter. A serious one.

'Well, we'll have to be moving now, I'm going for the bags,' I spurt out. I have to cut this conversation short.

We deposit our bags in the two rooms. Martin and I take one room, Veronica and Paul the other.

We head back out to the car, and drive the mile into town. The centre is alive with tourists, so we head down to the harbour. Towards the Ashauny Restaurant. A restaurant which I am familiar with. We have an enjoyable meal, what with the Irish stew and fish specialities, which are available.

Leaving the restaurant, I am leading the way towards the front door.

'Hey, you guys, let's check this out!' exclaims Martin.

I turn, and see him pointing towards a small poster, which is pinned on a display board. I retreat, and move closer to see the object of Martin's attention.

'It's, it's John Hannon,' Martin is surprised as he gesticulates towards the poster, 'he's playing here tonight, I don't believe this. We've got to check this one out!'

I move and look at the poster. One look and the face on the photo is instantly familiar to me. Just as it is to Martin. John was one of the neighbours' children at Marian House, was Martin's age, they'd been to school together, been to London together, flatshared together, played and enjoyed music together in the mid-seventies.

And then he'd lost all contact with him. Martin hadn't been back to Marian House for twenty-three years. He hadn't seen John Hannon either for nearly as long.

Neither had I. The last time that I'd seen him was at the Donilaun Hotel during the summer stint of 1974 that I'd done there. John was there with a group, all geared up with their bodhrauns and old Irish traditional instruments playing for another of Martin's classmates who was married that day. The function had finished so late that I was the only staff member around, and the musicians were so hungry that I went for a raid on the hotel kitchen, and they'd all settled for apple pies.

That too was the last that I'd seen of John Hannon.

But Martin had recognised him without a doubt. So had I.

I wonder if he'd recognise Rhona on the street in Castlebarry without such a doubt?

'My God, it's him all right,' I acknowledge.

'We'll have to come back for that, they're playing this evening,' says Martin.

'No problem,' I say, noting the time, 'I don't want to miss him either.'

On the way into town, I explain to Veronica a little about what I know of traditional Irish music. We wonder if Paul will be able to stay up late, as our B&B is a stretch away from the harbour.

We return to the restaurant at the announced time. The musicians are running late, but that's not a problem as we allow ourselves some comfortable seated places. A few pints of the cool stuff, and the conversation gets going. Then the band arrives. There are eight of them altogether, and they have taken the seats reserved for them opposite.

John Hannon is there amongst them. He hasn't seen us yet, but Martin and I recognised him instantly. The instruments are now being tested and tuned, the guitar strings adjusted, the opening notes played. Words go back and forth, eyes staring and straining into the emptiness, cigarette smoke rising from butts held in mouths, all hands busy holding instruments and busy strumming. A hand goes to one of the pint glasses of the cool stuff which have appeared out of nowhere, and which is then lifted to a mouth, savoured slowly and then calmly replaced on the table. Back to more strumming of chords, notes to be played, glances are exchanged and heads then nod in agreement, minds concentrate on the serious job ahead.

Then the opening burst starts. The whole place goes silent as the musicians give the best of their strumming and their voices for all to hear, admire and appreciate.

A pair of hands starts clapping. Then the crowd bursts in too. The musicians keep up the tempo, they've heard the feedback from the bar patrons.

The clapping subsides as all settle in to a taste of the best Irish traditional music that I, and I judge many others, have ever heard. I glance at Martin. It would appear that he has settled into a kind of calmness. I'm happy about that. It will help him, and us all, to forget what has happened these last thirty-six hours, and that we can enjoy some of what one might call the better side of what Ireland has to offer. Let's forget the human hypocrisy for a short while, let's enjoy some of what the human being is good at too. Like playing music.

The strong notes continue for another while. Martin asks the barman if he couldn't ask John Hannon to play a few notes for him.

'Martin who?' John raises his eyes towards the barman who is crouching over the low tables. He points in our direction. John sees Martin seated opposite me and smiles, then stares in disbelief. He changes the tune and starts playing.

After this one the group takes a break. John comes over to greet Martin, and then sees me too. It's been a while, but that soft peaceful Irish accent hasn't moved much, and we are sure all happy to see each other once again. I introduce John to Veronica and Paul. A short chat and John has to get back to the music. To the work.

After a good session the music winds up, and John doesn't delay in joining us again. After so many years, there are many things to talk about, many things to be related. I just hope that this is helping Martin to keep his mind off the event, which is planned for tomorrow.

It's late night when we finally leave the restaurant bar, and head back to our small B&B. John has explained to us that his sister Brenda has a small restaurant in town, so a meeting is fixed there for mid-morning. We head over and what a pleasure for Martin to see Brenda again. I remember her too. More chat, which helps me keep my mind off this afternoon. But the time moves by incredibly fast, and soon it's time to leave.

In the direction of Castlebarry. To Marian House.

'I don't know,' says Martin as we head out of town and eastwards.

'You were the one who initially asked and talked about your interest in coming back to meet Daddy,' I remind him.

He doesn't reply, and we keep moving. I switch on the car radio.

The few remaining miles are quickly covered, which is probably better that way. Soon we are the open driveway gates, and I manoeuvre the car in towards the house.

Marian House.

Twenty-three years.

The time is shortly before three o'clock.

We approach the house by the front door. Martin would not have dared done such since the mid-sixties at least. During the early years we could use only the side door to the kitchen for access to the house when allowed. Or the door to the annexe building.

Daddy opens the door. He smiles at the sight of us all, and I wonder if he was against us coming to the extent that Rhona was on the phone to Jane only two days ago. Maybe he wasn't even aware of those discussions. We enter the kitchen, where Jane is already seated at the top of the kitchen table. She smiles at me. Rhona rises from her seated position as we cross the room. I'm ahead of Martin, and then I retreat a little to let him pass.

'Hi Rhona,' says Martin.

'Oh, hello Martin,' she has to offer.

Handshakes are exchanged all round.

Greetings too for Veronica and Paul.

Daddy has started pulling up chairs, and aligning them in a semi-circle in front of the Aga. It's summertime here, and I don't have a winter jacket on my back. So Rhona can't get to ask me what I'm taking my jacket off for. But she might try something else.

I sit down nearest Rhona. Veronica to my right, then Daddy and Martin beyond him. The chair furthest from Rhona.

The chat gets under way slowly. Daddy, who is seated beside Martin, is curious to know what life is like down in Miami. Rhona is sitting in the corner, fidgeting and adjusting her seated position regularly. Jane is still smiling every time I take a glance in her direction. Rhona, who has already met Veronica before, gets talking easily with her.

At a point in time I have the feeling that the conversation is getting a little strained.

I have an idea.

'Daddy,' I say, 'why don't we take a quick trip out to the airport, Martin and I'd be interested to see the place, how it has changed?'

He agrees.

I cast a glance at Veronica. She says that she'll stay with Rhona and Jane with the children.

'Just a half an hour or so,' I say as I look towards Rhona. Her head is still wagging all over the place.

We three leave through the front door, and take seats in the car. Daddy is up front beside me, Martin sits behind. I'm about to turn the ignition key when the rear left passenger door flies open.

'I'll be having a seat with ye,' says Rhona as she slides in beside Martin. My God, I think! How will Martin react? Her sitting beside him?

What's she coming for? What's she after? Can't she trust us both with our father for half an hour? Is she afraid of something? What? Something that might be said about her? Against her?

One thing is sure. She doesn't have the intention of leaving us three alone, and together, even for a short while. She has to be present, to hear everything that will be said, told, questioned or debated.

There's no way that we two sons can have a father to son discussion, without interference from her.

Even after twenty-three years of absence and separation.

It's total control. Total manipulation.

I turn the key, and engage reverse gear.

This little rental car is a tight fit for four adults. Martin is right near her. Will he explode with anger? I'm slightly worried about the possibility of that happening. After all, I'd invited Daddy to join Martin and me. I hadn't mentioned nor asked Rhona to come along.

She'd decided to invite herself and trot with us.

It's self-service.

We ease out onto the road leading into town, and by now

Daddy is already busy with explanations about all the changes in the town. The new roads, the new housing estates, the new factories.

After all, a lot can happen in twenty-three years.

We arrive at the small county airport. The single Cessna 172 sitting out in front is a sharp contrast to the queue of long haul jets that Martin gets to see each working day at Miami International.

We order a few glasses of beer at the bar, and sit chatting. General chat, until we decide to pick up Veronica and Paul as we'll have to start heading out.

We don't mention the phone calls and the messages that Jane had received at her house two days ago.

No fights so far.

We arrive back at Marian House again, and announce our departure.

Handshakes and some hugs in the kitchen and again in front of the house. Jane and Aisling will be staying in Castlebarry. Rhona is busy looking at the surrounding houses, hoping maybe that the neighbours will notice and recognise Martin, whom they haven't seen either for so many years.

Martin is holding one of Daddy's hands, and his shoulder with the other.

'I'll be back next year with the girls,' he says.

'That'll be fine,' says Daddy.

It's half past four as I turn the ignition key.

With many thousands of miles and worries behind us in preparing for this and we've spent roughly one and a half hours at Marian House.

We stop in town and without delay order a few pints of the cool stuff. We're surprised but pleased that things did work out better than expected. Martin then says that he'd have preferred if we had done this at the beginning of the trip instead of this late in the week. Now I know why he was so nervous these last few days.

Then we hit the road, direction of Shandon airport.

Dying

It's early summer again and as on a number of occasions before, Jane and Aisling come to visit us in Geneva. As usual we enjoy having them join us for a few weeks, so many things to talk about, the goings on in Ireland and so forth, and time to spend at the swimming pools, parks and shops in and around the city.

I ask her about Daddy.

We're seated comfortably at table one evening and she tells me that healthwise he's not doing too well at all, and I can sense that she's worried about the continuation of the situation. This news doesn't worry me too much though, Ireland and Daddy are a long way from here, I don't feel enormously concerned by events going on over there.

They have hardly returned a fortnight to Ireland, when the phone rings, and Jane is on the line one evening. I'm expecting her to say how things have been going since returning home, but she is going on about Daddy's health condition, how he's hospitalised at the hospital in Galway, that he's really going downhill now and that it's a question of days only, and that I have to come home without delay. Why in Galway, which is miles down the road from Castlebarry, I wonder?

So here I am standing in front of a decision that would probably have turned up in my lifetime anyway, but that's not what's the difficult part.

To go or not to go, that's the decision that is disturbing me. Why should I go? What for? To talk to my father? To talk to my daddy? Is he my daddy or just my father? To talk about what? To listen to him, and wait for the moment when we're just the two of us if that is manageable at all, and maybe he might tell me that he's sorry? Sorry for the way things have turned out for me and Martin? Sorry for having ruined the half of my life, and that I still am having to carry the burden of my earlier sufferings. To go home and confront Rhona once again, and listen to her great gab, and her Christian way of thinking and be running in and out of churches and praying at every given possibility?

So now I have to go to him?

When I'd see him strolling through his vegetable patches at the end of the back garden years ago, I'd have enjoyed it if he might have come over to Martin and myself and kicked the ball around with us, but did he ever come? No, he didn't, preferring, it would seem, to care more for his rhubarbs, scallions, and the blackberry tree at the centre top of the vegetable patch than for us, the first children of the household!

Did he ever take me on his knees or hold my child's hand and ever express any kind of fatherly love towards me. No, he didn't!

When Martin dared the evening ban to come downstairs after we'd been sent to bed, but still did it and asked him one June evening many years ago to talk for a few minutes because we were fed up with our miserable lives, and we needed him to listen to us and hopefully sort out the situation, did he accept to hear us out? Did he come to us? No, he didn't.

Where was he or what was he thinking, or what had he been told to think, when I'd write to him from secondary college asking for a few more shillings because I didn't even have any more money to buy enough exercise books for my homework? At one time I had so few coins left that I was forced to split one book into four chapters, starting with my sums on the front page and then turning to start the history from the rear, and the Irish and the geography somewhere in between. Which might have been just fine, but when two teachers asked to have my copybook handed over for checking during the evening, I couldn't possibly give my book to both at the same time, which made me the laughing joke with the teachers and others too.

'What's with ye at all Duignan, you a doctor's son with no money?' Did he reply without delay and send the coveted sums? No, he didn't!

When I wrote him to tell him that I was getting married to Veronica in London, did he show any signs of happiness and wish me (or us both) good luck or send us a greeting card? I didn't receive any card, but a letter in which he expressed his astonishment that I couldn't find an Irish colleen like everybody else instead of a Continental girl, who have no morals at all over there. Was he prepared to accept Veronica, who might have been good enough for my Catholic upbringing? No, he wasn't.

When Martin wrote to him from America years ago and sent a few photos of his wonderful daughters, did he reply? No, he didn't!

When I'd write from the Shandon airport address asking for money because I'd soon be running out entirely, none left with the postage stamp paid for, the few pennies left wouldn't even buy me a small packet of biscuits at the airport self-service, saying I have nothing else left to eat until the morning and am still hungry, did he reply without delay? No, he didn't! He dallied!

When I phoned him from the Glenilaun Hotel one afternoon during the month of October 1979 to talk about the hotel management graduation conferring ceremonies that he was invited to, and as the invitation letter apparently never arrived at Marian House, did he accept what I had to tell him or judge it not important enough to even check it out with the college and then turn up for what should have been a joyful day, an important step in my professional life? No, he didn't!

Did he accept our invitation when Veronica and I were preparing our church wedding in February 1980? No, he didn't!

Is that what anybody could expect from their daddy? Or was he just a father to me? The Gardai told me many years ago that a father is obliged by the law to provide shelter, food and clothing to his child, and unless negligence can be proved thereon, the law doesn't provide alternative care or support. But those are the laws of this earth, man-made laws, they cannot be God's laws. Even Rhona, who is an adult, has her own set of laws. God's laws tell us, through the Holy Bible, that we must love each other, care for each other... But does a daddy love and care for his child more than a father does? Is a father a lesser person than a daddy? I don't know. I know the way things went in my family, I know how things went for Veronica in hers, and how they accepted me into their household, without hesitation or reserve.

A daddy?

A father?

And now I'm expected in Ireland!

Why should I spend a fortune of my money and time off too to go back to visit him at his hospital bed? When I was at the same hospital many years ago, sent there to be out of the way from

Marian House because of a tummy pain, he didn't come down to visit me. When I was in need, he never was aware of my distress and never made a move towards me to console me.

I tell Jane that I'm not coming and I leave it at that.

I spend my days and time saying that he was hard to me, and there's no reason why I shouldn't be so hard with him too. In the Holy Bible they talk about an eye for an eye, a tooth for a tooth. I find all kinds of excuses to justify my thinking and consistently block all of Veronica's arguments and suggestions.

The days continue to go by, and with a 'special mission' at my workplace keeping me extremely busy I don't have much time to think about Daddy, nor my father, or anybody else in Ireland.

Jane phones again as she doesn't see me or hear anything of my intentions at all. At first I refuse to budge on the matter, but continuing with the phone discussion I then accept to give it a little more thought.

I'm listening to the music coming through my headphones in the trolleybus on my way to work early Monday morning of the week. Many of the other passengers have their eyes closed, some have their heads leaned against the side windows, their subconsciousness probably still well alert for their own bus-stop. A young black boy is having a laugh or a joke, his mother seated to his right, she starts smiling, as does the man who must be the father, and is sitting in the row behind. They're communicating, they seem to form a normal and happy family. I feel happy for the young fellow. He's one of the lucky ones.

'In the name of love…'

The lead singer of a rock group is giving a throatfull of his strong and vibrant voice for his song and message.

'In the name of love, oh oh, in the name of love…'

Then I notice the elderly gentleman standing a little further away from me. He is grey-haired, and he reminds me of Daddy. I wonder where an old man would be going to so early in the morning. To work? At his age? He must be on an old-age pension, for goodness sake! I look around in the bus and I see elder men everywhere, old men all over the place, some grey haired, some darker, some without any hair at all but in every elderly face I see Daddy.

I'm barely aware of the bus moving onwards to its next stop, or how far I still have to go to arrive at work. I'm not aware either of the total calm which reigns in the public transport bus at this hour of the morning, but I'm aware of the images going through my head.

A face.

I haven't seen Daddy for many months now, but I can still remember his greying hair, and he may have changed somewhat since my last visit home.

I know however that I'd recognise him anywhere.

Daddy's face.

He's to be seen everywhere on the faces of these elderly men who surround me.

The drummer's sticks are keeping up their perfect rhythm without missing a beat, and the guitar chords are being strummed with a consistency and increasing energy.

'In the name of love, all in the name of love…'

The bus pulls in at another stop, and when I look out through the window, I see a man, another old man moving slowly along the footpath, leaning upon a walking stick as he quietly continues his leisurely pace across a nearly empty pedestrian area.

Daddy's face again.

Then I decide.

Right now.

I have to go.

I have to get back to Ireland before it's too late.

I decide that I have to do this for myself, for my own conscience. Jane and Veronica were right after all. There's not much that can be done for Daddy now, but if I can get there before it's too late then maybe I can get to hold his hand and touch him, talk with him and tell him that it wasn't all his fault, and that despite all my current and continuing inward suffering and exile I forgive him for what he did wrong to me and for what he never corrected down through the years now bygone, and if either the nurses and doctors or a shot in the arm can't do much, well what I have to say might just be what he needs to hear during his final days before leaving this earth and joining my mother Noreen in the cemetery in Ballinagarry way up in the Midlands.

Don't I have to go now because all of a sudden it might just have been too late and I would regret my stubbornness for the rest of my life? Of course I can't get through to him and talk just like that right now, and put the question to him, so I don't know, can't possibly know his thoughts and feelings about his situation and his life. When I'll get there I'll have lots of news and stories to tell him about what Veronica, Paul and myself have been up to since our last meeting in August 1994. Maybe he'll have a story to tell me too. The story of his life, what he's had for one, what he'd been going through and thinking all those hours and years of life that we hadn't spent together, what might have been better for him and us all in our lives together at Marian House. I know that he has a story to tell. My cousin Patricia visited him a few years ago at Marian House. During the afternoon and whilst Rhona was out preparing the tea and cake in the kitchen for the visitors, she and Daddy managed to take advantage of the few minutes of calm and discretion to get talking. He had told her about the things and events that had gone wrong during all those years and that he'd wished that they'd have been otherwise.

But fate had its hand decide that it wasn't to have been otherwise.

Then he had started to cry.

That's how I know that he has a story to tell.

A story which covers part of his life. Because all of it, I don't believe that it'd be covered in a few spare minutes.

A lot of lines and words, tears too.

I too have a story to tell. A whole lot of lines, a whole lot of words.

Tears too.

Not necessarily the same lines or words as in Daddy's story, because he can't know all of the story that I have to tell, as he doesn't know all of the details that I've had to live through in my life. I've had to live it, suffer it, bear it out and when I've had enough and can't take any more I'd just go overboard. He's never seen me cry, never seen me kick a wall, nor thump and thump endless times my fist so hard into the concrete until the blood flows from my white knuckles and I have to bandage my hand to cover the wounds. He's never seen me the days when I just don't want to have anything to do with hardly anybody on this earth, when I couldn't look or smile at a girl without blushing and turning the other way, nor bear to have friends or any company around me, nor talk with the stranger who has just greeted me, nor greet the other motorbike rider who has just pulled up beside me and waits too for the traffic light to go to green, the days that I'd rather sit in my corner and brood upon my life on this shitty earth, not being able to fit in anywhere. The days when once again, I'd live my internal exile, physically present with, but socially cut-off from, those surrounding me. A waste of time from the short life we spend on the face of this earth.

My internal exile.

Many lost years.

Many empty ones, except for the free violence.

But unlike my daddy, I'm not on my deathbed yet, so my story can wait until I have more time to spare.

But it will have to come. It will, for my serenity, my sanity, that of my family and those surrounding me, have to come one day. For the sakes too, of all those who had to spend their childhood's growing up being uncared for, unloved, rejected, discriminated against, beaten physically, psychologically and emotionally. Destined to grow up and become a black sheep in the family. Being thrown into the mainstream of adolescence and adulthood as a social freak, totally unprepared either for any of the joys or for the roughness of social and professional life in the great wide world the other side of the twin lawn gates at Marian House or elsewhere.

But I decide that it's Daddy I want to see and not just my father. Somehow I believe that if he had been allowed to do so during his lifetime, maybe he might have managed to be a real Daddy to Martin and I and not just a father who provides shelter, food and clothing to his boys. That would be practicing God's laws, and not just the earthly ones. Nor Rhona's laws.

'In the name of love…'

I have to act, and fast.

'In the name of love…'

I tell my department boss that I need a week's holiday, I tell him about Daddy's sickness and he obliges by giving me the following week off. When my coffee-break comes I'm on the phone to a good friend who works in a travel agency in town, and without delay he gets me a seat for a charter flight the coming Saturday, a rental car too, and he'll have the travel documents within twenty-four hours. I then phone Veronica, I don't tell her about the old men I've met on my way to work nor the images of Daddy's face to be seen everywhere, but she seems mighty pleased that I've decided to go.

'But you really have the tickets?' she asks.

'Sure, the seat is reserved, ticket and documents coming tomorrow,' I confirm.

Veronica's parents are staying with us just this week, but when they hear of my departure they decide to stay on a few extra days. I know that Veronica will enjoy the company whilst I'm trying to see what could possibly become of a lightning trip to the auld sod.

Finally I'm even looking forward to the trip, am happy with the decision that I've taken, and I need a break from the sheer amount of work here too. I phone Jane to tell of my impending arrival. Saturday morning out to the airport with us all, and then through check-in and goodbyes before customs. Through the tunnels, security checks, and shortly thereafter I'm seated at a right-side window on board and can see Paul, Veronica and her parents way away on the public terrace. I wave a white handkerchief from time to time, but I don't believe that they can see me, as I don't get any waves back. The flight is running late for air traffic reasons and I start getting worried about the whole drive I still have to put in before arriving in Galway this afternoon.

A lot of people on this flight. A lot of chatter going on around me. A lot of people, each of them travelling for their own personal reasons. Holidays? A wedding? A funeral?

All of a sudden I feel terribly alone, and want to cry. But I don't know what or whom to cry for, and could I possibly have a meal tray and something to eat or chew to get my thoughts off my suffering? But no meal tray can appear whilst we're sitting on the ground, so whilst the two seats to my left side are empty I am left to my thoughts, which isn't too bad either.

After some time the captain announces over the P.A. system

that he is cleared to go, and I hear the jet engines which have started to whine.

I want to go too.

Through my window I can now see the hot exhaust gases streaming rearward from the starboard engine. A gentle rumble from the twin engines and we start moving away from gate thirty-four, two left turns and we head out to the runway. The weather is excellent today, very few clouds to be seen, and we head for Runway 05, which will lead us out over Lake Geneva and then over towards France. A right turn and we are now aligned with the centreline. A few seconds later, a roar is to be heard as the throttles are opened to takeoff power, and the big jet starts picking up speed with an increasing tempo towards it's pre-determined take off speed, which leaves me pinned hard to the rear of my seat. As the nose is rotated into the air I can still see Paul, Veronica and her parents on the terrace. A few seconds more and we're gaining speed and altitude so quickly that there's no point in straining my neck rearwards any more.

Next stop, with this wonderful flying machine, is Ireland.

The excellent weather means that there's no turbulence today, and mind you that's the last thing I'd want right now, and whilst climbing there's a fantastic view out towards the Swiss and French Alps, and the Mont Blanc behind.

The Mont Blanc.

Europe's highest mountain peak, straddling the French and Italian border area. For the many years that Veronica and I had been living in Geneva, we had hoped that Daddy might come one day to visit us and that I'd show him the majestic mountain. It sure beats Slieve Nephin any day. I'd even take out the car, and we'd go for a day trip down the sixty miles, through the Mont Blanc tunnel and into the Aoste valley in Italy. But he never came to learn of the ninety per cent standby discount that he was entitled to because of Martin working in the aviation business, and never came to these parts, so now I'm wondering what sort of a perspective he might be having of the snow-capped peak or Slieve Nephin in the near future.

No turbulence in the air, in my stomach only.

Then a left turn, levelling off and we're over the French Jura mountains and are already settling into cruise altitude.

'What will you be having to drink, sir?' comes the polite suggestion.

The soft Irish accent is something I hadn't heard recently, and already I'm feeling like I was already on the auld sod. Feels like the real thing.

The turf fire can wait.

'Oh, I'll have a cool Harp if it's available.' The can and goblet are soon handed down. Meal service follows, and then some time to meditate.

'Ladies and gentleman, this is your captain speaking, we will shortly be starting our final descent into Dublin, so would you please fasten your seat-belts, check that your seats are in the upright position and ensure that your tables are folded in their position,' the message booms over the cabin paging system.

Into Dublin, car pick-up, get lost once again in the west end before I pick up the motorway, and start keeping the speed pedal down at maximum. Then I swing onto the main road bringing me towards Galway, crossing towns and quiet villages as I move westwards. I have but a little time to admire the countryside here, it certainly hasn't changed much since my last visit, and for some things it's just as well that way indeed. For other unchanged things I guess it's sad, even too bad, but there's little than you can do sometimes.

Now I'm driving along through the lush green open countryside, overtaking the odd tractor or the odd horse-trailer being hauled by big jeeps. Red painted barns to be seen on both sides of the road, their great volumes stocked high with some of the summer's hay crop. Odds and sods of farm machinery idling by gable ends of the red barns.

Lots of cars sporting checkered flags, which are dangling from their aerials, or through open windows. Drivers and excited children all sporting the same colours on their tee-shirts, all caught up in the weekend match fever. I don't know which team they're supporting, or who they intend to give a slashing and show how to play ball. There's a young boy out kicking his ball in his front garden behind the low whitewashed walls. The goal posts are up in one side of the garden. A garden, which I think, might be big enough to put a full-sized football pitch in there. A car parked up at the top of the long majestic driveway. Smoke drifting lazily up from the chimneys. People are at home. I'm not home yet. Flags posted high up on the ESB electricity poles out the front. Flags up in the neatly trimmed garden too, attesting to the same team fervour. I think of Marian House, where Daddy would often listen to the Gaelic football matches on a Sunday afternoon if we weren't going down to visit Mrs Ganaghan's that is, but he'd never put up the Mayo nor Longford colours out the front of our neat lawn. A great match, as the wireless man would be heard to say.

'This is a great match here in Crooke Park,' he'd be heard to say, 'a match of two halves, the first half and the second half.'

The third half always starts and finishes in the local pubs. Except for Daddy.

The neat lawn that Martin and me helped to trim and keep in shape all down through the bygone years. Now that he's getting nearer to death I wonder who's going to do all the gardening now?

I see hitchhikers by the roadside from time to time with their cardboard signs, but I don't have time to slow down and stop and ask them where they're coming from and where they're going to, and sure if there's anything I can do for an Irishman or a tourist who's come from far-away places to visit this beautiful land sure I'd be happy. I might even enjoy the company along the many miles ahead, but I have to keep up speed and push forwards.

Groups of sheep grazing leisurely in the meadows, one black-headed fellow is down on his front knees to get his share of the fresh green grass. Something must be giving him a pain in the neck. They sure seem to be taking their time about it, but Irish stew isn't on my mind right now anyway. I'll try one later. As the saying goes, where one sheep goes, they'll all follow.

Bars and lounges straddled all along the way, both sides of the road, some fine old country manors to be admired, striking contrast to the small groups of tinkers caravans, parked on lay-bys and sometimes selling garden ornaments.

Just like the generations of people around, I see the generations of houses straddled near the roadside, starting with the primitive one and its tiny windows, some of the stones have stumbled down around its ruins in the field, then the intermediate one with a red corrugated iron roof which might hold a few cows or other farm animals. Then the modern one adjoining the first two, great windows letting the sunlight stream through, the walls of many colours, and some having pebbles or sea-shells set into the cement, or ivy creeping and growing slowly on the facade. These are the modern bungalows of Ireland, with their satellite dishes fixed high up on the gable, the booms pointing skyward, towards the heavens, the bad weather and all the rest.

Is this rural Ireland, or is it global Ireland? Do people still go to Holy Mass on the Sunday, or do they watch it on a satellite chain? Tomorrow will be Sunday. How will the parish priest collect the Mass Offerings? Via the Internet?

But not all the houses have had the same destiny. There are many others to be seen on both sides of the road, with great sheets of grey corrugated iron blocking their windows and doorways. Houses in a considerable state of disrepair, nobody there anymore to take care of them, whitewash their walls, nor trim the briars, the thistles and the general wildness about the place. Those sons and daughters must have moved on further afield, one way tickets on the B&I boats or Aer Lingus's wonderful flying machines to far-away lands and the fortunes waiting to be made, the sufferings to be endured, the lifestyles to be enjoyed.

I've moved on too. Further than some, a lot less than others. Does that still make me a son of Ireland, or a tourist amongst these meadows, the rushes, the thistles, and green vales? A prodigal son maybe? The prodigal son did return, didn't he?

But Veronica and Paul aren't here to admire the settings.

Billboards up advertising B&B and hotel accommodation, B&Bs for the tourists. Am I a tourist? In my own home country? But then I never had much of a chance to visit and get to know this country. Mostly all I got to learn during my early summer holidays was to cut turf north of Baltrina. Never got to visit Longford nor the other fantastic regions that this beautiful country must have to offer. So now I'm back as a tourist.

'Ah, a pint of Harp please.' I need a drop of the cool stuff to cool my nerves.

'Where would you going to at all now, and hasn't the weather been holding on just great the last few days praise be to the Lord himself?' asks the middle-aged barman, his left hand around the glass, the other clenched around the wooden tap.

'Galway,' I offer, and as I've just hopped off a plane I haven't a clue of what the weather's been up to at all in these parts over here.

'And where would ye be coming from at all on such a fine day?' says yer man, eyeing me as he certainly hasn't seen me in these parts recently.

'Geneva, in Switzerland,' I fill him in.

'Jasus, do they have any jobs going over there?' he asks. 'Sure, the whole country here is going to the ruins now.'

So he's taken me as a tourist and he wants the whole story I think, but at his age I wonder if he'd care to pull up his roots and move on. I did it when I was young, and wouldn't care to now.

'Ah no, it's not the way it was years ago,' I explain, hoping that he'll he satisfied with my reply.

'Ah, sure I'll take that,' he says, and I know it's worked. The questions stop.

A few chaps are crouched around a table near the window facing the street, a television screen fixed high up on the wall shows some training sessions for tomorrow's Grand Prix somewhere. Otherwise hardly a word to be heard.

The pint is up front and its coolness adds to that of the temperature inside the quiet room.

Leaving the pub I brandish my car key and once again I head towards the wrong side of the car to find the driver's seat. When I find the right seat I'll still put my right hand down groping for the gear stick. Wrong again! The thought amuses me, as this isn't the first time that it has happened, every year it's the same. Too much Continental driving in between. Maybe I should come back to Ireland more often.

Some dark clouds have appeared on the horizon since I'd walked inside, pushed onwards by the strong westerlies which I can feel on my cheeks, and I guess that we'll be in for a rinsing fairly soon. I continue. An old tractor and trailer are parked by the roadside. The odd shower would do them no harm to wash some of the country earth off the wheels and sides.

The N4. Westbound.

Across the bridge over the Shannon river at Tarmonbarry.

'Welcome to the Warm, Wild, and Wonderful West of Ireland,' the huge road sign reads.

My destination is Galway.

The green fields of Mayo with the thistles and rushes will have to wait.

A railway line appears to my left, its double tracks carving out a track through the wild countryside. No train to be seen, maybe none more comes this way. I wonder.

A series of sharp bends is ahead. SLOW, SLOWER, DEAD SLOW, is painted on the road's tar surface.

Then:

SLOW
ROADWORKS
AHEAD
300m

A sign announces roadworks coming ahead. So there is some work to be done in these parts. What I'm wondering however is whether I have to slow down, or is it that the roadworks are advancing slowly? Approaching the site I can see the telescopic arms of the huge yellow excavating machines which have been swinging back and forth with their earthly charges. I stop at the provisional red traffic light, put my gear stick into neutral position, pull the parking brake, cut the engine and have time to admire the works which have been going on. Yes, the great machines have being tearing down trees, ripping up what's left of stubborn roots, removing bushes and grass and clearing great expanses for the widening of the road. Must have been a bad patch I think. A few poor souls may have even lost their lives on these winding stretches, and now the strain of all the ever increasing traffic and the continental-registered trucks is just becoming too much. The living souls just like myself are after the quest for higher speeds, live more stressful lives than the earlier generations. But I've travelled along some great stretches of road today, some parts have been widened, and widened again so much that some walls of the older cottages are now right up near the hard shoulder of the roadside.

Ireland of the changes. Money from Brussels being pumped into EEC improvement schemes. Ireland of the Eurospeak. What's with the Gaeilge nowadays? Is it of use anymore?

The light is perched atop its metal pole, controlling the one-way traffic, the base secured by a few sandbags. Propped neatly up in front I see a great metal panel with the inscription WAIT FOR GREEN. I wonder if you have to tell and explain everything to the people in these parts or what? This might be one for the Guinness book! I smile as I see my light going to green, I restart the engine, slide the gear into first position and advance slowly through the work site strewn with loose chippings and past more giant machines, their tracks having rumbled over the coarse ground, steam hissing as they had laid a strip of fresh tar, and the journey continues.

The threatening clouds have moved away by now, having showed very little signs of rain for this end of the county, and looking skyward towards the widely dispersed clouds which cast their meandering shadows over the meadows, a high-flying aircraft is seen heading west. The low clouds are moving too, just like the four wheels below me, and for a moment I think that the big jet is nearly motionless in the sky. But a few short seconds, another look and its white jet streams clearly leave a mark of its onward passage and journey through the air and time. I've been up in the air and back down again today, and my journey continues too. A few miles further, and the few droplets of rain left on my windshield have become part of memory.

Other people journeying too, as I get overtaken by a fast moving foreign registered car. Is he a son of Ireland returning home too? For a funeral? Maybe for a wedding at the Donilaun Hotel down at Baltrina?

I arrive late afternoon in Galway, only to find that there are two big hospitals here, and I'm in the wrong one right now. Back to the car and I hurtle through the maze of traffic and am trying to keep my thoughts in line. Then I recognise where I am, and the building too. This is where Rhona packed me off for ten days stay many years ago because I had a pain in my tummy at Christmas. Why the hospital in Galway, which is miles down the road from Castlebarry, and not the smaller one at home? I spot a B&B place nearly across the road from the hospital and enquire for lodgings.

'How long will you be staying?' enquires the young lady.

'Oof, no idea,' I say honestly, 'two nights maybe more, I have a family member in the hospital.'

The girl nods, she's probably heard that line before.

'I see,' she says, and then we're talking prices.

The price isn't cheap, but I need to be near to Daddy, so I accept.

I leave the car in the parking to the rear, and briskly walk the short distance in the hospital direction. Going through the huge parking lot out front I can see that the buildings haven't changed at all in so many years, and the front door is easily found. There's nobody attending the reception desk at the moment, so I continue further into the corridors beyond.

Towards St Enda's ward.

But the ward names above the doors are all written in Gaelic, and I don't understand it much anymore. I see one door, which is marked as being the intensive care ward, still unchanged too since those early days. A nurse appears out of nowhere.

'Excuse me, but where is St Enda's ward?' I enquire hurriedly. Having sat for so many hours and now having to rush through endless corridors has me panting now. She guides me towards the right area, and I stop at the nursing station.

'Hello, I'm looking for James Duignan,' I am still heaving for breath.

'Oh, you mean Doctor Duignan don't you?' a nurse questions.

'Yes, yes.'

She guides me to the ward door, and the first bed inside to the right.

I stare at the person who is lying prostrate and still in the bed and nearly covered by the drab hospital sheets, his head propped up slightly, the strands of his thin white hair still straying down on his forehead. I thought that I'd recognise Daddy anywhere I'd meet him, but I can hardly recognise him now in this state. Then I remember the elderly men in the trolleybus in Geneva, which is a long way away by now and the images of Daddy's face that I saw there, and then that I'm looking at an old man here too.

Daddy! Is this him? Can he really have become so?

Then my gaze wanders slowly around the bed. Aunty Mairéad is seated there to my left side, Rhona seated opposite with her white hospital gloves all on and fidgeting like mad, her hands fidgeting as if she wasn't expecting me, the boys are leaning against the walls at the bed's foot and to the right.

Aunty Mairéad then retreats a little, which allows me to move up the length of the bed, and I reach forward to take Daddy's hand in mine and lean downwards to kiss his cheek.

'Hello Daddy, Gerry's here, I've just arrived,' I say aloud.

Another kiss on his cheek.

I straighten my back waiting for a reply, but there's no movement from him, no sign of a reaction. Is he sleeping, or what? A long heavy breath out and a violent heaving of his chest shows me that he is still alive, but what is happening here?

A hug for Aunty Mairéad, I shake hands with the two boys but having not seen them in so many years and my current emotional state means that I get their names mixed up, one of them says it's all right and that it happens all the time.

A light kiss for Rhona.

More heavy and drawn out breathing as I stare again at the bed.

Daddy!

'What's happening here, why isn't he talking?' I enquire.

Aunty Mairéad speaks up.

'He's been like that since Tuesday, a sort of a coma, won't talk nor anything, do you know?' she whispers.

No, I didn't know, and it's not helping me here.

Tuesday.

Tuesday was the day that I'd bought my ticket, with the hope of getting to meet Daddy again. When I was a boy in my younger years I was always shut out in the annexe building which they called a playroom adjoining Marian House, or down the back garden when the weather was fine enough, so I didn't get to meet Daddy often, except mainly after saying the Holy Angelus in the evenings at six o'clock, and often thereafter I got cruelly beaten for things which I didn't do or weren't my fault anyway and to see him before prayers often put the frights in me because I never knew what was coming my way. In any case there was never any contact or fatherly love, and I don't think at this stage of the day that things are going to change because Rhona is still around the place, she's gazing such a lot at the bed. But I wanted to meet him again, especially as it may be the last time to hold his hand and touch him and have a talk about the country and how green it still is looking at all, or about anything else that might get his mind off his current medical state, and maybe a chat too between father and son which I believe happens in all normal families. Even though our family was never a normal one I was looking forward to listening to whatever he'd have to tell me, and I could tell him that I want to forgive him for all the wrong things he had done, and the undone things too, and that it wasn't always all his fault.

But now he's not talking nor chatting any more, and I won't hear his soft Irish voice again, and that was part of what I came for, not part of a bargain, just part of what I was hoping for from him and for me.

No contact here. Nothing doing.

'Can I have a word with his doctor?' I ask.

'He doesn't have a doctor,' replies Rhona.

I don't believe what I hear. As a doctor my dad spent his whole professional life down at the County Clinic in Castlebarry and travelling around and up and down the whole county giving schoolchildren in school halls sugar tablets for vaccinations, and giving older people shots in their arms, and listening to their pains and giving them advice and tablets or ointments of all sorts to ease their sufferings.

Who cares about his suffering here?

He doesn't even have a doctor!

'You mean, no doctor for him?' I say in astonishment.

'No, all we can do is wait, nothing but the waiting now,' she adds, 'it's his heart, which is strong, that's what's keeping him going.'

Rhona is sitting there with her head nodding all over the place, adjusting her plastic gloves and looking smart indeed. I wonder if she's going to start smiling soon about the whole thing or not.

'Well, isn't it great now that you came now yourself?' is all she finds to say.

I hear other people moving about the ward, some coughing and groaning too as they try to support their physical pains, and then Aunty Mairéad offers me a chair. I falter a little, and then she beckons me to join her outside in the corridor. I follow her to a point where we are well outside hearing distance of the others.

She asks me what I think of the situation.

'I haven't been expecting it to be this bad and hopeless,' I have to say, 'but have you seen the way Rhona is?'

Since my arrival she has just sat there, with total coolness and offering little to say.

'That's the way she's been taking it,' she says.

I'm not sure, but I think that she's rather cool for someone who is about to lose her husband. But maybe she has been waiting, and preparing for this moment for over thirty years now.

We return to the ward.

So here I am back in this hospital where I had to spend a week for a pain in my tummy many years ago, a long way from Castlebarry, and I'm slowly getting another pain in my tummy again, this time from the hunger. I haven't eaten since leaving the plane and it's telling.

But right now I just have to sit down on the chair which Aunty Mairéad kindly pulled up for me, taking Daddy's outstretched hand into my palm, and I slowly start to cry.

Rhona doesn't move an inch.

I gently squeeze Daddy's hand once again whilst watching his face, hoping for something. Maybe there will be a change for the better. I caress the back of his hand with my thumb.

Nothing.

'Mind yourself, you should be putting on gloves you know,' says Rhona as she adjusts hers once again.

I'm still looking at her, and wonder what kind of a joke this is.

'It's an infectious ward here,' she says.

I stare at her with puzzlement.

I think that she's overdoing something here. Just outside in the corridor I have seen the lines of potted plants which are being attended to by an elderly man, who judging by the identity bracelet on his wrist must be a patient himself. The staff here don't seem to be too concerned by germs floating around any potted plants and why not further down the corridors and into the wards? If I want to hold my daddy's hand in my palm during the last few hours or even days whilst he's still with us then Rhona won't stop me. He doesn't have a doctor coming near the bed anyway, so they aren't very concerned about the germs and viruses.

Time seems like an eternity here now.

Then suddenly Rhona says that they should be going now. They're not hungry at all, as they were in and out of the hospital during the afternoon nibbling bits and pieces, but it's time to start heading home to Castlebarry.

She enquires where I'm staying and as I've found the small B&B just opposite the hospital I let her have the phone number there, and as they're all off to Castlebarry now we agree to meet tomorrow in the morning.

'And will you be all right, now?' Rhona is enquiring, seemingly very concerned about my well being.

I'm nearly forty years old now I think to myself, so should manage, I think. I nod.

When they leave I return to Daddy's bedside and sit again holding his hand crying. This is the hand that would beat me, on many occasions, many of them trumped up by Rhona. The hunger pains in my stomach are a reminder that I still haven't eaten. A nurse appears to empty a bowl of water into the sink in the corner. I ask her if I can come back later in the evening.

'Ah sure, yes,' comes the reply.

I lean forward towards Daddy's head.

'Listen Daddy, it's Gerry here, I'm going out to get a bite to eat, and will be back in later on, okay?' I whisper to him.

No reaction.

A kiss on his cheek, and I rise to head out. Before leaving the foot of the bed another look, still hoping, and I turn to reach the ward door. A word with the station nurse, and through the long corridors towards the exit.

Out into the fresh evening air. It's a cool evening and the fresh air is welcome, and sure is a hell of a change from the suffocating insides of the hospital. I go back to the B&B place to have a look at the bar downstairs, but they don't serve any food evenings, so I'm not even going to sit down for a pint of Harp, I mightn't manage to stand up again. The city centre is a short walk away, and I stroll over there in the quest of a bite to eat.

I return later to St Enda's ward and Daddy. I pull up my chair, and move towards him.

'Daddy, it's Gerry here again, just got back from the town, and can spend some time with you now,' I say, squeezing his hand gently. Still no reaction.

So I stay seated, stroking the back of his hand from time to time, talking to him when I find some courage and desire, sometimes leaving my hand beside his, hoping that he would know where to find it if desired, but he doesn't come, other times I just remain silent, my hands clasped and upon my knees.

It's getting late, darkness has fallen outside, the amount of activity and noise in the ward is now decreasing sharply. It's been one long hard day, physically, emotionally and I'm knackered.

I lean forward and start whispering in his ear, because what I have to say doesn't concern anybody else in this ward.

Just the both of us.

I tell him what I think about the way that things have been happening all these years, I let him know that I have an impression that he might just already understand most or all of what I've just told him. I tell him not to worry, that finally I don't hold any grudge against him, and that for my part I pardon him.

'Okay, Daddy?' I question, but I know that he won't be able to confirm reception of the message that I brought in my heart all the way from Geneva, a city where amongst others he never came to visit me and Veronica or Paul, and where we have set up our home. I doubt he will ever.

I can't be sure, but I have a feeling he's got my message, and I'm happy about that.

I rise from my seated position.

'Okay, Daddy, I'll have to call it a day, I'm staying at the B&B

just across the road,' I explain. 'I'll be in early to see you in the morning, all right?'

A kiss on the cheek, a squeeze of his outstretched, and still motionless hand and I bid him goodnight.

I leave the ward, and head for the exit.

Arriving at the parking gates, I fix my sights on the pub in the B&B place opposite, and right now I need a pint or two of cool Harp to soften my emotions.

I'm happy about my monologue but especially I'm happy that Daddy wasn't shoved off and left to die at the hospital in Castlebarry instead of the one in Galway. That way I can talk to him more than I've ever managed to do whilst growing up in the playroom or out weeding and picking the leaves in the gardens at Marian House.

Dying II

Seated comfortably at table in the morning and having a hearty Irish breakfast is indeed an enjoyable way to start one's day. Today is starting well for me indeed, with the cornflakes, the rashers and lads, toast and tea galore. No stress, no rush. I am the only client in the restaurant at this time, so the service is fast and well-attentioned, and I take all my time to savour the meal, the hospital of course just across the road so there's no rush.

After breakfast I head over across the road. A beautiful day is announced weatherwise, and I nearly feel like I am on holidays. Arriving through the front door I note that the hospital's new day has gotten off to a busy start and there's a lot of activity in the main hall even if it's only Sunday. I head to the right for the chapel where I take some time and kneel to say a few prayers for Daddy.

Many minutes later and I'm on the way to St Enda's ward. The gardener is still there tending to his potted plants out in the corridor. I pass him and stop at the nurses station. Everybody is busy at this hour so I go directly into the ward and towards Daddy's bed.

'Good morning, Daddy, Gerry's here with you again,' I whisper into his left ear, before sitting down beside him. I continue by taking his hand into mine from time to time.

A little later I tell Daddy that I'm going out for a short walk, and will be back again in a short while. On the parking lot in front I meet the boys, and Jane, who has taken her turn to come down to visit Daddy. I tell them that there is no change. I'm happy to see Jane again, but saddened by the fact that it had to be so soon again after our meeting in Geneva such a short time ago.

The rhythm of Sunday and Monday repeat themselves very much indeed. The hearty Irish breakfast to start the day, then visiting the chapel and Daddy in his bed, popping in and out from the hospital to break up the day a little. Before leaving each time and upon returning I tell him about my intentions, so he'll always know what I'm up to. Taking time to go for walks in the city, and finding quaint little bookshops and restaurants down by the city centre and the docks. The weather is really keeping up, and strolling the time away through the clean city streets and alleys is a real delight indeed. The whole place is bustling with tourists and young people, and there's a permanent air of holidays and joyousness around. At lunch-time the others will join me to grab a bite and we always enjoy a good meal, and we spend time strolling down by the Corrib riverbanks, and as I haven't met the two boys in so many years we have lots of things to talk and laugh about.

Just like real brothers.

Monday it's Rhona's turn to come down, as Jane will stay with Aisling in Castlebarry. The young girl is still too young to understand what's happening here in St Enda's. Early evening we head down towards the Spanish arch and find a table in a fine restaurant where we enjoy an excellent meal. Thereafter we stroll leisurely back to the hospital where we spend some more time at Daddy's bedside. As usual they will be heading back to Castlebarry for the night. I tell them that I'll stay on a while with Daddy and that we'll be seeing each other in the morning again.

The hours are punctuated by me heading out from time to time, telling Daddy that I'll be back shortly.

'Goodnight Daddy, and I'll be seeing you in the morning,

okay?' I say as the darkness has fallen, it's late, the ward is quietened down now, and I have to get some sleep.

He is still lying there motionless, just as he has been since my arrival in these parts. The long heavy breathing process is punctuated and separated by what seems to be a lifelong silence. But he's still alive and I feel that within the last three days I have managed to spend more minutes, more hours of my lifetime with him alone, and be able to talk without interference from Rhona nor others.

It wasn't to be so for long more.

Tuesday morning, the 10th September 1996, my alarm clock goes off and I'm looking forward to another good Irish breakfast. I don't know what is the reason, but I have a real good appetite here, maybe it's the fresh clean air, I wonder, as I settle in at table.

I stroll over to the hospital and arrive at St Enda's ward. I'm approaching the ward door, and I grab a sight of lit candles which have been placed on a high table which is placed at the foot of the bed. I notice a part of a black garment sleeve, which is moving around. I have a feeling that something is wrong. I retreat a few steps and see a nurse in the station. She rushes to me, takes my arm and we move slightly rearwards towards the wall.

'I'm terribly sorry, Mr Duignan, but your daddy has just died,' she announces, and now I know what the candles are for.

'When?' I ask.

'Just a few minutes ago, if you want to use the phone you can use our one in here,' comes the reply.

Firstly I want to go to Daddy.

I go to the bedside, and kiss him on the cheek. I have to sit down and cry. I start talking to him, and I hope that he can hear me.

This is the inevitable point in his life. Nothing I can do anymore, but I've already said to him what I had intended to do before leaving Geneva. So that's a success.

I have a cooling feeling in my heart that I have been allowed to live, and nearer my father than never before, even if it was for the final hours of his life.

But mine has to continue.

I return to the nursing station.

'Do you want to make a phone call?' the nurse asks.

'Yes, please,' I accept.

The nurse gives me the switchboard operator. I call Veronica in Geneva.

'It's all over,' I announce, 'Daddy has just died.'

A silence.

'How are you keeping?' I ask her. 'Are your parents still with you?'

'No,' she says, 'they left for the railway station half an hour ago.'

I know that when her parents leave after visiting us they always leave an emptiness behind in our flat and hearts, and now I know that there's another emptiness too in Veronica's heart.

Even if she had met him only twice.

I don't stay long with her as I have to make other calls, including Castlebarry.

'Were you there?' enquires Rhona when talking about the precise minute of Daddy's death.

'No, I arrived a few minutes afterwards,' I tell her.

From her voice I sense a deception and have the impression that that's the only thing that counted for her. Or is she maybe afraid that Daddy might have come out of his coma, even if only for a short while, and somehow managed to talk to me, to tell me something? Something, which I shouldn't hear of, know of? Might he have told me his feelings, as he had done to my cousin Patricia many years ago, and as such ask me for my pardon, before he goes to meet his God and maker? But Rhona doesn't know what I had said to him the other evening.

I'm the last one of the family to see him alive, and the first to see him on his deathbed, isn't that enough? Was I expected to sit and pray for a whole fortnight at Daddy's bedside like Aunty Mairéad did with old Uncle Terence down in Rathagan?

The other children are already on the road down to Galway she says, and they don't delay in arriving. When they arrive here Jane seats herself on the left side of the bed, and looking at her I can see that she has real difficulty in assuming and accepting what's just happened. She keeps looking at Daddy's face as if hoping for another sign of life, just one. But now there's even less sign of life than that of the preceding days.

More phonecalls to be made, and Fintan joins me to go to the phone box which is just at the parking entrance. At the exit I hold the door wide open for a young couple who are leaving with a newborn baby.

Death and life.

'Have you ever read Arthur Hanley?' I ask him.

I talk about one of his books, the setting is in a big hospital, and you have all the ingredients for an excellent novel.

Life and death, and the rest in between.

We agree to meet in Castlebarry later in the day, as the funeral parlour people will be driving down to Galway for the corpse during the day.

I want to head out to Carraroe to meet my mother's family who are still living out there. I go to visit Megan who is living in the house where my mother grew up. Amongst other things I talk to her about the letter she wrote to my Aunty Sally in the spring of '58 talking about the hardship after my mother Noreen died in another hospital on the 17th February 1958.

Today's date is of course 10.10.1996: Daddy had married my mother Noreen on 10.10.1952. Forty-four years earlier, day for day.

When I arrive in Castlebarry late afternoon I get to the phone box beside the Post Office. I have to call Martin in Miami and I know that with the difference in time zones I should find him now at his flat.

'Oh hi there Gerry, what's up?' he says when he picks up.

'Daddy died this morning,' is all I can manage.

'Damn it!' he says.

'Will you able to manage it over for the funeral?' I ask, telling him that it's for Thursday.

He seems terribly mixed-up about the whole situation.

'The girls aren't going to forgive me, I had promised them to visit Daddy, and now this,' he adds. On the 1994 visit when Martin had met Daddy for the last time he had promised before leaving Marian House that he'd come back in 1995 with his two daughters. Daddy was even looking forward to that.

He doesn't know what kind of time that he might get off from work, and if he could possibly make it to Shandon by Thursday morning.

'Call me again in twenty-four hours,' he says, and we decide to leave it at that for the moment.

Wednesday morning and the local and national newspapers carry Daddy's name in their Deaths columns, and there will be a wake at the funeral parlour late afternoon.

I'm wondering where the two boys have gone to. Rhona says that they've gone down the town. I head off with the car and start a light pub-crawl. But I don't find them anywhere. Later on I learn they've been off on their own to Westbary.

I'm dressed in my best clothes and a dark tie and standing beside the boys. Rhona and Jane are seated to our left and nearer the door. There's a near total silence as people start coming in through the open doors and come along the line of ladies seated and on towards us boys before continuing towards the coffin to pay their respects to Daddy.

People.

Loads and loads of them coming and going, loads and loads of hands meeting mine, loads of serious faces staring at mine. Loads of people that I don't know nor have ever seen, many of them of an older generation, but I have a feeling that Daddy certainly knew a lot of people in these parts, people whom he had probably treated at the Clinic or at their homes during the many years that he was a doctor in this town and county. Fintan, with an accountant's precision, stops counting when he'd shaken the four hundred and fiftieth hand, and then gives up.

With a pre-arranged signal we know that we'll have to proceed with ceremonies and the corpse will be transferred to the Church of the Holy Rosary in Church Street. Whilst Rhona is at a discreet distance I move forward to look Daddy in the face for the last time. Brushing the tears out of my eyes, I incline towards and kiss my right palm, and then place it on his forehead.

He is lying there, and despite the cold deathly look I find that there's a peaceful and serene look to his facial expression.

'Dear Dad, may your rest be eternal, and that you find the total peace that has eluded you whilst on this planet,' I have to say in French, and then I move on. But God apparently knows all men, therefore many languages, and I'm sure he'll translate.

The coffin lid is put in place, and the screws are tightened, as I start to leave.

We all decide to meet again in the evening and go to have a meal down at the Trader's Rest Hotel.

I have to get to a phone again and call Martin.

I can sense that he's in a real state of distress and is very unsettled, he says that he just won't be able to make it, and even if he could he wouldn't be sure as to what he wants. I don't force his decision but quietly I admit to myself that it's probably better for him that way.

'No, I'm not coming,' he says, 'carry on without me.'

I feel a strong sense of relief sweeping through my whole system.

It would be better for him. I know that much.

Evening time comes, and we're getting ready to head out for the meal.

'Off ye go now,' says Rhona, 'I'll be minding the house, in case any of the neighbours come around.'

'You're not coming with us?' Fintan asks.

'No, no,' she affirms.

I remember the day when we are all together for Mother Alouise's funeral in 1984, and Daddy said that funerals are great occasions because they bring people together.

Now we are all together again, this time for Daddy's wake, but Rhona doesn't think of it that way it would seem, or she's just feeling awkward about sitting at table with her three brothers. So we are not really together as a family.

We leave for the restaurant without Rhona.

When we arrive back up at the house sure there are neighbours who are in for the tea and biscuits and the chat.

'Oh, Gerard I'd like you to meet the Donoghues,' Rhona introduces me to the couple, 'you know, the neighbours?'

'Hello,' I greet them, but as this is the first time that I meet them, I don't know who they are. I later discover that they have been living in the house next door to Marian House since the early seventies.

Never got to meet them before today.

So I guess that not all the people living along the Western Road are bogside people for Rhona.

Tomorrow it'll be Thursday and burial will take place after Holy Mass. Each of his children present will get to say a short prayer which has been composed for the Mass. I'm sitting in the kitchen with Rhona seated opposite me behind the Aga fire. The others are out of the kitchen for the moment.

'I'd like Martin's name to be mentioned at the Mass, especially as he can't be with us today,' I say to her.

'Oh, you couldn't possibly be doing that,' she objects.

'What do you mean, and why?' I want to know more.

'Sure you can't be mentioning names of those who are absent, only those who are present in the church, that's the way they do it, do you know now?' she tries, weakly, to defend her position.

The other children suddenly arrive into the kitchen, the conversation stops there, and I'm left with a terrible frustration in my mind.

Time to get ready, so I head upstairs to what was my bedroom in those earlier days. I have a view through the window and out over the rear lawn. To the right I can see the hedge which separates our garden from the neighbours one. The hedge through which my messages wrapped around two stones went many years ago to be intercepted by the Hannons.

Messages?

Whilst being alone in the kitchen downstairs one afternoon I had used a knife to cut a banana in two parts which didn't please Rhona at all and I got beaten for it. My message to the neighbours was a cry of help on that occasion, as Martin wasn't here with me then, and I just needed to talk to somebody. The neighbours certainly did react, but the news for me was just going from bad to worse as it resulted in me getting the worst beating of all the beatings in my whole life.

I look at the bed, which is located in front of the window. This is the bed where lying prostrate on my tummy, with Rhona's powerful hand behind my neck pinning my young and weak body down, and with my arms and legs swinging and thrashing in all directions from the pains and suffering being inflicted upon me, that Daddy with the heavy electrical cable mustn't have been sufficiently satisfied with the lesson being meted out to me, and went downstairs to fetch the broom handle.

Then the intensity of the beating went onto an ascension, a higher level, a crescendo and tornado of blows raining down upon my young and fragile back, excruciating pain, a feeling of total helplessness and lack of any self-defence to confront my torturers. The rat that I'd cornered in the schoolyard, after a slight scare, went free. This was a beating and a thrashing non-stop. Non-stop, until the broom handle broke and Daddy cursed, because that wasn't the way he was expecting things to turn out. Did it have to be the broom handle or my back?

Why so much pain and suffering for me as a child?

Because I talked to the neighbours and cried out for help.

The beating stopped, but not the pains. The physical pains continued for many hours and days, even whilst the man from the ISPCC came to ask me questions and asked me to strip in front of him in the comfort of the warm sitting room and show him the traces left by the blows. The Holy Bible tells me that before being sent to his crucifixion Jesus was beaten and that his back showed the traces of the blows that his executioners left. He had even to carry his crucifixion cross through the streets and along the road leading to Mount Golgotha. Jesus's marks on his shoulders and back were there for all to see, but whilst walking to and from school the marks on my back were covered by the clothing that I'd wear, so nobody ever saw them.

There were marks in my heart too. But they are marks that are not visible to those around me. They are the marks that I can't describe in total detail. They are the marks that I can't quantify, can't deduct them neither on any tax declaration form.

The marks on my back.

But whilst I have clothes on my back, shoes on my feet, shelter and food there's not much that the law can do to help me as they told me in the Garda station in the month of June 1970. My physical pains may have stopped and the marks on my back disappeared too, and that many years ago, but I still have to carry the pains of my cross and chains in my mind every day of my life since that day. Jesus's torturers, the Roman soldiers, were only carrying out orders, but I believe that after all Jesus would have pardoned them.

But I'd already lost some twenty plus years of my life. As for my healing, it cannot be achieved by simply filling out a magic prescription form.

Many lost years.

An internal exile, so to speak.

'*Let us forgive those who trespass against us…*'

Orders are orders. When the German panzers rolled into Poland in 1939 and with their blitzkrieg started the Second World War, the soldiers were simply following orders. Daddy too was simply following orders and satisfying his own motivations and those of his new-found darling wife during all those years when he remarried after my mother Noreen died, and partly that's why I made up my mind whilst still in Geneva to forgive him, and to tell him such I'd have to travel further than I'd ever travelled in all my younger years and spend sums of money in the making, sums of money that would have then bought me tons of chocolate bars or kilos of oranges, and boxes full of biscuits too, things that were denied me even when I earned them in the school exams at the end of term, or simply when I was hungry and had nothing else but thin air to nourish me.

Daddy has now gone to meet his God, and I don't know what he'll make out of all this earthly mess.

'*Let us pray for the sick and the suffering…*' Standing in front of the full-length mirror on the wardrobe I start practising my prayer for the Holy Mass.

I may not be really sick so to speak, but I'm still suffering from a lot of things, and if I have the right to pray for myself then the world isn't too badly off at all, and I believe that anybody who'd be working in the medical profession as my daddy did for so many years in his professional life would call it automedication. Help yourself, and the Lord will help you. That's what the priests used to say in St Joseph's. There have been many days when I had faith neither in the Lord, not to mention the ISPCC nor the Irish Gardai.

'*Let us pray for the sick and the suffering…*'

I have to rehearse my little prayer that I'll have to read from the liturgy block during the Holy Mass for my daddy's soul.

Be strong Gerard, I tell myself, be strong.

Even if Daddy didn't ever show you or give you the chance to learn how go to grow into a strong person and affront life with its multitude of problems, situations and difficulties on the professional and social scale, you'll have another try one day and you might just make it, but there's an urging now. I'll have to pull through all of today with its Holy Mass first.

Martin isn't here with me either now, just like that day when I got the broom handle broken over my back, he's far away from Castlebarry, his tranquillity broken by the events of these last few days, and Daddy is lying in his coffin down at the church in Chapel Street and ready for his final earthly journey.

But now it's time to go.

Straightening my jacket and adjusting my tie I have a final look out through the rear window onto the lawn that Martin and I cared for, picking all the leaves during the long cold Irish winter evenings and trimming the lawn edges too, whilst the others studied their books, played the piano, learned the traditional Irish jigs, or managed to participate in the school plays down at the National School before Christmas holidays.

Then down the flight of stairs that I daren't use during the early years at the house, once I'd been sent up to bed in the evening.

We arrive in a succession of cars in front of the church, and quietly proceed to our assigned places in the front row, and to the right of the coffin which is now placed on the catafalque. Rhona is seated nearest the centre aisle, then the boys, myself, and Jane is to my right.

People are still to be heard shuffling far down the aisles behind me, to their seated places and I have the impression that the church will soon be overfilling.

Time passes slowly. Life seems to be at a standstill, going on forever.

Raising my head high above, because I can't keep my eyes for ever on the American oak coffin resting on its pedestal to my left at the altar's base, I watch as the late morning sunshine streams through the panes of stained glass behind the altar, the curved tops of the tall windows pointed skywards towards the roof, and the heavens beyond.

There are even three priests concelebrating Holy Mass for Daddy. How many will I have? Deserve? Whilst the mourners are still taking seats to the rear of the church one of the priests comes over to our row of seats.

'Are all of the children here now?' he enquires, looking at Rhona and along the line at the rest of us.

My right hand flies up skywards.

'Are you Martin?' he asks.

'No, I'm Gerard, and Martin is stuck in Miami, can't be with us here today and I'd like that his name be mentioned,' I speak up aloud so that he'll hear me clearly.

For Rhona to hear too.

Because Martin is more family to me than Rhona ever was or is.

She won't win this one.

He approaches me.

'I'll see to it,' he says as he crosses his hands and then turns toward the coffin and the altar beyond.

I have a funny feeling that Rhona's heard my words, I don't know if she's turned her head in my direction, but I couldn't care less.

My eyes turn again towards the coffin resting on the catafalque. Here I am sitting in this Holy Church, waiting for Holy Mass to start. How many times in so many years did me and Martin ever walk down the mile from Marian House to attend Holy Mass here on a Sunday morning within these imposing and majestic walls, whilst Daddy would drive Rhona and the other children down for their Holy Mass in the church at the Mental Hospital which is only a short distance from Marian House, and this even on a Christmas Day? But this was neither Daddy's, Rhona's nor the others' church in those days, and they could never have heard the same sermon about the sins and the Christian values in the Catholic families as I could have heard. I remember the day that Daddy drove down with Rhona from Marian House and left me just inside the great brown wooden doors, it was the day of my Holy Confirmation, but Rhona said that they had to go to Westbary to talk to a man, and that they'd be back later in the day. I had spent my time of day of what is supposed to be an important point of my religious upbringing, simply being dumped at the church. I remember coming home, and that Mrs Glavney picked me up with her car near the river crossing, had already bought some potato chips for me to gobble down. She had then invited me into their house, but as I didn't know how long Rhona and Daddy would be having with the man back in Westbary then I preferred to refuse and wait outside Marian House until they arrived back late evening.

It was the 10th May 1970.

I was twelve years young.

And thus I sadly realise that this is probably the third time only in my life that I've been inside these church walls with Daddy, generally for short strips of a few minutes, and now it's going to be a long one for a Holy Mass.

A funeral Mass.

His funeral.

This wasn't the church where Daddy would attend his Holy Masses in those earlier years, but now it's the church for his funeral Mass. I guess that maybe the church in the Mental Hospital wouldn't have been grand enough for such an event, so they've brought him further down the town. But this time he's near to me during a Holy Mass.

And now the Holy Mass is for him.

The church up at the Mental Hospital might have been too small for all the mourners.

Holy Mass starts and we all kneel and pray for James Duignan, but I hardly hear the words, only the thoughts and suffering going on in my own mind.

'...thy faithful servant...'

The Mass, and prayers continue.

Shortly thereafter it's time for the children to take their turn at reading the short prayers that Rhona has prepared for each of us.

I rise from my seated position, move left towards the central aisle, and then move forward towards the altar.

Past Daddy's coffin.

It's my turn to go to the front and the microphone placed on the ambo.

Placing my hands squarely on the edges of the ambo, I raise my eyes and look through the massed crowd seated down in front and filling the big church. The whole way back to the great brown wooden doors. A feeling of total cool, of total control fills my mind, strangely. Not a trace of stage fright here. Many faces out there, most of them totally unknown to me. Question is, do they know me, of me, what I have suffered, what I have become? Am I a tourist here in my hometown? What are they expecting of me? What do they want to hear? Is it the truth that they want? Sure, if that's what they want they can have it, but is this really the moment or the best occasion, it's not a speaker's corner here is it? They'll have it, I decide, but later. It'll be taken down and written on tablets of stone. Well documented. But some of them present surely already know a lot of it. None of it was ever published in the local papers, but I know that some people up and down the country out there know more of Rhona and her ways and means, her intentions too, than she herself could ever imagine. Some of those people might even be in here with us. I keep glancing around, and to my left and a few rows behind Rhona I can see Aunty Brigid.

Then I know that I am not alone within these stone walls.

My eyes turn towards the coffin.

I slowly unfold the small square of notepaper, which I am holding squashed in the palm of my hand, and flatten it out.

'Let us pray for the sick and the suffering, and for all those who care for and comfort them, Amen.'

My voice comes alive for all the congregation to hear.

I wonder if they've heard.

The sick and the suffering! Who cares for what I've suffered and what I'm still suffering? Who cares or even knows about my internal exile, all those lost years, all those lost smiles, lost chances, never to be reclaimed? Which law could possibly replace all those lost chances, on a social, personal and professional level? What can this church offer me to ease my suffering and pain, not just this funeral day, but every other day which will follow until one day too I'll be lying in a coffin and hoping that others will pray for the sick and the suffering, and maybe for those who have suffered?

I feel like a pressure-cooker.

Steamed up inside.

Here I am announcing a prayer for the sick and the suffering! But where are those people if they're sick? They must be lying in their hospital beds somewhere out there and waiting to be cured or that we healthy folks will pray so much for them that one day they'll be strong, and maybe after eating loads of buttered slices of bread they'll be so strong again that they'll be picking up their hospital beds and going walking as if it were Jesus who had ordered them. Then all the doctors and nurses will suddenly be out of jobs, and the unemployment situation will be getting even worse, and all the people in the pubs will be gabbing about the poor state of the whole country itself, and what on earth is the government up there in Dublin doing about the whole affair at all, and isn't that what we elected them for? But that'll be a problem for the government and not one for the church whose holy and persevering Catholic members prayed so hard for all the sick and the suffering.

The sick and the suffering!

What else could Rhona have possibly invented for a prayer? What hypocrisy!

But this morning whilst I was seated in the kitchen in Marian House Rhona had said that I can't mention people that are absent from the church like Martin, it's not the way it's done do you know, you mention only those who are present, so why am I talking about the sick and suffering? I don't see them around me in the church here, they all seem to be doing grand, well for themselves, and if you're sick, well, you should be going to see a doctor now shouldn't you? My daddy was a doctor, you know? So why couldn't I talk about my brother Martin too, and have his name mentioned at Holy Mass? I wonder how he's keeping. Why did she want to have his name banished from the ears of those who have come to pay their respects to my daddy? If he did suddenly turn up on a miracle flying machine would he have to ask Rhona's permission to take off his jacket and have a seat amongst his brothers and sisters in the front row, like I was asked when I'd driven home some seventeen hundred miles in the middle of December 1981, and where he could also see Daddy's coffin waiting to go on its final earthly journey?

'Amen,' the churchgoers reply.

I leave the altar, and whilst approaching the coffin I kiss the palm of my right hand. I gently place it on the highly polished American oakwood as I pass by.

Before turning in to pass Rhona I notice that Brigid still has me within her sights.

Dying III

The Holy Mass is finishing and Rhona and the children present will of course be the first to follow, or to carry the coffin, as it is being carried down the church aisle. I am in a poor state at this time, I can feel the tears flowing down my cheeks. At first I want to hide them, wipe them away before they'd be noticed by the congregation, but stop at the thought that part of my worldly suffering is now out here in the open, ready for all to see. Hiding emotions was part of my growing up, I couldn't talk about them then, had nobody to show them to, didn't even have the chance in those early years, but that is now a thing of the past, be it at my daddy's funeral right now and here, or with my whole life. But now I feel more present with my daddy than I ever was allowed in my whole life. I know that Jane is also having a hard time here, so I take her left arm firmly in mine to support her as we continue proceeding towards the big church entrance doors.

Rhona is her usual self, total cool, total control, not the least outward emotion visible.

No tears there whatsoever. Any regrets, I wonder?

The church bells can be heard tolling as we approach the exit. I leave Jane as I have to help load the coffin into the waiting hearse. Steady footsteps take us over to the rear-opened door.

Rhona calls me over towards her as there's an old lady waiting to see me.

'Meet Mrs Agaddy,' she says.

I gawk at Rhona before I hold out my hand, eyeing the lady curiously.

I'm hesitating here.

'You know, Henry's mother,' Rhona adds as she tries to help me out, I hardly knowing anybody in this town anymore. I feel like a stranger here.

'Oh yes, pleased to meet you,' I greet her.

'I'm sorry,' she says, 'about your daddy.'

I nod.

I don't know who Henry is and even less of his mother, and am still wondering as I retreat to my rented car, where the boys join me. Rhona and Jane are in the first car behind the hearse, and we start threading down the rest of Chapel Street, two right turns and we are now into Main Street. The funeral parlour owner walks in front of the hearse right through the whole town. Fintan say's that this is a sign of respect for Daddy, as they were great friends, he'd hardly do it for the whole townspeople. We are of course moving at walking speed, and I am aware of the great number of shoppers and other strollers on the footpaths at this time of the day. Strollers. I wasn't allowed to stroll around the streets of this town when I was growing up at Marian House, wouldn't be caught dead in these streets and so have to discover the place as a tourist. I try to keep my eyes pinned ahead but it's not easy, so from time to time I just stare at my steering wheel, the speedometer too, and through the emptiness beyond, because if I look further I might see the hearse.

The coffin too.

The American oak coffin.

I keep talking about things and anything to the two others, but it's just a distraction for me really.

'I understand,' Fintan says.

That helps me, nearly just what I need.

We stop at the traffic lights at the top of Main Street, where the funeral parlour owner hops into the passenger seat of the hearse. A left turn by the Mall, and we will soon be approaching the town boundary. Shortly thereafter we are crossing the humpbacked bridge over the railway line, and upon leaving town the hearse driver puts his foot down hard on the pedal, and now we are all moving with ever increasing speed to keep up with the black car up the front. Speed. A sharp contrast with the way the time was moving whilst waiting in the church, waiting for the Holy Mass to begin. That was an eternity.

Now we're moving.

Out the road to Ballyheane.

Not out the Dublin road which would have brought us towards County Longford and Ballinagarry where my mother is buried. I know she's buried over there, and as I could never find her name on any tombstone I had to ask Daddy one day where she really is buried. After some hesitation and a choking voice as if I was after a State Secret, he had told me that she was buried in the Duignan plot over there. But because I'd always go down to Mrs Ganaghan's so-called farm every summer, instead of getting to visit my real relatives up in Longford like the other children did, I hardly ever got to visit my mother's grave. It had to wait until I'd grown up, and could afford to come back home on holidays with one of the Aer Lingus's wonderful flying machines, pick up a rental car at the airport that I'd visited for the first time a certain June of 1970 when I'd ran away from home, and be able to decide for myself where I'm allowed to go, with whom I may associate and what I can do with my time. That's when I found about my mammy's grave.

The road to Ballyheane.

I'd asked Rhona this morning why Daddy was going to be buried out in Ballyheane instead of in the Duignan family plot in the cemetery up in Ballinagarry.

'Because he has so many friends buried out there,' she had answered earlier in the morning, sitting at her usual end of the kitchen with her cup of coffee in hand before we got ready for the Burial Mass, 'that's the way he had wanted it, do you know?'

Why not the cemetery just down the road in Castlebarry? Does he get sent to be buried out here, like he got sent off and left to die at the hospital way down in Galway?

It would be so much nearer Marian House, easier for Rhona when she might want to visit and pray! After all, praying, for her, is very important.

But maybe he doesn't have many friends buried in that cemetery. Maybe only in the other one out in Ballyheane.

I didn't know it of course, and now can understand it even

less. This road has the usual bumps, twists and bends just like any Irish country road, so I have my concentration on the rear of the car ahead, which isn't too bad as it keeps my mind off the hearse and the coffin further on ahead.

The coffin. It's American oakwood, with the fine brass fixtures, signs of Daddy's fortune available for all to see, now going with his corpse on their last few miles to their final resting place.

'There we are, over there,' Fintan motions with a wave of his hand.

'Where?' I ask.

'Up over there to the right, the cemetery, you see where the tall trees are?' he asks.

'Oh, yes,' I say as I have now located the trees on the top of a hillcrest well set back from the road. Tall trees they are indeed. Their trunks half bent, and pointing towards Dublin.

The motorcade starts slowing down as we enter the village of Ballyheane. It doesn't seem to be the biggest place around. It starts with a few houses to the right, then the inevitable local pub. A schoolhouse, and here we are already turning in to the right beside the church, which by itself seems to be the largest building I've yet seen in the village. There's a large parking place to the rear, and the hearse has already positioned itself rearwards towards the cemetery gates. We wait until all the following cars are parked, and then begin unloading the coffin from the hearse, and I'm now holding the same rear left brass handle again. There are great tall trees all around the cemetery just inside the greying stone boundary wall. We start walking in a slow procession through the great wrought iron gates. There is a great crop of nettles growing just inside the wall to the right side, I think that they have must chosen that shaded and warm spot sheltered somewhat from the wind and the gardener's lawnmower. Their strong pervasive odour abounds and stings my nostrils as I bypass them.

Then we start into a slight climb. The coffin is heavy. This is the first time in my life that I have had to help with carrying a coffin. It's also one of the rare times that I have had to assist at a funeral, the last time was Mother Alouise's funeral in 1984, and emotionally speaking I'm not used to this sort of thing. Even if funerals are great events for reuniting people. I don't even know if I managed to assist at my mammy's funeral at Ballinagarry because she'd died only five days after I was born, in a place called Tury, from God only knows really what kind of an illness, and at that young age I wouldn't understand anything about what was going on nor have any emotions either. Right now there are still things which I can't understand either, like why Daddy comes to this godforsaken place to be buried, instead of near his home country where he'd be nearer the boreens and roads that he'd have walked, jumped and ran along all through his childhood and growing-up years, and he'd even be lying beside his own parents and my mammy too. So whenever I'll be coming back to this country that'll make for two cemeteries to be visiting. That's not even all of what I can't understand, but right now not much time to think, have to concentrate on my step, aren't used to this kind of manoeuvring, not much time to try to reason things out. Is there any point in trying? Time for emotions here though. When my mammy died I was too young for any emotions. When I was growing up at Marian House during the early years there was no time for emotions either. No right to have emotions. I had to live all my life in silence, bear out my internal exile, not showing any outward emotion or doubt of any sort to the other children, nor Rhona and Daddy. My daddy never came to me either, asking me what my emotional state might be, how I'm feeling, if I am enjoying school, or what did I learn today?

What have I learnt so far from this life? Much, very much in school and college, and a lot about what it's like to live a life of terrorism and violence, the segregation and humiliation at Marian House, but they don't teach you that at any school.

Hate too. Maybe my father hated me, as my birth in a clinic in Tury was responsible for the health complications that led to my mammy's suffering and eventually to her death. Maybe she was too much of a darling wife to him, and in Rhona he found only a second-class one, and that he couldn't accept, nor live with it.

Maybe the cruelty, the segregation and humiliation that he meted, and allowed Rhona to mete out, was his reaction of outburst to the unfairness of life?

We keep moving, taking a gentle right turn as we head up the slope towards the top of the hill where the tall trees are swaying gently as the westerlies whistle softly. From this point I can see the mound of freshly dug earth, which shows me without doubt what will be Daddy's final resting place. It's hard for me to look in that direction. I lower my head, and continue the pace. I can't stop and say that I can't any more, I'm part of this team. My daddy hardly ever took my hand in his throughout my life, I managed to hold his through the last few days whilst he lay in his bed at the hospital, waiting. But now it's over with holding hands. All I get to hold now is a brass handle. Four brass handles to the coffin. Four hands holding, carrying. Four minds grieving, each in their own manner.

The coffin is weighing on my hand, and my wrist is having some difficulty taking the strain, having a quarter of the corpse's weight and that of the heavy coffin with me. As far as I can remember my daddy never carried me on his knee nor lifted me in his arm when I was a young boy, and I might think that the only bodily contact we had was when he would hold my head between his knees and with my bare knees on the cold kitchen floor after saying my Holy Prayers at the Angelus at six o'clock in the evening, and thereafter I'd get beaten by him for a hole in my cardigan elbow or something else that often wasn't my fault. I was never good enough to be carried by him, but now I'm sure good enough to help carrying him to his grave. Good enough to show all the family and strangers who haven't seen me for years that I've grown into a strong man myself indeed now, and isn't this a fine family altogether indeed, and they're doing well with their grieving now tonight, and arrah, sure Gerard himself is looking well, isn't he at all?

Little time to talk now, but the words, the lines and the paragraphs will come later, one day, just to let them all know what I'm really going through, really thinking and not just what my face shows.

Moving slowly uphill I have all the time to think and reflect about life and things, so when I consider that I've had to carry, just like Jesus, my cross upon my shoulders all down through those early years and am still doing so, why should I be overwhelmed by helping to carry Daddy's coffin? But I still don't know what nor whom I'm supposed to mourn here. Feelings of love and hate are running through my mind, my muscles, my body. What to think? Is this the end of something? Is this the closing of a chapter? Part of my life? Death is part of life, like everything else, but did my life have to become such? What has Daddy given me, he gave me life, physically. But is this life, as it is being lived, worth living? If God is just, He who is all about loving and caring, then why did He let so much happen to me? Maybe the sufferers inherit the earth, and have their place already reserved in Heaven? I don't know whether to mourn the loss of my daddy, a daddy whom I've met but never have been allowed to get to know, associate with, or play ball with, nor talk about all the things that I think a boy should or might be able to do when growing up in a normal childhood and family.

Like travelling.

Apart from driving down to Mrs Ganaghan's place on the Sunday afternoons, or to St Joseph's College in Tury, or the days he brought me down to the Donilaun Hotel, or to the airport in Dublin to catch one of Aer Lingus's wonderful flying machines, or to the Hotel College, I hardly ever went anywhere travelling with him. Except once in 1965, when I went back to Gaigue to visit Mrs Brigid and her family on a Sunday, but I didn't really get talking to them that much, as I was sent out to play on their tennis court whilst they sat at table for lunch.

Travelling.

Right now we're travelling at a slow speed, half shuffling through the grass. I hear the crows making noises high above my head. I can't see them though, so I guess that they are nesting somewhere up in those branches, concealed by the green lushness.

Their cawing continues. It's the way of communicating that nature has given them.

But at least they're communicating.

That's something, which we couldn't do between us, neither I, nor my daddy could do with the neighbours along the Western Road. Having anything to do with the so-called 'bog people of North Mayo' wouldn't have been the right thing to do at all, do you know? So Daddy never got to know them all really, even if he'd spent college years with Willy Conlon who lived only three doors down from Marian House who too was a Longford man, but now he can get along with all his real friends and all the others buried out in the cemetery here, and even Rhona won't be able to interfere with that, for a while being at least.

I'm travelling with my daddy for the last earthly time, won't be able to make up for all the lost travels and chances that had slipped by through the years. No going back now, it's a one-way street. A slow-lane to heaven for him? Or elsewhere?

I don't know.

We let the coffin down gently on the transversal beams. The priest goes through the ritual prayers. One of the funeral men comes over and explains how I should grip my end of the thick cloth straps, which are passed underneath the coffin. He tells me to be careful, because the weight might catch me by surprise upon lowering the coffin into the tomb. One strap near the top of the coffin and I've got my end near the bottom.

After a hand signal, we lift the coffin up a few inches until the supporting bars are retrieved from the ground, and then we slowly let the coffin lower into the grave. I know now why yer man came to give me some advice, because it's even harder letting down whilst I'm overlooking the pit than just carrying the coffin. At one point I let slip a little too much and the coffin is tilted a few inches to my side, but no one except us four notice. A few moments later it's resting at the bottom and all that's to be done is to fill in from the mound of earth, which is piled up behind me.

I look at Rhona. She's still her usual self, total cool, total control. A game of bingo or a burial, it seems to be much of the same to her. It's not normal, just like many other things going on here.

I dally for a bit as people are now starting to talk and chat a bit, and then move towards Brigid. Someone who will comfort me a little.

After a short while the group starts splitting up and moving down the slope towards the gates. Rhona is talking to two distant cousins from Longford. They are about to leave for their homeward trip and then she invites them to join us for lunch at the Brandon House Hotel. They hesitate as they weren't on the original booking list for the hotel.

'Don't ye worry about that,' she says, 'Jim had lots of it.'

For good measure she insists that they should come along.

She's buried her husband just a few minutes ago, and here she is already talking about his money.

Jim had lots of it! But nothing apparently to pay for my third year college education.

Aha! So now I've an idea what's going on here!

Let's see!

We all get back to our cars, where goodbyes are said to some, and then we head back to town, over the humpbacked bridge again and then a right turn to take up the other road out to the hotel.

The hotel is situated in a splendid setting indeed. A long driveway takes us from the main road through a large wooded area, which then opens up into the huge grounds and garden. The building's stone-cut facade is there to be admired, and having left the parking lot I move into the lobby within the majestic walls.

To my right I recognise the lounge area where on my last visit to this manor I sat with Daddy late one evening having a pint of the cool stuff. But now he's dead and gone, and my emotional state is so bad here that when over at the 'open bar' I'm going to have a pint of the cool stuff for meself, and one for Daddy too.

Maybe he'll understand, especially as he had lots of it anyway.

I'm hardly aware of the time passing or the other people chatting, and suddenly it's time to sit for lunch. The tables are laid out in a banqueting room overlooking the garden. The starched tablecloths, napkins, and silverware remind me of the dining room at the front of Marian House at the other end of town. There's a great view out to the well-kept gardens. Just like at Marian House. They pay a gardener here for picking the leaves and so forth. But we aren't many guests so we barely fill half of the room. Rhona says that Daddy had lots of friends buried in the cemetery out in Ballyheane, but not many friends are invited to lunch here.

Maybe all, or most of his friends are dead, and are further back the road at the cemetery in Ballyheane.

'Not more than one glass of wine per person with the meal,' is the instruction that Rhona gives the headwaiter.

The manor hotel, the splendid hundred acres of secluded grounds and well-kept gardens, the cut stone facade, the relaxed and luxurious surroundings, the cloth napkins and silverware, the fine meal, but only one glass of wine per person!

What a show!

I'd have preferred to go to the Central Hotel, one of the good pubs, or even the local fish and chip shop for a today's special in town but have the right to two glasses of wine if I so desire.

A good job that I didn't dally in having a pint of the cool stuff for meself, and another one for Daddy too at the 'open bar' before the meal, and that I didn't have to pay for it either.

After all, Jim had lots of it.

Dying IV

Friday the 13th September 1996.

We are all seated in the kitchen at Marian House. Rhona is over in her usual place by the Aga.

'Oh, Tadgh, would you be going for those bits and pieces for Gerard?' she asks of him.

I react as I've heard my name being mentioned, and without delay Tadgh has reappeared in the kitchen with a small plastic bag.

'What's this about?' I ask.

'Oh these are some of Daddy's personal effects, I thought that you'd like to have some of them,' Rhona explains.

'Look those glasses, they're special now, he'd bought them only the week before he fell. The week before he'd gone to the hospital,' explains Tadgh.

I'm still very under the emotions of what has gone on these preceding days, but I open and inspect the contents.

I choose to accept his watch, reading glasses and a pair of cufflinks.

'Here, have some more,' offers Rhona as she sees other items, which are spread out, on the table.

'No, no, I don't want to have everything,' I say, 'we should share them around.'

She insists. But so do I. I want to stay with what I already have in my hands.

I had brought some chocolates with me from Geneva, and as I don't want to delay in hitting the road, I share them around. Especially as the conversation has cooled off considerably.

I bid my farewells. Tadgh will come down to the town centre with me. Jane and Fintan stay in the driveway whilst I'm reversing out.

Rhona has chosen to stay inside the house as I start reversing the car out towards the Westbary road, and is now nowhere to be seen.

Luv

It's late afternoon, and I'm sitting comfortably at the bar counter in O'Reilly's pub on Main Street. The 'soup and sandwich' trade has been over for a while now, but it's still too early for the happy hour clientele.

There's a low hum of background music and chat going on, the not so numerous patrons are settled into their armchairs at various places in the lounge side of the bar, and there's a tinge of pipe and tobacco smoke in the air. I think that if it were possible, the addition of a peat fire in an open chimney place would be a welcome part of the furniture, a final touch so to speak, but even so, I feel as if on holidays. I feel relaxed, a world away from the rumble and hectic ways of life, and a cool pint of Harp lager, which is worth savouring. Harp, 'Way Out In Front', and I remember my stint in Donegal.

From my seated point I can hear some agitation which is going on behind the central bar counter, more to the public bar side. Heavy footsteps and a girl shouting.

A man giggling out loud.

Then suddenly this barman appears in front and to my left, and streaks right in front of me and before you can say 'Jasus tonight', sure he's disappeared from my sight again.

The girl still can be roughly heard from a distance.

Then again yer man coming back again, back this time in the other direction. There must some sort of a maze behind there, separating the two main bar counters. This time he stops, and I can see that he has some sort of a photograph in his hand.

He's grinning a grin as wide as the Shannon River is at Tarmonbarry Bridge.

'Padraig,' the girl's call is now loud and clear, and seems to be getting closer.

Padraig, who I now assume is the barman, and who seems to have some price on his head, is still staring at the photo.

Now he's splitting with laughter. I hear shoes skidding, and now a young lady appears around the corner. Yer man takes a fast half turn, and with his great legs he's gone out of view before the waitress even can count to two.

'Oh come on now, Padraig I want it,' the young lady is panting from all the running around she must have been doing to catch the sprinter.

She wants it? What's all this?

I thought that the sprinter might be a mile away by now, but the quietness is broken again by a loud rail of laughter and giggles galore.

Here he is again in front of me ready for another furlong's run, and he's still clutching the sought after piece of conviction.

'Haha, did you see yerself then, haha!' he calls aloud.

'Padraig, come on, over here will you now,' she still has some wind in her breath.

Never heard nor saw anything the likes of that craic going on at the Donilaun bar, or the Shannaun Hotel either, as far as I can remember.

What's yer man got in his hand anyway, I wonder?

More feet shuffling, yer man's pounding around the place by now, yelling and laughing his head off. The poor little stubby waitress just can't keep up with him.

Ah, so I think that maybe the little girl just wanted to show off her holiday photos to her other workmates and yer man probably grabbed the one with her having not much to do all laid out in a monokini on a sun-scorched sandy beach in Greece or other foreign parts, and having a good grin at the camera and thinking about all the others working their butts off with the soup and sandwich trade in the pubs of Castlebarry and others up and down the country. If it's a good photo then I can hardly imagine it being taken over on the beach at Louisburgh, not enough sun in these parts. Maybe she's having a good grin at the photographer there, but right now she seems to be somewhat surpassed by the lightning speed that Padraig is managing around and between the bar counters. She's not grinning now to say the least. That bastard, if only I could catch him, and when I get my photo back again, I'll never show the likes of anything more to that devil now. If he wants to have a gawk of young ladies doing some topless sunbathing, he can either buy *The Sun* newspaper for the girl on page three, or book a ticket to Crete down at the travel agency.

'Padraig, oh!' she shouts.

'Haha, come and get it!' is all he has to offer.

'Ah, come on will you, I want it now,' she's really had enough of the chase, 'ah Padraig, come on give it to me, give it to me will ya?'

A client has been sitting quietly behind his pint of beer at a table to my left and like myself must have been observing the goings-on for a while.

'I'll give it to you, Luv, any time that you want it, Luv,' he offers as a consolation price to the waitress, his strong cockney accent betraying his origins.

I don't know if she's heard anything of his offer, but right now I'm grinning and laughing just as much as Padraig.

Another sup of my cool lager, and I'm settled in for another few moments in my comfortable chair, the strain of the preceding days having released a little.

The Estate

Tuesday the 27th May 1998.

I'm already back on the auld sod for a week's holiday and

investigation.

I'm becoming impatient about the lack of information concerning my father's estate. I do not believe that I can bring myself to talk to Rhona about it without extreme difficulty, and anything that she'd have to say will probably be pure lies, so I'll have to find another way of getting to the will. I get a suggestion that I should go to the County Registrar's office in Castlebarry. One phone call, and an appointment is made.

I get seated in the chap's office, and out comes the file.

The Affidavit of James Duignan, deceased.

Nearly twenty pages of paperwork.

I get to see Daddy's last Will. It's signed on the thirtieth day of December 1966. Therein amongst other texts can be read:

I appoint my wife Rhona as sole Executrix of this my last will. I bequeath all my property both real and personal of every nature and kind that I may become entitled to or die possessed of to my said wife Rhona absolutely.

There are two witnesses.

One of them, the solicitor, is an uncle of Rhona.

For a Christmas present, Daddy could hardly have done better! Rhona has signed many of the other papers, including government forms for Capital Acquisitions Tax, and so forth, which I'll have to shift through.

Marian House's gross value is indicated at one hundred thousand pounds. Marian House's contents are valued at ten thousand pounds.

The auctioneer's letter, dated the 25th August 1997, confirms such.

She has signed on part five, and thus claims that my father, who was a doctor, died with not a single fiver in any bank account.

No monies, no savings, no bonds, no stocks.

Then comes the Certificate of Discharge from Probate Tax for Rhona.

My daddy died a poor man indeed.

He had spent all of his working life down at the Clinic, ever since the early fifties, up to the date of his retirement on the 16th May 1977. Which means that whilst I had to be saving my hard earned money whilst in Geneva, and not being allowed to enjoy life and its pleasures like my classmates during the whole year, was it because he had no money to pay for my third year college education, whilst he was still earning a full salary? And what did he get for a pension? During a further nineteen years?

The other children came through secondary school, and later higher education more than I did. Did they have to contribute towards their education, or was the roof at Marian House keeping itself up in a grand way indeed?

The undertaker's bill. All the details are there. The American oak coffin, an outward sign of some of my father's wealth that it is supposed to be. The undertaker even rounded off the bill by forty-five pence, from £1,887.45 to £1,887.00. That was very kind of him I think. That small sum of money would have gotten me two or three small packets of biscuits at the freeflow staff restaurant at Shandon airport in the winter of 1977–78 when I didn't have enough money to buy me same and stave off the hunger pains in my tummy then, but there you are.

Where have the sums of money gone, those that I'd earned during the summer months during the earlier years down at the Donilaun Hotel. Rhona had said that she'd be minding them for me indeed. But the years had passed, I'd had many other worries on my mind indeed, and now there's nothing there! He never travelled, never entertained, according to the neighbours, so he had lived a frugal lifestyle indeed.

Leafing further through the wad of papers, my eyes settle on a copy of the death certificate signed by the doctor at the hospital where Daddy had died. I examine the columns. Then I arrive at column eight, the one where the Certified Cause of Death is mentioned.

Then comes the slammer.

My memory goes back to the day that we were seated all around the bed, waiting for God knows what.

'Can I have a word with his doctor?' I had asked on that occasion.

'He doesn't have a doctor,' she had replied, coolly.

'You mean no doctor for him?'

I had stared at her in amazement.

'No, it's his heart which is strong, that's what's keeping him going, all we can do is wait, nothing but the waiting now,' she had offered.

Then I remember that foolishly, I had forgotten to take the matter up with the station nurse later. The opportunities were there, to say the least.

I finally find out what were the real causes of my father's death. There are two causes.

Pneumonia. And Alzheimer's disease, certified.

The Death Certificate is signed by a doctor from the University Hospital.

It's taken me slightly over a year and a half to learn this. Just this scrap of information. But like all information concerning my father and his and my family, I was used to the blockages during so many years.

Amongst the rest.

Alzheimer's disease.

I don't have a medical training nor background, but I know what that means.

It means that Daddy was suffering from problems with his memory.

Like adding figures, and doing the sums.

Like how much is seventeen pounds and eighteen pounds?

'I don't know, and what's the point of it anyway?' he might have replied to Rhona, had she ever asked the question.

He probably couldn't do that sort of sums anymore.

Or even remember what use money can be to anyone, less even himself.

My hand goes backwards through the preceding pages, and I stop again at the one where it's clearly stated that Daddy had no money in any bank account at the date of his death.

No monies, no savings, no bonds, no stocks!

It's all gone! Including the sums of money that I'd saved whilst working summers at the Donilaun Hotel! My money!

Don't I have the right to any heritage?

Or do I have to happy with Daddy's glasses, his watch and the cufflinks which I was given shortly before leaving Marian House, and that's all that I'm entitled to?

I have to find a solicitor!

I manage it without delay.

A real estate man too.

He tells me that the house is worth far nearer £250,000, two and a half times the sum of £100,000 certified.

The house's contents, full of antiques, is easily way above the £10,000 certified.

Why? To avoid Capital Acquisitions Tax? If so, then it's tax fraud!

Then my attention turns to the bank accounts once again.

I feel that this whole story smells of fraud, thievery, selfishness, and egoism.

I get onto my solicitor. I'm told about Section 117 of the Succession Act of 1965. According to that, I'm entitled to a share of my father's estate.

Which means that the Will signed by my father, nearly thirty years ago now, wasn't even respectful of the laws which were enforced at that date.

All of that drawn up and typed out by a solicitor's office in Baltrina. Who's none other than Rhona's own uncle.

I've been denied many things in my life, but now I'm going to act. It's my right, and I'm going to take affairs right into my hands.

I want my part of this estate. The memories of all the square yards of the garden out front, and the few square yards of floorspace of the inside of Marian House that I knew is not sufficient.

But firstly, of course, it will have to be revalued by real professionals.

Saturday 30th of May 1998. I am staying the night at Jane's house in Longford. On every trip to Ireland I look forward to this stop. Firstly to meet and have time with Jane and Aisling. Aunty Brigid lives a few miles away, and that's practical too. Secondly, the town is an interesting one for shopping. Thirdly, it's most convenient for the early morning return trip to the airport at Dublin, where a wonderful flying machine will be waiting to take me back home to Geneva.

It's now late evening and we're sitting in the lounge. I ask Jane if she has heard anything new about Daddy's will. She tells me that she had approached Rhona on the point.

'He told me to mind it for him,' was the reply that Rhona had given on that point. For an empty, useless answer it's hard to do better. But I keep my gob shut.

Tuesday the 23rd June 1998. Jane and Aisling have since joined us here in Geneva for their holidays. I have a day off from work today and suggest to Jane and Aisling that we take a drive out of the city and spend the day at the swimming pool in Nyon. They'd be happy with that.

We are settled down on the well-kept grass lawn. In front of us the pool grounds stretch down to Lake Geneva. A great number of sailing boats and motorboats are plying the waters beyond. A big cruise ferryboat eases its way amongst the others, destined certainly for one of the next picturesque and quaint little villages, which adorn the lakeshore. To my right I can manage to see the city of Geneva on the horizon, its world-known water fountain able to be picked out. Down below us I can see Aisling, who seems to be enjoying herself in one of the children's pools.

The mid-afternoon sun is hitting hard.

'Does Rhona know that you're here?' I ask Jane.

She laughs loudly.

'Oh, I couldn't be away for a week without my mother knowing where I am!' comes her reply.

'That is what I am afraid of,' I say. 'She seems to know everything of what you do, and where you are.'

'Well, that's my mother,' she says.

'Have you heard anything new from Rhona on Daddy's will?' I ask her.

'No, I haven't,' she says.

'Jane, since I was in Ireland last May, I've been finding out a whole lot of information concerning the will,' I tell her.

'Oh, really, where?' she is surprised.

'It's simple, at the County Registrar's office in Castlebarry,' I explain, 'it's information which is available.'

'In Castlebarry?' she asks curiously. 'Rhona knew that you were in Ireland, and she's furious because you didn't stop at the house.'

'Oh, yes?' I continue.

'She came down on me like a ton of bricks,' she tells me, 'as if it were my fault.'

'I don't have to stop at the house if I don't want to,' I say. 'Besides, I was busy anyway; if I don't stop there it's not your fault, and your mother has no right to come down on you for that.'

'Oh, but that's her,' she says.

'Do you know that according to the Irish laws and all that I've found during my May trip, I'm entitled to my part of Daddy's estate, just like Martin, you and the boys?' I ask her.

'Yes, I do,' she replies.

'And what do you think of that?' I then enquire.

'I think that you are wholly entitled to your part, it's only fair,' she nods in agreement.

'Yes, but Rhona isn't very forthcoming on any of the information concerning the will,' I say, eyeing her for a reaction.

'I'll agree on that,' she says.

'I'm not sure, but for me she's hiding something,' I say. 'I feel that on the morning after the funeral, when we were all, except Martin, present in the kitchen, she had an opportunity to talk about the will. That way we would all have heard the same version of the story.'

'Yes, I see that as being a communications failure on her part,' says Jane, 'she could have used that chance.'

'Well, as she's not coming forward with anything, I guess that I'll have to go after her,' I add.

'Well, I don't know now,' she says.

A glance down towards the pool, and I see that Aisling is still busy and seems to enjoying herself there. That's what I need right now, so that the conversation can continue.

'I'm not sure, but I have a feeling that she's intending to keep it all, hoping that Martin and I will just both fade away like the early morning fog, and then distribute all the estate upon her death to her children. That way we get nothing,' I say. 'I'm of the impression that if I do nothing, I'll get nothing, and that is unacceptable for us.'

'I can understand that,' she says.

'I could consider taking legal action against her,' I continue.

'If you take any action against my mother, then I and Aisling will be very sorry not to be able to continue coming to visit you here in Geneva. She's my mother, I love her, and I'll be obliged to stand by her,' comes the direct reply, as she shifts herself in her seated position.

She hasn't said so much, but for me this means that I won't be welcome any more in her home in Longford, and that I'll lose her as a sister, and the contact with Aisling, who is my goddaughter too.

Biologically speaking, Jane was only a stepsister, but in reality she was much more than that to Veronica, Paul, and I.

Images flitter through my mind, us visiting her, she being with us regularly with her good humour and character. She'd joined us for the trip when Martin had turned up in August 1994. She'd spent much time with us near Lough Allen in May 1998. She'd even been brought to visit Veronica's parents' house high up in the Swiss Alps. Been to Miami to visit Martin. She was the only one of Rhona's children who dared to let me know through the bushes that she has understood what went on at Marian House during all those earlier years, and could realise what Martin and I had suffered in our upbringing. She let it be known by the fact that she accepted my opinions of her mother and what she is capable of doing, what evil she represents. She had even suffered herself when things turned sour between her ex-husband Danny and her parents a few years ago. And now she is about to say her goodbyes to Martin, Veronica, Paul, and myself.

The crunch has arrived. Flat in front of me.

I know that I've rocked the boat. But I'll have to make a firm decision someday. Not today. Not whilst she's still enjoying her holidays with us. I don't want to ruin what is left of her time here. But I know that a sentimental nerve has been hit.

Badly hit, and damaged, maybe irreparable.

'Jane, for the moment I'm just considering things, weighing it all up, I have an enormous amount of reflection to go through, but I preferred talking to you about the situation directly, as you're with us here, than trying to talk over the phone when you'll be gone back. I don't want to lose you as a sister, nor

Aisling, can you understand that?' I ask.

She remains silent for some time.

I don't like this silence. I look towards Aisling, I listen to the water being splashed by happy children, the crystal blue lake still abounds with big sailboats gliding silently, with the other shore and the French Alps beyond. The Mont Blanc is still tipped with some snow. Beautiful scenery in a beautiful part of the world indeed. But deep down inside, I feel profoundly saddened.

I've had to take the beatings, the segregation, the humiliation during so many years, paid for my third year at college from my own savings, and now not one single shilling from the heritage without me having to ask for it.

It's the final straw.

'But I don't want to lose my share either of the heritage,' I say.

'I can understand that,' she adds. 'Listen, I have a suggestion. If you don't do anything for the moment, when I get whatever share in the future, then I'll split it between you and Martin.'

I think that it's more than reasonable on her part. But it's also a way of buying my silence.

'Thanks for your offer, Jane, but it's not your moral responsibility to split your share with Martin and myself. It's up to Rhona to come forward and let us have what we're entitled to. Whatever you'd get at any time in the future is yours, and I can't reasonably expect any part of that,' I explain.

'I might try and speak with her,' she says.

We change the subject, but things aren't like before, and the remaining hours until our departure back to Geneva pass very slowly indeed.

It's back to work the following day, and I'm on a series of late shifts for the remaining days of Jane's holidays, so we hardly touch the subject at all. Deep down, I have a feeling that it suits me fine that way.

Jane and Aisling leave on Sunday, the 28th June. On my way into work I bring them to the railway station.

'I'll phone you next week,' she says.

'Fine,' I say.

We say our goodbyes at the station.

But she never phoned.

Homeward Bound

Sunday 1st November 1998

I've passed through Longford town, which seems to be still fast asleep just like many of the others that I've already seen and covered during my journey this morning. But it's still the very early hours here, and I keep heading eastward. This is the first time in many years that I haven't made the overnight stop at Jane's house, to visit her and Aisling too, but since our conversation by the beach at Nyon I'm not welcome to stop here anymore, so I've had to cover the whole width of the country in one go. But, by now, I've covered half of that distance, so psychologically speaking I'm over the mountain ridge. I'm heading home again from another flying visit to the auld sod, and again, there's another wonderful flying machine waiting for me at Dublin Airport, destination being Geneva. Another one that I don't want to miss. Just like all the earlier ones.

Once again, I'm emigrating from my homeland. But this time, it's my choice. I'm hereby expressing my choice of freedom of liberty and speech!

Speech, because I've had many discussions this last week! Speech, and group sessions with various neighbours still living at Western Road, or within reaches.

I have been so busy, however, that I simply haven't had time even to find a birthday present for Paul! This saddens me. Daddy never gave me any sort of a present for any of my birthdays during the early years at Marian House, but now I don't even find the time to buy something small for my boy! Daddy had three of them, did he manage better?

At this early hour there's no traffic, and nothing much moving on the N4 except my little rental car, and the odd car that overtakes me, often at considerable speed, as if there were an All-Ireland match on today at Crooke Park in Dublin and the last available tickets are about to go.

And of course the black crows.

They're to be seen perching in numbers, as spectators, on the roadside posts, on the field gates, and in the middle of the road too. The little car's engine has long warmed up to the ideal temperature, which allows me to gently keep the pressure on the speed pedal, and thus gain ground yard by yard, curve by curve, mile by mile. The huge black crows don't seem to like me arriving though, and the middle of the road ones and some of the others decide to scatter and live for another day. They don't delay however as I see them resettling behind me via my rear-view mirror, until the next axle and set of wheels will give them the fright of their lives.

The intermittent swishing of my windscreen wipers clears my view as I continue cutting forward through a light greyish mist that seems to be hanging over the whole of the countryside, upwards to the heavens beyond, and back down again to cover all of the horizon. Gripping a tighter hold on my steering wheel, I grab, for a moment or two, the liberty to observe the serenity of the countryside around me. A little of the scenery, which I am about to leave once again, for an undefined length of time.

I see groups of heifers and cows grazing lazily on the fresh green pastures of this Emerald Isle, the freshest pastures to be found for miles around now. Some others are sleeping, maybe just like the farmer himself, who might be stirring his great bulk, by now from his comfortable Sunday morning's bed, just in time for the parish priest's Sunday mass, just like all the other good Irish Catholics should be doing now, do you know? A perceivable calmness and serenity exists in this part of the world, and now part of it is in my mind too.

A few miles further east, and I'm driving in Edgeworthstown. No traffic here either, but I let my speed automatically drop. I'm now at the first junction in the town, where the Ballymahon road heads right to the countryside beyond.

My thoughts go to Aunty Brigid. A kind lady she is indeed. A good lady. She'd taken great care of me since I'd left that hospital in Tury, in February 1958, and until I was brought back down again towards the warm, wonderful and wild west end of Ireland in 1960. And to live for many years thereafter.

To Castlebarry I had to go. But Rhona was neither a caring or a loving mother to me whilst I grew up during all those lost years at Marian House. What a fate!

But the calmness and serenity which surrounds me in these

fields and pastures all the way towards the horizon do now exist in my heart and mind too. I know they are there. I can nearly put my hand on them. As, judging by all the earlier departures from this Emerald Isle and this all down through many years, many of them lost, many of them with pangs, belly pains, and soul-searching, I know that a lot has been done, and much has been achieved for the better. I have finally managed to fight harder than some, which sadly was and still is necessary, but I still have to win what I am entitled to of my father's estate, and there are many people who will have to stand in a courtroom, like myself, and answer impending questions.

Through these group sessions, phonecalls, mails and e-mails, a 'support group' is now set up. There is still much to do, but there's growing intention and motivation to have all this affair 'outed'; brought public.

What do I want?

I want my rightful and fair share of my deceased father's estate!

I want the whole light and maximum exposure be made of my case, it may help others to realise what has happened, what is still happening, and what people, even in seemingly very Irish Catholic households, are still capable of!

I want answers as to why unofficial and state organisations failed in their moral and legal responsibilities to me during my younger years!

I wish a judge would reasonably estimate that I have suffered unquantifiable injustice, and that he might also be allowed to decide what sum of monetary compensation might be offered me!

I want a written, or less a verbal, offer of excuse from Rhona, for all the physical and appalling psychological and mental treatment and abuse that I have been subjected to over many years, points of which have had irrevocable effects upon my well-being, be it socially, professionally, or financially!

I want after all, my father, who is no longer with me on this earth, just as he never was anyway, to remain in his Eternal Peace.

So some battles have been won, the weight is a little lighter on my shoulders now, but there's a hell of another one to be fought! And to be won!

The weight is lighter in my mind now, the rest will have to be set up.

I wonder how long it's still going to take to sort out the rest? Will we make it? Do we have enough time upon this earthly planet?

But now, I have my 'support committee' behind me, and beside me too, and their words will count for a lot indeed.

Because for many years, many lost years, I wasted time on worthless efforts, and now I have a real chance to get this whole story out into the open.

But, by now, the dice are laid, and I believe that I'll be getting high numbers, and have already more witnesses than can be counted on any dice cube. These witnesses are set and prepared: they too are waiting for justice!

The battleground has now been prepared; we now have but to await the final attack! The final onslaught! For my rights, but also for the justice of others! To show others who too have suffered that there is a way, that there is a justice out there, and not just injustice! It's for them too!

It's been a long time since I've been in such a calm state of mind, and I guess that this must be one of the better moments of life.

The first time I'd ever been so far in these eastern parts, travelling the eastbound N4, which leads the way from Castlebarry to Dublin, was an awfully long time ago. It was the 30th May 1976. I was a young boy then, seated by the rear passenger window, with Daddy upfront at the car's driving wheel. I had spent many lost years living and growing up at Marian House by then.

But now this widened road brings me once again to Dublin, to another great flying machine whose destination is again Geneva, and the whole great wide world beyond, whenever I want!

In those early days, I wasn't allowed many chances to learn much at all about life, the great flying machines, nor cars or driving licences, and even less of the rules of the road.

Just like the black crows.

Epilogue

It's half past nine on the morning of Tuesday 21 September 1999, as Veronica and I arrive at the doors of the Castlebarry Courthouse for the sitting of the Circuit Court. The sky is overcast, rather grey, but once inside the time starts moving very quickly indeed, especially with the arrival of all my witnesses and others who have come to show Rhona and her group the support that I have, and deserve.

Shortly before 3 p.m., with barely a few minutes left to go before entering the courtroom, and after many hours of detailed negotiations, I learn of an 'eleventh-hour' settlement, which has been wrenched from Rhona's unwilling hands and mind and is thus awaiting my acceptance. I have but a few seconds available to decide, but this is something for which I am prepared. I know that I can count upon the seriousness and professionalism of my solicitor and my barrister-at-law to squeeze this much out of Rhona. For a 'poor' woman indeed she has to find her bank before closing time and settle.

Awakening on the Wednesday morning, I appreciate, with delight, the success that has been achieved, a battle that has been won and that holidays and life can begin once again.

Driving eastwards past Marian House, I think of the bygone summer season and of the leaves which will soon start falling again upon the lush green garden. Maybe the crows will pick them up, and use them to line their nests to shelter them and their young from the harsh westerlies which will soon be blowing in from the wild Atlantic beyond, and spending endless hours howling during the long evenings and dark winter nights ahead, against the western gable of Marian House.